BETRAYED

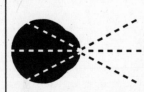

This Large Print Book carries the
Seal of Approval of N.A.V.H.

BETRAYED

ROBERT K. TANENBAUM

THORNDIKE PRESS
A part of Gale, Cengage Learning

 GALE
CENGAGE Learning·

Detroit • New York • San Francisco • New Haven, Conn • Waterville, Maine • London

GALE
CENGAGE Learning

LIBRARY OF CONGRESS CATALOGING-IN-PUBLICATION DATA

Tanenbaum, Robert K.
   Betrayed / by Robert K. Tanenbaum.
     p. cm. — (Thorndike Press large print thriller)
     ISBN-13: 978-1-4104-3269-8
     ISBN-10: 1-4104-3269-6
   1. Karp, Butch (Fictitious character)—Fiction. 2. Ciampi, Marlene (Fictitious character)—Fiction. 3. Public prosecutors—Fiction. 4. New York (N.Y.)—Fiction. 5. Large type books.
   I. Title.
   PS3570.A52B48 2010b
   813'.54—dc22
                                       2010036994

Published in 2010 by arrangement with Gallery Books, a division of Simon & Schuster, Inc.

Printed in the United States of America
1 2 3 4 5 6 7 14 13 12 11 10

To those blessings in my life:
Patti, Rachael, Roger, and Billy;
and
To the loving Memory of
Reina Tanenbaum
My sister, truly an angel

ACKNOWLEDGMENTS

To my legendary mentors, District Attorney Frank S. Hogan and Henry Robbins, both of whom were larger in life than in their well-deserved and hard-earned legends, everlasting gratitude and respect; to my special friends and brilliant tutors at the Manhattan DAO, Bob Lehner, Mel Glass, and John Keenan, three of the best who ever served and whose passion for justice was unequalled and uncompromising, my heart-felt appreciation, respect, and gratitude; to Professor Robert Cole and Professor Jesse Choper, who at Boalt Hall challenged, stimulated, and focused the passions of my mind to problem-solve and to do justice; to Steve Jackson, an extraordinarily talented and gifted scrivener whose genius flows throughout the manuscript and whose contribution to it cannot be overstated, a dear friend for whom I have the utmost respect; to Louise Burke, my publisher, whose enthusiastic support, savvy, and encyclopedic smarts qualify her as my first pick in a game of three on three in the Avenue P park in Brooklyn; to Wendy Walker, my talented, highly skilled, and insightful editor, many thanks for all that you do; to Mitchell Ivers and Jessica Webb, the inimitable twosome whose adult supervision, oversight, and rapid responses are invaluable and profoundly appreciated; to my agents, Mike Hamilburg and Bob Diforio, who in exemplary fashion have always represented my best interests; and to Paul Ryan, who personified "American Exceptionalism" and mentored me in its finest virtues; and to my esteemed special friend and confidant Richard A. Sprague, who has always challenged, debated, and inspired me in the pursuit of fulfilling the reality of "American Exceptionalism."

PROLOGUE

The trim, dark-haired man in the tuxedo and white gloves walked into the mansion's library and immediately absorbed all that he saw. He noted the standard dark walnut paneling and the leather furniture, the massive hickory desk, and the obligatory wall of important and/or obscure books. The decor was a bit old-fashioned for his taste but understandable given that the house was more than one hundred and fifty years old.

He glanced at the fireplace, where, in a single concession to modern times, blue flames of natural gas licked around ceramic logs; then he turned his attention to the cliché bearskin rug in front of it. He took note of a pair of cherry-red high-heel shoes — *Gucci, I believe* — cast aside at the end of one rear claw, waiting for their owner to retrieve them. *Unfortunately, that will never happen,* he thought, more as something else to file away rather than any sentiment.

The mantel above the fireplace had been decorated for the Christmas holiday with what smelled to be real cedar boughs but with suspiciously uniform, and therefore fake, red berries attached. A few more holiday items — a flickering, cinnamon-scented red votive candle surrounded by plastic mistletoe, as well as a stack of Christmas cards — adorned the desk that dominated the room. There was also a photograph of the man who lived in the mansion, as well as his blue-eyed, blond Barbie of a wife and their three college-age daughters. The smiles on the faces of the parents looked about as real as the berries and the logs.

Now for "the talk," he thought. He had a carefully honed ability to assess a situation and make a decision almost instantaneously. This was, after all, what made him success-ful. His business card stated: "Discreet risk assessment and mitigation." It was an ambiguous way of saying that he made prodigious amounts of money by quietly and definitively "fixing" problems for wealthy and powerful people who messed up.

In fact, most of those who received a busi-ness card, which bore only the inscription and a toll-free telephone number, knew him as the Fixer. That's how he was referred to — usually by satisfied former customers, who then passed on his information to others in need of such services. And it was how he preferred the relationship to remain, though as he also traveled in some of the same social circles as his clients, they occasionally bumped into one another. His clients had been instructed on what to do in the event of a chance meeting. They knew better than to behave as if they'd ever met him anywhere else or as anyone else. For all intents and purposes, he was Jim Williams, a quiet and unassuming investment banker.

Of course, that was not his real name, but it was perfect in its forgettable-ness. Physically, the Fixer didn't stand out, either. He looked like the typical middle-aged businessman who kept in shape at the local health club and watched what he ate but was otherwise unremarkable. Average height. Average looks. Average slightly receding hairline above a bland oval face. Then again, it was an asset in his line of work *not* to be noticed or remembered from a casual glance.

If there was anything that stood out about him, it was his heightened state of alertness, evidenced by the way his dark eyes seemed to record everything they saw, and the calm confidence he exuded when dealing with clients and their issues. But even that he kept under wraps unless he was working. He did have a way of standing that a trained eye might have concluded meant a military background, and indeed he'd gone from Special Forces many years earlier to the Company before going into the business of fixing problems for people with money. *Speaking of which . . .*

The Fixer's attention shifted to the man in the plum-colored smoking jacket sitting on the edge of a Chesterfield leather chair in a dark corner of the room. The object of his attention was bowed over, his tanned, ruggedly handsome face buried in his hands, as his shoulders and silver mane of hair shook with each muffled sob.

Crying . . . and with good reason, the Fixer thought clinically. There was a young woman lying naked, and in a state of rigor mortis, on the master bed upstairs, and this apparently despondent family man had killed her. *And for what? A shortcircuit between his brain and his balls?*

The Fixer shook his head. It never ceased to amaze him how people with as much station, power, and money as the man in the corner could be so good at throwing it all away for some ass, or more power, more recognition, or a few more bucks they didn't need. Like heroin junkies, they were addicts: the more they got, the more they needed. Then they'd refuse to acknowledge that they had a problem until they *really* had a problem.

Good thing, he told himself as he began to cross the room toward the man. *Or I wouldn't be in business.*

Upon arriving at the house, he'd spoken briefly with his new client's assistant, a young man named Peter, who'd placed the call to him. *Thank God someone in the house was thinking with something other than, well, you know.* The Fixer had then directed the semihysterical client to make himself a stiff drink and have a seat in the library. "Don't make any calls. Don't touch anything," he'd warned.

After that, he'd gone upstairs with the members of his team and Peter to view "the problem." She was lying on her back, her head and waves of auburn hair hanging over the edge of the four-poster bed. Her pale blue eyes were wide open and upon closer inspection revealed subconjunctival hemorrhaging, which occurs when tiny blood vessels break just underneath the clear surface of the eye — a common feature of death by strangulation. *As if the bruises around her neck weren't proof enough of what happened here,* he thought as he knelt beside the bed.

Despite the waxy pallor of her skin and the bluish tint to her lips, he could tell that she'd been a real beauty. *But all she is now is a liability.* He stood and left the room to make his way back down the stairs to the library, leaving his men to begin their work.

He'd put on gloves before entering the house, as had all of his men. Their job was to remove evidence, not add to it. However, the tuxedo wasn't his normal business attire. He'd been at a holiday party in Manhattan when he got the call, and there wasn't time to change clothes before climbing into his Porsche 993 and rushing to this home in Westchester County. He wasn't happy about the call, as it meant leaving his beautiful girlfriend surrounded by wealthy, better-looking men who thought that she could do better than a boring, if financially well-off, middle-aged banker. But part of being the Fixer was that he was on call anytime of the day or night; for the kind of money he commanded, he had to be.

There will be an extra fee for that tacked onto tonight's invoice, he noted in his mental ledger. The bill would go to the people Peter really worked for, and they'd gladly pay it. They had a lot invested in the man's future potential.

At least they'd had the sense to keep someone on the payroll to monitor their prize rooster. Peter might have saved the day. He was a little surprised it had taken so long for the proverbial shit to hit the fan with this man. The rumors about his serial philandering had been out there for years, but a friendly liberal press had not tried very hard to confirm the allegations, and the missus was apparently resigned to the role of a stoic cuckquean.

However, that was before her famous husband killed a young woman. Now neither she nor the press nor the police would be able to look past this transgression.

"What was her name?" he asked, sitting on a corner of the desk. His voice was quiet but firm.

The man looked up through tear-filled eyes. "I didn't mean to hurt her."

It was a pretty typical reaction, and the Fixer let it go the first time. In these sorts of situations, clients felt the need to express remorse for their fuckups. But part of his job was to remove the emotion from the moment and keep the client focused.

"I'm sure you didn't," he said dryly. "But it doesn't matter now, and it's not my concern. Most respectfully, sir, my job is to make sure the problem goes away. Was this an affair or a 'professional' relationship?"

"It was . . . it was both," the man said. His lip trembled, and he moaned. "Oh, God, help me . . . she was a call girl, but I fell in love. I was going to buy out her contract so that she could be with only me. And maybe someday, when the timing was better, I was going to divorce my wife and marry her."

Now the man was starting to annoy him. Most of the people he had to help were idiots, but some were worse than others and needed to be brought down to earth, or they could make his job impossible.

"Yes, and let me guess, the two of you would then ride off into the sunset and live happily ever after," he said, his voice still flat and emotionless. "Instead, you killed her. Judging by the bruises on her throat and the position of her body, I'd say you were engaged in something pretty damn kinky, things got exciting and before you knew it, she wasn't moving anymore."

"It was an accident," the man said, now scowling slightly. He wasn't used to being dressed down. "She liked it rough, to the point of passing out just as I . . ." The scowl faded as the man rubbed his eyes; his lip quivered again. "But we loved each other.

You make it sound so cheap. I should just . . . I should just turn myself in."

The Fixer remained still as stone, but he allowed the intensity of his voice to turn up a notch. "Cut the shit. I need you to wake up and smell the coffee. We've got a real problem on our hands, and just because I'm here now doesn't mean it's over. You choked the life out of an expensive prostitute while getting your rocks off. It was not a beautiful thing, and it ended in murder. If you don't get your shit together, they're going to lock you up and throw away the key, *if* they don't stick a needle filled with poison in your arm to execute you. Is that how you want to go out?" The Fixer looked down at his client. "You knew this was bound to happen," he said. "People like you are so seduced by your power and money that you believe you can do anything you want and get away with it. But then the high isn't high enough, so you do just a little bit more. And the more you get away with doing, the more you think you can."

"It wasn't like that."

"Oh, no? You want to tell me that you didn't get an extra kick out of screwing a prostitute your daughter's age, in your marriage bed, while the wife and kids were out of the house? Why not a hotel or her place?

In fact, I'd bet it was a thrill to think that even if the chance was remote, your wife might come home early and catch you. Of course, you would have been up shit creek if she had, and they would have called me then, too. But that still would have been better than this; making a sordid little affair go away is a lot easier than hiding a murder. So right now, I need you to quit sniveling about your hopeless love for a hooker and answer my questions as quickly and accurately as you can. Now, I asked you once before if you knew her name; I need an answer."

"Brandy," the man replied. "Brandy Fox."

The Fixer blinked once. "Brandy Fox? Now, that doesn't sound like a stage name, does it? Any idea about her real name?"

The man held up a small black purse that he'd had in his lap. "This was hers. Maybe there's some ID."

The Fixer's eyes darkened. "Where did you get that?"

"She left it on my desk."

"You were told not to touch anything."

The man looked frightened. "I wasn't thinking . . . this is such a shock . . ."

The Fixer held up his hand. "I don't want to hear it." He took the purse as he continued to glare at his client. "Did you touch

18

anything inside this purse?"

"What?"

The Fixer let his breath out slowly. "Did you put your hands inside this purse for any reason? Would your fingerprints be on anything other than the outside?"

The man swallowed hard and shook his head. "I didn't open it."

"You're sure?"

"Yes."

The Fixer opened the purse and removed a wallet. He glanced through the contents and placed it back. "Fake ID. You said she was a call girl. Was she an independent, or did she work for a service?"

"I was introduced to her through the Gentleman's VIP Club," the man said. "It's an online, um, dating service."

"Do you know if she told them or anyone else that she was coming here tonight?"

The man shook his head and offered a slight smile. "Tonight was . . . she said it was her Christmas present to me, off the books."

"I saw the jewelry box on the floor, so I presume the two-carat diamond earrings were your Christmas present to her. Not exactly a freebie, but I guess it's a matter of perspective. . . . The people who run this club, were they aware that 'Brandy' was seeing you? They know who you are?"

"The owner is a woman. Actually, an old acquaintance, and I'm sure she can be counted on for discretion."

"I'm sure . . . at least under normal circumstances, but that might not include someone killing one of her girls," the Fixer responded. "But the 'Christmas present' could be a bit of luck. Tomorrow I want you to contact this woman and try to make another date with 'Brandy.' Two reasons. One, you'll know then if 'Miss Fox' was telling the truth and her boss didn't know about this Christmas present. And two, if you'd just killed a prostitute, would you call her pimp and ask for that girl again?"

The man nodded. Hope crept into his eyes. "I see. Of course. That's clever."

"Clever is what I do," the Fixer said. "In fact, I want you to try to get a date a few times over the next couple of weeks. Get angry when it can't be arranged. Accuse them of holding out on you. . . . And I'll need to know how to contact this club. I'll want to keep an eye on this friend of yours. Did Miss Fox ever say anything to you about her personal life — tell you about her friends or family, maybe a boyfriend she actually fucked for free?"

The man's eyes hardened, and his lips set

20

in a tight line, but he shook his head. "We didn't talk much about our other lives."

"Yet you were going to marry her someday," the Fixer said with a hint of sarcasm. He was purposefully goading his client and was glad to see that, like many powerful men with big egos, he functioned best when angry.

"Why is it important?" the man demanded.

The Fixer smiled slightly. "Because I'm going to have to invent a plausible story to explain her disappearance, and to do that, I need to know who's going to miss her and what lengths they will go to in order to find her. She's obviously not someone you picked up at the bus station. She had some pretty expensive dental work, I would guess when she was a teenager. Not exactly a Forty-second Street hooker. I want you to rack your brain and see if you can come up with anything she might have told you about her 'other' life."

The client seemed about to say something, but he was interrupted by the appearance of a muscular-looking young man in the library doorway. He, too, wore white gloves, as well as a knit cap, a black turtleneck, and warm-ups.

The young man held up a plastic lawn

bag. "Sheets, pillowcases, mattress cover. Danny's vacuuming the carpet now."

"Thanks, Josh. Will we be able to match the linens?" the Fixer asked.

"Yes, sir. Dreamsack silk sheets, pricey but easy to find. The comforter can be bought at any decent home-furnishings store. How much time do we have?"

The Fixer looked at his client and said, "Your assistant, Peter, told me that the family is due back from the Bahamas on Christmas Eve. Is that correct?"

The man nodded. "In the afternoon. I'll have Peter check on the exact time."

The Fixer smiled; he liked to reward co-operation, make the client feel like part of the team so long as he did what he was told. "That gives us until tomorrow, practically an eternity." He leaned forward so that he was nearly at eye level with the man. "Did you use a condom?"

"What?"

"A condom . . . when you were banging this girl, did you use a rubber? I don't intend for anybody to find the body, but it's always good to be thorough."

"She didn't make me wear one," the man said. "We both took blood tests to show we didn't have any diseases. It's part of the requirements with the VIP Club."

The Fixer looked incredulous. "You submitted to blood tests so that you could fuck a prostitute?" He gave Josh a knowing look. "Add it to the list of gets."

The young man nodded.

Turning back to his client, the Fixer said, "I need you to think carefully about this next question. I need to know where else we should look for any body fluids."

The man looked puzzled. "Fluids?"

"Yes, semen, blood, sweat, urine, hers or yours, anywhere you might have had sex or deposited some bit of DNA. That includes the kitchen counters, toilet paper, or the sheets like my friend Josh has in the bag." He pointed at the bearskin rug. "For instance, did you have sex on old Smokey there?"

"Um, yes, I suppose there could be something," the man admitted.

The Fixer nodded and looked at Josh. "Get a photograph of the bear and send it to the Russian and see how close we can get. If he has a suitable replacement, let's get it out of here; if not, clean it the best you can. I assume the high heels are Miss Fox's, yes? Okay, get them packed up. Now, where else was there sexual contact?"

The man pointed to the ceiling. "The shower in the master bathroom."

The Fixer turned back to Josh. "We'll want those towels and whatever looks used. Make sure the tile gets scrubbed, and run drain cleaner down the pipes." He looked back at the client. "Anywhere else?"

The client shook his head.

"All right," the Fixer said. "We're making real progress. We'll be wiping obvious areas of fingerprints, and we already found the champagne flutes and bottle in the bedroom. What else did she touch? The refrigerator? The good china? Maybe you let her fondle the wife's jewelry? No? Well, let's walk me through what you did from her arrival up to the moment I got here. You'll be surprised what will jump out at us."

After the man had provided the chronology of his evening and had been asked to repeat it several times, the Fixer moved on.

"Now, what about her clothes? I saw what I assumed to be her underwear upstairs. We'll pick up anything we see there. But did she undress anywhere else?"

"Her coat is in the hall closet. The black mink," the man said.

The Fixer favored his client with another smile. "Very good. We might just get away with this." The man smiled back like a school-boy praised by his teacher, who now said, "I assume the smoking jacket could

24

have something on it, her hair perhaps? Please, take it off and hand it to Josh, as well as any other clothes you might have worn in the young woman's presence."

The man started to do as told but quickly reached into his pocket. He answered the Fixer's questioning look by holding up a silver charm on a necklace. "My kid's," he said. "She wanted me to fix the clasp. I better not lose it." He casually walked over to his desk, where he hung the jewelry from the lamp's switch.

The Fixer looked at him for a long moment, then nodded. "Take off the robe."

The man did as he was told until he was standing naked. The Fixer motioned him over to a floor lamp that he switched on. "Stand in the light, and turn around slowly," he commanded.

The man blushed but complied. "What are you doing?"

"Looking for scratches, bite marks. Do you remember anything like that?"

"Not sure," the man said, continuing to turn.

"Okay, I don't see anything." The Fixer looked at his watch. "It's two A.M. I want you to drive back with me to New York, do a little Christmas shopping in the morning, where you'll be seen. I'll have my people contact the press and make sure they get wind of the photo op. I have a friend with a hotel who'll make sure his books say that you checked in earlier this evening — alone — so remember to tell the media that you came down early to shop before picking up your beloved wife and kids. Right now, I want you to run upstairs and take a shower, and I mean scrub every nook and cranny, and make the water as hot as you can, with plenty of soap and shampoo."

Ten minutes later, the man walked back downstairs, towel-drying his hair. He was dressed casually in slacks, a button-down shirt, and a cardigan and was carrying a small suitcase.

Young men were carting several lawn bags out the front door as the Fixer stood in the foyer, talking to Peter and another sandy-haired young man. He signaled for the client to come over and nodded to his employee. "Jason, would you explain what you've been up to, please?"

The young man turned and said, "Basically, I wiped your security tapes clean from shortly before the young lady showed up; they won't start recording again until about five A.M., long after we're all gone."

"What if somebody notices?" the client asked.

The Fixer shrugged. "Unless there is some reason for somebody to go back and review the tape — like a break-in — I think we're pretty safe. They recycle every seventy-two hours. Besides, Jason here is a master at making it look as if such things were caused by power spikes or viruses." He took the man by the elbow and guided him over to another young man he called Lex, who, like the others, was dressed in a black knit cap and a turtleneck, clean-cut but unremarkable. "How did the young woman get here?"

"She drove."

"Then I assume that's her BMW parked around the side?"

"Yes."

The Fixer pulled a set of keys from his pocket and handed them to the young man. "Lex, would you do the honors? Park it in our garage until I decide what's next. Remember, keep it under the speed limit, full stops — we can't have you getting pulled over."

"Yes, sir," Lex replied as he took the keys and left the house.

The Fixer's attention turned to Josh and another young man coming down the stairs with a large zipped bag between them. It was apparent what was in the bag.

"What . . . what are you going to do with

her?" the man stammered.

"Better you don't know," the Fixer replied. He clapped his client on the shoulder. "I believe it's time for us to go. We have a lot to talk about."

1

The sky was overcast and threatening more snow on Christmas morning as the three-car motorcade pulled out from the garage beneath the Varick Federal Detention Center at Foley Square in lower downtown Manhattan. The armored sedans turned left onto Centre Street and headed north, leaving a cyclone of flakes in their wake.

New Yorkers who had hoped for a white Christmas had had their prayers answered during the night. It was as pretty as the city got in the winter; the four-inch blanket of white covering the sidewalks, streets, and buildings was still pristine and virtually untrammeled, as traffic was light and most citizens were home with their families.

Christmas decorations hung from streetlights and overhanging wires or blinked with holiday cheer from shop windows and restaurants as the convoy passed through Chinatown. It wasn't as hip or ostentatious as the displays uptown at Saks, Barneys, Bloomingdale's, or Bergdorf Goodman, but the neon *Buon Natale* hanging above the door of the Italian restaurant at the corner of White and Centre and the electric menorah in the window above the shoe-repair shop across the street were more quintessentially New York.

Only a few pedestrians trudged along the sidewalks, huddled against the cold, their breath puffing from their mouths like old locomotives, as the sedans plowed forward as fast as traffic and road conditions would allow. At the corner of Centre and Canal, a man dressed in a Santa Claus suit, talking on a cell phone, waved merrily as the convoy turned left again and rolled west.

In the second car, a skinny black man stretched out his long, lanky frame and smirked at the decorations, sentiments, and Santa. *Good riddance, New York. Allah curses the air you breathe. We tried to ruin Christmas for you this year, but it was not his will. So enjoy your false religions and peaceful streets a little while longer, but we'll be back.*

Spotting a sign for the Holland Tunnel ahead, Sharif Jabbar licked his thick purple lips and smiled so widely that his large white teeth protruded from his thin face like a skeleton's grin. He wanted the others in the car to see his triumph and know that there was nothing they could do about it. There were three U.S. marshals in the vehicle and four each in the sedans in front and back. But they weren't there as his captors, not anymore. He was an important man, and it was their job to make sure nothing happened to him until he was safe and on his way out of the cursed United States of America. That's why they'd chosen this morning, when no one was around, to spirit him from his cell and take him to Fort Dix in New Jersey, where a jet was waiting to fly him to freedom.

Apparently, there had been several threats to assassinate him for his role in the attack on the New York Stock Exchange the previous September, including a plot by NYPD officers because of their colleagues who'd been killed in the battle. His attorney told him that there was also a rumor that some of his former congregation at the Al-Aqsa mosque in Harlem were after *thar,* or "blood vengeance," because some of their sons, and one daughter, had died for Allah because of him.

A bunch of uneducated ghetto niggers and stupid African immigrants, he thought, *who don't understand that jihad requires sacrifices; they don't remember that* Islam *means "sub-*

mission."

Jabbar wondered what it was going to be like living in Saudi Arabia or wherever he ended up. He'd never been out of the country before. He'd been born in Harlem Hospital and christened DeWayne Wallace in the Abyssinian Baptist Church on 138th Street and only converted to Islam some twenty-five years later while serving time in Attica for manslaughter and armed robbery.

Released with time off for "good behavior," he'd decided to study to become an imam, then founded a "mosque" in an abandoned liquor store in Harlem. For ten years, he'd preached a virulent anti-Semitic, anti-white, and anti-U.S. screed that found a small but enthusiastic audience with some of the young men in the neighborhood. His congregation grew to include families and even a few Muslim immigrants looking for a place to pray with others of their faith, even if Jabbar's political rants made them uneasy.

Still, it had been a meager living until he met with certain foreign "Islamic scholars," who questioned him about his beliefs in the late 1980s. The mosque had then received a sudden infusion of money from the governments of Saudi Arabia and Libya, as well as private contributions from wealthy men in other Muslim countries. The funds had paid for a comfortable, even luxurious, life for Jabbar, as well as millions for the construction of the Al-Aqsa mosque on 126th and Madison.

At first, he'd been asked to show his appreciation for the "gifts" by hosting various visitors supposedly in town to raise money for "Muslim charities" overseas. He knew that these were just the front men for terrorist organizations, who were also using fundamentalist mosques in America like his to create networks for sleeper cells. It was easy money for a while. But then he received word from a visiting imam, a radical with the conservative Wahabi sect, that his benefactors wanted him to assist the "Sheik" with a plot that, if successful, would destroy the economy of the United States by crashing the stock market.

The Sheik turned out to be terrorist Amir Al-Sistani, who had arrived in the United States acting the part of a meek, subservient business manager for a Saudi prince, Esra bin Afraan Al-Saud, who'd come to check on his vast holdings as principal owner of a hedge-fund company. Of course, the trip had been at the suggestion of Al-Sistani, who had then manipulated the prince into insisting on a private tour of the stock market. The prince had not known he was being used to gain access to the most sensitive area of the market, the computer room, until Al-Sistani revealed his plan and killed bin Afraan.

It had been Jabbar's job to recruit young men from the streets of Harlem and brainwash them into believing that it was a martyr's mission to destroy the stock exchange. Once he realized that most of the danger would be to others and that he would be amply rewarded, Jabbar had no objections to doing as he was asked or to using the mosque as the staging ground for training and the attack.

But something had gone wrong. The attack had failed, though he still wasn't clear why. The last he'd heard, everything was progressing according to plan, and he'd left Harlem for a private airfield in New Jersey toting a suitcase filled with large-denomination currency. U.S. authorities were certain to trace some of the *jihadi* foot soldiers to the mosque and Jabbar, so Al-Sistani had arranged for the two of them to leave after the attack aboard a private jet and fly to a friendly Muslim country.

However, Al-Sistani never showed, and Jabbar had been surprised when federal agents had appeared to arrest him. In short order, he'd been indicted by a federal grand jury for murder, conspiracy to commit murder, kidnapping, and terrorism. He was denied bail, and the future looked bleak from his cell in the federal detention center. Indeed, some of his guards made sure to talk near his cell, wondering aloud what it would feel like to be put to death by lethal injection. "Like a dog at the pound."

A federal agent named Jaxon had shown up one day early in the month and asked what he knew about Dean Newbury, who'd been the mosque's attorney. Apparently, the old man had been arrested, and the agent wanted to obtain any information Jabbar could provide regarding a group called the Sons of Man.

Jabbar had played dumb. He was aware that the lawyer and the Sons of Man were connected to Al-Sistani's plot, which had initially surprised him because Newbury — and, he supposed, the group he represented — was a rich old white man, who didn't really fit the image of a religious zealot or terrorist. But he'd been kept out of the conversations between Newbury and Al-Sistani and had no real information to trade.

Then, a little over a week ago, his lawyer, Megan O'Dowd, a heavyset white woman who'd described herself to Jabbar as a "radical activist" attorney, had visited and told him that Al-Sistani had just been captured by the federal authorities. The Sheik had disappeared following the stock-exchange attack, but apparently neither the feds nor Al-Sistani's friends in the Muslim world knew what had happened to him. The news that he'd been apprehended was an answer to Jabbar's prayers to Allah, because now he would have someone to turn state's evidence against and cut a deal with the feds. But what O'Dowd had said next was even better. Al-Sistani had some sort of information that the people who had hired O'Dowd to represent them both didn't want out.

"Just sit tight," O'Dowd had told him. "Something's in the works." Otherwise, he wasn't to speak to any law-enforcement agents about Al-Sistani . . . or anything else.

A few days later, the attorney had returned and informed him that U.S. charges against him and Al-Sistani were being dropped and that they were to be turned over to Saudi authorities and tried for the murder of Prince Esra bin Afraan. Jabbar's bulbous eyes had nearly popped out of his skull. "How is this better?" he'd demanded as a ripple of fear shook his bony body. The Saudis were known to behead murderers, especially the murderers of members of the royal family, no matter how low-ranking. It wouldn't take twenty years of appeals, as it would in the United States, before the sentence was carried out.

O'Dowd had told him that Al-Sistani and, by association, Jabbar were folk heroes in the Muslim world. The attempt on the New York Stock Exchange had been greeted with dancing in the streets of Gaza, Tehran, Tripoli, Beirut, the West Bank, and Damascus. After Al-Sistani's recent arrest, there'd been large demonstrations in Muslim capitals in support of him, amid claims circulated on Al-Jazeera television that he was being tortured by the Americans. The radical imams of Saudi Arabia had pressured the royal family to insist that Al-Sistani and Jabbar be brought to the kingdom for "a fair trial."

However, O'Dowd had said with a wink, the trial would be for show. It was widely believed in the Muslim world that Prince Esra's death, as well as most of the other fatalities, actually had been at the hands of the Americans, who'd overreacted as usual and gone in with guns blazing. More important, incurring the ire of the imams, who kept the populace in check, wasn't worth the life of a minor prince of the royal Al-Saud family. At worst, the two "heroes of

Islam" would receive a slap on the wrist and be "forced" to seek asylum with another Muslim regime.

Jabbar had a feeling that there was more to this stroke of good fortune than his sudden popularity in the Muslim world. This had been confirmed the next day, when he was surprised to find himself in the detention center exercise room with Al-Sistani. Up to that point, they'd been kept apart, but now they were allowed a private meeting without any other inmates or guards present. That was when Al-Sistani revealed his "secret weapon" that would result in their freedom.

The next morning, O'Dowd had told him that Al-Sistani had been quietly flown out of the country. Apparently, the authorities who might have been expected to object — particularly New York District Attorney Roger Karp — had been distracted by the most recent terrorist attack on New York City, when *jihadis* tried to sail a ship filled with natural gas up the East River to blow up the Brooklyn Bridge. They, too, had been stopped by the police, according to news accounts Jabbar saw on the television in his cell, with the assistance of a group of armed Russian immigrants in tugboats.

Jabbar had had to fight off a panic attack

when he learned that Al-Sistani was gone. He knew that back in September, Karp had agreed to hold off indicting Jabbar on state murder charges in case the U.S. attorney needed to be able to offer him a carrot to testify if Al-Sistani was apprehended. The district attorney had been tight-lipped when the media found out that Al-Sistani had been flown to Saudi Arabia and asked for a reaction. His spokesman said only that Karp was "disappointed" with the decision by the U.S. Attorney's Office and the State Department.

Then O'Dowd had showed up on Christmas Eve and told him to be ready to leave in the morning.

"What about Karp?" Jabbar had asked.

"He's afraid of getting his ass kicked by the feds." O'Dowd laughed. "He's not even in town, and you'll be long gone before he hears about it."

As the sedans entered the east end of the Holland Tunnel, Jabbar rubbed his eyes and yawned. He'd had a difficult time getting to sleep that night worrying about Karp. When he finally drifted off, his dreams were haunted by Miriam Juma Khalifa.

Miriam, the young widow of one of Jabbar's followers, had been murdered in the basement of the mosque by the Russian terrorist-for-hire Nadya Malovo, a.k.a. Ajmaani. Miriam's husband had blown himself up in a Third Avenue synagogue months before the NYSE attack, and Malovo claimed that Miriam had dishonored her husband's martyrdom by carrying on an affair after his death. But Jabbar doubted it. He knew that Miriam, who'd immigrated from Kenya with her family, was not the sort of Muslim woman to have a lover. Her father was a respected elder in the mosque, one of the voices countering Jabbar's politics within the congregation. And Miriam was a modest young woman who followed her father's example.

Jabbar suspected Ajmaani had other motives for murdering the girl: preventing Miriam from disclosing anything she had learned about the impending stock-exchange attack from her husband, raising the bloodlust of the *jihadis* who would take part, and warning anyone who might contemplate betraying Ajmaani. The brutality of the act — cutting her throat in front of the men and himself as a video camera recorded the event — also suggested that the woman simply enjoyed killing.

Personally, Jabbar hoped he'd never meet Ajmaani again. But the same held true for

Miriam Juma, whose ghost had troubled his dreams. She'd often been accompanied by another woman dressed in a burka, and they'd followed him in his nightmares as he tried to escape from a menacing presence.

Thinking of the women while sitting in the sedan, Jabbar felt a chill run down his spine. He glanced at the man next to him. He knew that the marshals were none too happy with what was going on. They'd hardly spoken to him except to say what was necessary to lead him from his cell, cuff his wrists behind his back, and place him in the car. He suspected that if they had their way, they would have rather thrown him off a bridge into the Hudson River than escort him safely beneath it.

His stomach knotted when the female U.S. marshal sitting in the front passenger seat, who seemed to be in charge, turned to the marshal next to Jabbar and nodded. For a moment, he thought that his fear of assassination was about to come true. But instead, the man ordered him to turn around so that he could get to the handcuffs with a key he'd produced from his pocket.

Jabbar smiled. "I *was* getting a little uncomfortable," he said, and smirked as he rubbed his wrists. "I'll make sure to send you a postcard from Mecca."

The man tensed but didn't say anything as he turned his head to look out the window. Jabbar laughed and made a face for the driver, who was looking in the mirror at him.

He started to hum a tuneless melody as the car emerged from the tunnel on the New Jersey side of the Hudson, but then he jumped at the sudden sound of sirens behind them. A moment later, a dark unmarked police car with a bubble light on top sped past. He started to relax, thinking the cops were responding to a call up ahead, when a Newark patrol car pulled alongside. The passenger window slid down, and an officer indicated that he wanted the marshal's sedan to pull over.

There was another quick blast of a siren behind them. Jabbar whirled around in his seat and saw that a third patrol car was trailing the last sedan with its red and blue lights flashing. His escort's radio crackled on. "Marshal Capers, this is Marshal Joe Rosen in car one. It appears that the locals want us to pull over. What do you want to do?"

The woman in the front seat picked up the microphone. "It's their turf, Joe. If they want us to pull over, pull over."

Jabbar's eyes grew wide. "What are you doing? Don't stop!"

The woman turned around. "We've been asked by local law-enforcement officers with jurisdiction over this road to stop, and we will comply."

"You're the feds, you don't need to pay attention to those New Jersey pigs," Jabbar said as the car rolled to a halt off the side of the road. "I demand that you continue!"

"I don't appreciate you referring to any police officers as pigs," said the woman, her dark brown eyes flashing with anger. "And I suggest you relax until we can find out what this is about."

With that, U.S. Marshal Jen Capers opened her door and got out of the car. By craning his neck, Jabbar could see her talking to a large black man in a suit as two uniformed Newark cops stood listening. The black man handed several papers to the marshal, who turned around and pointed at Jabbar's sedan.

Capers and the man walked back to the car, where she opened her door and looked back at him. "Mr. Jabbar, I'm going to have to ask you to get out of the car."

"What for?" he whined, shrinking back against the seat.

"This is Detective Clay Fulton with the New York Police Department, though if I'm not mistaken," she said, turning to the large

43

black man who'd come up to stand behind her, "you actually work for the district attorney."

"That's right, Jen," Fulton replied. "I head up the detectives who conduct investigations for the DA."

"And Clay, I believe you have an arrest warrant for Mr. Jabbar?"

"Yes, ma'am."

"Then Mr. Jabbar, I'm afraid you're going to have to go with these men. Please step out of the car. Clay, would you help Mr. Jabbar out of his seat?"

Fulton smiled and stepped to the door, which he opened. "Let's go," he said, offering a large hand.

Panicking, Jabbar tried to avoid the detective's grasp. He looked past him to Capers. "I'm still a federal prisoner," he said. "I insist that you take me to Fort Dix and hand me over to the proper authorities there."

The marshal pursed her lips and shook her head. "Well, actually, that's not true. Once we passed through the Holland Tunnel and into New Jersey, we were no longer in the Southern Federal District, nor were you my prisoner. At this point, we were merely escorting you to Fort Dix as requested by the U.S. Attorney General's Office. But that was as a favor to the Saudi

44

Arabian government. As you know, U.S. federal charges against you have been dropped, but NYPD Detective Clay Fulton and these officers from the Newark PD have what appears to be a valid warrant, and we're in their jurisdiction."

Fulton grabbed Jabbar firmly by the upper arm and half slid, half pulled him from the car.

The imam blinked. "I'm not your prisoner? I can leave?" he asked Capers.

The marshal scratched her head and grinned at Fulton. "I suppose you could try to leave, and I won't even try to stop you — unless, of course, the detective requests my assistance as a law-enforcement officer. However, seeing as how these men are here to arrest you for murder, I would caution you that there is the potential for them to use deadly force to prevent you from escaping."

Jabbar stared from face to face, noting the smiles. "This was a setup!"

Capers shook her head. "I can honestly say that I had no idea that this would happen," she said. "I admit that I'm not terribly disappointed to be deprived of a trip to Fort Dix, and it's nice to see my old friend Detective Fulton on a Christmas morning. But if this was a setup, I wasn't in

45

the loop. Perhaps, Clay, you'll be kind enough to fill me in on how you knew about our plans someday?"

Fulton laughed and shrugged. "I'm just following orders. How's your daughter? You going to be at church this evening?"

"Wouldn't miss it," Capers responded. "I love singing Christmas carols."

"Me, too," the detective said, and then nodded to the Newark officers. "Want to do the honors?"

The Newark cops grinned as they spun Jabbar around to face the trunk of the sedan. One of the officers ordered Jabbar to spread his legs and place his hands on the vehicle as they patted him down.

"I just came from jail," Jabbar protested as they cuffed him. "What do you think I'm carrying? I want to call my lawyer *now!*"

Fulton stepped forward, grabbed Jabbar by the front of his shirt, and pulled his face within two inches of his own. "I don't give a shit, you phony fuck," he growled. "You'll get your call *after* I've tossed your ass in the Tombs."

Immediately, with barely controlled violence, Fulton rattled off the Miranda warnings. "You are under arrest for the decapitation-torture murder of Miriam Juma Khalifa, committed in concert with

46

others, in the basement of the Al-Aqsa mosque in Harlem, of which you are — you son of a bitch — the so-called imam. You have the right to remain silent. If you choose to say anything, it can and will be used against you in a court of law. You have the right to an attorney. If you cannot afford an attorney, one will be appointed for you."

Two minutes later, Jabbar was being stuffed into a Newark patrol car as Fulton turned to the federal marshal.

"Thanks for making that easy," Fulton said. "We were concerned that some by-the-book guy might want to call the U.S. attorney or Jabbar's lawyer, and this could have got messy. I didn't know it was going to be you in charge, or I wouldn't have worried."

Capers shrugged. "Happy to turn the bastard over to someone who will nail his hide to the wall. To be honest, I don't think you would have got much resistance from the marshal's office no matter who was riding shotgun today. Nobody likes these kinds of 'politics over justice' cases. All we needed was a legal excuse, and the warrant worked. I'm glad whoever the little bird is who told you about this figured it out. What's next for the son of a bitch?"

"The boss will go to the grand jury for an

indictment as soon as he gets back from his vacation," Fulton explained.

"Knowing Karp, I'm surprised he goes on vacation," Capers said with a smile.

"I practically had to threaten him with my resignation to get him to go." Fulton laughed. "Even then, he was looking for excuses until Marlene put her foot down and insisted he join the family. If there's one person on this planet who can tell him what to do, and maybe get him to do it, it's his wife. It helped that the courts are closed for the holidays until Monday, which gives him three more days to relax. He needs the rest."

Fulton stuck out his hand to Capers. "Thanks, Jen. I need to get this dirtbag over to the Tombs and call Butch. Then I can go home to the family."

"Hey, thanks to you, I'm going to be home a lot sooner than I would have if I had to go to Fort Dix," she replied. "See you tonight. I look forward to hearing that lovely baritone. Merry Christmas, Clay."

"Merry Christmas. And thanks again."

2

As he waited for Fulton's call that morning, Roger "Butch" Karp perused the *New York Times,* which had been delivered that morning to the family's suite in the Kit Carson Inn, a luxury hotel in Taos, New Mexico. The *Times* and the presidential suite were both courtesy of a man he'd never met, who owned the ranch west of town where Ned Blanchett, his daughter's fiancé, was foreman. The generous offer had been tendered after their wealthy benefactor had learned the family would be staying in Taos over the holidays.

Karp had resisted the trip to New Mexico. After all, as he'd pointed out to Detective Fulton and his wife, Marlene Ciampi, they'd just weathered another terrorist attack conceived by his diabolical archenemy, Andrew Kane, who'd joined forces with Islamic terrorists and tried to blow up the Brooklyn Bridge. To make sure that Karp understood the personal nature of Kane's animosity toward him, the sociopath had also abducted Karp's daughter, Lucy, in an effort to make him choose between her and many other innocent lives. Fortunately, as a result of the heroics of some brave men, it hadn't come to that, but it was one more reminder that evil seemed to have a personal vendetta against the Karp-Ciampi clan.

And if the terrorist attack had not been enough to deal with, Karp had just finished up with a high-profile murder trial. An eccentric, well-known theater producer, F. Lloyd Maplethorpe, had murdered an actress in his Tribeca hotel penthouse but then claimed that she'd committed suicide. Karp had presented a bare-bones, "just the facts, ma'am," case based on the incontrovertible evidence and then counted on the jurors' common sense to cut through the defense's endless string of "expert" witnesses — with his guidance. In the end, the jury had sided with the prosecution and convicted Maplethorpe.

Karp had looked forward to the sentencing, but then Maplethorpe had been murdered in the Tombs, as the Manhattan Detention Complex was known. Thinking about Maplethorpe's death now caused him to frown as he glanced back down at the

Times. The suspect in the killing was a member of the Inca Boyz, a Hispanic gang out of Spanish Harlem, whose one-time leader, Alejandro "Boom" Garcia, was yet another of the unusual characters whose fate seemed woven into the fabric of his and his family's lives. It didn't take Sherlock Holmes's assistance for Karp to suspect that Garcia had ordered the hit.

Alejandro's girlfriend, Carmina Salinas, another aspiring actress, had also been assaulted by Maplethorpe and testified to that effect after the producer tried to have her killed to silence her. Garcia had wanted to go after Maplethorpe himself, and only the intercession of Marlene and Carmina had persuaded him to let Karp and the justice system handle it. But apparently, the gangster-turned-rap-star had decided not to wait for a judge to pronounce sentence. Maplethorpe had been stabbed to death while waiting in line with other inmates.

Nothing could be proved regarding any involvement Garcia might have had in Maplethorpe's death — saving Karp the dilemma of having his office prosecute a young man who'd risked his own life for Karp's family in the past. He just hoped that the truth that he suspected was buried with the producer.

Karp shook his head at the thought. There'd been a time — back when the color of his hair was still dark coffee, not pewter, and the lines around his gray gold-flecked eyes were far fewer — when the concept of hoping that a murderer would go unpunished was unthinkable. However, somewhere along the line, he'd reached an uneasy compromise with his sense of justice. So long as it did not impinge on his duty as district attorney to prosecute crimes committed in New York County, he wasn't going to shed tears for the violent end of evil men and women.

He still abhorred the concept of "street justice" (though there'd been plenty of it meted out by his own wife), and if the evidence ever warranted charging Garcia, he wouldn't interfere. Maplethorpe's death had occurred in his jurisdiction, and if a case could be made against Garcia, he'd have no choice but to ask that a special prosecutor be appointed and then step out of the way. But until, and if, that day arrived, Garcia's involvement in the death of Maplethorpe was nothing more than a hunch.

Nor had it kept Karp in New York over the holidays. His arguments that it was a bad time for him to go on vacation had

52

fallen on the deaf ears of Fulton and Marlene. The stress was all the more reason he needed to go, they'd insisted, and they'd finally convinced him that the DAO would not collapse in the two weeks he would be gone.

Now, sitting in an overstuffed leather chair in the presidential suite of a New Mexico hotel, Karp turned back to his newspaper and noted that the attack on the Brooklyn Bridge and Maplethorpe's murder had finally dropped off the front page. However, there was still plenty of carnage and scandal to report, alongside the annual feel-good story about some multimillionaire basketball player giving away a few toys to underprivileged children. The major political parties were, of course, blaming each other for the economy being in the toilet, while at the same time increasing massive government spending on entitlement programs and handing out taxpayer dollars by the billions to financial institutions, apparently to reward mismanagement and malfeasance.

As he turned the page, a photograph accompanying a short news story out of Westchester County, a suburb just north of Gotham, caught his eye. The photo was of the Westchester district attorney, Harley Chin, seated behind his desk during a press conference. According to the story, a young debutante named Rene Hanson, from the upscale town of Purchase, had been reported missing by her distraught, and wealthy, parents. The twenty-two-year-old had disappeared shortly before Christmas and had not been heard from since.

Chin had called the news conference apparently for the purpose of announcing that he was "putting all the resources of my office, working with the Westchester, state, and federal law-enforcement agencies, to locate Miss Hanson. And if, heaven forbid, her absence is due to criminal activities, to put the perpetrators on notice that this office will not rest until justice has been served."

Karp rolled his eyes. There was no reason for a district attorney to be issuing statements at that point — *or ever* — in a missing-persons investigation. For one thing, there was no clear evidence that Hanson was the victim of criminal activity, and certainly no one had been arrested or charged with a crime that would have involved Chin's office. There was simply no point to holding such a news conference and making those kinds of statements, except to grab the media spotlight, which, given the personality of the man involved, did not surprise Karp.

He had known Harley Chin for years. The tall, forty-five-year-old Chinese-American's immigrant parents owned a small grocery store on the Lower East Side in Alphabet City between Sixth and Seventh Streets on Avenue B. They had scrimped and saved to put their only son through Harvard Law School. After graduation, he'd come to work at the New York DAO.

In fact, at one time, Karp, who was then head of the DAO Homicide Bureau, had taken Chin under his wing, intending to groom him to run the bureau himself someday. The younger man had seemed to have all the right stuff. He'd graduated near the top of his class, and he possessed a sharp mind, a keen intellect, and a willingness to learn. He was an eloquent speaker and a pleasure to listen to as he deftly put together his cases so well that much more experienced attorneys in the DAO were usually at a loss to find any flaws at the weekly meetings of bureau chiefs.

However, much to Karp's disappointment, Chin also possessed an enormous ego, and a lot of gray areas when it came to his ethics eventually undermined his attributes. Although Karp wouldn't learn the full extent for some time after his former protégé had left the office, Chin saw nothing wrong with taking "shortcuts" and using morally questionable tactics if that's what it took to "win" at trial. Some of his former colleagues had later confided that Chin equated his success in the courtroom with climbing the ladder at the DAO — a means to an end rather than dedication to justice.

Chin loved the limelight. Nothing seemed to make him happier than getting his name and face in the newspapers or on television. He usually ignored, or tried to get around, Karp's admonishments to stop talking to the media about his cases. That included one instance in which Karp suspected his protégé had leaked a grand-jury indictment, a misdemeanor, to a *Times* reporter before it was filed with the court. But Karp had no solid evidence to back up his suspicion.

Karp couldn't prove it, and after another stern warning, he chalked the publicity seeking up to youthful immaturity and continued to work with Chin, hoping he'd wise up and see the light. But it turned out that Chin's problem wasn't just liking a little ink. He stepped over the line when he showed a witness to a murder photographs of a suspect before the witness was to view a police lineup. The witness then picked the man in the photograph and became adamant about the identification.

The defendant had an airtight alibi and proved it in court. Karp didn't learn about the corrupted lineup until he read a post-trial article in the *Times* quoting the witness, who claimed to have been "intimidated" into identifying the wrong man. Karp was livid. Not only was the real killer still walking the streets — and probably could never be successfully tried because the defense would use the impeached witness — but an innocent man had gone through the misery of jail and a trial and had nearly lost his freedom for life.

Chin, in his arrogance, had explained it all away as a "gut instinct" that he'd had the right man, but the witness had been a bit iffy about his ability to identify the killer and needed a little help. "Win some, lose some," he'd said, shrugging, as he sat in the chair across from Karp's desk. Twenty minutes later, he was slinking out the door with his ears still burning and no longer employed by the New York District Attorney's Office.

After leaving the DAO, Chin had gone into private practice, mostly minor criminal cases from well-heeled clients who liked the idea of a former hotshot with the New York

DAO defending them or their kids. Then, several years ago, he'd popped up in Westchester County, where his sudden, well-financed entry into the district attorney's race there had surprised the incumbent, a lazy, multiterm good old boy who didn't recognize the threat until it was too late. Chin won the election handily.

Now, according to the office grapevine, Chin was angling to get the governor's nod to replace the current New York attorney general, who was intending to run for the U.S. Senate in the spring. And, according to the *Times* article, the missing girl's parents and their wealthy friends were major contributors to Chin's political war chest.

Karp shook his head. *That pretty much explains it,* he thought, turning the page.

The antics of Harley Chin were hardly his concern. He'd awakened at four that morning unable to sleep, thinking about events that would soon be transpiring in New York City regarding one Sharif Jabbar.

Leaving the warm, gently serene presence of his wife, he'd wandered out onto the deck off the suite's expansive living room and let the frigid predawn air shock him fully awake. Looking up, he'd marveled at the clarity of the New Mexico night sky. In New York, stars — if they could be seen at all —

were dim facsimiles of these brilliant spots of light. On the high plains of northern New Mexico, stars stood out as individual entities, their light as crisp and as brilliant as diamonds even though they were millions of light-years away.

Karp lowered his gaze. The deck overlooked the snow-covered Taos Plaza, which he'd learned had been in existence since the late 1700s. The plaza was set up in the traditional Spanish style, with a park in the middle, surrounded by a narrow lane and an outer ring of shops and cafés occupying what had been the adobe homes of early inhabitants. It had once been the town's and the region's center of government and was still a favorite meeting place for locals.

A coyote howled in the desert on the outskirts of town. Karp shivered with the cold and with pleasure at the wild, independent cry. Ever since he was a child growing up in Brooklyn, he'd dreamed of someday visiting the wide-open spaces of the American West. In a neighborhood populated by immigrants and their children, most of whom had never been farther west than New Jersey, he and his friends had spent many summer days and evenings fending off Indian attacks and bravely dying in gunfights against the bad guys.

Karp had learned his moral values from his parents. But their values were reinforced and magnified by his heroes on the silver screen, such as Gary Cooper in *High Noon* and Alan Ladd in *Shane.* At the top of the list of heroes was John Wayne as he appeared in westerns and World War II movies. Karp had lived for the Saturday matinees at the Avalon and King's Way theaters on King's Highway in Brooklyn, just a few blocks east of Ocean Parkway, where he grew up.

They were simple stories pitting virtue against evil. Heroes were often opposed by their mirror opposites, evil that they had to destroy. Villains often had the advantage or cheated, but heroes played by the rules and were defined more by their integrity, courage, and toughness than by even their exceptional prowess with a Colt .45 Peacemaker. The hero was a leader of men, but if necessary — especially in the defense of those who had no one else — he would stand alone and never, ever compromise his principles for expediency, personal gain, or safety.

Such morality tales were not lost on Karp as a boy, nor was their deeper meaning ignored by the man. Many years later, as an adult, he'd recognize these themes as allegories for the potential for evil that resides within every human. While most resisted their baser impulses, those who didn't were the sorts of criminals he prosecuted on behalf of the People.

Karp's appreciation for the romanticized hero of the Old West wasn't the result of his belief that such a man had existed. It was what that hero represented. An ideal of living up to principles. A role model to aspire to. And if you failed at first, then, like one of Karp's screen idols, you picked yourself up, dusted yourself off, and climbed back into the saddle again.

It had carried over into his choice of profession. His one goal upon finishing law school was to work for the New York District Attorney's Office, where the legendary DA Francis Garrahy was the "sheriff" in town who ran his office according to a strict moral and ethical code, what Karp came to think of as the institutionalization of virtue. There would be no cheating, no shortcuts, no compromising of principles for the sake of expediency, self-aggrandizement, or glory. Ever since, Karp had made his living putting the guys in black hats behind prison walls, though even in his wildest dreams as a young assistant district attorney, he'd never imagined that someday he would be the old man's actual, as well as philosophical, heir.

Karp had left the deck and retrieved the *Times* from outside the apartment door. As he began to read, he paused and noted the nearly absolute quiet surrounding him. Even with the windows closed in New York City, there was no escaping the sounds of traffic and the constant hum of the machinery that supported millions of people packed together on an island.

He liked it in Taos and had even entertained what it would be like to move there and go into private practice, maybe hang his shingle outside some small office down the street from the house where Kit Carson and his wife, Josefa, once lived. Or perhaps he'd apply for a job as an ordinary prosecutor for the local district attorney. *Why not?* he'd mused. *What's the difference between bringing a murderer to justice in New York City or in New Mexico?* The victims were just as deserving of justice, the killer just as deserving of punishment.

The fantasy didn't last long. It was a question of scale and of being where he was needed most. Certainly, a victim in New Mexico was just as deserving of justice, but there were a lot more of them on the island of Manhattan. And that was where he could have the greatest impact against the evil that lurked in some men's souls. For better or worse, he was the chief law-enforcement officer for the County of New York, responsible for directing the efforts of some five hundred assistant district attorneys to prosecute more than one hundred thousand criminal cases every year.

In the years between the old man's and Karp's terms in office, Garrahy's institutionalization of virtue had succumbed under the leadership of less principled men, who had precious little, if any, trial experience and who corrupted justice by engaging in excessive plea bargaining to manage the massive DAO caseload. So, believing that to return the DAO to its former glory he needed to lead by example, Karp took on high-profile, complex, and legally significant cases himself. Not for personal or ego-driven reasons, like Harley Chin, but to set the standard for what he expected of those who worked for him, as well as to take on such issues as organized crime, public corruption, terrorism, and disingenuous defense tactics such as the "big lie frame defense" and the "insanity of the insanity defense." He hoped to leave a legacy of well-trained trial-lawyer prosecutors who would someday replace the old guard like himself, while carrying on the principles of Garrahy.

The article in the *Times* reminded him that he'd once imagined Harley Chin was one of those, only to be disappointed. *Maybe Kenny Katz,* he thought. So far, his new protégé, an Iraq War veteran and Columbia Law grad, seemed to have Chin's legal brilliance without the warts. He could be impatient and brash, but to date, his ethics were beyond reproach.

Karp glanced at the clock on the wall. Six-thirty, eight-thirty in New York. At that moment, Katz was supposed to be working with Fulton to apprehend Sharif Jabbar. If the caller was accurate and had the time right. He rapped his knuckles on the wooden lampstand next to the chair. As if on cue, the telephone rang. He grabbed it before it rang again, hoping not to wake Marlene and his twin boys while he talked to his longtime friend.

"Merry Christmas, Clay, what's cooking?"

"And a Happy Hanukkah to you, too, boss," came the reply. "And that burned smell is Sharif Jabbar's chestnuts roasting. He's being processed as we speak, and then, as per your instructions, Mr. Kenny Katz is waiting to see if he wants to answer a few questions before he lawyers up."

"Beautiful," Karp said. "Glad to hear that Mr. Katz was able to drag himself out of bed on a cold winter holiday morning."

"As a matter of fact, he went above and beyond the call of duty," Fulton answered with a chuckle. "He insisted on getting to be the guy who dressed up in a Santa Claus outfit and stood on the corner of Centre and Canal to watch for the motorcade just in case they took another route. I'm told he looked somewhat like a deflated red balloon."

"Has to be the skinniest kosher St. Nick on record," Karp said, and laughed. "So I take it Jabbar's attorney wasn't along for the ride?"

"Nowhere to be seen," Fulton replied. "I thought it was a little odd, but I guess she figured she'd cut a deal and there was no reason to leave her cozy cave. It wouldn't have mattered. Even if she could have found a judge willing to listen to her on Christmas morning, I was dragging Jabbar down to the Tombs and booking him. In fact, I was sort of hoping I'd get the chance to watch her face turn that lovely shade of eggplant when I bounced her boy off the hood of the car and cuffed him."

Karp noted the bitter distaste behind Fulton's words. The detective had been a rookie police officer walking a beat in central Harlem many years earlier when self-proclaimed black nationalists murdered four cops in cold blood. The killers had walked up behind the unsuspecting officers who were patrolling a section of the projects and executed them without warning. One of the murdered officers, a black thirty-year-old father of two, had been Fulton's first cousin.

The killers' defense attorney was Megan O'Dowd. She'd argued that the shootings were justified as self-defense, that the cops had "invaded" the projects for the purpose of harassing young black men like her clients because of their political beliefs. She'd also claimed that the police department had knowingly sent officers into the projects to incite a violent confrontation. And when the officers came out on the losing end, the department and the DAO had framed her clients to make it appear that "justifiable resistance to government provocation" had been an act of premeditated, cold-blooded execution.

Opposing O'Dowd had been a young, idealistic prosecutor named Roger "Butch" Karp, who had only recently been appointed to the DAO's Homicide Bureau when the case fell to him. Surprisingly, because there were many more experienced assistant district attorneys in the bureau, Garrahy had gone against the advice of his senior bureau chiefs and put Karp on the case.

O'Dowd had since made a career out of defending every antigovernment, anti-U.S. group who'd have her. Communists. Black Panthers. And a plethora of terrorists from Puerto Rico to Croatia to the Middle East. After September 11, 2001, she'd been quoted in the media contending that terrorist groups like Al Qaeda were "national liberationists," whose only option to defend Muslims against the military and economic tyranny of the West was to attack "by unconventional means." Violence, she said, aimed at the institutions that perpetuate capitalism and contribute to the oppression of Muslims all over the world was "justified."

"It turned out that the U.S. marshal in charge of the detail was an old friend, Jen Capers, and she was only too happy to cooperate," Fulton said. "I think you met Jen at our house on the Fourth of July last year."

"Yeah . . . tall, nice smile, striking eyes, looks like she could have been a model," Karp recalled. "I didn't get to talk to her much, but she seemed real sharp."

"That's her." Fulton laughed. "And also tough as nails. If my memory hasn't completely left me, she's been shot twice in the line of duty, but both times the shooter came out on the losing end of the gunfight."

"Well, glad it went smoothly, but sorry you had to do this on Christmas morning. Apologize to Helen for me."

"Oh, I intend to as soon as I get home," Fulton replied. "In fact, I'm blaming it all on you, so that maybe she'll still give me that special gift she's been promising."

"Then by all means, I'll take the rap," Karp said.

"Right, so happy holidays to Marlene and the kids."

"Thanks, Clay. Merry Christmas, and I'll see you in a few days."

3

The Fixer's cell phone buzzed just as he sat back in the Italian leather recliner and began to unwrap his Christmas present — a Scotty Cameron Newport 2 golf putter signed by Tiger Woods, who had once carried it in his bag as a backup. The Fixer had won the Internet auction with a bid of $35,000, which he considered a steal for the club with the flawless German stainless-steel head weighing in at exactly 350 grams.

He'd then allowed his current girlfriend to wrap it up in gaudy Christmas paper "so that you have something under the tree." The delightful Miss Sherry Maxwell now stood in front of him, watching with a vacuous smile on her pretty face, giggling as if she'd had something to do with the purchase. She did look great in the skimpy Mrs. Claus lingerie she was modeling, so he smiled and said with only a trace of irony, "Thanks, babe, it's just what I wanted."

The phone buzzed again from the pocket of his silk robe. "Don't answer it, Jimmy," she pleaded. "It's Christmas."

Jimmy, he thought. *Yes, that's who I am now.* When choosing a name for his current incarnation, he'd gone for forgettable. James, John, and Robert were the most common male names in the United States; he'd settled on Jim as less formal, and therefore even less memorable, than James. Although Smith was the most common last name, there was a catch in that the very commonness of "Jim Smith" might cause someone to note it. Johnson was number two on the list, but Jim Johnson had too much alliteration, so he'd settled on number three, Williams. *You are Jim Williams; doesn't get any more vanilla than that.*

He pulled the cell phone out of his pocket and glanced at the caller ID. "Hold on a moment, baby, duty calls," he said, standing. Patting her bare bottom with the putter as he moved past her, he headed for his office. "I'll only be a minute."

"You better not be talking to another girl." Sherry pouted.

"Never, my love," the Fixer promised, and winked. "This is all business. You like that necklace, don't you? Somebody has to pay for it."

70

The fingers on Sherry's right hand shot up to the three-carat diamond solitaire pendant hanging from the platinum chain just within the shadowy cleavage of her generous breasts. She'd hoped for a ring with an even larger stone, but the pendant had been a nice consolation prize. So she smiled and gave him a suggestive wiggle and a toss of her platinum-blond hair before turning back to the small white plastic Christmas tree she'd persuaded him to put up in a corner of the living room of his Fifth Avenue penthouse apartment across from Central Park. Gazing lovingly at the mound of assorted boxes on the floor in front of the tree, containing expensive baubles and items of clothing she'd already plundered, she sighed and smiled to herself, having momentarily forgotten the phone call.

The Fixer shook his head as he opened the door to his office and went inside. *Looks like we both got what we wanted this Christmas. She got twenty-five thousand, two hundred and ninety-six dollars' — rounded up — worth of shiny objects. And I woke up to the body of a woman half my age, who wouldn't give me a second glance if I didn't have money. And I now own a Tiger Woods Scotty Cameron, which I'll still be admiring when she's long gone.*

Sherry wasn't the brightest bulb in the room, but he didn't mind that so much. In fact, it was better for him if she wasn't particularly inquisitive — and her curiousity seemed to be limited to what presents he brought home for her when he returned from his "banking" business trips. Nor did she show much more initiative than determining what she was going to wear at any given moment, and even that could take hours to decide. Then again, he hadn't wooed her after he met her at the gym where she was an aerobics instructor because he wanted a brilliant conversationalist or best friend. A warm, energetic body in bed that also looked good on his arm was all that he required of her. And Sherry delivered.

However, there were signs that it was time to move on. Having found her sugar daddy, she was now thinking of the future. Her future. The little comments about her friends' weddings and finding "soul mates" and "not getting any younger" were growing more frequent and more pointed. She had not been able to hide her disappointment that morning when he handed her the long rectangular jewelry box, obviously made for a necklace, rather than a little square box with a rounded top that would have contained the engagement ring of her dreams.

The wedding comments he could handle, not that he planned ever to marry her. Why bother? A girl like Sherry would hang on as long as he wanted her to if she thought there was a chance of landing the big fish. But lately, she'd added a new ingredient with the little asides: jealousy. Even though she tried to disguise it with humor or fake pouting, she was always asking him whether he was seeing someone else, and he knew it meant that she was getting worried about his commitment.

A jealous woman could be a dangerous woman, he reminded himself as he took a seat behind his Parnian desk. He paused for a moment to admire the exotic wood inlays and burls of the world's most expensive "power desk." *Two hundred twenty thousand and worth every penny,* he thought. His preference in furniture, like his taste in women, was contemporary, beautiful, and expensive.

The Fixer recognized that Sherry and his other extravagances were counterintuitive to keeping as low a profile as possible. Instead of maintaining a safe, obscure double life as an accountant living in Yonkers with a dowdy, middle-aged wife and a couple of snot-faced kids, driving an SUV and golfing on public courses, he allowed himself to enjoy the fruits of his labors. He liked beautiful girlfriends, expensive furniture, nice toys, dream vacations, membership at the exclusive Trump National Golf Club in Westchester, and, though he generally drove unremarkable sedans when working, he was a collector of rare sports cars.

Most of his life had been spent pulling in a government salary, beginning with his days in the 1980s as a lieutenant in the U.S. Marines Central Intelligence Division, "unofficialy and off the books" training Contra guerrillas to fight the Communist Sandinista government in Nicaragua. When the Iran-Contra affair blew up, he'd left the Corps for the Agency and was reassigned to Cold War games of cat-and-mouse that took him from Latin America to Europe, Asia, and Africa.

As a spook, he'd proved to be particularly adept at cleaning up messes created by other agents or "friends" of the U.S. government, which might mean removing any and all traces of an embarrassing sexual affair by an ambassador or eliminating witnesses to a botched assassination. He became so good at it that he'd earned the in-house moniker of the Fixer.

However, being good had not earned him the kind of lifestyle he coveted. During his time with the Agency, he'd managed to put aside a private stash of funds he'd skimmed from the seized assets of drug dealers and tin-pot dictators. But that was all small potatoes compared with the cash he was raking in now, thanks to his training with the Agency.

When the Cold War ended, the Fixer's talents were not as much in demand, and in fact, some of his previous dealings were something of an embarrassment as old enemies became friends and vice versa. So he was allowed to "retire" and pursue his avocation of taking care of other people's problems for a lot of money.

The idea had come to him while he was still employed by the government, and a U.S. senator, considered "friendly" toward the Agency and its budget, had run into a little trouble. He was being blackmailed by one of the male Senate pages who had worked at the Capitol the year before. Apparently, the senator, a "family values" man, had a thing for buggering the young man, now nineteen, in his office in the Russell Senate Office Building after the rest of the staff had gone home for the evening.

The Fixer had contacted the young man, a student at George Washington University, and they arranged to meet one night at a coffee shop in Foggy Bottom. Being a rookie at the blackmailing game, the young man had agreed to allow the senator's representative, "Bob Johnson," over to his apartment to "settle up privately." Excited about the riches Bob was surely carrying in his briefcase, the young man hardly noted the well-built men strolling behind him.

Not until they began to walk down a poorly lit side street and a dark sedan pulled alongside did the young man grow wary. Suddenly, a back door was flung open, and Bob and the young men grabbed him and threw him into the backseat, where another well-built man spun him around and choked him into unconsciousness. The Fixer climbed in next to his victim.

When the young man regained consciousness a few minutes later, he cried out, "Where are you taking me?"

While the well-built man on the other side held the young man's head up with a painfully tight handful of his hair, Bob leaned close so that he was staring into his victim's frightened eyes from a foot away. "A little ride up the George Washington Memorial Parkway along the Potomac River. In fact, in a few minutes, we are going to stop the car at a place near the river, and then you and I are going to have a brief conversation. I am going to ask you a question, and I am only going to ask it once. If you want to live, you will answer me immediately and truthfully. I will know if you are lying, and there will be no second chances. Am I clear?"

The next morning, the young blackmailer's body was discovered by two kayakers, washed up on the shore at a popular access point off the parkway. The assistant medical examiner who performed the autopsy determined that the deceased had died as a result of "accidental drowning." The AME wrote in his report that the victim's blood alcohol content was well above DUI limits. He had been drinking in his car — found parked nearby with a half-dozen empty beer cans and a partially drunk bottle of tequila — then walked over to the water, where he'd apparently stumbled and fallen in.

Left out of the report was any notation about the bruise marks around the victim's neck. And the blood alcohol content was false. The young man had been sober when he died. But the AME, who received a generous wire transfer to an offshore bank account, had been doing this sort of work for the Fixer and others for years, and there was simply not going to be a determination of homicide.

Of course, there was a small amount of press coverage. That couldn't be helped. A U.S. Senate page getting drunk and tumbling into the Potomac River was going to make the news. But for some reason, the newspaper could not locate the kayakers at the address given to the police. And the Fixer and the public relations experts at the Agency prepped the senator on what to say. He issued a brief statement about "the tragic loss of a fine young man due to the ever-present danger of alcohol in our society." The senator vowed to introduce a bill aimed at an education program for college-age students on "the dangers of binge drinking" and name it after his former page.

The important thing was that the problem was fixed and the senator duly impressed. When a wealthy friend of the senator needed help out of a sticky situation, the politician had called the Agency and asked for the Fixer. His boss had shrugged and told him the Fixer could take it on as a freelance job if he wanted. The Fixer had then called the wealthy friend, who didn't bat an eye when, after explaining the problem, he was told it would cost half a million dollars to fix.

It was then that the Fixer began to consider the benefits of free enterprise over his government job, and he'd put in the paperwork and retired. Any concerns about making the leap into the private sector disappeared quickly as he was pleasantly surprised by the amount of business after word got out. It seemed that the more power and money various politicians, CEOs, actors, ministers, and blue bloods had, the bigger the trouble they got into. His initial fee had gone up to a cool million dollars plus expenses just to take on a case. No negotiating. No guarantees. Half the money up front, the rest immediately upon completion, wired into an account in the Cayman Islands.

Of course, some of the money was used to lure former colleagues to join his growing business, though he was always careful to ask permission of the Agency, which sometimes granted permission and sometimes did not. He filled in his other personnel needs with other former law-enforcement, intelligence agency, and military types. He was even allowed access to some of the Agency's computers and technology. Of course, that meant he still took care of certain jobs for the Agency when the higher-ups wanted something done while keeping a distance from the outcome, just in case some congressional oversight committee came sniffing around.

If the case turned out to be more difficult than normal or the client messed up and created unnecessary obstacles, the price went up, as it had done automatically with this client calling him on Christmas morning.

"Jim Williams" didn't answer his cell phone, nor did he call the client back on it. Cell conversations were too easy to monitor. Instead, he punched in the caller's land-line telephone number from his own land line after checking it with the telephone analyzer he'd borrowed from the Agency. Years ahead of any commercial version sold, the analyzer instantaneously detected whether the line was being tapped and even continuously swept his office for any radio-frequency bugs to prevent remote eavesdropping.

The phone rang only once before it was picked up. "Have you seen the *Times?*" the client asked. His voice sounded as if he was on the razor's edge of panic.

"Not yet," the Fixer replied calmly. He reached for the newspaper lying on his desk. "What's the problem?"

"There's a story about . . . about our arrangement."

"What page?"

"Inside . . . with the photograph of that piece of shit Harley Chin."

"Give me a moment," the Fixer said. He read the story. "Okay, so it's a story about the disappearance of a young woman named Rene Hanson, and this . . . Harley Chin is trying to get in the spotlight. But there's no photograph of the girl, so how do we know this is your friend?"

The Fixer thought the girl would turn out to be one of the thousands of pretty young women who arrived in New York City every year hoping to make it on Broadway or as a model but ended up doing whatever it took to make a living. And if she was pretty enough, and willing, there were plenty of wealthy men — many of them older, like himself — willing to pay for their bodies.

Wherever this girl was from, he'd thought, *it might be weeks before her family reported her missing.* So he hadn't worried when a friend at the Agency told him it would be the day after Christmas before he'd get the results of the fingerprints his man had taken from the dead girl, whose body had been taken to a mob-operated farm in New Jersey to be dismembered and fed to the hogs.

Apparently, the fingerprint identification

would no longer be necessary. The girl's name was now in the news. He recognized the names of the missing girl's parents from the social circles he moved in. They were wealthy and very involved on the political scene, as evidenced by the way this district attorney, Harley Chin, was dancing around like a marionette. He sensed that something had slipped, like a gear in a machine.

The client hesitated long enough before clearing his throat that the Fixer knew the other shoe was about to drop, and his bill was about to rise.

"I forgot to tell you that I —" the client started to say.

"Forgot?"

More hesitation. The bill grew larger. "Well, the truth of the matter is that I knew her real name, Rene . . . um . . . in fact, I knew her before . . . uh . . . before I started seeing her through the VIP Club."

"How did you know her?"

More throat clearing. More zeros on the end of the check. "She was the daughter of one of my golfing foursome," the client blurted out. "It just sort of happened —"

"Bullshit!" The Fixer intended the word to hit like a bullet. "You liked the idea that you were screwing your buddy's daughter. Just a little extra excitement, isn't that right?

Like screwing her in the family home. You're a sex adrenaline junkie. But unfortunately, this Rene wasn't just some runaway kid from Ohio. Her family has wealth and influence, and they're going to want to know what happened to her. Now I have to work even harder, and that's going to cost the people who are footing this bill a lot of money. I hope you're worth it."

"So what do I do now?"

"Get in touch with the escort service, and demand to see 'Brandy Fox.' Otherwise, go about your business as usual. At some point, we might need to reach out to this district attorney, Chin. What do you know about him?"

"A real climber," the client answered. "Stops at nothing to make himself look good. Wants to be state attorney general when the current AG steps down to run for the Senate this spring."

The Fixer thought about it. "That could be important — ambitious men can be reasoned with." He hardened his voice. "But it was a mistake not to tell me everything. As I told you in the beginning, there are no guarantees that I can fix every problem, especially if I don't have all the information I need. If you do that to me again, I will have one of those nice young men you met the other night cut out your tongue for lying to me. Understood?"

After hanging up with the client, the Fixer sat at his desk for a minute, thinking. Then he picked up the telephone and dialed another number. A woman answered.

"Merry Christmas, Amy. How are you doing?" he asked. "Good. I know this is spur of the moment, but I'll make it worth your while. I need you to take a trip to Mexico for me today. I think Guadalajara. Rob will pick you up and will have the necessary documents, but take your own passport to use on the way home. You'll be flying back into San Diego and then home. Oh, you'll need a shoulder-length auburn wig. Bundle up and wear sunglasses so no one gets too good a look at you, though I don't want you to avoid security cameras. Rob will fill you in when he picks you up. We good? Okay. Thanks, baby, you'll have a great Christmas present waiting for your return."

He hung up and placed another call. This time, a man answered.

"Merry Christmas, Rob," he said. "I know it's the holiday, but I have to ask you to go pick up Amy Lopez and take a trip to Mexico. Stop by the Jew's and pick up a passport with Amy's photo in the name of Rene Hanson. There will be one for you under the name of Enrique Salazar — look the part. I'll call the Jew and say you'll be over. Then come here. But first stop by the garage and pick up the car we brought the other night. Apologize to Kate and the kids. Tell her Uncle Jim will make it up to her."

After a few more calls, the Fixer emerged from his office.

Sherry stuck out her lower lip when she saw him. "Who's bothering my sweetie pumpkin on Christmas morning?" She pouted, though the suspicion in her voice was clear.

The Fixer smiled. "Just one of my clients calling to wish me a Merry Christmas. Wants to make a change in his investment strategy before the New Year. Oh, and my buddy Rob is going to drop by. He's headed out of town and wanted to wish us a happy holiday first."

"Does he have to?" Sherry pouted some more.

I can't take this much longer, he thought. "It'll just be for a moment, love bunny. Then I promise, you'll have me for the rest of the day. And don't I see another unopened package over there behind the tree?"

Sherry's eyes lit up, her jealousy momentarily forgotten. She whirled around.

"Where? . . . Ooooh, baby, you're spoiling me!"

"That's what I'm here for," the Fixer said, and took a seat. He patted his lap. "Why don't you sit right here to unwrap it? I might have another surprise for you."

4

Marlene heard the telephone ring once and stop. She surmised that it was the call her husband had been expecting and that he'd picked it up quickly so as not to wake her or the twins. Nor was she in a hurry to get up. A petite woman, she was enjoying the feeling of being lost in a giant ocean of a bed on Christmas morning. Keeping her eyes closed, she nestled down into the luxury of goose-down comforters and German flannel sheets and smiled at the thought of her amorous visit from "Santa Claus" the night before, after the proverbial stockings had been hung by the chimney with care and a glass of Merlot had been enjoyed.

She could just make out Butch's deep, resonant voice and listened for a clue to how the conversation was going. When he laughed, she sighed happily. It meant that he could relax for the last few days of their vacation . . . and so could she, having insisted that he could leave Manhattan without the forces of evil overrunning the city.

As a result, they'd had the most peaceful, relaxed family time she could remember in many years, and now she could rest easy, knowing that her insistence hadn't back-fired. Butch had even been able to drop his official lawman visage and enjoy a visit from his uncle, Vladimir Karchovski, and cousin, Yvgeny — both of them Russian gangsters in Brooklyn, who'd helped Butch save many innocent people on more than one occasion. In Taos, they were just family members celebrating Hanukkah.

Inhaling deeply, Marlene savored the scent of knotty pine and fresh desert sage. *Why can't it ever smell like this in New York City?*

Butch wasn't the only one who'd entertained the idea of retiring to New Mexico. They could certainly afford it. After leaving the DAO, where she'd first met her husband when they were both young assistant district attorneys, she'd started a firm that specialized in providing security services for VIPs. The company had merged with a larger firm, and when its board of directors decided to go public with a stock offering, she'd cashed out of the security game for millions.

Butch made a good living at the DAO, too. Nothing like what she was worth or what he could have earned in private practice, but their lives would still have been quite comfortable without her bankroll.

Especially with their quiet lifestyle. They still lived in the same three-bedroom loft on the corner of Crosby and Grand in SoHo that she'd owned when they first met. He'd bought a small loft across Crosby for her to use as an art studio, and the kids went to private schools, but those were their only real extravagances. They didn't go on expensive vacations or own a summer home on Long Island or decorate the loft with expensive rugs and overpriced art pieces, though her collection of contemporary New York artists such as Robert Rauschenberg and Jasper Johns wasn't shabby, either. She had a truck that was usually parked in a garage two blocks from the loft for six hundred dollars a month, but Butch didn't own a car. As an old-school New Yorker, he preferred to let others deal with the hassles of owning automobiles and negotiating Manhattan traffic.

So money was not the problem if they wanted to move, but she doubted she'd ever be able to get her husband to leave New

York or the DAO.

Butch had spent a lot of his time off catching up on his reading — books he never seemed to have time for back in New York, reading two pages a night before falling asleep exhausted by his day at the office. He'd also taken an interest in Taos and its remarkable history. Like his twin boys, he'd been disappointed that they couldn't visit the ancient Taos Pueblo; a thousand years old, the multistoried complex of apartments built of red-brown adobe was the longest continuously occupied community in North America. However, while it was otherwise open to the public, during the winter months only the two thousand members of the tribe were allowed on the reservation by tribal law.

Not all of Butch's Wild West vacation fantasy was lost. There were the museums and places of historical interest, such as the plaza. And although he'd tried to hide it, she knew he'd been delighted to be asked on several occasions to "ride the range" on horseback with his future son-in-law, Ned Blanchett, who was the foreman of a local ranch, and their Indian friend, John Jojola, the former police chief of the Taos Indian Pueblo.

After the first invitation, Marlene knew

that her straight-laced husband would be too self-conscious to get into the spirit of the thing without a push, so she'd gone shopping and bought him a dark gray Stetson, size 16 cowboy boots, and a "Marlboro Man" leather coat with a fleece lining and collar. When he emerged from their bedroom dressed and ready on the morning of his first ride, he'd blushed and then tried to scowl as he muttered, "I look ridiculous." But the scowl had quickly turned into a boyish grin when she jumped into the arms of "my long tall cowboy" and told him that if he played his cards right later, she might let him keep the hat and boots on. He'd returned that afternoon with his eyes glittering as he described the mare he'd ridden as "a nice little filly" and told her how exciting it had been watching real horsemen like Ned and John race across the prairie while he and "Sally" trotted along behind.

Giggling at the memory, Marlene rolled onto her back and opened her eyes. She could hear Butch still talking, but judging by the tenor and occasional chuckle, it sounded as if the conversation was now purely social. There were no other noises indicating the presence of their fourteen-year-old twins, Isaac and Giancarlo. The trip had been good for the boys, too. They'd spent as much time as they could snowboarding at the Taos Mountain ski resort, guided by Jojola's son, Charlie, with whom they'd quickly bonded. Charlie was sixteen and could drive, so when they weren't on the slopes, they'd explored the surrounding mountains and prairie.

She wondered what they'd think of spending their high school years in Taos instead of New York. Gotham could be a rough place to grow up, even if you weren't the sons of the district attorney. But that fact seemed to destine them to having a target drawn on their backs for every criminal, terrorist, and wacko who had a beef with their dad.

Which brought to mind her first child, Lucy, who was engaged to Ned and planning a July wedding. She and Lucy had spent many happy hours going over plans, invitations, and guest lists. Yet each task brought with it a touch of sadness. Her only daughter had chosen New Mexico over Manhattan, a cowboy over a city boy; this was her home now, and there would be long periods of time between visits.

Who would have figured? Marlene thought as she glanced over at the big bedroom window, where the soft morning light was stealing in around the edges of the curtains.

Lucy had spent almost her entire life on the island of Manhattan, until the age of twenty-one, when she'd traveled to New Mexico with her mother, the two of them seeking to heal wounds both physical and spiritual.

That was when Lucy had been recovering from her ordeal at the hands of the brutal sociopath Felix Tighe. And there was no better way to overcome the depredations of an evil like Tighe than in the arms of a good and loving man, whom she'd found in Ned Blanchett, a ranch hand her husband later described as "the quintessential Western Man archetype." When Marlene had returned to New York, Lucy remained behind for Ned, and it was soon apparent that the move was permanent.

After what Lucy had been through with Tighe and, like the rest of the family, a plethora of other killers, kidnappers, and psychopaths, Marlene had been happy for her. She had hoped her firstborn would now enjoy a safe, secure life as a wife and mother ensconced on a ranch. But it wasn't to be, at least not for the time being.

Fluent in more than sixty languages, with varying degrees of fluency in more than a dozen others, Lucy, with her sharpshooting fiancé, had been recruited into a top-secret counterterrorism agency by an old family friend and FBI agent, Espey Jaxon. The small group was independent of the traditional agencies, including the Bureau and even the umbrella National Security Administration, with orders to discover and disrupt terrorist activities domestic and international. Apparently, Jaxon reported only to some entity so top-secret that even the young couple had not been told. But it meant that their lives would be anything but safe and secure. New Mexico would be their home, but their duties had already carried them far beyond the borders of the United States and into dangers worse than what even the Big Apple offered.

Marlene noted that the deep rumble of her husband's voice had stopped, and she assumed that his business with Clay Fulton was done for the moment. She allowed herself a brief fantasy that he was about to come into the room and announce that he wanted to stay in Taos, that the years of working in a pressure cooker like the New York DAO were over. But the thought lasted about as long as a soap bubble before bursting into reality.

For better or worse, her husband was the district attorney of New York County, a job he saw more as a calling than as a career. And that was just the half of it. In the past few years, and for whatever reason, he'd become increasingly entangled in terrorist plots against his city — often connected to his role as the chief law-enforcement official on the island and the point man for the Five Boroughs Anti-Terrorism Task Force but outside his official duties as district attorney.

Lucy, a devout Catholic who believed that she carried on conversations with the ghost of a fifteenth-century saint, thought that her father's and the family's roles were preordained as part of a wider battle between good and evil, of angels and demons and humans who lined up on either side. But for Butch Karp, being a religious person did not equate to observing the rituals of the Jewish calendar; religion to him was having a moral and ethical code of Judaism.

With a sigh, Marlene rolled out of bed and walked over to the window, where she pulled back the curtains and looked out on a breathtakingly beautiful Christmas morning with the town of Taos glistening under a blanket of new snow. As she turned, she caught a glimpse of herself in the mirror. She knew that she was still an attractive woman, with a lithe yet curvy body, but there was no denying the vanguard of middle age was upon her. It was getting harder to keep up with the strands of gray

that invaded her black curls; the lines
around her eyes and at the corners of her
mouth were deeper and longer. Her hand
went up to the side of her face where she
had lost an eye so many years earlier after
opening a letter bomb intended for Butch.
A glass eye stared back at her unemotion-
ally.

The bigger changes were those she
couldn't see. In the years when she had
been protecting important people from
threats, she also got involved in helping
abused women deal with violent men —
even taking the law into her own hands
when the police couldn't or wouldn't help.
The violence and darkness that had followed seemed to spiral downward from
there, whether it was protecting her family
from others or finding herself allied with
men like David Grale against Lucy's "forces
of evil." She'd killed men, and while it could
be argued, as Butch had, that much of her
violent tendencies had been brought on in
self-defense or in defense of others, she'd
increasingly been disturbed by the thought
that she was playing God, deciding who
deserved to live and who deserved to die.
And it had affected her relationship with
Butch, to whom vigilantes were anathema
to his belief that the rule of law was sacro-

sanct to Western civilization.

Marlene gave herself a smile in the mirror. *Yes, there's hope for you yet,* she thought.

There was still no sound from the twins. All of her children were growing up and would soon leave, like Lucy. In past years on Christmas morning, the boys had hardly let the sky grow gray before bursting into their parents' bedroom and jumping around like squirrels after nuts in their avarice. Butch had purposely made a game of taking his time getting out of bed, just to hear the desperate pleas in their voices before releasing them to wreak havoc on the poor presents.

What are you going to do with yourself when the boys are gone, too? The thought brought a lump to her throat, and tears filled her good eye as she opened the door of the bedroom and stepped out into the hallway. She found her husband in the living room, sitting in one of the big leather chairs, reading the sports section of the *Times.*

"Merry Christmas, Santa," she purred when he looked up and smiled at her.

"Merry Christmas, Mrs. Claus," he replied. "The boys must really be sawing logs."

"Teenagers," she noted. "They can stay up all night but need their beauty rest in the morning."

"When are Lucy and Ned coming over?"

"After mass," Marlene replied. In the incongruity of the Karp-Ciampi clan, their twin boys were still preparing for their bar mitzvahs — after their studies had been interrupted by the recent Karp family confrontations with evil — while their daughter was attending Roman Catholic mass.

After fixing herself a cup of coffee, Marlene sat down next to her husband and picked up the news section of the *Times*. "Hey, did you see this story with your old chum Harley Chin?" she asked.

Karp rolled his eyes. "Yeah, never met a camera he didn't like."

"So, did you get your Christmas present from Clay?"

"I did indeed. He will be waiting for me in the Tombs upon our return."

Marlene looked at her husband. She thought he was incredibly handsome, and that got her motor running. "I don't suppose you want to give me my Christmas present again?" she said, and nodded toward the bedroom.

Butch laughed. "I suppose you've been a good girl this year . . ."

"Oh, yes, Santa," she cooed, "so very

good. I think I want —"

Whatever she was going to say was interrupted by the sudden sound of the boys jumping out of bed and pounding their way into the hall.

"Guess it will have to wait." She sighed.

"Damn kids," he agreed, smiling before turning to where the twins were emerging from the hall. "Why, Merry Christmas. We were beginning to wonder if you guys had decided to forgo presents this year."

"No way, José," Zak replied.

"Nice try, Dad," Giancarlo added. "Now, which ones are mine?"

5

With a grunt, Megan O'Dowd hauled her body out of the yellow cab and up onto the sidewalk at 125 White Street in lower Manhattan, immediately causing pedestrians to veer sharply around her like schools of salmon skirting a grizzly bear in the river. They scattered even more violently when the assembled media spotted the bombastic defense attorney and swarmed to where she stood sneering up at the looming Manhattan Detention Complex, otherwise known as the Tombs.

O'Dowd paused dramatically, with her hands on her wide hips, so that the cameras could capture her scripted contempt for the building and all that it represented. "White man's justice, ain't no justice for the African man," she liked to say, and would again today when the moment was right. And she would deliver the line — as she did with all her speeches, except in the courtroom — in the patois of Ebonics, although she was as ethnically Irish as a bottle of Guinness Stout.

Her legal assistant, a thin, coffee-colored young man with Malcolm X glasses and dressed in a plain black suit with white shirt and thin black tie, scrambled out of the other side of the cab. Sweating despite the frigid air gusting in from the East River, he hurriedly unfolded a hand truck and loaded it with two file boxes, which he quickly secured with bungee cords. After plucking two briefcases from the backseat and placing one under his arm, he used his free hand to haul the cart around the cab as fast as he could walk.

His boss did not offer to relieve him of some of the burden. Nor did she wait for him to catch up as she pushed through the reporters. "No comment until after I've met with my client," she said for the microphones and notepads, and launched herself in the direction of the front entrance. The young man followed in her wake, his eyes locked on her watermelon-sized calves, the cart creaking along.

O'Dowd wore a purple traditional African dashiki blouse with a voluminous lime-green skirt and *gele* head wrap. She wanted everyone to see that she identified with "the

African experience in racist America."

Proceeding through the doors and up to the security screening area, she flared her puggish nose as if she'd caught a whiff of something particularly loathsome, and her dark green eyes — such as they could be seen in her fleshy face — sparkled with righteous indignation. She tossed her oversized purse onto the X-ray machine's conveyor belt and then squeezed through the metal-detector cubicle while glaring at the security officers.

Waddling across the foyer and up to the intake desk, she bellowed in a voice intended to be heard by the media that had followed her into the building hoping to witness one of her famous temper tantrums. "Megan O'Dowd. I'm here to see my client, Imam Sharif Jabbar, who is being held as a political prisoner of a racist regime."

The reporters caught their collective breath and smiled as one, sure that they were about to witness a monumental battle of wills. Known to the press as a "great quote," O'Dowd had been raised in the wealthy enclave of Riverdale, in the Bronx, the daughter of a wealthy hedge-fund manager and his glitterati wife. She'd attended Riverdale Country School, a private academy that boasted such past students as future president John F. Kennedy, actor Chevy Chase, Pennsylvania governor Ed Rendell, and musician Carly Simon.

Upon graduating from New York University with a bachelor's degree in ethnic studies, she'd gone on to Albany Law School. However, after passing the bar, she professed to be "ashamed" of her privileged upbringing and her "capitalist oppressor" parents, who, after trying and failing to get her "professional help," had disowned her.

For the past thirty-plus years, she had inserted herself into the African-American community of Manhattan, most of whose principled majority ridiculed her behind her back and sometimes to her face. However, certain criminal and political elements in the community found it convenient to have a loud, abrasive white lawyer who saw every arrest and every job or political appointment not given to one of their own as an act of racism. They tolerated her fawning and publicly lauded her as "a friend of the black community."

O'Dowd was known for her diatribes against the Man, in particular as represented by the men and women of the NYPD. But she was no slouch as a lawyer, having won several notable, and many run-of-the-mill, cases, often by portraying her clients as innocent victims of a racist police state. And she knew how to work the press to taint jury pools and garner public sympathy where none was deserved. Several of Karp's predecessors had simply refused to prosecute cases in which she was the attorney or quickly agreed to her terms for lesser charges, rather than deal with her public accusations and courtroom stunts.

However, the intake sergeant at the desk, one J. P. Murphy, was unimpressed and gave O'Dowd a dour look over the top of his half-glasses. An old-school Irish cop with the requisite ruddy cheeks and jowls, rheumy blue eyes, and bulbous red-veined nose, he'd walked beats in the worst neighborhoods Manhattan had to offer. He had kicked in doors of heavily armed drug dealers, had been shot twice, and was stabbed once by a Puerto Rican drag queen in Times Square. He feared nothing — except maybe his impending retirement and the thought of spending 24/7 with the missus until the good Lord called him, or Mary Louise Katherine, home.

Murphy wasn't about to make it easy on O'Dowd. There wasn't a cop in the NYPD who didn't know and despise the woman for her rhetorical attacks on their ethics and professionalism, as well as her defense of cop killers. "Is he an inmate?" he asked, and gave a sideways glance to the young male officer standing next to him.

O'Dowd frowned. "You know damn well he is."

"Do I now? He got a date of birth?" The sergeant's thick, callused fingers hovered ever so slightly closer to his computer keyboard as though he was trying to be helpful.

"What?" The attorney's face furrowed into numerous scowl lines. "Oh, I see how it's gonna be! Ain't that just like *the Man,* to make it difficult on the black man . . ."

"You're a white woman," the sergeant pointed out.

"I *represent* an African man," O'Dowd retorted, her face beginning to turn purple.

"Wait a minute, you say you represent an African man, but word on the streets has it that there's a Sharif Jabbar who was born in the Bronx. So, like I said, date of birth?"

"How many damn Sharif Jabbars do you have in this gulag?"

The sergeant's bored expression and tone didn't change. "We get a lot of perps with the same names. Jimmy Johnsons. Johnny McPhersons. Sharif Jabbars. And Pablo Espinozas by the dozens," he said. "Personally, I don't give a rat's ass, lady. I need a date of birth so I can make sure we're both talking about the same upstanding citizen."

O'Dowd started to sputter something in response but looked at the sergeant's face and realized she'd be wasting her breath and losing the battle in front of the media. She snapped her fingers for her assistant. "Elijah, I need Sharif's date of birth."

Her assistant's eyes widened in fear. "I . . . I don't have that with me," he stammered. "Unless it's in *your* briefcase."

His thin, worried face betrayed that he didn't have much hope of that. The two file boxes on the cart were for show and only filled with empty manila folders and a couple of reams of printer paper. Ever conscious of the press, O'Dowd thought it would make her look as if she was on top of the situation, rather than having been taken by surprise. Elijah's own briefcase was basically empty except for his lunch, and he doubted that O'Dowd had much more in hers than the writ of habeas corpus she'd dictated to him that morning.

Jabbar's arrest two days earlier, on Christmas morning, had caught O'Dowd sleeping, literally and figuratively. She'd been awakened by her client's angry, panicked phone call from the jail. He'd made several nasty threats and hung up. She'd immediately called Elijah and demanded that he drop everything and start trying to find a judge who would grant a writ of habeas corpus *ad subjiciendum,* essentially a court order demanding that Jabbar's jailer bring him immediately to court for the judge to decide if he was being legally detained. However, finding such a judge on Christmas morning had proved impossible. All but the most activist liberal judges were no more thrilled with O'Dowd than the police were. Elijah had been told to wait until Monday, "like everybody else."

In terror, Elijah had called O'Dowd to relay the bad news and, as anticipated, had been subjected to a stream of vitriol so foul that the devout Muslim took his second shower of the morning immediately afterward, even though most of the verbiage had been directed at "that racist cracker," New York District Attorney Roger "Butch" Karp. So now he cringed when he had to tell O'Dowd that he didn't have Jabbar's birthday memorized.

Indeed, she looked as if she might strangle him before she hissed, "Then get your ass on the phone and call the office. Maybe someone there can actually be of some use to me."

Elijah's eyes filled with tears of anger as

he stepped back and flipped open his cell phone, hitting the speed-dial number for O'Dowd's office on Adam Clayton Powell Boulevard in Harlem. He spoke briefly, and after a pause, in which he kept his eyes fixed firmly on the ceiling, he wrote down the answer on a piece of paper and handed it to his boss. She glanced at it and turned to Sergeant Murphy. "Five ten sixty-five," she said tersely.

The sergeant typed in the numbers, hit the Enter key, and nodded. "Oh, *that* Sharif Jabbar."

O'Dowd glowered one last time at the sergeant, walked over to the security door leading into the Tombs, and was buzzed through.

When she was out of earshot, Murphy turned to the young officer. "Sweet Jesus, Mary, and Joseph, that woman's got a better mustache than you do, Gleason."

"Up yours, Sarge," Gleason replied. "But she is one foul human being."

"Inside and out, me boyo." The sergeant nodded grimly. "Enjoys getting cop killers off when she knows they're guilty as sin."

"Well, then, I guess she better hope she never needs a cop," Gleason replied.

Murphy grunted and smiled. "We won't exactly come a-runnin', now, will we?"

■ ■ ■ ■

Sharif Jabbar feigned indifference as one of the two guards following him stepped past to open the door to the interview room. Eyes straight ahead, chin tilted up, face set in what he hoped passed for a look of disdain, he sauntered into the conference room without a word and circled around the table, sitting down on a stool facing the door. He gave a bored sigh when the guards turned and left, closing the door behind them.

It was, of course, an act. In reality, he was sweating bullets, sure that every inmate they'd passed since they pulled him from his isolation cell had a shiv up his sleeve and was preparing to assassinate him. And he was positive the guards would do nothing to stop it. They hated him. Two cops had been gunned down during the attack on the New York Stock Exchange, and that was something they weren't going to forget. Although they said nothing to him, made no threats, he could see the hatred in the eyes of the police and the guards he'd come in contact with. In fact, he was sure that if an inmate tried to kill him, it would probably be the NYPD who put him up to it.

Just being a high-profile prisoner put you in jeopardy. In fact, it was a good way to get killed. A few weeks earlier, a famous Broadway producer got his liver sliced up just standing in line with a bunch of other prisoners. The Puerto Rican who killed him claimed he'd done it for the notoriety. *Though others say it was a gang hit,* he thought. *And if some rich white-ass mutha fucka can get jacked up like that, sure as shit in this racist hole, so can I.*

He couldn't even count on protection from other black Muslims. Most of them didn't like him or the Al-Aqsa mosque. They were home-grown Muslims and didn't like his ties to the Arab world. *Envious,* he thought. *Jealous of my benefactors in Saudi Arabia and Libya.*

Even black street gangs like the Crips and the Bloods would just as soon see him dead because he'd encroached on their territory and recruiting pool. There were some incarcerated members of the Rolling 777s, a gang he'd created for protection and to fund his "ministry" through criminal activity before his Middle Eastern benefactors made it unnecessary, but they were too few to impose their will on other gangs.

And as if he didn't have enough enemies already, his anti-white tirades in the press had certainly made him a target for white supremacists. That had been okay as long as he stayed in Harlem with his bodyguards. But the Tombs housed plenty of Aryans, Klansmen, and other dangerous white crackers, and his bodyguards were dead, on the run, or in jail themselves. *You got a damned circle painted on your back, and In-shallah — God willing — that fat white bitch better bail you out of here quick, or someone's gonna fuck you up.*

Waiting for O'Dowd to show, Jabbar felt bitterness rise in his throat like a bad case of indigestion. He should be enjoying his hero status in some foreign country, but instead, he was waiting for his lawyer in the Tombs. Raised on New York streets, he had a mind as suspicious and shrewd as a sewer rat's; he wondered if it had been Al-Sistani's plan all along to abandon him.

Well, if Al-Sistani and his wealthy benefactors thought they could just leave him to take the fall for everyone, they were mistaken. He'd been kept out of the planning meetings between Al-Sistani and the old white lawyer, Dean Newbury, at the mosque. *My mosque.* But that hadn't stopped him from secretly taping them, and some surprising names had come up in conjunction with the Sons of Man. If he didn't like what he heard from Megan O'Dowd, he'd make a deal with the feds.

In the meantime, the tapes plus a very incriminating video were well hidden. *My ace in the hole.*

O'Dowd had shown up shortly after his arrest following the attack on the stock exchange and said he didn't have to worry about her fees. "They're taken care of," she'd said with a wink. He had rich and powerful friends who were going to see to it that nothing happened to him and Al-Sistani. He'd said nothing then about his tapes and only planned to use them if necessary.

Now Jabbar looked up as the lock in the door clicked and the door opened. O'Dowd moved ponderously into the room, followed by her skinny assistant. She smiled, which made her tiny eyes disappear behind her fat cheeks. "Sharif! Brother!" she exclaimed.

Scowling, Jabbar pointed at the stool across the table from him. "Sit your fat ass down. Where the fuck have you been? And why ain't I out of here already?"

The smile left O'Dowd's face for a moment, but she glued another back on. "I understand you're frustrated . . . as am I. This was all supposed to have been arranged, but now we have to deal with it in a different way."

"Different way?" Jabbar hissed, his bulging eyes threatening to pop out of his skull. "Get me the hell out of here."

O'Dowd tapped the table, and her assistant, Elijah, placed her briefcase on it. She opened the case, pulled out a piece of paper, and slid it across the table to Jabbar.

"Writ of habeas corpus?" Jabbar frowned. "What's it mean?"

"It's a demand for a hearing in front of a judge claiming that you've been unlawfully detained."

Jabbar nodded. "Okay, so I get out after this hearing?"

O'Dowd heaved a sigh and shifted uncomfortably on the insufficiently wide chair. "Well, probably not. You were arrested for the murder of Miriam Juma Khalifa, whose decapitated corpse, as we know, was found in the basement of your mosque."

Jabbar licked his lips. He was thinking that it had been stupid that his people hadn't gotten rid of the woman's body. But he'd planned on being in some Arab capital enjoying life before she was discovered.

"The grand jury is meeting this morning, and I expect they will hand down a murder indictment against you," O'Dowd continued. "That fascist pig Karp is apparently handling this himself — the man's a racist, no doubt about it. There's a good reason they used to call him KKK Karp."

Jabbar swallowed hard. He didn't like the way this was going. "Then what?"

"You'll be arraigned," his attorney replied.

"After that, I can get out?"

O'Dowd sighed and shook her head. "Sorry, but I think Karp will request that you be held without bail. You'll be charged with the capital crime of murder, and he'll point out that you were getting ready to leave the country aboard a private jet owned by an accused terrorist and carrying a large sum of money. It's going to be tough to get bail."

Jabbar blinked as if he'd been hit on the head with a stick. "You're telling me I'm going to have to stay here until they put my ass on trial?"

"Yes," O'Dowd said with a nod. "We'll try to get you out of here, certainly. I will point out that you're a respected religious leader in the community, and we could put the mosque up for a surety bond. But I think we're fighting an uphill battle. So, yes, we'll go to trial, where I'm sure we'll prevail."

Actually, O'Dowd was struggling to sound more confident than she was feeling about facing Karp. The New York District Attorney's Office probably had the best-trained prosecutors in the United States, but she'd had her share of successes against them. Except Karp. She was zero-for-whatever when it came to the Man himself.

The closest she'd ever come had been many years earlier, when they were both young attorneys. She'd taken on a case of three black "nationalists" who'd ambushed and shot to death four police officers in a Harlem projects complex. As they'd explained to her at the first interview, they'd killed the "pigs" hoping that the enraged members of the New York Police Department would overreact and come down hard on the black community, which would in turn riot. A riot in Harlem, they'd said, would spread to every black-dominated urban center in the United States and set off a race war. The result of that war would be a free and independent country, "where the Afro-American man is in charge and honkies may visit only with permission."

Megan O'Dowd was enthralled with the revolutionary rhetoric. A devotee of a not-so-subtle form of casuistry, she convinced the killers that she needed to spin their story in a somewhat different way in the media. Yes, they were black nationalists hoping that someday there would be a separate nation where their people would not be subject to racism. However, the central theme core of their trial strategy would be that the police officers had been shot in self-defense.

"The storm troopers of the racist, capitalist white society entered the projects intending to provoke a violent confrontation that would provide the excuse for a wholesale attack on the Afro-American community of Harlem," O'Dowd had argued. "My clients were providing armed patrols of the projects at the request of local residents to protect them from the criminal element. They were confronted by the police officers, whose aggressive behavior caused my clients to believe that their lives were in danger. They fired upon their oppressors in self-defense."

She had, of course, ignored the fact that the first two officers were shot and killed from behind, never having seen their attackers, much less confronted them. The other two had died in a hail of bullets without pulling their guns from their holsters. It was, she said without batting an eye, "justifiable resistance to government provocation."

The whole argument was ludicrous, of course. But she wasn't trying to prove her clients' innocence. She only wanted one thing: a single juror. Someone who would believe enough of her story, or who held enough of a grudge against police officers or government, to vote for acquittal.

Karp was a formidable adversary. However, in this case, he'd made some mistakes, and the jury hung. Her experience in the retrial was a different story, not one she wanted to repeat.

Normally, a hung jury is a good thing for the defense. The defense has a chance to see all the evidence and cross-examine the witnesses based on their testimony in the first trial. The defense can take any witness inconsistencies between the first and second trials and argue to the jury that the witness was lying. Or, if the witness testimony is consistent, the defense can argue that the testimony was scripted.

In the ordinary course, the DAO would usually come back with a sweetheart plea bargain or in some cases decline to retry the defendant. However, to O'Dowd's surprise, Karp had immediately refiled the case. No attempt to get a plea, no lesser charge, just four counts of murder. This time, he'd learned from his mistakes. The verdict: four counts of guilty, four life sentences.

It had been a humiliating defeat but not the last one. Over the years, there'd been a half-dozen other battles, and she — or, more accurately, her clients — had come out on the losing end. She hated Karp more than any human being on the planet. Her cop-killer clients had referred to him as Captain America, and she detested his personification of American values. Nevertheless, she also feared him and would not have sounded anywhere near as confident with Jabbar if not for other information she'd received.

When Karp's men had intercepted and arrested Jabbar on his way to Fort Dix, O'Dowd had worried what the men footing the bill would say. She knew from Al-Sistani and Jabbar that their benefactors were extremely wealthy and extremely powerful. She thought they would be upset that the plan to free Jabbar had gone awry, and she had cursed Karp as never before.

However, while not pleased, they had said that she would continue to be paid — at the generous rate she was already charging them — to represent Jabbar at trial. When she'd noted the difficulty she would have, they'd said not to worry, they had a "plan" that would not only free their man but humiliate and frustrate Karp as well. And it was that last notion that had truly appealed to her.

The men wouldn't tell her how this plan

was going to work. "Better you not know," she'd been told, "so that you will be able to deny anything that might come up. You will be contacted by a woman, Natalie Stiefelmaier, who will give you instructions."

They had said that the end game would be to cause a mistrial, at which point a federal judge would immediately issue a writ of mandamus ordering Karp to hand Jabbar over to federal agents who would be present at the court. Jabbar would be taken to Fort Dix and turned over to Saudi authorities.

"So, how you gonna beat Karp?" Jabbar demanded now.

O'Dowd smiled and leaned forward. "Can you keep a secret?"

6

John Jojola sat patiently at the table in the front of what would have passed for a small lecture hall at a college. He looked up at three rows of tiered seating set in semicircles, in which twenty-three people now sat, all attentively waiting for him to speak. Also waiting, off to one side, was a stenographer who would record every word.

At the back of the grand-jury room, behind the jurors, stood DA Butch Karp, who appeared to be studying his notes but in a moment would be asking him questions about the death of Miriam Juma Khalifa. Then it would be up to this grand jury whether to indict Sharif Jabbar for her murder.

Jojola closed his eyes for a moment, his wide, bronzed face framed by straight shoulder-length black hair. He appeared composed, though his mind raced. This was not Taos; this was a grand-jury room at 100

Centre Street, New York, the Criminal Courts Building, which housed New York County's criminal courts as well as the DAO. And he was no longer the police chief of the Taos Indian Pueblo but an agent of a secret federal counterterrorism agency headed by former FBI special agent in charge Espey Jaxon.

Along with a few trusted men he'd known at the Bureau, Jaxon had been looking for agents who would be "under the radar" of spies both within and outside the government. And after fate threw them together battling the Sons of Man, Jaxon had asked Jojola, a former Vietnam combat vet, to join his group for his tracking and guerrilla fighting skills.

Lot of good they did Miriam, he thought. He pictured her face in the moment before her death and felt a stab of shame . . . and an intense hatred for her killer, Nadya Malovo, and the man he would be testifying against for participating in her slaughter.

An immigrant from Kenya, Miriam had been the widow of Muhammad Jamal Khalifa, an American-born Muslim who'd blown himself up inside the Third Avenue Synagogue. Her father, Mahmoud Juma, had taught her since childhood that Islam was a religion of peace and that terrorists in

121

her native Kenya and elsewhere were guilty of a grievous sin by misinterpreting the Koran to support the murder of innocent people. She'd been wracked with guilt at her husband's act.

Miriam had also been angry at Jabbar, who, as the imam of the mosque, had recruited a cadre of young men from the congregation — poor, disenfranchised, and impressionable men like her husband — for "jihad" against the United States. She had argued with her husband as he grew more radicalized and spoke about a "big event" that would make him and Jabbar heroes in the Muslim world. Their arguments had become more heated and degenerated into violence. No longer willing to suffer his verbal and physical abuse, Miriam had finally moved out. So she hadn't known that he'd been kicked out of the *jihadi* cadre for drinking alcohol and then had decided to prove his worth by strapping on a "martyr's vest" filled with plastic explosives and ball bearings and detonating it in the synagogue.

A dozen men had died. But in the end, Khalifa's murderous act had probably saved many other lives, and even the economy of the United States. It had pointed Jaxon at the Al-Aqsa mosque and then paid off big when Lucy Karp befriended Miriam. The two had met when Lucy, posing as a translator for "private security analyst" Jaxon, attended a social function at the mosque.

After her husband's death, Miriam had been given the job of receptionist for Jabbar so that he could keep his eye on her. But that plan had backfired on the imam a few days after her husband's death, when a package addressed in his handwriting arrived for Jabbar. At considerable risk, she'd taken the package, which contained a videotape her husband had made of himself with his "last will and testament."

In the tradition of such tapes made by suicide bombers in other parts of the world, Khalifa had announced his plan to "offer myself in jihad against the Zionists." But more important, after Miriam had handed the tape over to Lucy, he'd included coded language meant for his "mujahedin brothers" that Jaxon and his men were able to crack enough of — along with what Miriam told them — to know that a major attack was in the works. They had also learned from the tape that a Philippine terrorist, Azahari Mujahid, was involved and would be arriving by ship a few days prior to the event. They just didn't know what the attack would entail or exactly when, other than near the beginning of the Muslim holy days of Ramadan.

In the days between Miriam handing over the tape and intercepting the terrorist Mujahid, John Jojola had met with her several times as she gathered evidence for them at the mosque. In case anyone followed her to these meetings, they'd made it appear as if she was meeting her secret lover, though in truth they'd spend most of the time talking and playing chess. He'd grown to like the young woman, who talked often about her dream of attending college and raising her young son, Abdullah.

But then Malovo had accused Miriam of carrying on a sexual affair that disgraced her "martyred" husband and announced that the young woman would pay for the sin and "bring Allah's blessing on our plans." At the same time, a plan was devised in which Mujahid and his men were intercepted and their places taken by Tran Vinh Do, a Vietnamese gangster who also had joined Jaxon's group, and Jojola. They had been taken to the mosque and then found themselves unwilling witnesses as Malovo pulled Miriam's head back and prepared to cut her throat.

Jojola had tensed, ready to attack, though he didn't have a weapon and others, including Malovo, did. He knew it would give away his cover, but he could not witness the execution of a young woman without intervening. He'd sensed his comrade, Tran, who was standing next to him, prepare to die in defense of the young woman as well.

What had happened next, however, was inexplicable. A distinct spirituality had possessed Jojola. When he'd looked into Miriam's eyes, a woman's voice had entered his head, telling him that Miriam did not want him to give himself away in what would have surely been a futile attempt to save her. He could hear the voice still: "She is prepared for martyrdom in the hope that her one death may save thousands, even millions. She asks that you remember the lessons you taught her from chess: that sometimes one piece must be sacrificed for the good of the many. This is her last request, and she asks that you honor it so that you will live to do as you must tomorrow."

So Jojola had done nothing and prevented Tran from taking action as well. A moment later, Malovo had decapitated the young woman.

As a result of Miriam's sacrifice, in their presence, with their identities unquestioned by murderous *jihadis,* Jojola and Tran had been able to save countless lives and keep the United States and even the West from plunging into economic chaos. But the shame of it had never left Jojola, nor had he forgotten his promise to bring her killers to justice someday.

Nadya Malovo had escaped after the stock-exchange attack and again more recently when she was involved in an attempt to blow up the Brooklyn Bridge. *Someday,* he swore now, as Karp cleared his throat in the back of the auditorium, *she will pay.* In the meantime, justice would begin with Sharif Jabbar.

"Mr. Jojola," Karp began, "would you tell the jurors your current occupation?"

"I am an agent of a federal counter-terrorism agency."

"In that capacity, were you in the basement of the Al-Aqsa mosque on 126th Street in Harlem?"

"Yes, I was."

"And could you briefly explain what you were doing there and what occurred?"

The heat of shame crept into Jojola's face, but he nodded and responded.

An hour later, Karp waited outside the grand-jury room with Kenny Katz for the verdict. New York law required that anyone charged with a felony must be indicted in order to be tried in the state supreme court.

The only exception to proceeding by way of indictment was if the defendant "voluntarily, knowingly, and intelligently" waived the grand-jury process. However, defense attorneys usually wanted to see the entire grand-jury transcript, hoping for a legal infirmity or that a witness's trial testimony was inconsistent with the grand-jury testimony.

Karp knew that the grand jury would indict Jabbar. After all, he only needed twelve of the twenty-three jurors to vote to indict. That would bring the defendant to trial in the New York Supreme Court.

"If you're prepared, it should be about as tough as making a ham sandwich," he said to his protégé Katz.

With a grand jury, the prosecutor is in total control. He is by statute its legal advisor. There is no judge, no defense attorney, no defense witnesses or cross-examination of prosecution witnesses. No need to prove the defendant guilty beyond a reasonable doubt. A much lesser burden of proof is necessary before a grand jury to obtain an indictment. In law, it is a "probable cause" standard requiring sufficient evidence that a crime had been committed and that the defendant committed it.

Not a very high threshold. Karp understood that the quantum of proof presented to the grand jurors should warrant the triers of fact, be they trial judges or trial juries, to find the defendant guilty if the evidence he presented went unexplained or uncontradicted.

He didn't believe in wasting a lot of time and effort "trying his case" in front of grand juries as some prosecutors did. As a young assistant district attorney assigned to the Indictment Bureau at the DAO, he'd often present more than a hundred cases a month to GJs. Given the immense amount of crime occurring on a daily basis on the island of Manhattan, the supreme court impaneled four grand juries — two morning GJs and two afternoon GJs — to listen in the general course to presentations by assistant DAs of the garden-variety felonious mayhem inflicted upon the innocent citizenry of Gotham.

Throughout his career, grand juries had responded appropriately. Much of that was because he adhered to Old Man Garrahy's insistence that on his legendary watch, before a case could proceed even as far as the GJ, his prosecutors be absolutely certain, "one thousand percent," of the defendant's factual guilt *and* that they had the legally admissible evidence to prove it at trial beyond a reasonable doubt. And those two factors didn't always go hand in hand. On occasion, a prosecutor might have factual guilt, but because of legal, constitutional infirmities — such as acquiring evidence without a valid search warrant or an improperly obtained confession — the DA lacked sufficient evidence to convict. In those situations, the case did not go forward. It wasn't about winning; it was about justice.

Having to satisfy that burden before a case got that far — a standard Karp had reinstated when he took over the DAO — made persuading grand juries to issue indictments a cake walk. It also was the reason he'd never lost a felony case.

Karp had other reasons to believe in putting on a bare-bones case for grand juries. "Whatever the witnesses say is recorded, and, as you know, that transcript is turned over to the defense," he'd said to Katz. "Why give them any more insight into our strategy than we have to? Plus, between now and the trial, witnesses might alter their testimony somewhat as they remember or forget details. The defense will jump on these as 'inconsistencies' and try to attack on cross-examination. So, keep the testimony — and therefore the transcript — as brief and limited as possible."

Karp had started the case against Jabbar by calling to the witness table the first police officer to discover the remains of Miriam Juma Khalifa in the basement of the Al-Aqsa mosque. Then he'd called an assistant medical examiner, who testified that Miriam Juma Khalifa was the victim of a homicide and the cause of death was decapitation with a sharp instrument, "probably a large knife."

When he'd finished with the AME, Karp wondered briefly what had become of the videotape of Miriam's murder. *Probably in the offices of some terrorist Web site waiting for the right moment to be broadcast as yet another so-called courageous act of jihad lunacy,* he thought.

The next witness had been Mahmoud Juma, the father of the victim. He'd testified that Jabbar, the imam of his mosque, had recruited young men, including his son-in-law, for the purposes of "violent jihad." Juma said that he'd had numerous arguments with his son-in-law, who'd quoted Jabbar, regarding the use of terrorism in the name of Islam prior to the young man blowing himself up in the Third Avenue Synagogue.

The old man had held together pretty well until Karp had asked him about the last time he'd seen his daughter, on the day she was murdered. He'd said she'd asked him to take her son to Chicago to visit relatives "until the danger has passed," and then she'd left for the mosque. "I never saw her alive again," he'd said, beginning to weep.

Then Karp had called his last witness, John Jojola. Giving as comprehensive but terse an answer as possible for what he was doing at the mosque, Jojola had also kept the graphic details of Miriam's death to a minimum. Karp had asked him prior to his testimony to limit his responses. "If I want more, I'll ask."

Karp had not asked Jojola why he hadn't tried to save Miriam. "I doubt Megan O'Dowd will be so kind," he'd told Katz. He wondered if the jurors had caught the strain that seemed part sadness and part rage in his friend's testimony. He knew Jojola's history with the girl and had heard the spiritual story about the woman's voice urging him not to act. It ate at Jojola, and Karp sympathized.

As part of the process, grand jurors were allowed to ask questions of the witnesses by raising their hands. While allowing them to exercise this right, Karp kept a tight rein on what was asked and answered. He always self-edited what he said and did in the grand jury and at trial in the supreme court, because he was constantly concerned with keeping a legally impeccable record that would pass appellate muster.

"For instance, it's pretty common for grand jurors to ask if the defendant has a criminal record," Karp had said to Katz. "I gently explain that such information would be highly prejudicial and inadmissible at trial. We don't want to taint the record here."

After he was finished with the witnesses and his case presentation was completed, Karp had taken a few minutes to inform the jurors about the law regarding homicide. In part, he explained that based on the evidence presented, Jabbar was guilty of common-law intentional murder by acting in concert with others to cause the death of Miriam Juma Khalifa. And in fact, he did cause her death, by decapitating her, even though Nadya Malovo had wielded the knife.

"Jabbar and Malovo both possessed the requisite intent to murder the deceased and participated in this execution together, even if only one of them held the knife," he'd told the jurors.

He'd closed his presentation by telling the jurors "to keep in mind that an indictment is an accusatory instrument used to bring a defendant to trial in New York Supreme Court, part of the process that will lead to a fair due process hearing affording the defendant the right to question all witnesses and any physical and/or documentary evidence presented against him. And if the defendant so chooses, to present evidence to advance his cause."

Karp had walked out of the room and sat down at the table with Kenny Katz to wait while the jurors deliberated. Their verdict would be announced by means of a buzzer: one buzz for indictment, two for dismissal, three for a question.

Relaxed and calm, Karp now read over the indictment document he'd already prepared. One buzz, and he and the jury foreman would head up to Supreme Court Part 30, the designated courtroom where indictments were filed.

The buzzer went off. Once. He and the jury foreman headed up to Part 30, where Karp requested that the presiding judge set Jabbar's arraignment for the following day.

At that arraignment, Karp was going to ask that the defendant be remanded without bail, and he would state that "the People are ready now for trial and intend to expeditiously move the case. Any delays, therefore, in a speedy trial would be at the hands of the defense."

After returning from Part 30, Karp looked at Katz. "Care for lunch across the street?"

"Sure. Anything you'd like me to do?"

"Yeah, give O'Dowd's office a call, and say we're going to arraign her client tomorrow and to check with the court clerk to see what time."

7

"Did you talk to O'Dowd?"

Katz shook his head at Karp's question. "No, spoke to her legal clerk, Elijah. He actually thanked me for the heads-up."

"I imagine working for Megan O'Dowd is a challenge," Karp said, and then sank his teeth into a potato knish he'd bought from the vendor cart in the park across Centre Street from the Criminal Courts Building. He was enjoying a rare, for late December, "balmy" day in the mid-forties with blue skies.

Street preacher Edward Treacher stood nearby on his milk crate, his eyes rolling wildly and his frizzy hair standing on end as he rained fire-and-brimstone biblical passages down on the heads of passersby. At the same time, he held out a hand for "donations to my Godly mission" and offered a smile and a "God bless you" for every charitable contribution. As Karp watched, Treacher climbed down and used some of his mission money to buy a warm cup of cocoa from a vendor.

The Walking Booger, an enormously filthy giant, was working the lunchtime crowd, too. His huge hands, protruding from the sleeves of multiple layers of shirts and coats, were covered with thick dark hair, as all parts of his body apparently were — at least, the exposed parts Karp could see, including his face — and he gave the impression of a large, very dirty bear. One of the Booger's hands went up to his face, and he inserted a probing finger into a nostril. The demonstration of how he'd earned his nickname nearly cost Katz his lunch.

"I just don't get how attorneys like Megan O'Dowd live with themselves," Katz said to distract himself. As part of his training for the current case, Karp had him look at some of the more famous cases she'd defended, including the cop shooters he'd convicted. "There's a complete lack of integrity, and I don't understand why the black community puts up with her acting like she speaks for them."

Before Karp could answer, a short, slightly stooped young man with a long, pointed nose, pale skin, and large, watery blue eyes magnified by thick glasses interrupted.

"Missed you . . . fucking asshole whoop oh boy . . . this morning, Karp," he said cheerfully.

"Sorry, Warren, was running late to a grand-jury hearing," Karp replied. "I'll buy two papers tomorrow."

Dirty Warren smiled. He owned the newsstand in front of the Criminal Courts Building and, despite his outburst, was a friend of Karp. His unfortunate nickname was inspired by the fact that he suffered from Tourette's syndrome, a brain disorder that, along with facial tics and muscle spasms, interspersed his speech with obscenities.

Karp didn't know much about Dirty Warren except that he was in his thirties, lived in an apartment in Manhattan's Lower East Side, and, as one of a certain group of street people who either panhandled or worked around 100 Centre Street, was a conduit to David Grale and his army of homeless Mole People. Most people shied away from Dirty Warren with his tics and language, as well as his shabby clothes, scruffy face, and stringy hair that poked out from beneath a moth-eaten New York Yankees stocking cap. But over time, Karp had learned that looks were deceiving, and his friendly, verbally abusive news vendor was a bright, funny young man with a good heart

who on several occasions had acted courageously to protect others.

"Oh boy oh boy whoop shit piss," Dirty
Warren said. "And by the way, the public
doesn't give a . . . flying fuck lick me . . .
damn about integrity."

Katz was taken aback. "Oh, I wouldn't
say that."

"Save your breath, Kenny," Karp said with
a smile. "Our clever friend here was trying
to pull a fast one on me. Isn't that right,
Warren?"

The little man started hopping from one
foot to the other, and his face went through
a series of gymnastics. Then he grinned.
"Damn, Karp, you're sharp. But I want . . .
oh boy oh boy ass tits . . . film, actor,
character, and year."

Karp shook his head. He'd been playing
the movie-trivia game with Dirty Warren
since they'd met years before. The little man
had yet to win a round, but he was up
against years of experience. When he was a
boy, Karp and his mother had loved going
to shows and discussing films and theater,
and movie trivia remained an avocation in
adulthood.

"You forgot the rest of the quote," he said,
" 'The public doesn't give a damn about
integrity. A town that won't defend itself

deserves no help.' Way too easy, Warren, the cold weather must be slowing you down. It's *High Noon* with Lon Chaney Jr. playing the character of Martin Howe. And the year was 1952."

"Ah, crap," Dirty Warren swore. "I didn't expect to see you today, so I just came up with that one off the top of my head when I heard . . . oh boy whoop asshole . . . Kenny talking about integrity."

"Well, a great film, one of my favorites," Karp replied. "Okay, you finish the quote: 'And in the end you wind up dyin' all alone on some dusty street. For what?' "

Dirty Warren grinned and, hooking his thumbs in an imaginary vest, said, "For a tin star. It's all for . . . whoop whoop screwed your sister . . . nothin', Will. It's all for nothin'."

Karp laughed, then his face grew serious, and he lowered his voice. "Speaking of all for nothing, is there any word on the street about what happened to Andrew Kane?"

For a moment, Dirty Warren's face looked troubled. A wealthy white-shoe lawyer, Andrew Kane had once been the darling of New York and a candidate for mayor. But Karp and others had revealed him as a sociopathic monster who, as a member of the clandestine Sons of Man, stopped at nothing, not even mass murder, to achieve his savage goals. He'd been thwarted again — this time failing to blow up the Brooklyn Bridge — but had since disappeared, as had the assassin Nadya Malovo, who worked with Kane and the Sons of Man.

Dirty Warren shook his head and scratched the end of his long nose. "Not a . . . balls whoop ass . . . peep."

"And nothing from Grale?" Karp asked.

Dirty Warren began hopping from one foot to the other again, like a little boy who needed to take a piss. "Haven't . . . lick me bastard . . . seen him," Warren said, and pointed to his newsstand across the street. "Got to go. Have a business to run, ya know." He turned and left, dodging through traffic to reach the other side.

Karp's eyes narrowed as he watched him go. Then he shrugged and stuffed the last of the knish into his mouth and washed it down with orange soda. "Ready to get back to work?"

"Champing at the bit," Katz replied.

Ten minutes later, they were sitting in Karp's office on the eighth floor, talking about the arraignment the next afternoon, when there was a knock at a side door that led to a private elevator. "All hope abandon, ye who enter here," Karp called out.

The door opened, and a good-looking man, with a gray crew cut that complemented the clean angles of his tan face and equally gray eyes, entered the room. "Quoting Dante Alighieri, are we?" he said with a smile.

"Agent Espey Jaxon," Karp said, standing. "To what do we owe the pleasure?"

Jaxon crossed the room, moving with the grace of an athlete — nothing forced, smooth as silk — and held out his hand, which Karp shook warmly. "Just thought I'd stop by and see how things went with our friend Jabbar."

"We have an indictment and will be arraigning him tomorrow. And by the way, thanks for the Christmas present."

Jaxon gave him a puzzled look, but before he could say anything, there was a loud knock on the office main door, followed by the entrance of two more men. The first was Assistant District Attorney V. T. Newbury, a New England blue-blood whose blond hair still flourished, as did his boyish face and bright blue eyes. Somehow he was beating the aging process. He'd just rejoined the DAO as the head of the Frauds Bureau after successfully infiltrating his own family's law firm to bring down his uncle Dean Newbury for the murder of V.T.'s father.

The second man actually appeared older than his age, which was close to the others', with his white hair and frail body. Assistant District Attorney Ray Guma, formerly known, at least in his own mind, as the Italian Stallion, had once been the proud owner of a thick, curly mane of black hair and a thick, muscular body. A bout with an intestinal cancer had aged him almost overnight, but he'd retained his acute mental faculties — specializing in cold cases for the DAO — and his legendary libido, which he was exercising now by pausing at the door to say something to Karp's unseen receptionist, Darla Milquetost.

"We'll see you later, my little sugar blossom," Guma said, which elicited giggles from the woman. He turned and saw the other men looking at him with amused expressions, which caused him to grin and say with his thickest New Jersey accent, "What? What? Can't a guy say something to his girlfriend without the world eavesdropping? You jealous or somethin'?"

"Most certainly," Newbury replied in his driest patrician voice. "We all wish we could be you."

"Well, that's obvious," Guma replied. "But there is only one Goom."

"Thank God," Karp added. "Anyway, we seem to be having an impromptu meeting. I just asked this of Espey, too, but what brings you here this afternoon?"

"Turn on the TV," Guma replied. "Your old pal Megan O'Dowd is going to be letting loose, live in front of the courthouse, any moment. We were watching the tube in V.T.'s office and saw a news teaser. We think she's probably going to rip you a new one, and I wanted to watch your face when she calls you a racist pig."

"Like I should care?" Karp said, though he picked up a remote and pointed it at the small television mounted in the corner next to the bookshelf. A moment later, the angry face of the defense attorney appeared on the screen. She was standing in front of the courthouse and holding up a piece of paper that Karp thought was a copy of the indictment.

"This," she said for the camera, shaking the piece of paper, "isn't about the unfortunate death of a young woman in the mosque where my client is a respected leader and spiritual guide. This is about freedom of speech and freedom of religion and the lengths our government will go to to suppress those freedoms, especially as they apply to the formerly enslaved men and women of African descent. We all know my client is no fan of this government and courageously speaks out against the oppression of people of color, especially the 'new niggers' of the white establishment, black Muslims.

"This," she said, again shaking the indictment document, "is how the government seeks to silence that voice. It seeks to shut him up and take away his freedom by suggesting that he took part in the activities of a small, misguided group of men who, while understandably frustrated, sought to bring attention to the bloated cow of capitalism and its role as the white man's chief mechanism of oppression, the economy, by carrying out a protest against a symbol of that oppression, the New York Stock Exchange."

"Protest?" Jaxon scowled. "Murdering nearly a dozen people in cold blood and trying to destroy the lives of millions of Americans was a protest?"

O'Dowd looked down and dramatically shook her big head before looking up again for the cameras, her eyes glittering with indignation. "What do we know about what occurred in the basement of the Al-Aqsa mosque? We know that a woman whose husband finally could not tolerate the abuse any longer and, regrettably, took his life to make a statement was murdered. We also know that at least two federal agents were in the mosque at that time, but we don't know why, and their presence at the mosque might very well be unconstitutional. What were they doing there? Was the murder an act of revenge by our government? A way to silence my client, Sharif Jabbar, while sending a message about the lengths white America will go to in its misguided, oil-driven, racist, so-called War on Terrorism? These are the questions my client and I look forward to answering in court."

"Ah, the old 'agent provocateur' defense," Guma noted. "Government agents committed the crime and are trying to pin the blame on someone else to destroy them. It's a setup, a frame job."

"She'll be looking to seat that antigovernment juror," Newbury added. "A member of the Tinfoil Hat Society who believes in UFOs and massive government conspiracies."

"Or an angry black man or woman," Katz said.

A question was shouted by a member of the press. "Are you saying your client is innocent?"

"Sounds like a planted question," Guma said.

"My client is innocent of this charge," O'Dowd replied. "He wasn't even present in the mosque when this incident allegedly took place, and we can prove it, and he in no way participated in its planning or execution."

Another question was shouted. "When Imam Jabbar was first arrested at the airfield in New Jersey, why was he carrying a suitcase full of money?"

"And the answer," Karp said, "to the sixty-four-million-dollar question is . . ."

"He was leaving for Yemen with money that had been raised on behalf of several Muslim charities, including one for orphans," O'Dowd answered. "It was perhaps unwise and even a way to circumvent the government of the United States from getting its greedy hands on the cash, but his intentions were good."

"Admit to tax evasion to deflect attention from the more serious crime," Newbury said.

"What about his association with the terrorist Amir Al-Sistani?" another reporter yelled.

O'Dowd scowled. "First of all, Mr. Al-Sistani has yet to be convicted of any crimes in the United States, which the last time I looked at our Constitution meant he should be considered an innocent man. But even if the allegations against Mr. Al-Sistani are true — and I have my doubts — my client hardly knew the man. Mr. Al-Sistani was introduced to my client as the chief financial officer of Prince Esra bin Afraan, who was visiting the mosque. As we will prove in court, my client was kept out of the meetings between Mr. Al-Sistani and Dean Newbury, a man who *suspiciously* will likely be one of the government's primary witnesses. Of course, Newbury, who is facing a number of charges, including murder, just happens to be a wealthy, *white* lawyer with familial ties to the New York DAO. But what else would you expect of this particular district attorney, who, if memory serves me right, has been justifiably known in the past as . . ."

"Uh-oh, here it comes." Guma chortled and looked at his boss.

". . . KKK Karp because of his racist policies."

Guma waited for a reaction, but when Karp's expression didn't change, his smile faded. "Spoilsport," he grumbled.

Karp pointed the remote at the TV screen, and it went blank. He turned to Guma and winked. "Wouldn't give you the satisfaction, Goom." He turned his attention to Katz.

"Okay, what did we just learn?"

"Well, as Guma pointed out, I think we can assume that the defense might try to create a scenario in which government agents — Tran and Jojola — infiltrated the mosque for illicit purposes and might have even contributed to, or caused, Miriam's death."

"And what obstacles can you foresee for us in countering that?"

Katz furrowed his brow and thought for a moment but then shrugged his shoulders. "I'm not sure what you're driving at."

Karp looked over at Jaxon. "Care to explain?"

Jaxon, who had once worked for the DAO as an assistant district attorney before becoming an FBI agent, said, "I think you're talking about that in all likelihood, Tran and Jojola will not be able to say much about why they were present in the mosque if it leads to a discussion of the attack on the stock exchange. Jabbar is not being tried in this instance for his participation in the attack, only the death of Miriam, and therefore, any mention of crimes committed in association with the NYSE attack will be prohibited by the judge. Our guys might be able to say that they were working under-cover on a federal antiterrorism case, but even then, O'Dowd will probably raise hell about their connecting the word *terrorism* to the mosque and Jabbar."

"Anything else?" Karp asked the agent.

"Well, because of the secretive nature of my little group, they also won't be able to say much about who they work for or in what capacity," Jaxon added. "We tried to keep our existence completely secret for as long as we could, but we're pretty sure that our enemies are aware of our presence. So now our hope is to keep them guessing about our mission and who we report to."

"Which means that not answering questions on national-security grounds or being too vague will make them appear to be uncooperative, secretive, and sinister," Newbury said.

"Just the sort of thing a conspiracy buff would latch on to," Guma added. "And I don't know how far O'Dowd will get with Tran, but I'd guess it's going to be a little problematic that he's a Vietnamese gangster, too. Shades of mob involvement in the Bay of Pigs sort of thing."

"Exactly," Karp agreed. "O'Dowd will try to use the fact that John and Tran can't tell the whole truth to make it look as if they're covering up and lying about the rest. And of course, she'll be looking for anything she can find to impeach their characters . . . if I can't keep it out of the testimony." He turned to Katz. "What else?"

Katz furrowed his thick eyebrows. "She said her client wasn't present at the murder and they will prove it. So I guess that means he'll have an alibi witness."

"Correct," Karp said. "But they'll have to abide by reciprocal discovery rules and detail for us the alibi with witnesses' names, addresses, and whereabouts."

"Well," Katz said, "I gather from that little diatribe about our wealthy white witness Newbury and her poor oppressed black client that she will press the racism button whenever she can."

"Which is why Dean Newbury gets zippity-do-dah from this office in exchange for his testimony." Karp nodded. "If she asks him what, if any, 'deals' he received, all he'll be able to say is that he will be entering guilty pleas in this case, as well as for the murder of V.T.'s dad, with no deals. And that I have agreed I will tell the judge at his sentencing whether or not he told the truth at this trial. That's all. What the feds do with him after this trial will be up to them, but he will be a convicted felon in the New York State corrections system."

The meeting broke up just as there was

another knock on the door and Clay Fulton walked in. "Well, this gives me a chance to wish you all a happy new year," the detective said. "And a late Merry Christmas to those I missed last week."

"That reminds me," Jaxon said to Karp. "What was that about a Christmas present? You're Jewish; I didn't buy you a Christmas present."

"Okay, my Hanukkah gift." Karp laughed. "I'm saying thanks for tipping us off that Jabbar was going to be moved Christmas morning."

Jaxon's mouth dropped open. "We didn't call you."

"Sure you did. On Christmas Eve," Fulton replied. "My telephone ID said the call came from the federal lockup at Foley Square."

Jaxon shook his head. "Not me or my gang. Wish we could take credit for that, but the people handling the transfer for the State Department kept it real quiet. We didn't hear about it until the car was already on the move Christmas morning. I thought Butch was going to have my head after promising to keep tabs on that son of a bitch. Did the caller identify himself and say he was with my group?"

"No," Fulton replied. "And it was a she.

But she didn't identify herself. Just said that Jabbar was being taken to Fort Dix in the morning, and the transport would be going through the Holland Tunnel."

"Remember anything else?" Jaxon asked.

"Well, she spoke funny, like she was trying to disguise her voice a little," Fulton replied.

"Somebody with another agency?" Newbury asked.

"Well, I know the marshals weren't real pleased about the assignment," Fulton said. "I think Jen Capers would have hog-tied him and tossed him into the Hudson if I'd asked."

"It could have been one of the guards, for all we know," Guma said. "There's not a lot of affection for terrorists in this city. What do you think, Butch?"

All eyes turned to Karp, who shrugged. "I think I don't know enough to hazard a guess."

8

The tanned, ruggedly handsome man with the mane of silver hair raised his champagne glass to the crowd gathered on the back patio of his mansion. "On behalf of myself and my friends with the Center for Missing and Exploited Persons, I thank you all for coming tonight and for your generous donations to this worthy cause."

Keeping his expression somber, he waited for the polite applause to die down. "Every year, according to the FBI, there are nearly one million missing-persons reports filed with police agencies," he continued. "And while we are all aware of the tragic fact that eighty percent of these involve children, not many people know that twenty percent are adults. They are truly the forgotten ones."

The man bowed his head, and when he raised it again, it was with tears in his eyes. "Tonight we remember one of our own, Rene Hanson, a beautiful, loving, gifted young woman, whose parents, Tom and Rebecca, are living the ultimate nightmare and asking, 'Where is Rene?' " He pointed to a tearful couple standing off to the side, who managed weak smiles and a slight lifting of their champagne glasses.

"I realize that most of you know the story, but to recap: Rene disappeared shortly before Christmas, just four months ago and, except for a few text messages, has not been heard from since," the man went on. "I'm sure you are aware of the news reports that her car was discovered parked at LaGuardia and that security tapes at the airport show her in the parking lot and on a concourse with an unidentified man. According to FBI agents I have been in contact with, she boarded a plane bound for Guadalajara, Mexico, with the man, whose passport said he was Enrique Salazar. We have since been told that the FBI believes this was an alias for a man called the Bishop, a known trafficker in the human sex trade that is epidemic in Mexico."

He paused in his speech, gazing sadly at the somber audience. Since Rene's disappearance, there had been a media frenzy to discover what had happened to the young woman. The story had everything the press looked for when deciding what to sensationalize. The victim was pretty, wealthy, "clean," and white. The parents were hopeful and proactive, even traveling to Guadalajara to pass out flyers offering a reward as the television cameras rolled. The tabloids had competed to see which one could print the most incredible unsubstantiated rumor. Meanwhile, the major television newsmagazines had investigated in Guadalajara and reported that it was a city rife with crime and drug gangs, with an extremely high murder rate, and infamous for trafficking in sex slaves.

But they couldn't find Rene, nor could any of the others who tried as the cameras followed their attempts. Not the forensic teams with bloodhounds and ground-penetrating radar, not the psychics or private investigators or amateur sleuths. Not even legendary "reality television" bounty hunter Michael "Gator" Gleason, who was arrested and expelled from Mexico for assaulting, pepper-spraying, and handcuffing a man he claimed was the Bishop. "Give me ten minutes with him in a cell, and I'll find Rene," the muscular and well-coifed Gator had told the cameras when he was handed across the border to U.S. authorities. The man had turned out to be a day laborer who had never been out of the city.

And America ate it up, the speaker thought, pausing his speech as Rene's mother barely stifled a sob at the mention of "sex trade." Coming up with the story and then pulling it off was pure genius. The news wasn't about Rene's disappearance anymore, it was about the search for Rene, and all the tracks led away from him.

The man sighed. He felt bad for Rene's parents. They'd never know what really happened to her, if she was dead or living in hell. But he didn't feel bad enough to turn himself in. *What would be the point of that except to punish me and waste my talents for what was basically an accident?*

"We're honored tonight to be joined by Westchester County District Attorney Harley Chin, who has kept the Rene Hanson case on the front burner," the man said, pointing to a tall Asian-American in the back of the room, who bowed slightly to the smattering of applause. "As well as Senator Wade Tinsdale, all the way up from the great state of Arkansas, who some of you may know was recently appointed to the Senate Subcommittee on Missing and Exploited Americans. I also recognize and deeply, deeply appreciate that many of you took time from your busy schedules to come here tonight as a show of solidarity and to demand that this administration put the heat on the Mexican government to end this travesty and bring girls like our Rene home to the people who love them."

The applause was louder, with a few "Hear, hears" thrown in. The man bowed his head and shook it slowly side to side. The emotion wasn't entirely feigned. He missed Rene. The idea that he might divorce his cold and shrewish wife had been a fantasy; the real money in the family was hers, and there'd been a prenup. But he had loved Rene — at least, her body and the way she made him feel good about himself again. Like a new man. Younger. Bolder. *Best sex I ever had . . . though I have to say that new girl, Maria, is a firecracker. Exciting.*

At the thought of his new girlfriend, the man looked over at the blond woman standing at the edge of the crowd near the entrance to his house. She looked troubled, her blue eyes catching his and asking questions he didn't want to answer.

He thought about the possible slip he'd made while talking to some of his guests earlier about a vacation to Portugal he'd taken shortly after Christmas with his wife and daughters. He hadn't seen the woman come up to the group, and even when he noticed her, he hadn't realized he might have made a mistake until he saw her frown. He hoped she hadn't noticed.

However, after he finished his speech and was working his way through the crowd, shaking hands and hugging, she waited for him to be alone and then walked up to him. "Can I speak to you privately for a moment?" she'd asked.

The man glanced around with a half smile, as if listening to a mildly amusing joke. "Well, I'm supposed to be mingling, and the wife might not appreciate me leaving the party," he said.

"There are many things your wife might not appreciate," the woman replied evenly. "I think we should find a quiet place to talk."

The man widened the smile on his face. "Fine," he said under his breath. "I'll see you in my library in five minutes."

At the appointed time, he made his way to his library and entered. The room was stuffy, and he saw that despite it being an unseasonably warm April day, someone had the natural-gas flames lit and flickering over the ceramic logs. He looked at the bearskin rug and had a momentary flashback to the Fixer pointing to it and saying, "I assume the high heels are Miss Fox's, yes?"

The man passed his hand over his face.

What does she want? What has she guessed?
He sat down at his desk and saw the photograph of his wife and daughters. He reached out and put it on its face just as the door of the library clicked open and the woman walked in.

He smiled and pointed to the chair in front of his desk. "Have a seat," he said. "So, what do we need to talk about?"

"That was quite a moving speech," the woman said. "Especially the part about the travesty of the sex trade. Ironic, don't you think?"

The man's smile disappeared. "You are certainly in no position to lecture me on morals," he said with a growl. "You're a high-class pimp. You made money by getting young women to sleep with men like me."

A shadow passed across the woman's face. "I'm well aware that what I've done will assure me of a seat in hell," she said. "But as you know, I'm out of that business, and, if possible, I want to do what little I can to make amends."

"What do you mean?" the man asked. He could feel the sweat beading up on his forehead.

The woman leaned toward the desk and looked deep into the man's eyes, searching.

"The Hansons deserve to know what happened to their daughter."

"I couldn't agree more. That's why I'm involved with the CMEP. As you know, I had . . . strong feelings for Rene."

"And she obviously had them for you," the woman added. "But she was young and vulnerable and . . ."

"A call girl who charged a lot of money for sex," the man said. "Let's not gild the lily. I think she was a wonderful person, too, but —"

"It was, after all, a business arrangement," the woman said.

The man's eyes hardened, and his mouth set. He wasn't used to being challenged, and now, while his mind urged caution, his ego took over. "Yes. In the end, that's what it was, and she obviously took her business to Mexico."

Mutual dislike hung in the air like a noxious gas. The man was the first to speak again. "What does all of this have to do with what you wanted to talk to me about?"

The woman's eyes also narrowed. "As I was saying, that was a nice speech, but I was more interested in the conversation you were having when I first arrived."

"I've had quite a number of conversations

this evening," he said. "Could you be more clear?"

"This was the one about your vacation in Portugal with your wife and daughters."

She knows. "A lovely place, and we had a nice time," he said. "What about it?"

The woman studied his face. "What about it is . . . I am absolutely sure that you were trying to schedule 'Brandy Fox' — Rene — for times when you obviously knew that you'd be on the other side of the Atlantic."

The man's smile twitched. "Maybe you misunderstood the dates I was requesting."

The woman shook her head. "No, I don't think so, and I still have a good memory. I'll check when I get home — I kept a record of all client requests, even if the girl already had an appointment, just in case someone canceled, and to monitor client tastes — but I'm sure I'm right."

The man thought for a moment, then shrugged. "My wife and I were having marital problems, and I was thinking about not going on the trip and sending them ahead. I loved Rene, and she loved me. I wanted to spend more time with her."

"Loved? Past tense. Not love," the woman said.

"Let's not play word games," he retorted. "I think we're all aware that the chances of

Rene returning from Mexico are pretty slim to none."

"If she ever went to Mexico."

"What are you implying?"

This time, the woman hesitated before she answered. "I'm not sure, but something's not right, and it's not just you asking to see her when you knew you'd be gone." She shook her head. "I should have put a stop to it when I found out that you knew her from before and that you were friends with her dad."

"Quit with the moralizing." The man scowled. "What's the difference if she was screwing me or some other middle-aged man with a bitch for a wife?"

"Nicely put . . . true love. But unfortunately, I think you're right. Rene did love you. She told me that you two had talked about buying out her contract so you'd have her exclusively."

He bit his lip. "That was my plan. So that makes me the bad guy here?"

"I think you know more than you're saying," she responded.

"Why? Because I was hedging my bets on going to Portugal? Pretty flimsy case, if you ask me."

"Maybe, but a lot of things aren't adding up," the woman replied. "After she disappeared, I went back and looked at her file, and there is no record of her seeing anybody else but you for two months leading up to Christmas. She's excited about you buying out her contract and all this talk about marrying her. But suddenly, she meets some Mexican slave trader, and without saying a word to you or me, she goes off with him to Guadalajara?"

"I have to admit it hurt," the man said sorrowfully.

She looked at him balefully. "You seem to have recovered. I saw you in Manhattan with a pretty little Latina last weekend. Starbucks at Washington Square in the Village. I was sitting at the window seat, and you were kissing her at the curb."

"So what?" the man said impatiently. "She left. I've moved on."

"My girls didn't make their own arrangements, for their own safety . . ."

"And to make sure you got your cut," he noted.

She took a deep breath and let it out slowly. "Yes, my blood money . . . but let me finish. So she works for me for a year and follows the rules, then just skips out with some guy she meets?"

"I'm told the Bishop is quite manipulative," the man said. "He comes to the

United States and promises riches and even movie deals and wealthy husbands, and then, once he gets them to Guadalajara, he abducts and sells them to the highest bidder. Those Mexican drug lords like white girls."

"Maybe," the woman replied. "But in this case, add it all up, and it doesn't make sense. And now you're fudging around because I overheard you talking about your trip to Portugal."

"What is this really about?" he said. "You think you can shake me down for money because you've thrown together some disparate pieces and believe you've solved this case? How much are you looking for? A hundred grand? Five hundred thousand? A million? Sorry, I'm not buying."

"No," she said sadly. "I've already done enough evil for money. I certainly don't want any of yours. I'm going to think about all of this and decide what to do."

"I would strongly suggest that you think long and hard," the man replied. "A defamation suit can cost a lot of money. Now, if you're done, I really should be getting back to the fundraiser. I'm at least trying to do something for Rene."

"I'm sure you are," the woman said. She started to rise from her seat, but a bright object hanging from the desk lamp caught her eye. It was a silver pendant of a Mandarin symbol.

The man's eyes followed hers, and he realized in that moment that he'd made another mistake.

"Rene had a pendant like that," she said. "She was superstitious and told me she never took it off."

"Yes, she gave me a duplicate," he replied. "She said that since we couldn't exchange rings, it would be the symbol of our commitment to each other. It's Mandarin for eternal love."

"Yes, I know," the woman said. "Yet another irony."

She stood and walked over to the door. When she reached for the knob, he said, "Don't do anything stupid."

She hesitated. "It's a little late for that, don't you think? For both of us."

The man waited for the door to close and then yanked the pendant off the lamp. He opened the middle drawer of his desk and angrily tossed the jewelry inside before slamming it shut. Then he reached for his business-card file and found what he was looking for: "Discreet risk assessment and mitigation." He dialed the number, then hung up and waited.

The return call came faster than he'd expected, and he jumped when his landline phone chimed. He answered it, listened, grimaced, and responded. "Um, we might have a problem. I don't know that we can count on the discretion of my acquaintance anymore."

9

U.S. Marshal Jen Capers glanced out the window of the small black jet as it touched down on a covert government airstrip near the farming town of Florence, Colorado. It was three A.M., and except for little green landing lights along the runway and a sky full of stars, the night was as dark as a cave. As the jet slowed, she noted the piles of dirty white snow melting off to the sides of the runway, proof that while it was springtime in the Rockies, it had only just arrived.

When the aircraft lurched to a halt, the runway lights winked out. She kept the cabin dark, too — no sense making it easier on a sniper. She and her young hotshot partner, Joe Rosen, were escorting a "high-value" prisoner from New York to ADX Florence, the "Supermax" federal penitentiary known as the Alcatraz of the Rockies, and there would be no relaxing until he was officially out of her custody.

ADX Florence housed the worst of the worst, the prisoners deemed the most dangerous to others or those most likely to stage a prison break with the help of outside sources. There were mobsters and gang-bangers, terrorists and drug traffickers, bombers, just plain cold-blooded psychopathic killers, and even a former FBI agent, Robert Hanssen, serving life for espionage. Among the other infamous occupants were Omar Abdel-Rahman, the "blind sheik" who had organized the 1993 World Trade Center bombing; Zacarias Moussaoui, the so-called nineteenth hijacker from the September 11, 2001, attacks; Richard Reid, who had attempted to ignite a shoe bomb on an airliner in flight; Theodore Kaczynski, the Unabomber; and Terry Nichols, who had helped plan the Oklahoma City bombing carried out by Timothy McVeigh, who'd also been held there prior to his execution in another penitentiary.

It was no "Club Fed." Most of the prisoners were kept in solitary confinement twenty-three hours a day in seven-by-twelve-foot concrete rooms with steel doors and a grate. They rarely saw other prisoners, and their only direct human interaction was with the staff. One hour a day, they were taken to another concrete room to exercise by themselves. They ate alone and prayed alone — religious services were broadcast from a chapel — and any visitors from the outside were separated from the prisoners by bulletproof glass.

There had never been an escape or a successful attempt to break anybody out, because any individual prisoner's exact whereabouts inside the thirty-seven-acre prison complex could not be determined. Prisoners had no way of knowing where they were in the complex; they never went outside, and even their windows opened only to the sky. They were not allowed to make calls to anyone outside the prison, and every last nook and cranny of the facility was monitored by cameras and motion detectors. Surrounding the prison was a twelve-foot-tall fence topped with razor wire, the space between it and the walls crisscrossed by laser beams and patrolled by big, vicious dogs.

Once she had her man behind the walls, Capers thought, there was no way he was getting out unless he was released or escorted by a U.S. marshal, a member of the agency responsible for transporting federal prisoners. And more important, she reasoned, no one was getting in to get to him. This prisoner was unusual; although he was in federal custody and under indictment, he had not yet been convicted and was, in fact, in the process of becoming a federal witness. ADX Florence was for those who had already been convicted.

Or someone they want to talk to real bad and think is a dead man if they can't get him locked away from the rest of humanity, she thought. *I guess it wouldn't have anything to do with the fact that he's also a former congressman and involved in an attempt to blow up the Brooklyn Bridge. It didn't go off as planned, but plenty of people died, so I hope whatever deal he works out is nothing more than a nicer cell at ADX Florence.*

A twenty-year veteran of the U.S. Marshals Service, Capers didn't spend a lot more time thinking about her prisoner or his past. She had a job to do: take federal prisoners into custody and deliver them safely to wherever she was directed — a courtroom, a prison, or into the hands of the branch of the service that ran the Witness Security Program, WITSEC, better known to the public as the witness-protection program.

She did her job well. She'd never had a prisoner injured or escape, and she'd shot it out with armed men to prevent both, surviving, though hurt, because in the end, she'd proved to be the better marksman. The closest she'd come to losing a prisoner was turning over Sharif Jabbar to her old friend Clay Fulton on Christmas morning, and she'd done that with pleasure.

"We have company off the starboard side," the pilot said over the intercom.

Starboard, huh? Didn't know Pete Todd was a Navy pilot, she thought as she remained in her seat near the rear of the jet and across the aisle from where her prisoner sat in handcuffs. She leaned back in her seat and saw two vehicles approaching with screens over their headlights to minimize their visibility from a distance.

The dark SUVs stopped twenty feet from the jet, facing the plane. She didn't like that they kept their lights, even dimmed, on the aircraft. "I see them, Pete," she said into her shoulder microphone. "Keep the engines revved."

Capers watched Rosen go to the door and look out the window. He was tall, with chiseled features as if he'd stepped off a Marine recruiting poster, and indeed was only recently out of the Corps, having served in Iraq and Afghanistan. He carried a big gun and had a tendency to flirt with any female who came within ten feet, including her. But she had to admit that while he was half her age, she enjoyed the attention; it had been a long time since her husband, Steve, a journalist, had been killed covering the war in Afghanistan. She was lonely, and it was nice to feel appreciated as a woman by a handsome young man, even if it was a harmless flirtation.

One of the vehicles — a black Hummer — flashed its lights in prearranged code. Rosen looked back at Capers, who nodded and spoke to the pilot. "Pete, turn on the audio for the outside, please."

"Yes, ma'am."

Rosen pressed a button, the door popped open, and the gangway lowered to the tarmac. Eight figures dressed in black exited the Hummers. Six heavily armed men immediately moved out and took up defensive positions facing away from the jet. The remaining two began walking toward the gangway.

Capers was somewhat surprised to see from the silhouettes in the cars' lights that one of the two was a woman whose shape she didn't recognize. She didn't personally know every marshal in the WITSEC program, who would be in charge of her prisoner's security from this point on, but she thought that any female assigned to this would have been Pam Ayres, who was short and stocky. This woman was tall and moved like a dancer. *Someone new,* she thought.

Rosen walked down the stairs of the gangway to intercept the two on the ground. "Morning, folks. Identification," he said, turning on a small flashlight. The two stopped in front of him and flipped open their wallets.

As her partner turned his light on the IDs, Capers glanced over at her prisoner, former congressman Denton Crawford. "When I tell you, stand up and proceed down the aisle ahead of me," she said.

Crawford smiled. "Whatever you say, officer."

Standing in the dark as the young marshal looked at the identification she'd handed him, Nadya Malovo waited patiently to make her move. She had no fear that the stolen ID would pass a quick inspection; after all, the document was real, even if the photograph had been quickly substituted for one of her own. And there was no danger of the real owner showing up; U.S. Marshal Pam Ayres was lying dead out in the dark along with five other members of her team.

Malovo considered herself the best at what she did, but even she had to acknowledge that she'd been plagued lately by a string of failures. She'd been in charge of training the Al-Aqsa Brigade for the attack on the New York Stock Exchange, as well as taking out a secondary target in Brooklyn. But both plans had been ultimately thwarted. As was the plan to incinerate the Brooklyn Bridge and both sides of the East River within a mile of it by blowing up a liquefied-natural-gas tanker.

Not my fault, she thought. The plans had called for her to escape early from what were little more than suicide missions for the others. She was the catalyst, the field commander, and, when necessary, an assassin. Seducing the head of building security and dispatching him with a letter opener in his brain. Personally guiding the progress of the LNG tanker right up to the moment when it entered U.S. waters, and then, by prior arrangement with a traitor U.S. Coast Guard captain, being "taken into custody" and transferred to his patrol boat. Safely away from the tanker and its rendezvous with fate in the East River, her accomplice had facilitated her escape but then died along with the rest of the small crew, whom she "terminated with prejudice" when her escape was secure.

All her accomplices had to do was complete a few simple tasks, but they had failed, and therefore, so had she. *Of course, much of that was because of that bastard Karp and his associates,* she thought. *And my old lover, Yvgeny Karchovski, who keeps interfering in matters that should not concern him. I wonder what his connection to Karp is. No matter. Someday soon, I will settle with both of them.* The thought of both men turned her stomach. Not only had there been a string of failures of late, but she had come increasingly close to losing her life.

Malovo suppressed the urge to shiver at the jolt of . . . a premonition? She needed for this new mission to be a success. She wanted to retire before it all caught up to her. If either the NYSE or the Brooklyn Bridge mission had come to fruition, she would have been out of the business and living her days in ease and comparative safety. But the people she worked for didn't reward failure, and she had even begun to worry about at what point they might decide she was a liability. *Like Denton Crawford.*

So this time, she would personally see to it that the missions were brought to a successful conclusion. And when it was over, she would be wealthy. *And I will begin to act out my revenge on Karp and Yvgeny.*

The mission this time wasn't as dramatic as attempting to destroy the U.S. economy or blow up a major landmark and portions of lower Manhattan and Brooklyn. However, the leadership of the Sons of Man considered it even more vital that she succeed. For the first time in its two-hundred-year history, the SOM council was in a panic. All those years, they'd kept their existence a secret as they'd evolved from simple smugglers who fled the Isle of Man to evade the British navy to leaders of American politics, business, and military with a goal of eventually controlling the United States and, if all went well, the world. However, mistakes had been made lately. Impatience, perhaps, to see the dream fulfilled had led to overreaching and complicated schemes that had backfired. The existence of the group, if not its membership, was known, and now the authorities had two members in custody, Crawford and Dean Newbury.

Compared with Newbury, Crawford was small potatoes, an empty suit, good for politics and doing what he was told by the council. But he wasn't privy to all the secrets or plans. If he talked, he could do serious damage, of course; he did know names and the basic structure and purpose of the organization. But SOM's public relations machine could make him out to be a nutcase, a criminal who'd worked with psychopath Andrew Kane to extort money and was blaming others to get out of trouble.

The real problem was Dean Newbury. He'd been one of the oldest and most powerful members of the council, and there was nothing he did not know about the organization, including access to documentation that would make denials futile.

However, according to sources within several federal agencies, neither man had talked yet. They were, in fact, "lawyered up" as their attorneys negotiated *quid pro quos,* such as being placed in the witness-protection program in exchange for their information about the Sons of Man and, in Newbury's case, testifying in the New York case against Sharif Jabbar. But it was only a matter of time before they did start talking. *Unless they're no longer breathing.*

Malovo had already probed the edges around Newbury's security. She knew he was being kept somewhere in upstate New York, but she couldn't find the exact location. Karp's man, the big black detective, Fulton, was in charge of security and had the old man stashed away so well that her spies — both on the street and SOM agents within federal law-enforcement agencies — could get no word of his whereabouts beyond a region. *So if I can't get to him, I need him to be brought to me,* she thought.

In the meantime, she'd been tipped off that Crawford was being brought to ADX Florence to protect him. If they got her target inside, it would be virtually impossible to get at him, and she would have already failed at half the mission.

She considered simply blowing the jet out of the air with a shoulder-fired missile, but she couldn't be sure that Crawford was on the aircraft. It would be just like the U.S. Marshal's Office to spread false information about a prisoner's movements to throw off anyone tracking them. And if she didn't get him, she probably would never have another crack at him. Her bosses had also asked her to ascertain, "if possible," if Crawford had already talked by seeing him face-to-face.

The world was full of men who would betray their duty and comrades for money, or sometimes sex, which was when having a beautiful body and a face like hers was a definite asset. She was wired to take advantage of the weak and corrupt. And so U.S. Marshal Ben Stopes was easy prey. For a cool million dollars, he had led the witness-protection team assigned to take custody of the target into an ambush.

Now, all she had to do was get past this young, handsome, doomed man and the U.S. marshal still onboard the jet. She'd been told that the latter would not be an easy task. Apparently, U.S. Marshall Jen Capers was tough and smart.

The young man handed her identification back. "Thank you, Marshal Ayres."

Inside the jet, Capers jumped up at her partner's words and pulled her gun. *Dangit! That is definitely not Pam Ayres,* she thought as she started to race to the front of the jet. "Marshal Rosen! I need to see you immediately," she said into her radio, which was set to Rosen's earpiece.

It was a code that something was wrong, and he was to get back onboard the aircraft. But realizing the vulnerability of Capers and the prisoner, Rosen reached for his gun and had it out before the others could draw.

As had happened before in her long and vicious career, Malovo's opponent chose the wrong partner, apparently believing that, between the two, the woman was less dangerous. He pointed the gun at Malovo's male companion, who was slow to react and was only just grabbing his gun when a bullet from Rosen's .44 Magnum caught him in the stomach and knocked him off his feet.

However, Nadya Malovo was not slow, nor was she less dangerous. Before the young man could turn his gun on her, she shot him in the throat. It didn't take the fight out of him, but as he tried to bring his gun to bear, her second shot hit him between the eyes.

Capers arrived in the doorway just in time to see her partner fall to the tarmac. "No!" she screamed, and fired at Malovo.

The shot might have been fatal to anyone else. But years of hunting and being hunted had fine-tuned the Russian's reflexes; she saw the movement at the door and turned her body sideways without hesitation, just as Capers pulled the trigger. She felt the bullet tug at the sleeve of her shirt as it whizzed past. But it was enough to throw off her own aim when she returned fire.

Two bullets crashed into the bulkhead next to Capers, who ducked back inside the cabin. A hail of bullets struck the fuselage as the rest of the ambush team began shooting.

"Pete, get us out of here!" Capers yelled.

"What about Joe?" the pilot replied.

Capers felt a lump in her throat. "He's gone. We have a prisoner to protect!" She fired a couple more rounds out the still-open door to hold off the attackers.

Suddenly, the jet lurched to the right and then down in front. Capers realized that the attackers were shooting out the aircraft's tires. Then there was a blaze of automatic rifle fire, which, judging from the surprised and then anguished shout from the pilot, meant that the people outside were determined to keep the jet on the ground.

Capers heard a shout from outside — "What are you waiting for? Attack!" — and took cover behind a row of seats. Her bosses in New York had considered escorting Crawford to ADX Florence under a large and heavily armed guard. But they were hoping to get him safely tucked away without gaining any attention. So it had been decided to smuggle him in quietly with only a small team.

Guess that was a mistake, Capers thought as she trained her gun on the door. A moment later, a man jumped into the cabin, his gun ready, but he didn't fire.

Capers dropped him with a shot to the head. *Didn't shoot,* she thought. *They want my prisoner alive.* She glanced back but couldn't see Crawford.

Another man, followed quickly by one more, came through the door. She shot one

181

in the chest but had to duck when the second man opened fire on her. Something punched her hard in the left shoulder, and she was slammed back into a seat. Leaning over into the aisle, she shot the second man in the leg. He fell, and she finished him with a bullet that struck him in the chin.

Capers sat back up. With her free hand, she reached up to touch where it felt as if someone was applying a red-hot poker to her skin. The hand came away covered with blood. She felt light-headed and couldn't react when someone threw a small canister into the cabin that landed a few feet from where she sat.

M84 stun grenade, she thought. A moment later, there was a blinding flash of light and a deafening roar as the cylinder exploded.

It took five seconds for her vision to return, and when it did, she was looking up into the face of the fake Pam Ayres. Even with a black stocking cap covering most of her blond hair and the black military-style clothing covering her body, the woman was quite beautiful, though the gun she was pointing at Capers was not.

Capers prepared to die. *I will not let her see my fear.*

However, the other woman leaned over and picked up Capers's gun where it had fallen. She stood and pointed her own gun at the marshal's head but then hesitated.

"Shoot — get it over with," Capers snarled.

The woman smiled and shook her head. "Not today. Today you live. It's good to meet another woman who knows how to fight. And I want you to take a message back to Butch Karp. Tell him that I will take my revenge against him one life at a time until he is the last one, and then I will take him, too."

"Fuck you," Capers said.

Malovo smirked. "Perhaps some other time, if you survive your wound." She turned to one of her men, who'd joined her on the aircraft. "Watch her." She then proceeded to the back of the jet, where Crawford was standing with a smile on his face.

"I knew my brothers would not let me down," he said as she walked up. "Now, get the key from the woman and get me out of the handcuffs."

"In a moment. First, I need to ask you an important question," Malovo replied. "What have you told the authorities about the Sons of Man?"

Crawford looked incredulous. "Are you kidding? I know better than that. Our reach is long, as is our memory. I pretended I was going to talk in exchange for a deal, but that was just a stall tactic."

Malovo looked into the former congressman's eyes, then said, "I believe you."

"But of course," he replied. "I would never betray my family or friends. *Myr shegin dy ve, be eh!*"

Malovo nodded. "*Myr shegin dy ve, be eh.* That's Manx for 'What must be will be,' correct?"

"Yes. Now, would you please release me? These things are killing my wrists."

Instead, Malovo raised her gun and pointed it at his face.

"What are you doing?" he screamed. "I told you I didn't say anything!"

"And I said I believe you, but unfortunately for you, this must be," she replied, and pulled the trigger.

10

Warren Bennett stood in the quietest corner of the ballroom, an untouched martini in one hand and a strained smile glued to his face, as he pretended to be interested in the swirl of guests carrying on animated conversations throughout the room. The muscles on the right side of his face twitched several times in a row, making it appear that he was grimacing. Without his consciously thinking about it, a finger on his free hand inserted itself between his neck and the unfamiliar and uncomfortably stiff collar of the tan button-down Brooks Brothers shirt the butler had laid out for him that afternoon along with a blue Saint Laurie blazer, blue tie, and tan slacks.

He would have preferred not to dress up, but he knew better than to argue the subject with his autocratic mother. It would have been a waste of breath and time. And as he rarely returned to his wealthy parents'

15,000-square-foot mansion in the town of Purchase in Westchester County, he didn't think it worth making what little time he did spend any more unpleasant than it already was. He'd be out of the suit and into his blue jeans, a stained World Champion Yankees '99 sweatshirt, and worn-out high-top sneakers soon enough.

Neither Purchase — one of the wealthiest communities in New York and thus the United States, with a median income of near $200,000 — nor the mansion was a happy place for him. It wasn't home, not even now in April, when the warming days and gentle rains reminded him of early childhood playing on the manicured lawns as the hardwood trees turned lima-bean green with new foliage. Back before he was "afflicted."

No, he was content living in a low-rent one-room walkup on the Lower East Side of Manhattan and operating his newsstand in front of the Criminal Courts Building. And to be honest, his parents were just as happy to keep it that way.

Turning slightly, Warren caught a reflection of himself in one of the room's many mirrors. A young man in his mid-thirties, with a long, pointed nose and pale skin, stared back at him with watery blue eyes magnified by the thick lenses of his glasses. He was a little surprised by the reflection, as if seeing someone he once knew in an unexpected place. As his father had remarked, he'd "cleaned up nicely" for the party, with a fresh shave and by combing his thinning brown hair back with what his sister, Shannon, called "product."

But the well-tailored, well-heeled son of a Top Ten insurance company president in the mirror wasn't him. He was "Dirty Warren," the Tourette's-afflicted, foul-mouthed, constantly twitching news vendor at 100 Centre Street. Laughed at and ridiculed by some, feared by others who thought he was "crazy." All because of a neurological disorder characterized by involuntary movements, or muscle spasms, and vocalizations called tics.

In his case, the tics included twitches in his facial muscles, the sudden jerking of his head to the side or up and down, and shrugging his shoulders for no apparent reason. When particularly agitated, he hopped from one foot to the other like a child needing to use the restroom. But it was the foul language and accompanying "whoops" and "oh boys" that had the most deleterious impact on his life, as it could seem to those who didn't understand the disorder that the cursing was purposeful or a sign of being mentally unbalanced.

The Tourette's had first manifested itself when he was about ten with mild outbursts at inopportune times, such as in the classroom at the private school he attended or while sitting in the pews at the White Plains Presbyterian Church or, most unforgivably, during his parents' many formal dinner parties attended by all sorts of important people. The most unfortunate example was probably the time when the governor had politely asked him about his studies, and he'd proudly replied, "I'm getting . . . eat my ass fucker whoop . . . straight A's, thank you for asking." The boy and the man had sat for several seconds blinking at each other — one of them involuntarily — and not saying a word until Warren's mother literally picked her son up by his arms and removed him from the dinner table. He'd been deposited in his room, where he received a "for your own good" spanking and no dinner.

Indeed, corporal punishment and verbal castigations were how the Bennetts had dealt with their once-perfect boy's "willful and inappropriate behavior" for the next year. Then, one day when he was in the fifth grade, they'd been called into the office of the vice principal. As Warren sat in a corner seat with his head bowed and tears streaming down his face, they were told that their son was being expelled because of "continued disturbances in the classroom." The final straw had been during the Pledge of Allegiance, when he said, "and to the republic for which it stands . . . oh boy ohhhh boy, my aching balls . . . one nation, under God."

The vice principal had shaken his head. "I'm sorry. The fact is that most of the time, Warren is a very nice young man and a good pupil. However, his . . . behavior of late has become too disruptive, and it's not fair to our other students and teachers. And to be honest, and I don't know if he's talked to you about this, we've received reports that his . . . um . . . language has resulted in his being assaulted by other students, off school grounds where we can't monitor what happens. Frankly, I'm concerned for his safety." The man had leaned forward and looked earnestly from mother to father. "I'm suggesting that your son see a psychiatrist who can perhaps determine the cause of his outbursts — it could be a chemical imbalance or something — and correct it before it affects his life more than it already has."

Even after that, Warren's parents had

resisted the idea of seeking psychiatric help. "There has been no madness in the Todd and Bennett families for three hundred years in this country, and we're not going to start having any now," his mother had declared, as his notoriously acquiescent father mumbled his agreement. But as the boy bounced from one private school to another — many echoing the suggestion of that first vice principal — it had become clear that his condition was worsening. So they'd finally bundled him off to a renowned psychiatrist in Manhattan who'd diagnosed Tourette's syndrome.

Told that there was treatment but no cure, the Bennetts had decided that a second opinion was needed, which led to a bevy of psychiatrists and neurologists, and even a "child whisperer," being consulted. Current research had pointed to "abnormalities in certain brain regions" disrupting the communication between nerve cells as a cause, but no one suggested that a cure was imminent. The Bennetts had been assured, however, that in ninety percent of Tourette's cases, the tics were worst in the early teens and then got progressively better as the patient got older.

Unfortunately, Warren fell into the ten percent whose condition didn't improve, and, in fact, it had grown worse as he went through his late teens and entered his twenties, despite all efforts to treat him. Under the guidance of a behavioral psychologist, he'd worked to control the tics by consciously suppressing them when he felt the urge coming on. However, there were two problems with that. One was that he didn't usually get much warning of the onset of tics or vocalizations, and by the time he tried to focus on the mental exercises he'd been given to maintain control, it was often too late. The second issue was that suppressing tics only caused the urges to grow until they burst from him in a torrent that was much worse than if he'd gradually released the pressure. And if he was agitated or frightened, or even when he was happily excited, nothing really helped; the Tourette's was likely to turn into a runaway freight train of spasms and swearing.

Warren had also tried several varieties of medications, but they'd made him feel sedated and dull-witted. So he'd decided that if he had to live as a zombie, he'd just as soon be dead and tried to kill himself by swallowing a bottle of the latest pills. But all it had done was make him ill, and after getting his stomach pumped at the hospital, he'd been forced under penalty of "eternal hatred otherwise" to promise his sister, Shannon, that he'd "never do such a fucking stupid, selfish, cowardly thing again!"

It wasn't always the easiest promise to keep. Tourette's had been tough on his social life. Even his most loyal childhood friends had abandoned him by high school. He was no River Phoenix, the teen male film idol he had most wanted to be at the time. He might have made up for his lack of looks with his quick-witted sense of humor and genuine smile, but his guy friends had been dealing with their own teenage insecurities and didn't want a foul-mouthed "spaz" to make it tougher. And girls hadn't wanted a boyfriend who might suddenly cut loose with "lick my ass" in front of their parents and then start twitching and hopping.

Lonely and ashamed, he'd spent much of his teenage years reading books and watching films alone. Even what little human social interaction he got going to the movies had ended because his outbursts disturbed other patrons, and he got tired of being asked to leave the theaters. After that, he'd been relegated to watching films he bought or rented in his room or the mansion's state-of-the-art home theater.

Tutored at home for the last two years of

high school and with so much time on his hands, he'd quickly gone through current films, then recent releases. Finally, he'd come to the black-and-white and early color classics — at first out of necessity and then from a love of the era. He'd had many favorites old and new, some of which he'd watched so many times that he could recite the dialogue, and his room's shelves had contained all manner of books on film, which he read repeatedly.

Even now, watching movies in his Lower East Side efficiency — where he kept them neatly and alphabetically arranged on a bookshelf — was still his greatest pleasure. That and reciting obscure movie trivia to his current crop of friends and acquaintances, most of them "street people" like himself who were tolerant of his behavior. He considered himself a film expert and knew of only one man whose knowledge and breadth of movies surpassed his own: Butch Karp, the district attorney of New York, with whom he'd been playing a movie-trivia game — without a single success by Warren — since they'd met years earlier.

Growing up, he'd had to rely on Shannon, his pretty, smart, perfect sister, for someone he could talk to without being judged first for his speech and physical quirks. Although five years his junior, she was probably the only human being who truly knew him, the only one who cared to know him. Even his street friends, such as the Walking Booger and Edward Treacher, only knew so much, and that didn't include his dreams.

The only girl who'd been kind to him in high school had been Michelle Oakley. She'd grown up in the neighborhood, the daughter of a brokerage-firm president, but they didn't become friends until seventh grade. A few days into the school year, he'd been off to himself on the playground when he noticed that a girl was being harassed by an older boy. Stepping in and demanding that the bully cease, he'd promptly got his ass kicked, but the pain was forgotten when the pretty blond girl helped him off the ground and declared him "my hero."

Michelle had captured his heart at that moment, but while he longed for something more, they'd remained "only friends." But they were good friends. She seemed not to notice his tics or his profanity — except when he'd occasionally catch her by surprise, which usually elicited a surprised look and then a laugh. She was the only person other than his sister whom he could confide in.

Although they ended up at different schools after he was expelled yet again, she would call to see if he wanted to hang out down at the park or take in a movie. That summer had been the best of his life. She'd even let him kiss her once, though when he tried for another, she'd laughed and gently pushed him away.

When Michelle entered high school in the fall, everything had changed. He was the recluse, ashamed of a condition he could not control. She was the cheerleader, dating the captain of the football team, a straight-A student and homecoming queen. She still called from time to time, sometimes just to talk but other times to see if he wanted to go to a party or just hang out with her and her friends. But he turned down most invitations that had meant interacting with other teens, so the offers had grown fewer with each passing year.

She'd remained friendly whenever she saw him. Although their friendship had begun with his interceding on her behalf with a bully, she was the one who defended him on the few occasions he agreed to meet her or if she and friends bumped into him in public. No one was allowed to laugh at or tease him when she was present without receiving her full fury, which could be considerable and accompanied by language that left even Warren blushing. She'd actually dropped the football captain when she learned that he'd been part of a group that harassed Warren on his way home once from the video store.

Of course, she hadn't always been around to protect him, and it wasn't just from mean words or teasing. The Tourette's had cost him beatings throughout his life. Without intending to or sometimes even knowing it, he'd say something offensive and get punched in the nose or be subjected to even more vicious assaults.

Once it had nearly cost him his life. And that was the first time he met David Grale.

It was a cold November night a few months after he'd moved to Manhattan. He was in his mid-twenties and living on the streets, unable to keep a job because of his outbursts. Penniless, he had nowhere to go at night and was trying to sleep in the alcove outside St. Bartholomew's Church on Park Avenue. Shivering, hungry, and tired, it had taken him a moment to see the robed figure materialize out of the shadows, the light of a streetlight glimmering off the long curved blade of a knife.

Warren hadn't known it at the time, but the man in front of him believed that demons inhabited the bodies of some men and that it was his God-given duty to send them back to hell. And Grale had been told by one of his "Mole People" — who lived with him in the sewers, tunnels, and caverns beneath the city of New York — of a new-comer who spoke in profanity-laced tirades and whose body twitched and jerked as though possessed. So he had come to St. Bart's, intending to send another demon back to hell if the reports were true.

His face twitching with fear and his head jerking to the side, Warren had sat up and looked upon the pale, drawn face and bright, haunted eyes of David Grale. And he'd believed that he was about to die. "I don't have . . . fuck asswipe . . . any money!" he'd cried out. "But you can have my wallet and shoes . . . oh boy whoop whoop kiss my balls . . . they're the only thing I have that's worth anything. But please don't kill me. I don't know why . . . cocksucking whore whoop . . . but I promised my sister I'd keep this fucked-up life as long as I could."

The executioner had paused and looked into his eyes for what seemed like minutes but was probably only a few seconds. Then the madman's eyes had softened as he lowered the blade, smiled, and extended a hand. "Come, brother," he'd said. "The night is already cold, and it's going to get worse. I can offer a warmer place to sleep and get some food in your belly." And that's how Warren Bennett, scion of a wealthy businessman and his imperial wife, had come to be living among the Mole People.

For the first time since the fifth grade, he'd felt as if he belonged. The Mole People came from all walks of life and bore many different types of crosses. Some had been wealthy and respected but lost it all to alcohol or drugs. Some had been born poor and disadvantaged or were abused as children and had never overcome their rough start. Some had been criminals, though Grale did not allow the unreformed to stay. Others had suffered physical deformities or mental illnesses. All of them had found themselves living on the streets, cast from the circle of "normal" society whose individual members could pass within inches of them on the streets and look right through them as though they were invisible.

Whatever they had been, whoever they were, they had come under the leadership of the charismatic but at least partly deranged David Grale, who had organized them into a community based on early Christian concepts of everybody working for the common good. Everybody had a job. It might be dumpster diving, looking for anything that was useful or could be sold. Or begging restaurants and grocers for food they would have otherwise thrown away. Or, for the stronger members, robbing criminals such as drug dealers and pimps, who counted themselves lucky if "those crazy bums" caught them unaware in some dark alley and they lived to tell the story.

Grale had instilled pride in them, preaching that they were the vanguard of the ultimate battle between good and evil. That they were not outcasts and derelicts but society's invisible saviors. And in truth, their "invisibility" on the streets and sidewalks was an asset — they saw and heard things when those being monitored thought no one was paying attention.

Everybody was expected to keep their eyes and ears open for useful information and to keep tabs on those "outworlders" considered friends and the activities of the "enemies of God." And for those Grale handpicked to do "God's work," there was the job of sending evil men to hell.

Grale and the Mole People ruled the honeycomb of caves, sewers, and tunnels — natural and man-made — beneath the city. Although there were several smaller communities scattered throughout subterranean Manhattan, the main living area was a large cavern that had been carved out as part of an abandoned subway station. It even had electricity, stolen by tapping into a nearby active subway line.

No official count had ever been taken of the Mole People. The city of New York unofficially estimated that there were between five thousand and twenty-five thousand of them scattered throughout the tunnels and caverns beneath the streets, with more arriving when the economy tumbled.

Grale did not demand that those who found a place in the underground community — and did their fair share of work — believe in his apocalyptic vision or join his crusade against evil-doers. Some eventually left the Mole People and returned to "the world," often following the practice of "tithing," giving ten percent of their income to their former benefactor's underground church and mission.

Warren was one of those. He'd never joined Grale's hunting parties, not that he shed any tears for the evil men who died. Whether they were actually demons in men's bodies, as Grale claimed, or simply evil men who preyed on others, it was one and the same to him, but he could not cross that moral line to take another life.

Ultimately, Warren's reasons for leaving had more to do with being too much of a loner to fit in well in a commune. Nor had he wanted to spend his life scavenging or begging for subsistence. He'd wanted a job and a place of his own where he could watch his movies and read.

Warren had found a job as a night janitor, and, with Grale's blessing, as soon as he could, he'd rented a walk-up efficiency on Pitt Street. He'd found a part-time day job helping the owner of the newsstand on Centre Street and finally saved up enough money to buy the old man out.

Warren loved working at his newsstand. It had come as a surprise to those who knew him — including his sister, who occasionally came into the city to visit — that he got into a business with so much public interaction. But he'd explained to Shannon that if he was going to "live in the real world," he needed to find ways to cope with his issues, not hide from them.

"And to be honest, owning my own . . . oh boy ohhhh boy piss on me bitch . . . business has made me feel like I'm as good a person as anyone and that I shouldn't have to be ashamed for something I can't help."

Along with tithing, Warren had repaid

Grale's kindness by being an invaluable source of information about the comings and goings at the Criminal Courts Building. But he was getting worried about his friend.

Having been examined by a dozen psychiatrists and psychologists, Warren thought they would have probably diagnosed Grale as bipolar, with a mental disorder manifested by wild mood swings. When he was up, Grale was a loving "father" and spiritual advisor to all who sought shelter and respite in his underground kingdom.

However, when the pendulum swung the other way, he brooded on his "throne," an old overstuffed chair set on the edge of an abandoned subway platform, in moods so dark that he would either not talk for days or would rant about the approaching Apocalypse and the need to prepare. Then he might leap up and go in search of the "Others" — a sort of evil version of the Mole People who vied for the territory beneath the streets — or hunt killers and other violent criminals on the streets.

It was widely known among the Mole People that Grale held a special affinity for Karp's family. He'd met Lucy in a soup kitchen where they both worked — she an idealistic teen and he a Catholic social worker on the verge of becoming a serial killer of murderers. He'd asked Warren and others, such as Booger and Treacher, to keep an eye on Karp, Marlene, and their children and warn him if they were in any danger. Warren knew that Grale sometimes kept vigil himself when he perceived the Karp-Ciampi clan was in jeopardy, watching their residence from the shadows of the alley across Crosby Street.

Several times in recent years, Grale's plans had coincided with Karp's efforts to thwart terrorist plots. But in the end, Warren knew, his friend had served only his concept of what God intended him to do.

The last time Warren had seen him, Grale was keeping Andrew Kane, whom he'd captured after the Brooklyn Bridge attack, chained by his neck to a wall on the old subway platform like some sort of dangerous junkyard dog. Occasionally, Kane, who was at least as deranged as his captor, would be dragged forward to crouch at the foot of Grale's "throne." There the two madmen would engage in theological discussions about the nature of good and evil and the end of the world. But Warren couldn't see any purpose to Kane's imprisonment other than as retribution.

Warren knew that Kane might have information that Karp and his colleagues could use, particularly regarding the workings and membership of the Sons of Man. He felt bad for lying to Karp about Kane's whereabouts. The district attorney was one of the few "normal" people who always treated him with respect and even friendship; he was a busy man, and yet he almost always took a few minutes to play their movie-trivia game or chat as he picked up his morning newspaper.

Personally, Warren thought that Grale should turn Kane over to the authorities. But when he'd broached the subject with his friend, who was in one of his dark moods, Grale had demanded that he keep Kane's existence a secret.

Warren's recollection of that last conversation with Grale was shattered now by an overly loud laugh from one of his parents' guests — a boozy blonde who'd been introduced to him as Sherry. Her boyfriend's name was Jim Williams. Warren's head jerked suddenly back and then down again.

It was a long way from the damp, dimly lit lair of David Grale to the Bennett mansion in Purchase. The last time he'd been home was for Christmas, four months earlier. He'd spent that morning pretending they were a happy family and then left as soon as he could get away gracefully.

Then, as now, his only real reason for returning was his sister. And today was her thirtieth birthday, which was as good an excuse as any from their parents' point of view to throw another of their VIP parties.

Shannon sometimes joked that she was particularly happy to have "a potty-mouthed brother who twitches," because it made her, by default, "the good child," despite her recent divorce and a failure to produce grandchildren. Up to those unfortunate events, or nonevents, she'd been an untouchable star — magna cum laude at Brown University and an MBA from Columbia.

Of course, their mother did nothing without an ulterior motive, and this party had two. It was an opportunity to bring the movers and shakers in local and state politics together — under her roof — with the movers and shakers with money. And as Clare Bennett had noted dryly, "It's a fabulous opportunity for Shannon to meet the new Mr. Right." When Shannon protested that "the body of my marriage is still warm," their mother had smiled in her icy way and added, "You'll get over it."

"What about me, Mom?" Warren had

asked, giving his sister a sideways glance. "Got me set up with . . . ass balls whoop whoop . . . any debutantes?"

Clare's smile grew tight. "I'm sure you'll do your best not to embarrass us. And do wear the suit I had the houseboy run out and buy for you."

"I'm sure I . . . oh boy ohhhh boy . . . will," Warren had replied with a smile that only his sister knew masked his hurt.

Sighing now, Warren looked around the ballroom, with its Strass crystal chandeliers, Italian marble floors, gilded fixtures, and valuable oil paintings. His mother was a big fan of eighteenth-century French aristocracy, and her grand ballroom reflected it. She was also a big fan of important people talking about her parties, so there was a smattering of film stars, Broadway actors, directors and producers, the male and female leads in *Madame Butterfly* now playing at the Met, and a variety of musicians. They were complemented by a cornucopia of captains of industry, white-shoe attorneys, and their wives, all of whom could be expected to donate large checks to the Party. And of course, there were a dozen politicians who coveted that money, including the governor, a U.S. senator, two congressmen, the entire Purchase city council and mayor, several judges, and, Warren noted with a frown, District Attorney Harley Chin.

He'd met Chin many years earlier when the young prosecutor was working for the New York District Attorney's Office. He was an arrogant, self-important prick, as far as Warren was concerned, who thought it was beneath him to talk to the news vendor when he picked up his morning paper.

Chin was engaged in conversation with a middle-aged couple whom Warren recognized as the parents of the missing girl, Rene Hanson. He'd read the story in the newspapers, which had been all over it, from the *Times* to the *National Tattler* (right next to a story about the bat-faced boy). She'd disappeared around Christmas, and there was something about her being sold into sexual slavery in Mexico. A horrible fate if true, and he felt sympathy looking at the drawn faces of the Hansons.

The Hansons were old family friends, otherwise his mother probably wouldn't have invited them, thinking they would be drags on the party. "I understand it's a very difficult situation," his mother had said with a sniff at breakfast that morning. "But they need to give it a rest. We know the story, there's nothing we can do that we haven't done. This is a social occasion; if they don't feel social, you'd think they'd just stay home."

Remarks like that, Warren thought, *are the reason I really dislike my mother.*

"Why, it's Warren Bennett! Where on earth have you been?"

The woman's voice coming from behind startled Warren. He was shocked that someone knew him and was actually trying to engage him in conversation. He turned and saw the pretty blond woman and smiled. Her body was thicker, her face fuller, her breasts heavier and her hips wider, and her blue eyes had been enhanced with colored contacts, but he would have known her anywhere. Nor had the changes detracted from Michelle Oakley's beauty, at least not in his eyes.

"Meesh! I didn't know you'd be here," he exclaimed, pleased that he'd been able to control the urge to swear.

"Ha ha, Meesh . . . I haven't heard that name in more years than I care to admit," Michelle said with a laugh that reminded him of the girl he'd had a crush on. "Yes, your parents are kind enough to invite me to these soirees. I think my folks must have made them promise before they died to keep me in the social loop. I don't think they really approve of me, though, at least not your mother."

"Why not?" Warren asked. The Oakleys and the Bennetts had been friends for several generations.

Michelle laughed and rolled her eyes. "Oh, I don't know, maybe it's four failed marriages by age thirty-six. Does it count as failed if one up and died on me during sex? Massive coronary, which I guess I should take as a compliment, poor Jacob. I think I've run out of men who would marry me or I'd want to marry."

Warren smiled shyly. "Ha ha, what am I, the . . . shit whoop bite me bitch . . . bottom of the barrel?" It took him a moment, and the surprised look on Michelle's face, to realize what he'd said. "I'm so . . . oh boy oh boy stop it Warren . . . sorry," he said, blushing as tears sprang to his eyes.

Michelle reached up and touched his cheek. "You forget who you're talking to . . . my hero," she said. "I'm not sure what other people might hear, but all I heard was an old friend being sweet. And no, you're not the bottom of the barrel — I've already been there. I think you've been floating on top, but I was looking down at the assholes. You were always too good for me."

Dropping his eyes, Warren blushed even

harder, jerked his head, and shrugged his shoulders. "I . . . I . . . whoop . . . don't know what to say." His face, all the way to the tips of his ears, felt as if someone had rubbed cayenne pepper on it.

Michelle laughed again. But it was unlike the hurtful laughs he'd heard since childhood and still got on the streets of New York. "See what I mean?" she said. "The type of jerks I marry might speak sweet words, but they'd have taken my compliment as an invitation to try to get into my knickers. But not my dear, sweet Warren. He just blushes and says all he has to without words." She sighed. "If only I'd been smart and snagged you before I became damaged goods."

Desperately trying to control his words while at the same time wanting to tell her that he'd had dreams like this, Warren looked like a poor student who for the first time in his life had come up with the right answer before anyone else. He hopped from foot to foot as his face twitched nonstop.

Seeing his discomfiture, Michelle touched his arm. "Sorry, I shouldn't have put you on the spot. I'm sure you have a lovely wife."

Warren shook his head. "No . . . whoo . . . no wife."

"A girlfriend, then? I mean, since me,"

she said with a giggle.

Again the head shake, but he managed a smile. "No, not since you. But we'll always have Paris."

Michelle guffawed loudly enough that several people nearby looked over with distaste. "Still a movie buff, eh?" she said. "I remember when we used to go to the movies; you would know everything there was about the film. I always found that so fascinating. So, let's see if I can get this. The film is *Casablanca,* and Humphrey Bogart's character . . . um . . ."

"Rick Blaine," Warren said helpfully.

"Right, Rick, but don't tell me the rest. Rick says 'We'll always have Paris' to Ingrid Bergman's character, Ilsa Lund."

"Very . . . crap craaaap . . . good." Warren beamed. Not sure where to go from there, he took a large sip of his martini and gagged.

"So, what *are* you doing with yourself?"

Warren blinked several times and grimaced. "I live in the city. Independent businessman."

Michelle playfully raised her eyebrows. "Independent businessman, eh? Maybe I can finally marry for love *and* money."

Warren laughed. "Well, one out of two . . . nice tits . . . ain't bad."

His friend's eyes narrowed, and she

wagged a finger at him. "You know, I never could tell when you were just saying what was on your mind and what you couldn't help."

Warren reviewed what he'd said, and his eyes widened in horror. "No, I didn't mean . . . oh boy fuck me naked whoop . . . I . . ."

"Don't worry about it," Michelle said, smiling coquettishly. "I'll take the compliment either way. Husband number two paid for them."

"So, how are you doing?" Warren asked, trying desperately to get off the subject of the breasts he kept glancing down at. "Living the life of leisure in Purchase?"

"Well, those are interesting questions," Michelle said as her smile disappeared. "You might not know this, but when Dad was sent away to Club Fed for running a Ponzi scheme and ripping friends and clients off for a billion dollars or so, the prosecutors left Mom with a house, a car, and a few hundred thousand she managed to keep out of their hands. There was no way she could keep up with the Joneses, or the Bennetts, anymore and didn't want to try; so she downed a bottle of sleeping pills and never woke up. Dad had a stroke when he heard the news and died two weeks later in a prison hospital bed. I was still with husband number one, but he was about a month away from being T-boned by a semi while riding his new Harley-Davidson. I guess you'd say I've had a bit of a rough patch."

"Oh, Jesus, I'd heard a little about your parents," Warren said. "But I didn't know . . . oh boy ohhh boy . . . about your husband. Sorry."

Michelle shook her head sadly. "That's okay. Funny thing is, he was the only one of them I actually loved. The other three were for money. I wanted to keep the house and some aspect of my pampered life, so I buried my heart and offered my tush to the highest bidder. But I did pretty well out of the divorces when both number two and number three found someone younger and moved on. Good riddance. And since that time, I've scraped by."

Warren thought he caught a touch of irony in the last sentence, but before he could inquire any further, he saw Michelle's eyes harden as if she'd seen something behind him that angered her. He turned and saw a tall, distinguished-looking man who seemed familiar, though he couldn't quite place him, and another shorter, balding man. *Sherry's boyfriend,* he thought. *Jim Williams.*

Why is that name so familiar?

Both men were looking at him or, more accurately, at Michelle. Judging by the look on her face, he wondered if the taller man was one of her ex-husbands.

"Are you okay?" he asked, turning back to her.

Michelle looked at him, and her eyes softened again. "Yes, I'm fine. Sorry, but I need to go talk to that man before he leaves the party." She looked past him again, but this time when he turned, the men were just a few feet away.

"We need to talk," the taller man said. The other just looked at her.

Like a snake eyeing a mouse, Warren thought. "Do you need help, Michelle?" he asked, placing himself between her and the men.

Reaching out, Michelle touched his shoulder and stepped past him. "My hero, always ready to ride to the rescue. But no, dear, this is just a business matter."

Warren suddenly realized that Michelle was about to walk out of his life again. *Now or never, you coward,* he thought. "Um . . . whoop oh boy ass . . . maybe you'd like to go have coffee or something?"

Michelle hesitated and gave him a curious, almost appraising look. Then she smiled and nodded. "I'd like that. We could gossip about old times and chat about what's new. I'd like to hear all about your mysterious independent business. But tell you what, why don't you come by my place tomorrow evening? You remember where I live? Good. I'll have the cook whip us up something delicious, and we can drink a bottle of wine and reminisce. Say seven o'clock?"

Stunned by the sudden turn of events, Warren could only nod and blurt out. "Sure. Seven . . . oh boy oh boy whoop fuck me naked . . . sorry . . . whoop whoop."

Michelle laughed loudly. "Hold that thought. And see you at seven."

11

Butch Karp paused outside the Il Buon Pane bakery on the corner of Third Avenue and Twenty-ninth Street. Crouching so that he was mostly hidden by a pair of elegant multitiered wedding cakes in the big store-front window, he peered between them to catch a glimpse of the old couple working behind the counter.

Neither was much more than five feet tall, though the man had a couple of inches on his wife. He had a full head of kinky gray hair that looked like a cap of steel wool with two large ears protruding. Her hair was ginger-colored and framed an elfin face with merry blue eyes.

Moishe and Goldie Sobelman were in their eighties, but they were sprightly and animated as they interacted with their customers. Karp's smile faded when he saw them coincidentally extend their arms toward customers at the same time. He noted the purple blemishes on their fore-arms, knowing the discolorations were old tattooed numbers placed there by monsters more than fifty years earlier.

Moishe did most of the talking to the steady stream of customers, although Goldie interacted in her own special way. Without speaking a word, she would smile as a hungry visitor walked up, and she would point to one delicious treat or another in the display case. Invariably, the customer would nod and grin.

Karp had never once seen a customer shake his head and order something else. He wondered if it was because she knew them and they always ordered the same thing or she just had a sense for what someone might like that particular morning. As he watched, he corrected himself about whether Goldie spoke or not. Maybe not with her voice, but she was constantly talking with her hands, which flitted around like barn swallows in a combination of American Sign Language and her own inter-pretations.

Moishe spoke to her and signed with his own hands. But he really spoke to her with his eyes, which followed her every move as if he was looking at a beautiful painting for the first time. Every so often, she would glance over at him and wink; then they'd both laugh.

Now, there's real love, Karp thought. And it was a love that they turned around and poured into their work, a love their customers returned.

It was always a wonder to him that the Sobelmans had any love for humanity. Goldie was the sole member of her family to survive the Nazi concentration camp at Auschwitz. There was no physical reason she couldn't talk, nor was she deaf, but for more than sixty years, she had refused to speak. "She is afraid that once she started recounting the horrors of what they did to her in their 'medical' experiments, she would not be able to stop screaming," Moishe once told him. "And she doesn't want to sully the world by recalling their evil."

Gentle Moishe was one of the few survivors of the infamous Nazi death camp at Sobibor in Poland. He and a few hundred of his fellow prisoners had staged one of the only "successful" concentration-camp uprisings and fled into the forests. However, they'd been hunted down like animals, and most of those who got away died fighting their former tormentors. Sobibor itself had been bulldozed shortly after the revolt in an attempt by the Germans to cover up their atrocities.

Karp had asked his friend how they could now exhibit so much love for their fellow men. "We will never forget and never forgive those who did what they did to us," the old man had replied. "But you can't blame all of mankind for the acts of individuals, even a nation of individuals. And if we'd let our experiences define the rest of our lives, then the Nazis would have claimed two more victims. Goldie and I are not going to give them the satisfaction. Instead, we will love each other and try every day to see the good in other people — that is how we will get our revenge on the cursed Nazi ghosts."

As Karp looked through the window outside the shop, Goldie suddenly turned toward him with a smile, as if she'd expected to see him drooling over the pastries like a little boy. She waved him toward the door.

Her hands flew as he entered the shop. He caught "Good morning" and "Wonderful to see you" and tried to sign the same thing back, though he knew his signing was woefully inadequate. Still, she clapped her hands and tapped her husband on the shoulder to get his attention.

"Good morning, Butch! Shalom!" Moishe exclaimed in his lightly accented English as his face creased into a thousand smile lines. "You're early. The others aren't here yet."

Karp laughed. "Well, I have a confession to make. I had a sudden craving that wouldn't wait for —"

Before he could finish the sentence, Goldie was handing a gigantic piece of cherry-cheese coffee cake over the counter to him. The sight of the warm, gooey pastry stopped him in mid-speech, something hundreds of defense attorneys had never been able to accomplish.

"I see," Moishe said, and nodded. "Trying to get a jump on the competition." He pointed to the doorway leading to a larger seating area. "The usual table has been reserved for the Sons of Liberty Breakfast Club and Girl-Watching Society. I'll send one of the girls back with a pot of coffee. I'll join you in a moment when the rush has died down a bit."

"Take your time," Karp said with a chuckle. "I probably won't be very good company until I've inhaled every last crumb."

"Enjoy," Moishe replied. Then his smile faded for a moment and was replaced with a look of concern as he glanced over his shoulder at Goldie, who was occupied with a customer. "There is something I would like to discuss with you before the others arrive, if possible. It's probably nothing, but you have more experiences with these things, so I would like your opinion."

Karp frowned and started to ask what was wrong, but his friend had turned around to join his wife. So he headed back to the table and soon was happily savoring the coffee cake.

Five minutes later, he had just finished the last morsel when Moishe appeared, wiping his hands on his flour-dusted apron. He saw the empty plate. "Would you like another? On the house?"

Karp shook his head. "No, thank you. My mouth says yes, but my stomach doesn't have any space left. And if Marlene found out I had two pieces, I wouldn't be allowed to eat for a week just to make up for the calories."

"Ach, who cares about calories?" Moishe dismissed the statement with a wave of his hand. "You look very fit and trim. And besides, once a man has reached a certain . . . maturity, he should be allowed a few transgressions against the almighty American obsession with weight."

"Well, thanks for the compliment, and all I can say is this blazer hides a lot," Karp said with a chuckle. "But regrettably, I still have to decline the generous offer." He pushed the plate away and took a sip of coffee. "So tell me, what's troubling you?"

Moishe sat down with a sigh. "It's probably nothing," he said. "Just the paranoia of an old man who has seen too much."

Karp knew that was no exaggeration. The concentration camp and the hardscrabble days following World War II before he was allowed to immigrate to the United States had been a terrible ordeal. But more recently, Moishe had been worshiping inside the Third Avenue Synagogue when suicide bomber Jamal Khalifa blew himself up and killed a dozen more innocent men "for Allah."

"I think you've earned the right to be suspicious," Karp said. "Go on."

Moishe leaned back in his chair so he could see that his wife was still behind the counter. He turned back to face Karp. "I think my store is being watched."

"What makes you think that?"

The old man shrugged. "A hunch? A gut feeling about people with bad intentions?" He paused and absentmindedly rubbed the tattoo on his arm. "We've been lucky. We've only been robbed once, and Goldie made him feel so ashamed by offering him an apricot strudel with the money that he left without taking anything except the strudel. My Goldie, she has that kind of effect on people. But there have been others — it's almost as if they give off a smell that I can detect — and you know they're thinking about robbing you, or worse."

Leaning forward, the old man continued in a low voice. "I am not as trusting as Goldie. I have recently purchased a gun . . ." He stopped. "We've never talked about this — you are not one of those authorities, like the former district attorney, who believes that private citizens should not have guns to protect themselves."

Karp shook his head. "Absolutely not. Even if I thought it wasn't a good idea, I believe that the right to own firearms is an individual right, guaranteed by the Second Amendment, not a favor granted by a state or the federal government."

"Ah, yes, but what about these gun-control advocates who say that the Second Amendment only applies to the creation of militias?"

"Moishe, I'd say that is a politically motivated, insincere argument," Karp replied.

"How do you mean?

"Let's go back to the founding of this country," Karp said. "America was a frontier nation. People needed weapons for their safety, particularly those on the edges of that frontier, which was about where the Appalachian Mountains are. Pretty close to home. Also, the patriots who fought for independence were reluctant to ratify the Constitution because they were afraid of a strong central government that might interfere with their precious rights. So, historically, it offends common sense to suggest that the founding patriots would give up the individual right to keep and bear arms. Moreover, the Bill of Rights itself was specifically designed to guarantee the most precious personal rights that the early Americans cherished and did not want to be limited by the government."

"Should there be any limitations?" Moishe asked.

"I do think that reasonable regulations are acceptable — such as not selling weapons to felons or people with a history of mental illness and violence. Moishe, by the way, I would point out that New York, which has the most stringent gun-control laws in the country, has a far higher rate of gun deaths than states like Colorado or Texas, where guns are more prolific and people have the right to carry concealed weapons with permits."

"So your argument is both historical and constitutional?" Moishe suggested.

"Yes. The act of protecting one's life and property, rather than relying on government to do it, is as American as my boyhood hero, John Wayne," Karp said. "It is an established fact that criminals prey on the weakest members of society. A gun changes the paradigm of who is hunted and who is hunter."

Moishe nodded. "Good. When I fled Sobibor, I promised that never again would I allow evil men to control my life without fighting back. But only since, well, since the bombing, did I think to arm myself. Perhaps I had grown soft in this beautiful country that welcomed me and Goldie; after all we had been through, this was a safe haven. But the attack on the synagogue woke me as if from a dream, and I remembered that you cannot count on the government to protect you from killers and thugs. I don't know that if someone in the synagogue had a gun, the terrorist could have been stopped. But maybe he could have been, and twelve good men would not have lost their lives."

"What does Goldie think about the gun?" Karp asked.

Moishe shrugged. "She doesn't like it," he said. "She's seen enough violence, she says, to last a hundred lifetimes. And she thinks I'm being paranoid about being watched and that if someone wants to rob us, I shouldn't try to stop them. But honestly, the money I don't care about. Any man wants what's in the cash register, he's welcome to it, and I won't raise a hand. But I will not stand by and allow someone to hurt Goldie or someone in my shop. Nor, like I said, will I let an evil man raise his hand to me."

"You and I have no disagreement," Karp replied. "So, what makes you think that your store is being watched?"

Moishe nodded. "There is a woman, brown hair, maybe forty-five years old, good-looking, but she dresses modestly as though she wants to hide her body. She rarely smiles, though sometimes she seems to respond differently to my Goldie, as does any person who walks through our door. She comes in some mornings with a newspaper that she barely reads, orders a piece of the cherry-cheese coffee cake — just like you — and coffee with lots of sugar."

"What's so odd about that?" Karp asked with a smile. "I've said it once, and I'll say it again, your cherry-cheese coffee cake is the best in the five boroughs and quite possibly the world."

"I thank you," Moishe replied, but did not smile in return. "But she hardly touches it, maybe one or two bites, and she leaves the rest."

Karp shrugged. "Well, personally, I can't imagine anyone being able to stop themselves once they have that first bite," he said. "Maybe she's counting calories — like I should be doing — but she can't resist having just a taste."

Moishe looked down at his hands clasped in front of him on the table. "Yes, perhaps you're right," he said. "Though if she's counting calories, why does she use six or seven packages of sugar in her coffee at a sitting? Then again, she's eastern European or Russian — hard to say, as I've hardly heard her speak — and they like sweet coffee. But it's not what she eats or drinks that troubles me, it's something more concrete. My staff says she asks a lot of questions when Goldie and I aren't around."

"Such as?"

"Such as do we live in the apartment above the shop, which as you know we do."

"Maybe she's just interested in historic New York buildings," Karp pointed out. Il Buon Pane was housed in a two-story red-brick building built at the beginning of the twentieth century, as were its neighbors, a surprising anachronism in midtown Manhattan. "It's pretty amazing that there are still these — no pun intended — mom-and-pop operations in big, impersonal Gotham City. And this woman might just be an architecture buff."

"Yes, this is true." Moishe was quiet for a moment before adding, "But she asked if we worked every day. She made it sound as though she was impressed that two such old people had such energy, but it seems more like spying to me."

"How often does she come in? Every morning?"

Moishe shook his head. "That's the other thing. Most of my regular customers have set times that they come in, but not her. Sometimes it's morning, sometimes afternoon, sometimes just before closing. Not always the same day, and in fact, some weeks she doesn't come at all."

"Weeks?" Karp asked, surprised. "How long has she been coming?"

The old man thought for a moment. "I would say several months, off and on."

Karp pursed his lips. "Is there anything else?"

"So, you think I'm making something out of nothing?"

"No, not at all," Karp replied. "I'm just in

my district-attorney mode and playing a bit of devil's advocate with you. But that doesn't mean you're not right. I was just asking if you had anything else to add."

"I see," Moishe said. "And yes, since this woman began coming to the store, there is also a man who watches."

"A man?"

"Yes. In a neighborhood like this, you know who belongs, who is passing through, and who is maybe up to no good. Sometimes when I am outside, sweeping the sidewalk or returning from an errand or the synagogue, I have seen him."

"Can you describe him?"

"A large man but otherwise not unusual. What was unusual is that one day, I watched as the woman left the shop and walked across the street, where he appeared to be reading a newspaper. She stood near him, and though she made no obvious gestures, nor did he, I know she said something to him. He nodded — just a little bit — but it was in agreement to what she told him."

Karp took a sip of his coffee and considered. He didn't think Moishe was just being paranoid. *You don't survive a concentration camp and being hunted by Nazis and terrorists without developing a heightened sense of awareness regarding danger,* he reasoned.

Then again, the explosion in the synagogue shook him up big-time; he could be a little gun-shy.

It was possible that the man and the woman were casing the shop for a robbery. Il Buon Pane certainly did a lot of cash business. However, if Moishe was right and they'd been watching for months . . . strong-arm robbers were rarely patient enough to watch a target so long.

"Have you talked to Goldie about it?"

"Not really. Oh, I've asked her about the woman, just innocently, but Goldie thinks the best of everyone. She told me that there is pain in the woman's eyes, and she believes that she has been abused in the past. I'm sure if she heard me now, she'd be convinced that I am jumping at shadows. But you know, Butch, you're not paranoid if they really are after you."

Karp nodded. "Well, tell you what, I'm going to ask Clay Fulton — you remember him, big NYPD detective who works out of my office — to see if we can't get a few extra patrols through here and send a detective over who can maybe contact these people and see what they're up to. You have my phone numbers. If this woman comes in or you spot the man, give me a call."

Moishe held up his hand to protest. "That

won't be necessary. I was asking your opinion on whether I am being a silly old man. I don't want to impose or ask for special privileges just because the esteemed district attorney of New York is my dear friend."

"Nonsense," Karp said, reaching out to pat his friend on the shoulder. "It's probably nothing. This city is full of people who march to their own drummer. But I'm a firm believer in paying attention to gut feelings. Let's not take a chance that these two are looking to get their hands on your cash register. If we prevent a crime from happening, then we're ahead of the game."

Moishe smiled and wiped at a tear that had appeared in the corner of his eye. "Thank you. I would insist that it is too much. But I do worry about Goldie if I am away on an errand or at the synagogue."

At that moment, a half-dozen older men appeared in the doorway. Moishe patted Karp's hand and stood up. "It appears the Breakfast Club has arrived. I'd better make sure the coffeepots are filled."

Several of the men were already arguing as they walked over to the table where Karp sat. "What is the point of contention this morning, gentlemen?" he asked.

"The concept of American Exceptionalism," said one. "Care to chime in?"

"Love to," Karp replied with a grin. "It's a favorite of mine."

12

As the cab pulled up to the gated driveway of the Oakley mansion, Dirty Warren glanced up at the rearview mirror and frowned. He'd done his best — scrubbed and shaved his face, borrowed some more "product" from his sister for his hair — but he was unimpressed with the results. He could feel the muscles around his right eye starting to twitch ever so slightly, which, unchecked, he knew would lead to full-scale grimacing.

Get your act together, Warren. He straightened the collar of the same Brooks Brothers button-down shirt he'd worn at his sister's birthday party — sans tie, which he'd decided was too formal and datelike — and the Saint Laurie slacks. He hadn't intended to stay at his parents' place any longer than necessary, but that plan had flown out the window with Michelle's invitation to dinner. The suit was coming in handy after all.

Lying in bed that night after the party, he'd gone over every word, every movement and smile, looking for . . . *I don't know. What I hoped to hear and see?* Then, after he'd fallen asleep, he'd dreamed about her leaning forward to kiss him, but to his chagrin, the shock of that had awakened him. No matter how hard he tried to go back to sleep to see how the dream would have ended, he could not.

She's just being nice, he reminded himself for the hundredth time since waking up, *and wants to catch up with an old friend. You're making way too much of this, and you're just going to be disappointed.*

"Hey, pal, is this the address or not?" The cabbie's face invaded the mirror.

"Uh, yes it . . . whoop oh boy . . . is," Warren replied. Michelle's house was only a little more than a mile from his parents', but he didn't want to show up sweaty or late, so he'd called the cab. He gave the cabbie the fare and a generous tip.

"Got a sweetheart waitin'?" the cabbie asked with a wink and a smile.

Warren felt his face blush as he shook his head. "What? Oh, no . . . shit crap whoop . . . just a friend."

The cabbie's smile disappeared, and his jaw fell. "I tell ya what, pal — and mind you, I have some experience in these here matters — I'd drop the foul language with the ladies. You'll get farther, if you know what I mean."

"Thanks, I'll take that . . . oh boy ohhh boy piss balls . . . to heart," Warren responded with an apologetic smile.

The cabbie shrugged. "Your funeral, pal. You want I should wait around? With a mouth like that, it shouldn't take long."

"No, thanks, it . . . whoop . . . won't be necessary."

The cabbie shook his head and drove off, leaving Warren standing on the sidewalk. The sun was dipping into the purple west, bathing the neighborhood in early-spring twilight. He could see the front of Michelle's house; the windows looked dark, and he wondered if she'd forgotten. *But no, she called this afternoon to make sure I was coming,* he thought.

Suddenly, his knees wobbled, and his throat went dry. *What the hell are you doing here? You're just going to embarrass her and humiliate yourself. All you are to her is a few good memories from a summer a long time ago, so quit acting like this is a romantic date or something.* He started to press the intercom button next to the gate, then hesitated. *Leave now, and no one gets hurt.* But before he could turn away, Michelle's voice stopped him.

"Warren, is that you?"

He bit his lip and pressed the button. "Yes," he replied. *Keep your responses short and sweet. Easier to control.* The lock in the gate buzzed and clicked open.

"Come on up and let yourself in. Sorry I'm running late. I had to go into Manhattan today on business, so I'm doing some last-minute girl things. I'll be right down."

Warren walked up the drive with the queasy feeling in his stomach growing. But somehow he made it, opened the door, and went in. He found himself standing in the foyer, wondering what he was supposed to do next, when Michelle appeared at the top of the stairs. She was dressed in designer jeans and a light gray cashmere sweater, and he thought his heart might pound its way out of his chest.

She walked quickly down the stairs and swept past the hand he'd extended to shake and gave him a hug instead. The gesture both frightened and delighted him as he became immediately conscious of the press of her breasts against his chest and the smell of her perfume.

"I'm so glad you could make it," she said, stepping back. "Sorry there was no one to get the door for you. I had to let the butler go."

"I . . . I didn't mind," Warren replied, blushing. "You look . . . fuck me . . . beautiful." Realizing what he'd said, his eyes teared up. "I'm so . . . so . . ."

Michelle touched his arm lightly. "Don't be," she said, and giggled. "It was maybe a little forward, but sometimes a girl likes a man who's not afraid to speak his mind."

Warren turned an even darker shade of red, which only made Michelle belly-laugh until he finally had to join her merriment. "Actually, I think that might have . . . whoop whoop . . . technically been classified a Freudian slip, not Tourette's," he said, wiping the tears from his eyes.

"Cute, very cute. Come on," she said, taking him by the hand and pulling him after her. "This is going to be such fun. I had the cook — I am just barely able to still afford him, thank God, or it would have been microwaved burritos for us — whip up a little something, and then I sent him home." She wiggled her eyebrows suggestively and laughed. "We'll be all alone. But first let's have a glass of wine out back in the garden."

His head spinning, Warren allowed himself to be tugged through the house and out the back door to a small table where a bottle of red wine, two glasses, and a cheese plate had been set. The two friends spent the next hour talking and laughing about the good old days. It was the first time in many years, maybe ever, that he could remember being so relaxed in the company of a woman he was attracted to; even his Tourette's faded to minimal slipups and almost no twitching.

"So, Warren, tell me about this business of yours that keeps you from having a wife or serious girlfriend," Michelle asked.

Warren's smile faded. He rarely drank, and he'd had two glasses of wine. Suddenly, he was self-conscious, very aware that he was one step above living on the streets and visiting a beautiful heiress in her Purchase mansion, which was undoubtedly worth millions. "It's just a . . . whoop . . . small business," he said dismissively, hoping they'd move on to something else.

"Just a small business? Just the backbone of the American economy?" Michelle replied. "Come on, why so mysterious? You really a spy? No, I've got it. You're a gangster, right? 'Come and get me, copper!' "

"*White Heat,* 1949, James Cagney in the role of Cody Jarrett," Warren said, and smiled again. "But no, I'm not . . . oh boy ohhh boy . . . a spy or a gangster." He hesitated but could tell by the look on her face that she wasn't going to let him change the subject. "I own a little newsstand on Centre Street."

The way she reacted, he thought he'd just told her that he'd bought the Yankees. "Really? Oh, my God, I always thought that would be fascinating!" she exclaimed with what at least sounded like sincerity. "I love all those papers and magazines — so many choices, from high-brow to trashy gossip rags. Ooooh, I love it all. Plus, I'm big into people watching. You must see some really interesting things on the streets."

Warren tried to play it cool. "It's not bad," he said. "I'm doing okay and making . . . oh boy . . . ends meet. But yeah, I'm right there in front of the courthouse, so there's all types go in and out of there all day. Sometimes it's . . . piss whoop whoop . . . like being in a movie."

"Well, I think it's really cool. And you're your own man. That must be nice."

"I like it," Warren said. "So, how about you? Successful businesswoman? Doctor? Or do you just lie around the house all day eating bon-bons?"

Michelle laughed, but then the smile evaporated and she looked troubled. "Oh, a little of this and that to generate some cash flow," she said. "But hey, it's getting cool." She shivered for effect. "Let's go inside and have dinner, shall we?"

Warren noted the change in expression and subject. He hoped what he'd said about lying around and eating bon-bons hadn't offended her and wondered if he should apologize. *That will just make it worse, and somehow I think whatever is bothering her, it was more than a dumb comment,* he thought.

Dinner consisted of stuffed capons with asparagus tips, a lettuce-and-tomato dinner salad, and rice pilaf, washed down with a heady red wine that had Warren grinning and laughing uproariously. Michelle had been her old flirtatious, bawdy self and had made a game out of trying to make him blush. He'd responded with a few risqué jokes himself, made all the more hilarious — at least in their partially inebriated state — by Tourette's insertions.

They talked a lot about movies they had seen and played trivia games, though it was quickly obvious that she was no match for him. He tried to even the competition by asking what he considered easy questions.

"What character did Jack Palance play for his second Oscar nomination?"

Michelle furrowed her brow and was tentative when she answered. "I'm not really sure, but I only know a few of his early movies, *The Halls of Montezuma* and *Shane,*" she said. "I'll go with *Shane,* because he was such a good bad guy as the cold-blooded gunfighter Jack Wilson."

"You got it!" Warren exclaimed.

Michelle laughed and clapped her hands. "You're making it too easy on me."

When dinner was finished and dessert tarts consumed, there was a pause that to Warren seemed full of both danger and potential. *It's now or never,* he thought, and steeled himself to ask a question he'd thought he'd never be in a position to ask.

"Uh, Michelle, um . . . oh boy whoop ohhhh boy you bitch . . ." Warren passed a hand over his eyes. "God help me," he muttered. He took another deep breath and then let it all out. "You know I always liked you, and I was . . . whoo whooo whoop . . . wondering if, maybe, sometime . . . fuck whoop whoop whore . . . would you go to a movie with me?"

Warren hung his head from both the strain of trying to control the Tourette's and his shame at not being able to do so. But Michelle reached out and lifted his chin with the fingers of one hand so that he was looking into her eyes. He expected to see pity, but all he saw was a deep sadness.

241

She sighed. "Oh, Warren, that's so sweet," she said. "Being with you tonight makes me wish I could turn back the hands of time. Then I might do a better job of not judging books by their covers or poets by how well they speak." She smiled. "You know, I toyed with the idea of seducing you tonight."

Warren's jaw dropped, but he quickly tried to recover. "I'd like . . ." he started to say, but stopped when she shook her head.

"But I'm sorry," she said. "I'm not someone you want to get involved with. I'm not the girl you knew that summer or even the stuck-up bitch from high school."

"You weren't . . . whoop asswipe . . . stuck-up," Warren argued.

"Well, I certainly wasn't humble and, in fact, was pretty full of myself," she said. "But it doesn't matter. What does matter is that that girl doesn't exist anymore. And the truth is that you don't know me, because if you did, you would want nothing to do with me."

"That's not true," Warren said. He didn't like the way this conversation had veered away from her thinking of seducing him.

"Yes, it is true," Michelle interrupted. "When my parents died and my marriages failed, I was desperate. I had very little liquid money, never finished college, and was therefore unqualified for anything short of department-store greeter, and to be honest, I wasn't willing to give up this lifestyle. So I made some bad decisions — horrible decisions, really — and now I'm going to have to pay for them, after I try to atone."

"We've all changed since . . . oh boy . . . high school," Warren argued. "But deep down, we're still the same people. Whatever you think you've done . . ."

Michelle's eyes filled with tears. "No, Warren, dear, sweet Warren. I know what I've done; there's no question of guilt or innocence. You know how in westerns, sometimes there's someone with a past, like Shane, who was obviously a gunfighter before he came to town? And you want him to succeed, or be happy, or get the girl, like the farmer's wife . . ."

"Marian Starrett, played by Jean Arthur."

"Yes, though I suppose that might not have gone over well with the farmer or audiences in the 1950s," she replied with a slight smile. "But what I was getting to was, you know that they're not going to be allowed in the story to live happily ever after, and the best they can hope for is the chance to atone for their past. Just like Shane has to go face the evil rancher and his hired gun, Jack Wilson, and gets shot."

Warren nodded. "It's a classic ending, Shane riding off into the coming night, slumped over his saddle, while the farmer's boy, Joey, runs after him shouting, 'Pa's got things for you to do! And Mother wants you. I know she does. . . . Shane! Come back!' "

"But you know he can't come back," Michelle added. "You know that he's riding into the night to die, having atoned for his sins."

"What about it?"

"Well, I'm Shane," Michelle said. "I'm going to have to atone."

"Are you in trouble?" Warren asked, alarmed. "Maybe I can help."

This time, she placed a finger on his lips. "My hero," she said. "But no, it's nothing I can't handle, and it's something I have to do myself. The point is, you're too good for me."

His hopes dashing on the rocks before his eyes, Warren pleaded, "Maybe you should . . . suck my whoop whoop . . . let me be the judge of that. Let me help . . . oh boy . . . with whatever it is. I have friends who . . ."

Michelle closed her eyes as a tear squeezed out and rolled down her cheek. "I'm sorry," she said. "I've ruined my life and others.

I'm not going to ruin yours."

Warren started to protest again, but cellphone music began playing in another room. His hostess cocked her head and pushed herself away from the table to stand.

"Excuse me a moment," she said. "I have to get that. It's a very important client."

Michelle disappeared and was gone for several minutes as Warren desperately thought of ways to get the conversation back to attending a movie together. But when she returned, he knew that his time was up.

"I'm so sorry," she said, holding up the cell phone, "but I'm afraid some of my 'this and that' business has come up with an emergency. It's practically a life-and-death matter."

Although his face was etched with disappointment, Warren smiled. "Sure. No sweat. I should be getting back to the city. I need to open the newsstand bright and early. A couple of my friends have been watching it for me . . . oh boy son of a bitch . . . and have probably run it down the tubes."

"I'll call you a cab," Michelle said.

"That won't be necessary," Warren replied. "I'll just . . . oh boy screw it . . . walk. I can use the exercise, and it's a nice . . . whoop whoop . . . night."

As they stood at the door, Michelle leaned

forward and kissed Warren on the mouth. He was surprised both by the gesture and by how closely it reminded him of his dream. But before he could say anything, she stepped back with a laugh.

"You still want to go to a movie with me?"

Warren grinned. "You . . . fucking . . . better believe it!"

Michelle narrowed her eyes and looked at him sideways. "Warren, was that really Tourette's, or have you also got a potty mouth?"

"I'll never tell," he replied.

"Well, if you're going to be that way, then you have to solve a film riddle for me."

"Fire away," Warren replied.

"Okay, here it is," Michelle said. "The key goes where the book editor sees his wife and son off to Maine."

Warren pursed his lips. "Hmmmm. Is that all I get? That's a tough one."

"Are you saying I'm not worth a little work?" Michelle pouted.

Alarmed that he'd once again put his foot in his mouth, Warren quickly backtracked. "No, no . . . whoop whoop . . . I'll get it . . . ohhhh boy! The keys . . ."

"Key."

"Right, the key goes where the book editor sees his wife and son off to Maine."

"That's it," Michelle said, and reached for the door. As Warren started to move, she suddenly grabbed his hand. "We'll always have Paris," she said, but somberly, without smiling.

Puzzled but happy, Warren lightly replied, "Here's looking at you, kid."

Michelle watched Warren go, smiling as she noted how he practically skipped down the drive. The smile disappeared as she walked into the library off the foyer and picked up an envelope, which she carried outside and dropped into the outgoing mail slot of the large brass mailbox in the entranceway.

My insurance policy, she thought. *If everything goes right, I'll retrieve it before the mailman picks it up Monday morning.*

Michelle looked at her watch. *I still have an hour.* She turned back to her computer and pulled up a file. The image of Warren Bennett's high school photograph appeared. She smiled, punched a button, and began to type.

13

Waiting that morning for the judge to appear, Karp rose from the prosecution table and sauntered over to where the court clerk sat reading a sports magazine. He was physically relaxed but mentally focused on what he had to do, and it showed in the way he walked.

He was well aware that everything he did in that courtroom was being watched by the jurors from the day they walked in until the day they walked out for the last time. They studied his body language, so he exuded confidence in the way he sat, stood, moved, smiled, and even poured water for Kenny Katz, his young co-counsel who sat next to him, the witnesses, and perhaps the defense attorney. And they noted the tenor of his voice, which was resolute and firm — with an easy laugh when dictated, unless the moment called for righteous indignation, in which case he avoided shrillness and was simply forceful and well reasoned.

Nothing was feigned, however; he was just himself. If he appeared at ease and unscripted, it was because he was prepared. For Karp, pretrial prep was a religious experience, as in total commitment. He couldn't countenance losing a case because he wasn't ready. He made it a point to outwork and outprepare every adversary. The defense bar knew it, which was why, more often than not, defendants pleaded to the top count, hoping to get somewhat of a break at sentencing.

"If you can't explain to a jury a case as you would to your family and friends while sitting in your living room, you're not ready," he'd told Katz when they started the process of picking the jury three weeks earlier.

"Good Monday morning to you, Al," he said as the burly clerk looked up.

"Good morning, Mr. Karp. We about done with jury selection?"

"Close. One more will give us the twelve tried and true, but don't forget the alternates," Karp replied, turning so he could see the gallery. Although he liked Al Lopez, who'd been with the courts since Karp could remember, his real purpose in visiting was so that he could nonchalantly "check out the house" and the fifteen remaining members of the jury pool sitting on the spectator benches. Eleven of their number already sat in the jury box waiting for one last addition, and then four alternates would be selected, before *The People v. Sharif Jabbar* got under way.

And just as the sworn jurors and prospective jurors were watching everything he did, he was studying them as well. In fact, he was something of a connoisseur when it came to jury selection; he approached it as an artist might approach a scene he wanted to paint — with patience, a plan, and an eye for detail.

Three weeks earlier, the supreme court trial courtroom known as Part 39 on the eleventh floor of the Criminal Courts Building had contained a pool of seventy-five prospective jurors, when Judge David Marvin Mason began the proceedings by asking Karp to give the *venire,* or jury pool, a brief description of the case and the main players in the real-life drama about to be played out in front of them.

"Thank you, your honor. Welcome to Part 39 of the Supreme Court, State of New York, County of New York. I am District Attorney Roger Karp, and I will be responsible for presenting the evidence on behalf of the People of the State of New York during the course of this trial. His honor, Supreme Court Justice Mason, will be presiding. Seated at the prosecution table is Assistant District Attorney Kenneth Katz, who will be assisting me during the course of the trial," he'd said, gesturing with his hand. "At the defense table is Ms. Megan O'Dowd, and next to her is the defendant, Imam Sharif Jabbar. Now, for purposes of understanding the nature of the charges, I will read to you the indictment in this case, handed down by the grand jury."

After Karp had essentially read the jurisdictional location, date, time, and place of the crime, he'd concluded: "That the defendant, Sharif Jabbar, acting in concert with other individuals with intent to cause the death of Miriam Juma Khalifa, caused her death by stabbing her multiple times about her throat and body.

"Now, ladies and gentlemen, please understand that the indictment I just read against the defendant is the accusatory instrument in this case. It is not evidence and should not be considered by you as evidence. The evidence in this case will come from the lips of witnesses, after they are sworn, while seated in that witness stand, and from whatever exhibits his honor receives and marks in evidence.

"At this time, I am going to read to you a list of prospective witnesses who might be called to testify at the trial. If you know any of them, please let us know when you are questioned during the *voir dire,* and we'll inquire as to the nature of any relationship that may exist."

Karp had then told the jury pool that chief court clerk Al Lopez would call off a dozen names at random. "Those of you who are called, please come forward and take a seat in the jury box." He'd looked over at the clerk and added, "Mr. Lopez, I believe that we are ready to proceed."

The twelve who had stepped forward and sat in the jury box had then been questioned as a group, first by the prosecution and then by the defense. They were asked personal questions about such things as their employment, education, and marital status and questions involving the justice system, such as whether they'd been victims of crimes, had previously served on a jury, and, in a case like this, how much of the pretrial publicity they had followed and what, if any, effect it had had on them.

They had been kept on the panel or dismissed based on their answers and their demeanor. Some prospective jurors had been excused for personal reasons and others "for cause," such as evincing a bias toward either side or expressing the inability to follow the law as given by the court. Still others had been sent away by the attorneys using "preemptory challenges," meaning that either Karp or O'Dowd did not want that particular individual to sit on the panel even if there was no cause to have the juror excused by the judge. The preemptory challenges did not have to be justified or explained.

The vacated seat had then been filled by one of the remaining prospective jurors, who, it was hoped, had been paying sufficient attention throughout, still sitting on the hard wooden benches of the gallery.

In addition to the general questioning, however, Karp had made a motion to be allowed to *voir dire* each individual prospective juror away from the others in chambers. He'd argued that "the massive amount of publicity surrounding this case and its sensitive nature — particularly in this city — greatly increases the potential for bias for and/or against either party given our post-nine-eleven world.

"I believe that they will be more forthright outside the hearing of others," he'd said.

"They won't feel the need or be tempted to conform their answers to what others around them are saying."

The judge had frowned at the request. He obviously wasn't happy about the motion, first, because it would greatly extend the time it would take to pick a jury, and second, because he simply didn't like Karp. Before his appointment to the bench, New York Supreme Court Justice David Marvin Mason had swum in the same political pond as Megan O'Dowd, in that he'd never met a left-wing cause he wouldn't champion. As such, he was no fan of the more conservative traditionalist Karp, and since being assigned to preside at the trial, he had bent over backward to accommodate defense requests and motions.

However, two issues had worked in Karp's favor for this request. One was that Mason knew the media were all over this case, and despite their liberal bent, they still blew with the winds of public opinion when it came to Islamic terrorists. Also, his last two rulings against a Karp-led prosecution team had been thrown back in his face by the appellate courts, and he was wary of being overturned again. Furthermore, the defense had offered little in the way of opposition to Karp's request for individual *voir dire,* so he'd reluctantly allowed it.

O'Dowd had also not opposed Karp's suggestion that instead of the statutorily mandated twenty preemptory challenges allowed to each side in a murder case, they would stipulate to increase it to thirty. It wasn't a new strategy for him and was one that defense attorneys normally didn't object to. It was their core belief that the majority of prospective jurors were pro-prosecution, and therefore the defense attorneys wanted more opportunities to keep "law-and-order types" off the jury.

However, Karp saw it differently. He'd learned his first hard lesson the first time he'd clashed with O'Dowd in court — in the case of the four self-proclaimed members of the so-called Black Liberation Army cop killers from Harlem. In that initial trial, which had ended with a hung jury, he'd made several mistakes, the first of which had been the way he'd approached jury selection.

It had started when he'd questioned the prospective jurors *en masse* and by the book: "Keep it short, straightforward, simple, and then sit down; let the defense bore the prospective jurors with a lengthy, tedious *voir dire*."

The problem was that the book had been

written before the cultural implosion that had begun in the 1960s and swept through the 1970s. That change had ushered in a general mistrust of the government, specifically police officers.

"If you'd asked a prospective juror in the 1950s if he would believe a police officer's word, at least nine times out of ten, he would have said, 'Sure, of course,' " he'd explained to Katz as they'd prepared for *voir dire* in the Jabbar case. "But after that, the mantra became 'Question Authority.' Add that to police scandals and corruption investigations, and suddenly, people didn't trust cops, or any other representatives of the government, including us. Cops got it the worst. They were referred to as pigs and bullies.

"It used to be that people didn't think a couple of bad apples spoiled the barrel; now they think they're all bad apples, except maybe a few. Up to the mid-sixties, it was the defense lawyers who would ask prospective jurors if they would believe cops more than anyone else and try to get rid of anyone who did. Now, we're the ones who need to ask whether the juror can fairly, without bias judge a cop's testimony and not automatically reject it."

If anything, jurors leaned more toward the

defense, Karp had told his protégé, especially in New York City, one of the most liberal populations in the country. But he had learned to deal with it, starting with the retrial against O'Dowd and her cop-killer clients when he "threw away the book."

In the retrial, Karp had argued that massive pretrial publicity had swung the door wide open for biases against either side. He had then won a motion that each juror be individually questioned. He'd painstakingly talked to each juror about all of his or her views: political, social, economic, religious, and philosophical — looking for anything that might affect that juror's ability to be fair and impartial, "without fear or favor to either side." And he'd paid particular attention to how they answered his questions about law enforcement. Had they had bad experiences with police officers? Were they *less* likely to believe a police officer than anyone else?

It had been a long, laborious process that lasted eight weeks and was still the jury-selection record for the State of New York. And he'd come up with a jury that after three months found the four defendants guilty of murder.

Selecting the jury in the Jabbar case had taken less than half as long, though certainly longer than it would have using the traditional method. But Karp had selected scores of juries since that other case, and he was much more zeroed in on what he was looking for and battling against when finding the magical twelve.

With O'Dowd loudly broadcasting her trial strategy in the media, Karp had known that once again, she hoped to capitalize on the public's distrust of government and its agencies, especially intelligence agencies. How he dealt with that would be vital to this case. Two federal agents — Tran and Jojola — had witnessed the murder of Miriam Juma Khalifa in the basement of Jabbar's mosque, as the imam led his *jihadis* in celebrating her brutal execution. The defense attorney's only chance was to claim that Tran and Jojola were lying and had even committed the murder themselves as part of a government conspiracy to use the War on Terrorism to silence the imam and destroy his mosque.

Once again, he was faced with the big-lie defense. O'Dowd would try to obfuscate the truth by creating a fiction so outrageous and mixed with half-truths and lies that some jurors might believe she couldn't have made it up — especially any who already tended to believe that federal agents regularly conspired to commit crimes to frame innocent people and that the DAO was a racist organization.

O'Dowd was not stupid; much to the contrary. She knew that if she faced a jury that would reach its verdict based on the factual evidence, her client would be convicted. So she needed jurors who were wired with a shortcircuit between their reason and their fringe political conspiratorial fantasies. The trial venue was on the island of Manhattan — advantage defense.

On the other hand, Karp wanted jurors who would work as a team and didn't deviate from the norm simply for the sake of being different. He hoped to root out potential jurors who might disregard the evidence and decide the case using their emotions and intuition. He needed mature, thoughtful people who could put their personal beliefs aside as much as possible and calmly, objectively see through the defense's smokescreen and judge the case solely on the merits of the evidence. He wanted people with a stake in the stability and safety of their community, who had respect for law enforcement and the justice system, and who were used to sizing up other people and their intentions, like shopkeepers.

They were the ones he hoped he'd placed on the jury so far, and whom he was now looking for in those prospective jurors who were left to fill the one remaining seat. Part of his approach to picking a jury included seeing how they dressed and acted. The guy in tennis shorts and a T-shirt was saying he thought the process was bullshit and had no respect for the system. He was not a good choice. But the women who every day appeared in nice dresses and the guys who wore slacks and button-down shirts were saying that they took their duty as citizens seriously and respected the system. Those were the people he was looking for.

However, there weren't many of them left in the gallery. And there was no telling which of their names Al Lopez would call if he didn't accept the juror whose name had been called to fill the twelfth seat shortly before court had adjourned on Friday. If he didn't keep that man, as Katz had urged, he wouldn't be able to do anything about whomever was called to replace him. Karp had used twenty-nine of his preemptory challenges and had only one left.

As Karp glanced around the courtroom, he noted that there was twice as many court security officers present as during a run-of-the-mill murder trial, even for a high-profile defendant. Many more were placed in the halls and the entry leading into the courtroom, and the officers were extra vigilant and thorough at the security checkpoint coming into the building.

When the media had asked about the additional security, which was prearranged with Karp's office, the court administrator had explained that precautions were necessary to protect Imam Jabbar from anyone with a grudge against alleged murderous Islamic extremists. Not a difficult story to believe in New York City.

In truth, there had been a number of threats against Jabbar worth monitoring, including some connected to the NYPD, whose officers were killed because of Jabbar's involvement in the attack on the stock exchange. And there were unconfirmed reports that some members of Jabbar's former congregation had sworn some sort of blood vengeance for the deaths of their sons whom he'd led astray and, in Mahmoud Juma's case, the daughter who'd been murdered in cold blood.

However, Karp's chief concern was about threats to one of his witnesses, Dean Newbury. Not from revenge-minded police officers and distraught families but from the organization the old man had once led, the Sons of Man, and they were far more dangerous. If he'd needed any further proof of that, it had arrived the week before with a telephone call from Espey Jaxon, who in a tight, angry voice informed him that Denton Crawford, the disgraced former congressman and SOM member, had been assassinated along with a half-dozen U.S. marshals.

Jaxon explained that Crawford was being moved to the Supermax penitentiary in Florence, Colorado, for his protection as a deal was worked out for his cooperation. The transfer was supposed to have been top-secret, given the same stringent security measures that the U.S. Marshal's Office used to transport the "worst of the worst."

"It was an inside job," Jaxon said, seething. "Apparently, one of their own betrayed his team, who were killed, and then this son of a bitch participated in ambushing the jet that was used to fly Crawford to Colorado. He was killed by Joe Rosen, one of the marshals on the Crawford security detail. Unfortunately, Rosen was also killed, as was Crawford. Another marshal, a friend of mine named Jen Capers, was shot, too, but it looks like she's going to recover fully."

"Thank God for that. I know Jen Capers,"

Karp had said. "She's a good friend of Clay Fulton's as well."

Jaxon had gone on to describe what happened as best as it could be pieced together by talking to Capers and the evidence at the scene. "Sorry to break the bad news," he'd added. "But there's more. Jen got a good look at the leader of the bad guys; we're pretty sure it was Nadya Malovo."

"Could have guessed," Karp had lamented. "I hope there will be a day when she sits in the docket and I prosecute her."

"That's the difference between you and me," Jaxon had said. "I'd rather put her six feet under."

"I wouldn't shed any tears at her funeral," Karp had replied, "unless it's for the innocent people she's killed."

"Apparently, the feeling is mutual," Jaxon had noted. "She let Capers live at least in part to pass on a message for you: 'Tell him that I will take my revenge against him one life at a time until he is the last one, and then I will take him, too.' Sounds pretty personal, so watch your back."

Karp had thought about it and then shrugged. There was no doubt that Malovo was extremely dangerous, and she had apparently fixated on him as her nemesis. But if he'd let threats get to him, he would have gone into private practice a long time ago. "When you find her, tell her to get in line, and it's a long one," he'd told Jaxon.

There was no question the Sons of Man would be even more anxious to silence Newbury than they had Crawford. In fact, they'd already tried. Several months earlier, Fulton had reported that various sources, including Dirty Warren passing the messages for Grale, were saying that some high rollers with a lot of clout were trying to locate Dean Newbury.

"The bastards are promising a boatload of money," Fulton had said.

Over the past couple of months, according to the detective, the reports of attempts to find Newbury had grown fewer. But even if Jaxon hadn't been around to point it out, Karp knew that the lack of new inquiries wasn't because the Sons of Man had given up. They had just backed off to try another route.

It worried him. He'd never intended to use Crawford as a witness in the Jabbar trial. But he did plan on calling Dean Newbury as the nexus connecting Al-Sistani, Malovo, and the defendant. And Newbury would be at his most vulnerable being transported between the Tombs, where he'd been moved for the trial, and the eleventh floor . . . and while in the courtroom.

Fulton had worked with the court security staff to ramp up precautions. Starting with jury selection, everybody — attorneys, clerks, court reporters, journalists, spectators, and cops not assigned to court security — passed through the metal detector. Then, when they reached the eleventh floor, they had to pass through a gamut of bomb-sniffing dogs and more officers with metal-detecting wands. All bags were X-rayed, searched, and sniffed. And anything resembling a weapon — including any liquids — was confiscated.

During the trial, anyone with access to the well of the court, the attorney tables, the witness stand, the jury box, and the judge's dais would have had to submit to a background check. Everyone else had to stay in the gallery on the other side of the bar, and even there, the first two rows had been reserved for defense and DA support staff, as well as detectives and police officers on the prosecution side. Fulton also planned to salt the gallery with plainclothes members of his bureau.

"Short of being able to read minds and get a jump on what somebody's contemplating," Fulton had said, "I can't think of anything more to do."

"I think you've got it covered. What else is happening?" Karp had asked.

"We've got a lot of other work in the hopper, and we're stretched pretty thin. I'll be bouncing in and out of the court during the trial, and I have good people assigned to the trial, headed up by Sergeant Cordova; he's as sharp as they come and as tough as nails. I'll check in from time to time, and I will be present for Newbury's testimony to keep an extra eye on the crowd. But unless you think I have to be there full-time, I'm probably of more use elsewhere."

"No, I don't see the need," Karp had replied. "Mike Cordova's a good man. Younger, probably better eyes, too."

"Hey, hey," Fulton had growled. "This bull is still king of the pasture."

Karp smiled at the remembered metaphor just as the court clerk announced the arrival of Judge Mason. The judge glared briefly at the prosecution table and nodded agreeably to O'Dowd, who returned the acknowledgment. Without further ado, Mason announced that they would now resume questioning of the man who'd been called to replace the juror dismissed before court had adjourned on Friday.

"Ms. O'Dowd, I believe you said you were

finished with your *voir dire,*" the judge said. "Am I correct?"

"You are, your honor," O'Dowd replied.

The judge turned to Karp. "Are the People ready?"

"We are, your honor," Karp said as he rose from his seat and faced the handsome black man sitting in seat twelve.

The forty-five-year-old looked back at him without expression, his eyes steady, neither smiling nor frowning. Hassan Malik had been the subject of a spirited debate between Karp and ADA Kenny Katz, who'd argued after court recessed for the weekend that they had to remove him from the jury.

"Why?" Karp had asked.

"Well, let me play devil's advocate here. The fact is, he's a black Muslim, obviously sympathetic to the defense," his protégé had replied.

It wasn't an unreasonable argument. The defense had obviously hoped to keep Malik on the jury; O'Dowd's questioning had been geared toward assuring the court that despite his religion, Malik could put aside his personal feelings and follow the law as laid out by Judge Mason. *Of course, that's not what she hopes if he does remain on the jury,* he'd thought.

They all knew that O'Dowd didn't hold

out much hope that the prosecution would allow it, but she wanted to make sure the judge didn't dismiss Malik for cause. That way, Karp would have to use his last pre-emptory challenge to knock him off the panel.

In this case, Katz agreed with O'Dowd, though for his own reasons. "You can't seriously be thinking about leaving him on," he'd insisted. "He's American-born, but as a Muslim, he is obliged to put God above country. And Jabbar, whether Malik agrees with his politics or not, is an imam — an imam who has sworn on the Koran that he was not responsible for Miriam's death. And the defense has been playing the racism and anti-Islam cards since January, which, by the way, has been a hit on Arab-language television here and abroad. Why take a chance that this guy harbors some resentment? It's pretty obvious that O'Dowd would pay us to let him on the jury."

Karp had been looking out of the eighth-floor window at the pedestrians below. *The People of the State of New York,* he'd thought. *The reason we do this.* "But she thinks there's no way in hell we'll do it," he'd said, almost to himself. "We'll let her prejudices work against her."

"How do you mean?" Katz had asked.

"Just this: Other than trying to set it up so that we'd have to use our last preemptory challenge to have Mr. Malik removed, Megan O'Dowd hardly bothered to question him with any depth for two reasons. The first is that she doesn't think we'll allow Mr. Malik to serve, so why waste her breath on an extended *voir dire.* But the more important reason is that O'Dowd is a racist."

"A racist? You mean she hates whites?"

"No, I mean she's your garden-variety radical white racist," Karp had replied. "She assumes that because Malik is black and a Muslim, he's automatically going to side with another black Muslim. No questions asked. She is in effect saying that because Mr. Malik is a black man, he is incapable of exercising his responsibilities as a good citizen who will listen to the testimony, look at the evidence, and decide if another man — not an imam — broke the law. The same law, by the way, that protects black Muslims from criminals also."

"And what's to say he isn't that guy?" Katz had asked.

Karp had shrugged. "Nothing," he'd admitted. "The same nothing that prevents any juror from ignoring the law or letting his or her personal beliefs dictate how he or she votes. All you can go on are their answers during the course of the *voir dire* and their demeanor. Did you read Mr. Malik's responses on the jury questionnaire?"

"Yeah, what about it?"

"You see his previous employment response?"

"He was in the army," Katz had said, "and served two tours in Iraq and one in Afghanistan, like me."

"He wasn't just in the army or a combat veteran, was he, Kenny?"

"No, he was a top sergeant and an MP . . . a cop. You think that's more important than his religious beliefs? I knew some black Muslims in my unit, and they caught a lot of shit from some of the other guys. A few were pretty bitter about it."

"Obviously, we'll have to feel him out about that. But let's look at the facts. The fact that he was a master sergeant suggests that he was promoted for good reason and then committed no offenses that would have got him demoted, right?"

"Right."

"And he was in for twenty years, all of it with the military police."

"Yep."

"As a top sergeant, he's a leader of men, and I assume that not all of those men would have been black Muslims. So he must have been a team player. Am I right?"

Katz had smiled, seeing the writing on the wall. "You are correct, sir."

"He got out with an honorable discharge and a full pension from the United States government. And he now owns his own garage, where he works as a mechanic, which also makes him a small businessman with a stake in the safety and stability of his community."

"Right on all counts. But that still doesn't mean his experiences as a black Muslim in the U.S. Army didn't make him angry. Maybe that's even why he got out."

"We'll ask him about it when we get our shot on Monday," Karp had said. "I think it will become obvious if there's a problem. But I've got a feeling that a military cop who saw firsthand the depredations of Islamic extremists isn't automatically going to side with another one. All O'Dowd sees is a black man. Besides, if we use the last of our challenges, the next juror called could be worse, much worse. And let me ask you this. You were a sergeant and saw combat. You were decorated; he was decorated. What does your gut tell you?"

"The good news is I like the fact he was a military cop," Katz had replied. "The bad news is I'm still concerned if he will follow the law." Having seen the light, Katz had asked, "Are you worried that O'Dowd will get suspicious if we don't remove Mr. Malik? Maybe she'll think you know something and decide to take her chances on the next person. Maybe she'll use a challenge."

"I've thought of that," Karp had replied. "We'll just have to use a little finesse."

An earlier prospective juror had set the stage for a little finesse when Karp had him in the judge's chambers for individual *voir dire*. He had asked if the middle-aged man, a history teacher at a Manhattan prep school, had any "political, social, economic, religious, or philosophical reasons" that he would not be able to reach a fair and impartial verdict.

"I am a twenty-five-year member of the American Workers Party."

"A Communist?" Karp had asked.

"Communist. Socialist. It's not against the law to belong to any political party of my choosing," the man had said defiantly.

Karp had held up a hand. "You're absolutely right; I was just trying to clarify. And do you believe that affiliation might prevent you from following his honor's instructions and reaching a fair and impartial verdict in this case?"

"Well." The man had sniffed as he adjusted his round eyeglasses. "As a member of the party, I am opposed to the current government of the United States."

"By your answer, I take it that you also believe our laws are illegal within the scope of your deeply felt political philosophy?"

"Yes, I believe it is an illegal government controlled by rich capitalists and their puppeteers, the international Jewish cabal. And therefore its laws are also illegal."

"Is it fair to say that as a committed Communist, you also believe that our government is immoral?"

"Absolutely."

"It follows, then, that law-enforcement officers are instruments of the government, used to control the population, like Cossacks serving to keep their masters in power?"

"Perfectly stated, Mr. Karp."

"I see," Karp had said, and turned to Judge Mason. "Your honor, it's clear from this gentleman's answers that he will not only *not* believe police officers who will testify, but he will also *not* follow the law as his honor will instruct. I ask that this man be excused for cause."

"I oppose," O'Dowd had chimed in immediately. "It's still not illegal, though perhaps we're almost there, to have a different political philosophy from that of the esteemed district attorney. He didn't say he'd refuse to follow the judge's instructions or that he would automatically disbelieve police officers."

Judge Mason had looked at the juror. "Sir, are you saying you'd refuse to apply the law as I instruct?"

The prospective juror had shrugged. "Depends. I would follow my own conscience, but I would certainly listen to what you have to say." He'd looked at Karp. "I, at least, am not some jack-booted authority figure trying to impose my will on the oppressed."

"Your honor, this fine fellow is clearly unwilling to answer the question directly, much less say he will follow the law," Karp had pointed out. He knew that judges in general didn't like to excuse potential jurors for cause, as it opened the door for appellate review post-conviction. And this judge would be even more reluctant because it was Karp who was asking.

Judge Mason had then asked the juror again if he would follow the law without question, "even if you disagree with it." At that point, the juror had realized that for him to remain on the jury, which he clearly wanted so that he could "fight the system," he would have to answer affirmatively. "Well, if you put it that way, then yes, I suppose I would," he'd said, smirking at Karp.

The judge had then ruled: "I decline to remove this man for cause. Mr. Karp, your request is denied."

Karp, suppressing the urge to engage further with Mason, had declared, "Then I will use one of my preemptories. I don't want him contaminating the rest of the jurors; I want him escorted out of the courtroom."

The judge's ruling had incensed Karp, given the juror's obvious bias, but it had given him an idea about how to handle Hassan Malik. He asked again to *voir dire* the man in chambers. Once there, he started by questioning Malik about his past leading up to his service overseas and experiences as a black Muslim in the U.S. Army.

"While you were in the army, did you have any problems because of your religion?" Karp asked.

"Officially, no, sir," Malik replied.

Karp noted the use of *sir*. "What about unofficially?"

Malik's expression hardened. "There were instances of some animosity, particularly after nine-eleven and later when I was over-seas."

"What sort of instances?"

"Taunting, things said so that I could overhear," Malik replied. "A dead rat placed on my bunk with a note that read, 'Watch your back, sand nigger.' "

"Did some question your loyalty?"

"Yes, sir."

"And how did that make you feel?"

"Angry."

"What did you do about it?"

The man shrugged. "Nothing I could do about it, sir. So I just did my job."

Karp furrowed his brow as though the next question troubled him greatly. "Mr. Malik, are you loyal first to the United States or to your religion?"

"As a Muslim, I place nothing before my duty to Allah."

Allowing his shoulders to sag just a bit, Karp looked at Judge Mason. "Your honor, I have concerns about his statement that his first loyalty would be to Allah."

Mason looked balefully at Karp but then turned to Malik. "In honesty, Mr. Malik, I understand that you place God before country. That does not exclude your partici-pation on this panel. However, I do want to ask on behalf of Mr. Karp here if you believe that you can listen to the evidence and, after being instructed on the law by me, reach a fair and impartial verdict."

Malik scowled and glanced at Karp. "My religion does not prevent me from serving on the jury and following instructions, sir."

"Very well," Mason said with a slight smile as he turned to Karp. "Anything more?"

Karp hesitated and then shook his head. "No, your honor."

"Then I suggest we return to the courtroom," the judge said.

When they'd reassembled in the courtroom, the judge asked Karp, "Are you going to use your preemptory challenge to keep this man from being seated?"

Karp bit his lip. "May I have a moment to confer with my co-counsel?" he asked.

"You may, but make it quick," Mason replied. "It's the eleventh hour and time to move on in this trial."

"Yes, your honor," Karp replied, and returned to the prosecution table, where he leaned over to whisper to Katz. "Don't speak aloud, but act as if we're locked in debate over this. I want O'Dowd to think that we are only reluctantly accepting Malik as the lesser of possible evils."

Katz pointed out, "Apparently, no one noticed that you didn't ask Mason to remove him for cause."

Karp kept the frown on his face, but his eyes twinkled. "Funny how that worked," he said, then shook his head and rapped his knuckles on the table. He looked at the remaining jurors and shook his head again, as if afraid of what prejudices against the prosecution might lurk in the gallery. Finally, he turned back to the judge with a sigh. "Your honor, Mr. Malik is acceptable to the People."

Mason barely hid the smile on his face. "Ms. O'Dowd?"

The defense attorney also smiled. "Your honor, the defense is satisfied with Mr. Malik's presence on the jury."

The judge rapped his gavel. "Okay, we now have twelve. Let's get on with selecting the four alternates."

14

Sitting back in his chair with his feet up on his desk, Karp watched his protégé alternately chewing on a pencil and scribbling on a yellow legal pad as he sat in a corner by the bookshelf. The young man shook his head and looked up.

"Spit it out, my man," Karp said. "You're squirming like a Times Square junkie."

Katz tilted his head and started to say something, then stopped. He tapped the legal pad with the pencil. "Well, it just struck me, the disparity between O'Dowd's fight to keep Jojola and Tran from testifying and her efforts against Dean Newbury."

"What do you mean?" Karp asked.

"Well, we just spent three hours arguing motions, and trying to suppress the testimony of Tran and Jojola probably took up two hours of that," he said. "But she was done with Dean Newbury in twenty minutes. Plus, over the past four months, I was buried with a mountain of paperwork attacking our guys but hardly a motion to keep Newbury off the stand."

"Maybe she's more worried about Tran and Jojola," Karp pointed out. "She'll have plenty to attack Newbury with while trying to make us look like we made a deal with the devil. She's also got a better argument against our *agents provocateurs,* which we've been battling since February."

Karp was referring to an *in limine* motion he'd made three months earlier asking the court to limit O'Dowd's cross-examination of federal agents Jojola, Tran, and Jaxon, "in respect to their counterterrorism activities except this specific case. They cannot give up sources and methods regarding pending matters that could endanger past and ongoing covert operations and law-enforcement personnel."

Karp had noted that such testimony under cross-examination could also be "highly prejudicial" to Jabbar, a reference to his part in the attack on the New York Stock Exchange that had resulted in the killing of two of New York's finest. Although the murder of Miriam Juma Khalifa was directly related to the stock-exchange attack, and Karp could have made a case that he should be allowed to present that evidence to the jury under the doctrine of "prior bad acts," but he chose not to.

O'Dowd could have rightfully pointed out that Jabbar had not been convicted of any crimes connected to the attack, nor was he charged with them now. More important, Karp had intended to make the motion *in limine* and knew that once he opened the door, he wouldn't be able to pick and choose where O'Dowd could go with her cross-examination of the agents.

However, O'Dowd had a good argument that granting the motion *in limine* would severely hamper her efforts to cross-examine Jojola, Tran, and Jaxon. She would necessarily be precluded from raising issues about background events and motivations to possibly frame her client.

Three months earlier, Mason had agreed with her and denied Karp's motion. The judge's decision had crippled the People's case. Mason knew that granting O'Dowd wide-open latitude in cross-examining the counterterrorism agents would preclude Karp from calling them as witnesses. He couldn't risk the blow to national security.

Without Tran and Jojola, two eyewitnesses, connecting the defendant to the execution of Miriam, Karp wasn't left with much. He'd felt his case would have the evidentiary impact of a feather.

So he had immediately filed an expedited interlocutory appeal, playing the national-security card. The appellate court had agreed and reversed Mason. It had surely antagonized the judge, but it also made him more gun-shy. Thereafter, Karp had mused that it was as if the ideological air had been sucked out of the judge's "alleged mind."

"So, obviously, she's spent more time on them than on Newbury," Karp pointed out to Katz as they debated the issue in his office.

"I understand all that," Katz replied. "However, I see two problems with your arguments. One, we all know she's staking her case on the 'government conspiracy' and *agent provocateur*' scenarios. So if I were she, I'd actually *want* Tran and Jojola on the stand. If she knows anything about their backgrounds, she probably thinks Jojola is some hick Indian from the sticks, and Tran, well, Tran's a Vietnamese gangster, and she'll have a field day going after him. And neither one is going to be able to say much about what he does with Jaxon's agency — at least, not the classified stuff — or talk about the stock-exchange attack, which is going to make them look suspicious and as if they're withholding information. And that should play right into O'Dowd's strategy."

"Good points," Karp said. "Go on."

"Well, I also think that if I'm her, and blaming the murder on these government agents, I'd rather not have a third party — Dean Newbury — provide the connections among Al-Sistani, Nadya Malovo, and Jabbar."

Karp took his feet off the desk. "All valid considerations," he said, "but I'm seeing it a little differently. Without Tran and Jojola — or that damned videotape that was supposedly made, and God knows where it is — we have no 'eyewitnesses' to Miriam's death. We have a body. A bloody knife with fingerprints on it that Jaxon has identified as belonging to Malovo. But very little evidence of Jabbar's involvement either before or during the murder, except some testimony that he was responsible for recruiting the Al-Aqsa Martyrs Brigade. Keeping Tran and Jojola off the stand would have been a devastating blow to us, a total and complete game changer. And as I said, Newbury's credibility will be an easy target."

"I'm surprised she didn't make more of the fact that Newbury was the mosque's attorney, and therefore Jabbar was his client and their conversations privileged," Katz said.

"To a point," Karp replied. "But attorney-client privilege extends only to Newbury acting in his role as an attorney. It does not extend to acting in concert to commit criminal acts. O'Dowd wants to preserve the record to give herself a chance to fight it on appeal, but she knows she's not going to win. Anything else?"

Katz again started to say something but shook his head. "No, it makes sense. It just seems as if she's not worried about Newbury. Anyway, I'm going to hit the road. I want to make sure everything's ready for tomorrow."

After Katz left the office, Karp kicked back again and thought about his protégé. He was pleased with Katz's progress. He had recently successfully tried a felony murder case where the judge had gone out of his way to write a complimentary note about his "professionalism and preparation."

In this, their third murder trial together, Karp had given the young man more to do than in the past, such as answering most of the motions filed by O'Dowd. Katz always checked his work with him before filing it with the court clerk, but Karp had found very little to critique.

Experience seemed to be Katz's only

shortcoming, and he was fast gaining on that. And his observations about O'Dowd's efforts thus far were sophisticated and intellectually penetrating.

Ever since Jabbar's arrest on Christmas morning, Karp had done everything he could to move the proceedings along as expeditiously as possible. He wasn't trying to rush the case, nor was he worried about the defendant's right to a speedy trial. He just didn't believe that it was appropriate for DAs to engage in pretrial detention willy-nilly because they had the power to influence the bail-setting magistrate. For him, it was a liberty issue, the belief that nothing was more important to a man than his freedom.

If he had not already believed it in a philosophical sense, he'd been convinced many years earlier, when he was fresh out of law school and newly hired at the New York DAO. His bureau chief, Mel Glass, had taken the newbies on a tour of the Tombs. An eye-opener, to be sure. The stifling heat and unbearable humidity of August and the stench of urine, unwashed bodies, and cleaning materials had nearly made him gag. It sounded like the inside of a cuckoo's nest, with screaming, loud yells, and insane laughter. The steel gates clanging and clicking behind and in front of him, and the walls and bars pressing in had given him insight into the isolation, loneliness, and fear felt by many of the inmates.

The Manhattan House of Detention, the Tombs, was occupied mostly by defendants awaiting trial. At tour's end, Glass had admonished all of them that they should seriously weigh requests for high bail and a man's freedom against the likelihood of a defendant absconding or allegedly presenting a danger to the public. "Knowing now the hell in which he'll live until his trial if he can't get out," Glass had said.

However, there were cases that justified the setting of high bail — such as a sexual predator — or, in the case of murder, no bail at all, only remand to the Tombs. The flight risk for such a crime and potential sentence, as well as the potential danger to the public and witnesses, was too great. But to Karp, that meant that ethically, he had to move even more expeditiously with a murder case than one in which the defendant could get out on bail. Each and every time Karp had asked the court to remand a defendant in a post-indictment murder case, he had informed the court that the People were "ready for trial."

Karp had been surprised that O'Dowd

had made little effort to postpone or delay this trial. In fact, he had noted that O'Dowd had not filed a motion for a change of venue away from New York County. Most defense lawyers with black Muslim clients charged with anything resembling terrorism had demanded a change of venue since September 11, 2001.

Karp had read somewhere that as much as forty percent of the people in the city thought that the government might have had something to do with the attack on the World Trade Center. If he intended to argue that his client was a victim of a government conspiracy, he might want to keep the trial there, too.

While the lack of a change-of-venue motion seemed explainable, Karp had also noted that O'Dowd was not using the usual defense methods to delay a trial. She had not attempted to raise a mental-competence argument, thus avoiding months of waiting for reports from mental-health experts. And she'd settled for a single defense forensic expert to look over the evidence.

The only surprise had been that afternoon, when she'd announced that the defense would be calling an alibi witness and handed over the information about the witness's statement and how to contact her.

"Megan, thank you for giving this to us on the eve of the trial. So typical," Karp had said.

"I only just learned of the witness myself," O'Dowd had retorted. "My client is married — to another woman — and had hoped to keep this assignation quiet."

The judge had allowed it, and Karp had looked back at Fulton, who'd been sitting behind the prosecution table. The big detective had nodded, and Karp knew he'd be all over the witness to catch her in her lies.

Still, all in all, Megan O'Dowd seemed as anxious to get this trial under way as he had been. Maybe Jabbar was simply confident that he'd be acquitted and wanted out of the Tombs so that he could wing off to some renegade Muslim nation and be feted as a hero like Al-Sistani.

The intercom buzzed, and Darla Milquetost announced that he had a call. "Moishe Sobelman on line one," she said.

Karp leaned forward and picked up the phone. "Shalom, Moishe," he said.

"Shalom, Butch," the old man replied.

"To what do I owe the honor of this call?"

"I wouldn't bother you with such a trivial matter," Moishe said at last. "But you told me I should call when that woman returned to my shop. She is here now, talking to my

288

Goldie. There is just something about her . . ."

"Say no more, my friend," Karp replied. "I'll call Clay, and he'll have one of his detectives there in twenty minutes."

"Well, it is probably nothing . . . oh, wait, she is leaving."

"Can you see where she's going?"

"Just a moment, I am walking to the front of the shop. Yes, she is crossing the street." There was a sharp intake of breath. "That man is over there. She walked past him, but he has turned and followed her. I do not see them anymore."

Karp frowned. It could be nothing. The woman might like a bite of cherry-cheese coffee cake before she met with her boyfriend, and it was nothing more than that. But he'd talked to Fulton after he got back from the Breakfast Club meeting last week, and the detective didn't like it, either.

"They do a lot of cash business," Fulton had noted. "And some of these older store owners are known for tucking their profits into the mattresses. Maybe this couple has heard a rumor that the Sobelmans don't use banks. I'll call my buddy who heads the patrol desk in that precinct and ask him for a couple extra drop-bys. And if this woman or her partner show again, call me, and I'll send a detective to check it out. If they are up to something and know we're on to them, they'll probably go away."

Karp punched the button on his phone for Fulton's office. "Hey, Clay, I just heard from Moishe," he said. "That woman was in the shop again a few minutes ago. She left and met her boyfriend across the street. . . . Yeah, just left. . . . Good. I'd hate to have something happen to those two."

He looked at his watch. Marlene was supposed to meet him in a half hour, and they were going to dinner in Brighton Beach with his uncle Vladimir Karchovski at the old man's restaurant.

He stood up from his chair, walked over to the window, and observed the many different people below from all walks of life and many different nations. Drawn here not just for the opportunity to make a better living but for a better life free from political, religious, and ethnic persecution.

Moishe's call reminded him of the main topic of conversation at the Breakfast Club meeting, "American Exceptionalism," a 180-year-old theory that the United States occupies a special moral place among nations because of its credo of freedom and justice for all, protected by two promissory notes, the Declaration of Independence and the Constitution, that guaranteed certain inalienable rights.

It was a typical topic of conversation for the Sons of Liberty Breakfast Club and Girl-Watching Society, a self-described group of "old codgers whose wives chase us out of the apartment once a week" to meet over breakfast and debate politics, the law, art, foreign affairs, and anything else that interested them.

The members were Frank Plaut, a respected former federal judge with the Second Circuit Court of Appeals; Saul Silverstein, a former Marine who'd fought at Iwo Jima and returned from the war to make a fortune in women's garments; a Jesuit priest, Jim Sunderland; a former top defense attorney, Murray Epstein; his conservative counterpart Dennis Hall, who was a former U.S. attorney for the Southern District in Manhattan; a retired editor of the *New York Post,* Bill Florence; and renowned Village artist Geoffrey Gilbert.

That particular morning, Hall and Epstein had been in opposing corners on the topic. The former U.S. attorney had argued that "the United States has a special moral and ethical role to play in world history." But Epstein had countered, "That's jingoistic and self-serving. It allows us to excuse our faults — such as slavery, civil rights, our treatment of American Indians, and even our refusal to accept Jews fleeing Nazi Germany — without owning up to them. It makes us appear arrogant to the rest of the world."

It was Plaut who'd asked Karp if he'd care to join the fray as the group settled in around the table. The topic was a favorite, and he'd begun by quoting the Puritan leader John Winthrop, who'd said around 1630, "We will be as a city upon a hill. The eyes of all people are upon us, so that if we deal falsely with our God in this work we have undertaken and so cause Him to withdraw His present help from us, we shall be made a story and a byword throughout the world." To which Ronald Reagan added in 1974, when still the governor of California, "You can call it mysticism if you want to, but I have always believed that there was some divine plan that placed this great continent between two oceans to be sought out by those who were possessed of an abiding love of freedom and a special kind of courage."

Karp had paused and reminisced. "Let me give you a down-home personal example of what I mean. My grandparents fled Europe's poverty, oppression, and anti-

Semitism to come to America to seek freedom and a better life for themselves and their family. They couldn't speak English, they had no place to live, but they worked hard and never took a government handout. They made a warm and comfortable home for their family and made sure their children were educated. 'Only in America,' they always said. Hitch your wagon to a star. Go to school, work hard, and your dreams can come true. There was always the notion at home that their children and grandchildren could do anything they put their minds to if they were willing to commit and sacrifice and be prepared to do that which was necessary to succeed on their merits."

"Yeah, okay, but what about slavery?" Epstein had said. "What about the treatment of American Indians?"

"And the ills that are still with us — racism and people trapped in ghettos," Gilbert had added. "How can we claim moral superiority with so much poverty and unequal access to decent health care and quality education in the inner cities?"

Karp had taken a sip of his coffee and looked down at the table, seemingly lost in thought. He'd placed the cup next to his cherry-cheese coffee cake and looked up at the Breakfast Clubbers, whose eyes were fixed upon him. "Yes, gentlemen, we have made mistakes, and we are still struggling to convert the promise of this country into reality for all of us. Without doubt, slavery is a stigma on our history, but we also fought a long and bloody civil war to end it, which saved our country's soul. We sacrificed our best and bravest against brutal and well-trained enemies at distant places like Guadalcanal, Midway, and Normandy, not because our borders were threatened but to save millions of others from death and enslavement on continents far from ours. I'm a firm believer in American Exceptionalism. We live in a country that cherishes freedom and liberty from governmental interference. We are a moral and virtuous people, committed to fairness and the eradication of evil. I can assure you that evil exists. I'm a volunteer soldier in the battle to destroy evil. As DA, I try to institutionalize systems in my office that will effectively combat evil in the framework of due process."

Karp thought of a man like Imam Jabbar, who spoke only of his perception of what was wrong with America and engaged in murderous violence to tear it down, and compared him to a man like Moishe Sobelman, a concentration-camp survivor, a man who'd witnessed the darkest side of human nature and fled to the United States for similar reasons to Karp's grandparents' almost a century earlier.

"It seems to me," Karp had continued, "that we are duty bound to honor and preserve our liberty and pass it on to our children. We are a moral people and must never waver in our commitment to do what is right, no matter what the threat or intimidation. I do believe that we are heroic and fearless in the pursuit and eradication of evil and the men who commit it, whether it is in the name of National Socialism or Allah."

"I'll drink to that," Judge Plaut had said, raising his glass of orange juice. "God bless America."

Karp's reverie was interrupted again by the intercom and Milquetost's announcement that his wife had arrived. The door opened immediately, and Marlene walked into the room.

"Now, there's the best-looking woman I've seen all day," he said with a smile.

"Hmmm . . . Keep talking like that, and you might get lucky," she replied. "You still working?"

He shook his head and stood up. "Nope.

We have a jury, and opening statements and testimony start tomorrow."

"Still feel like going out? I'd understand if you want to skip it and stay focused."

"Are you kidding me? Pass up a chance to spend a few blissful moments with the love of my life?" Karp took her into his arms and kissed her tenderly.

"Well, you're a lot closer to hitting a home run after that one, DiMaggio." Marlene giggled.

"Then the sooner we leave," he said, wiggling an eyebrow, "the sooner I get a chance to round the bases and score."

They were still laughing as they left the Criminal Courts Building. As they approached the curb to catch a cab, they came across Dirty Warren, who was humming to himself as he closed up his newsstand.

"Good evening, Mr. and Mrs. . . . oh boy assssss . . . Karp," he called out cheerily. "Beautiful evening. Love is in the air! Whoop!"

Karp and his wife looked at each other, amused.

"Why, Warren, you are positively aglow," Marlene said. She looked closely at him. "I do believe our Warren is in love."

Karp started to laugh until he saw the look on the news vendor's face. "I think you're right, he's blushing," he said. "Okay, give, who is she?"

"No one you know. Just . . . oh boy oh boy kiss my . . . an old friend," Warren replied. He kept working to make sure all his magazines and other merchandise were in neat, orderly stacks as he tried to redirect the conversation. "Hey, Karp, I got one for you."

"Let's have it."

"Okay. 'The key goes where the book editor sees his wife and son off to Maine.' That's . . . whoop . . . it."

Karp furrowed his brow. "That's not much to go on. Tell you what, I promise not to cheat, but we're running late, and I'll have to get back to you tomorrow on that one."

Warren grinned. "Well, I hope you get it right. I'm stumped, and I have a movie . . . whoop tits and balls . . . date riding on it."

"Well, then, I'll give it my best effort."

At that moment, two large men stepped up to Warren and flashed their gold detective shields. "Are you Warren Bennett?"

Surprised, Warren nodded his head. "Do you need a newspaper? I'm closed, but —"

"You're under arrest," said one of the men.

"What's this about?" Karp asked.

"Sorry, Mr. Karp," said the other detective. "But there's a warrant out for this man."

"What's the charge?" Marlene asked.

"Murder," the first detective said. "A woman named Michelle Oakley was killed sometime over the weekend —"

"Michelle! . . . Whoop oh boy fucking bitch . . . no, it's not possible!" Warren cried out. He started to twitch and hop.

One of the detectives stepped forward and grabbed him. "Hands behind your back," he said. "Turn around and hold still, or I'll have to put you on the ground."

"Take it easy. He's got Tourette's," Karp said. "He can't help the twitching or the language."

"You have the right to remain silent . . ." The second detective began to read Warren his Miranda rights as the first handcuffed him.

"No, no, not her . . . dirty whore whoop whoop . . ."

Realizing that Warren was digging himself a hole, Marlene stepped forward and addressed the detectives. "I'm his attorney. And he will not be making any more statements."

15

The uniformed police officer stationed at the front entrance of the apartment building on the Lower East Side placed his hands on his hips and shook his head. "I'm sorry, ma'am, but I can't let you in."

"Don't you know that women *hate* being called ma'am?" Marlene scolded, but with a smile. "Especially attractive 'mature' women when addressed by good-looking young police officers like yourself — as if you're talking to your mother or, worse, your grandmother." She held out her hand. "I'm a lawyer, my name is Marlene Ciampi, and I represent the tenant of the apartment."

"I don't mean to offend, mmm . . . Miss Ciampi," the officer replied, reaching out and shaking her hand. "You're nothin' like my mom or grandma, believe me, but I still can't let you go in. This is a homicide investigation, and I got orders."

Marlene contemplated whether it was

time to switch from polite and mildly flirtatious to imperious and demanding. She'd showed up at Dirty Warren's apartment — she was still getting used to the idea that he had a last name, Bennett — hoping to persuade the building manager to let her in to look around. But the cops were still on the scene.

She still had not had a real conversation with her client to figure out what this was all about. By the time Warren was transported to the Westchester County jail and booked the previous night, visiting hours were over, and she'd been told to come back after ten in the morning. She'd had only a brief few moments in the hallway, in which she reminded the distraught, twitching, cursing, frightened man not to talk to the police, and he'd begged her to go by his place in the morning to feed his cat, Brando, and his pet birds.

So far, most of what she knew about the case was from reading the *New York Times* that morning, which had carried a front-page story and a photograph of "brutally murdered socialite" Michelle Oakley, who had been found dead in her home in Purchase by her maid on Sunday afternoon. A "source close to the investigation" said that Oakley had been stabbed several times and possibly sexually assaulted. The police had taken a suspect, whose name was being withheld, into custody Monday evening. Other than that, the cops weren't saying much.

The newspaper had located Harry Lee, a Westchester County cab driver, who claimed that he'd dropped off a passenger outside the home at about seven P.M. on Saturday. The self-described "star witness" hypothesized that his fare was "obviously a very disturbed individual," who swore like a "Jersey longshoreman."

"I thought he was kind of creepy," Lee said. "But I have to say he did tip well, whereas a lot of so-called upstanding citizens are too cheap to throw a starving dog a bone."

District Attorney Harley Chin had, of course, chimed in for the story. He told the newspaper that he was "personally sickened by the vicious, senseless murder of one of Purchase's most upstanding citizens." He pledged that the killer would be brought to "swift and certain" justice and that his constituents could rest easy in their beds, knowing that the law never slept at the Westchester County District Attorney's Office.

As she finished reading the story that

morning over a cup of coffee, Marlene had wondered why she'd stepped in and said she was Warren's lawyer. It was obvious the poor man needed help — whether he was guilty or not — and was only digging himself a hole with his language. But while she'd kept her license to practice updated, it had been years since she'd been in a courtroom as an attorney. Yet there she was, acting like Clarence Darrow and telling her client to keep his mouth shut. Then she'd told Butch that she needed a rain check on their visit to Karchovski's restaurant and followed Warren to the Westchester County jail.

When she'd got home some five hours later, Butch was still up waiting for her and concerned about her and Warren.

"I personally don't believe that Warren is capable of murdering anyone," Butch had said. "Either way, he deserves effective counsel. He's lucky to have you."

Butch had turned in soon after. The Jabbar case was starting in the morning, and given the evening's sudden drama, he'd opted to catch some shut-eye. He'd kissed her good-bye that morning and wished her luck as he marched out the door ready to do battle with the forces of evil in the person of Megan O'Dowd and Imam

Sharif Jabbar.

As requested, Marlene had taken a cab to Warren's apartment to care for his pets but also to see if there was anything in the apartment that might help his cause. But it looked as if gaining entry was going to be difficult. *Might as well try imperious and demanding,* she thought.

"Look, I know you're doing your job, Officer O'Brien," she said, reading his name tag, her voice suddenly stern and rising in volume as she went on. "But I have a job to do, too, and a man's life might be at stake. Now, I insist that you either let me by or call someone with some authority, and perhaps he'll understand that I have a right to go into my client's apartment."

The officer looked confused, probably as much by the change in demeanor as by what she'd said, and was about to say something again when a gruff voice rolled out from inside the building. "What's going on out there, Eric? If it's the fucking press again, I'm gonna kick some journalist ass, I swear to —"

A big, rugged-looking man with olive skin and a dark seven o'clock shadow in an ill-fitting suit stepped out of the building with a scowl on his face. But he grinned when he saw the person confronting the officer.

"Well, ain't this a pleasant surprise, Cousin Marlene! Or, as we used to call her in the old neighborhood in Queens, Stinky Ciampi."

Marlene rolled her eyes and addressed the perplexed young officer. "That is *not* what they used to call me, although they did use several other words that weren't always appropriate for someone of my delicate nature." She stood up on her tiptoes to kiss her relative on both cheeks. "Cousin Bobby! I heard you'd left the NYPD for Westchester County, but I didn't know you were working homicides."

"The pay's a lot better," Detective Sergeant Roberto "Bobby" Scalia said, and laughed. "Also, Westchester is mostly full of rich people, so we get a better grade of criminal. Fewer gangs, dope fiends, and nutcases — though I have to tell ya, this current perp is a piece of work. He's got a mouth on him that would have made my dad — God rest his alcoholic soul — sound like the pope, and he jumps around and twitches like somebody stuck a live light socket up his keister. He ain't saying much, though, that ain't a surprise; his asshole lawyer already got to him and told him to keep his yap shut. But enough business. I ain't seen you since Pop's funeral. Where you been, and what the hell are you doing here?"

"I'm the perp's asshole attorney," Marlene said with a grin. "And by the way, he's got Tourette's syndrome, which is why he behaves like that."

"Perdonilo, cugina, io non ha saputo," Scalia apologized.

"È giusto. Forget about it, Bobby, obviously you didn't know," Marlene said, patting his shoulder. "And besides, there *are* plenty of asshole defense attorneys. I hear about them every night at the dinner table."

"What's Tourette's? Some fancy name they got for having a mouth like a Forty-second Street hooker?"

"For the record, Detective Sensitivity, Tourette's syndrome is a brain disorder that makes him blurt inappropriate things and have muscle spasms. He can't help it any more than you could ever help passing gas after a serving of your mom's meatballs. And now that I think about it, you're the one we called Stinky."

The detective laughed. "Well, I guess I had that comin'. But lay off my mom's cookin' — not every Italian mom is a great chef like yours. So, you think your guy's innocent?"

"I don't know yet. But I do know that it's

completely out of character for him. My husband has known him for years and considers him a friend, and Butch is usually a good judge of character."

"Well, if he didn't do it, I hope it comes out in the wash, but it don't look good," Scalia said. "We got his fingerprints in the house. And a cabbie putting him at the crime scene Saturday night."

"What's his motive?"

The detective shrugged. "I'm only second fiddle on this one, but I heard there was a sexual assault."

"Which would be even more out of character."

"Like I said, I'm just helping out on this one; the main detective is a guy named Jake Meadow. I don't like him much — sort of a blowhard and lazy, too. He likes his cases nice and easy. And just so you know, the DA's got a hard-on for your boy, too. He wanted the reports on his desk yesterday morning, and he's going to the grand jury this afternoon, but you probably already know that. I haven't seen a case move this fast in Westchester County . . . ever. Not that I give a rat's ass about what that little prick wants, but Meadow sure jumped when Chin called."

"Yeah, I'm on my way over there to talk

to my client when I leave here," Marlene said. "But I'd like to have a look inside, both for professional reasons and because my client asked me to feed his cat."

Scalia scratched his head. "There's no cat," he said. "I was the first one through that door, and the place ain't very big. There are a couple of birds but no felines. Come on in. We've about wrapped it. I'll take you back up myself. It's okay, O'Brien."

The young officer stepped aside. "I meant no offense."

"None taken," Marlene replied with a smile. "You were just doing your job. Lead the way, detective."

As they entered the turn-of-the-century brick building, Marlene noted the worn carpeting in the dim hallway and the cracked and peeling paint. After climbing the stairs, which creaked and groaned with each step, they reached the second floor, which was in about the same sad state of disrepair as the first.

Most of the doors in the hall were closed, though she could hear the muffled sounds of morning shows on a half-dozen televisions. About halfway down the hall, two men — one of them in an NYPD uniform — hovered outside the only open door.

Scalia led the way to the door, where the

two men looked at Marlene, shrugged, and stepped back.

"Careful where you put your feet," her cousin cautioned. "Your guy wasn't much of a housekeeper, and he has his stuff piled all over the place."

Marlene walked into the tiny apartment and immediately saw what the detective was talking about. Clothes and books and magazines were strewn about, and every dresser drawer and closet door was open, with clothes hanging out or lying on the floor.

Warren apparently had a large collection of films on DVD and video, but while there was a shelf that could have easily held them, most were scattered about on the small desk and on the floor, and many weren't in their cases. Recalling how neatly he stacked the newspapers, magazines, and other merchandise in his newsstand, it seemed odd.

She walked over to the small kitchen. Every drawer and cabinet door was open here, too. She was about to turn away from the scene when a puzzled look came over her face. "Hey, Bobby, notice anything strange about the kitchen?" she asked her cousin, who was talking to one of the crime-scene technicians.

Scalia walked over and glanced around. At first, his smile was merely one of tolerance for his cousin, but then his thick eyebrows rose. "No dirty dishes," he said.

Marlene smiled. "You always were a great detective," she said.

"Apparently, only second best in the family, or I would have noticed that. So, this guy is such a pig that he can't put his clothes away, and his prize film collection is scattered all over Timbuktu . . ."

". . . but there are no dirty dishes in the sink or on the counters," Marlene said, continuing the thought. "No food wrappers, spills, or rotting garbage. The place is a mess, but it's not dirty."

"Maybe he's afraid of germs, but he doesn't have a problem leaving his clean clothes all over the place?"

"That what you really think?" Marlene asked with a sideways look at the detective.

Scalia's lips puckered as if he'd just tasted a bitter lemon, and then he shook his big head. "No. I think the place was tossed before we got here. Which means somebody got in here last night."

"Looks like they were in a hurry, too," Marlene noted. "Whoever it was, he wanted in and out of here fast."

"Maybe one of the neighbors, or a not-so-good friend, heard your client had been arrested and used the time to rip him off?"

"The DVD and VCR players are both still here. I don't think he has much else to steal. I wonder what they were looking for?"

"Maybe they found it. And maybe they let the cat out when they came in."

Marlene nodded slowly. "Yeah, maybe. Nice exercise in deductive logic, Detective Sergeant Scalia. But do me a favor, and don't make a big deal out of our little observations right now. If someone else is involved in this murder, I'd like a little head-start."

"The other stuff is guesswork, so it doesn't go in my report," Scalia said, "*if* you promise to keep me in the loop if you find anything. It'd be funny to make this bust while Meadow's sitting on his fat ass. Meantime, have a look around, but don't touch anything unless you ask me first, *capice?*"

"*Si, capice.* And I promise I'll let you know if I find something."

Five minutes later, Marlene had seen enough. There was nothing in the apartment that was going to jump out at her to establish Warren's innocence or a clue to who might want to frame him. At least, nothing that wasn't going to be in the police report.

She hugged her cousin and turned to leave. "*Ciao,* Roberto. Say hi to your beautiful mom and sisters."

"I will," he replied. *"Vada con il dio, la mia cugina graziosa."*

Just then, Officer O'Brien showed up at the door with a large orange tabby in his hands. "Is this the missing cat?"

Marlene looked at the name tag on the collar. "It is," she said, accepting the cat into her arms. She held him up so she could look into his face. "Where have you been, Brando? And who did you see?"

16

The gallery section of Part 39 was buzzing with anticipation as those journalists and spectators fortunate enough to get through the screening before all the seats were taken eagerly awaited the start of the Jabbar trial. It was expected that sparks would fly when O'Dowd and Karp clashed, contributing to the prize-fight atmosphere. The *Times* had even done a special pull-out section with a look back at the cop-killer trial, a timeline for the current case, side-by-side columns on the respective careers of Karp and O'Dowd, and various legal experts weighing in on the likely strategies of the two sides.

When Karp entered the courtroom and took a seat at the prosecution table, he put away his thoughts and concerns about Marlene and Dirty Warren. He had a job to do, and his wife was as capable as anyone he knew. It was time to get his game face on.

Taking a deep breath and letting it out, he relaxed and chuckled quietly. *It's always been the same,* he thought, *regardless of the nature of the competition, whether as a kid in high school or college playing ball or here in the courtroom. Once the contest begins, all of the anxieties, uncertainties, and general angst evaporate.*

All of the preparation and laser focus always paid off. When the games began, he went into a performance zone and played it out with all of the zeal and vigor he could muster.

Kenny Katz sat to his right, fussing with the large three-ring binders that contained the thousands of pages of police reports, transcripts, motions, and photographs. Glancing back at the gallery, Karp saw several faces he recognized as detectives on Fulton's squad sprinkled in the crowd. Detective Sergeant Mike Cordova sat behind him in the first row, speaking quietly into the microphone clipped to his lapel.

Over on the defense side, a half-dozen members of Megan O'Dowd's staff occupied the first bench, including her chief clerk, Elijah, a decent young black man who'd introduced himself when Karp entered the courtroom, though not without first checking to make sure his boss wasn't present. Of the others, three were large black males whose main purpose seemed to be as bodyguards for O'Dowd; they spent a lot of time glaring at the prosecution table and staring down people in the gallery. The other two were white — a young man with Rastafarian dreadlocks hanging nearly to the middle of his back who seemed to be a gofer and a plump, dark-haired, middle-aged woman who sat quietly taking notes.

When his eyes flicked to the defense team itself, he saw that O'Dowd and Jabbar were both looking at him with smirks on their faces. He was reminded of the scene in his office before court, when he, Katz, Ray Guma, and his administrative assistant, Gilbert Murrow, had gathered to watch the news on television and witnessed the arrival of O'Dowd at the courthouse.

"This ought to be good," Guma had exclaimed.

O'Dowd did not disappoint him. Although there were empty places along the sidewalk, the cab she was in had conveniently stopped where a group of a dozen protesters, both black and white, were marching in a circle, carrying signs with such pithy slogans as "KKK Karp" and "Free Imam Jabbar from the Terrorist State" and "White Justice, Black Lynching."

314

Into this group, O'Dowd had emerged from the interior of the cab like a water buffalo climbing out of a mud hole. With a shout, the reporters and cameramen had converged on her. Someone in the crowd of journalists had yelled a question: "What do you think of the protesters?"

"My brothers and sisters on the streets know the truth," O'Dowd had shouted back as she adjusted her purple dashiki and green *gele* head wrap. "This government will do anything to silence its critics. It cannot be trusted to do the right thing. The black man has known this for more than three hundred years, and some enlightened white folks are catching on now, too."

"Bet ya a slice of pizza, she paid for that question to be asked." Guma had snorted.

"I'll see your bet," Katz had replied, "and raise you another slice that she also paid for her 'brothers and sisters' from the streets to be here."

O'Dowd had made a pretense of trying to push her way through the throng, though no one in their right mind would have really dared to stand in her way. She'd paused as though exasperated.

"Is your client a terrorist?" the same reporter had shouted.

"The only terrorists here are government

terrorists," she'd replied. "I expect to prove at trial that Miriam Juma Khalifa, my client's loyal and much-missed receptionist, by the way, was murdered by agents working for the United States government."

"Why?" the man had shouted again.

"I can think of a number of reasons," the defense attorney had said. "Possibly to prevent her from exposing them or to frame my client and others. But I suggest you ask Mr. Karp that question."

Now in the courtroom, with their expressions somewhere between arrogant and smug, O'Dowd and Jabbar were looking at him as if they expected an answer. But he gave them one they didn't expect. A wink.

It wasn't his normal practice to bait the opposition, but in this case, he wanted to judge their reactions. Jabbar's face clouded over with doubt before he regained control and casually looked away as if he couldn't be bothered. However, O'Dowd's countenance positively radiated hatred.

It surprised him a little that an old warhorse like O'Dowd wasted her time on such a useless emotion in the courtroom. He personally didn't like her or care for her ethical lapses, though she was an effective lawyer; but he didn't hate her or let his feelings for her enter the picture when it came to trying the case.

In general, Karp had enormous respect for the defense bar and believed that his adversaries should operate under different standards from the DAO's. His duty was to seek the truth, no matter where it led. But the defense obligation was to vigorously challenge the government's case, aggressively question the evidence, fiercely cross-examine the witnesses, and force the prosecution to prove a defendant's guilt beyond a reasonable doubt.

It was intended to be an adversarial relationship, but only rarely did that carry over to a personal level. He certainly had known defense attorneys who did not like him. He could be pugnacious and abrasive in court, and it didn't help his popularity with the defense bar that he'd only once lost a major felony case in a career where he'd personally tried to verdict more than two hundred felons. But even then, there was usually mutual respect, and both sides handled themselves professionally.

Only a few of the defense attorneys let their personal dislike for him affect their behavior in the courtroom. These were usually the ones who saw themselves as "radicals," and it was them against Evil Government, of which Karp and the assistant district attorneys who worked for him were the prime representatives. It wasn't about their clients so much as it was winning personal victories over their counterparts at the DAO, even if that meant bending the rules that might let violent criminals back on the streets.

O'Dowd was one of those. But Karp still didn't hate her; she wasn't worth it.

Jabbar, on the other hand, was a different kettle of fish. Karp had been fighting his kind of evil his entire career. The imam wasn't someone who in the heat of the moment stabbed or shot someone; he didn't plan a robbery and end up killing the store owner in a struggle for the gun. He'd help plan a terrorist attack that he knew from the onset would result in many deaths, including the young men he'd influenced to throw their lives away on a false cause by telling them they were dying for God.

Yet Karp didn't let his personal feelings for Jabbar get in the way of his duty. If he hadn't been one-thousand-percent convinced of the defendant's factual guilt and known that he had the legally admissible evidence to prove it, they wouldn't both have been in the courtroom that day. Disgust for Jabbar and the imam's hateful ideology had nothing to do with his reason for prosecuting him; justice did.

That didn't mean Karp couldn't use the hatred Jabbar and O'Dowd had for him to his advantage. And so he'd winked.

Twenty minutes later, Karp stood in front of the jury, placed his notes on the ledge extending out from the jury rail, and began to deliver his opening statement. Over the years, he'd come to believe that in a case like this, a good opening was almost like a summation. It covered the critical and damning evidence in narrative form that left no doubt in the jurors' minds of the defendant's overwhelming guilt. He gave his opening remarks with righteous and persuasive passion.

To heighten the drama and keep the jury attentive, after reading the indictment, he walked over to the defendant, looked him in the eye, and unequivocally assured the jury, "Simply stated, the People will prove and the evidence will demonstrate that this defendant, with his henchmen, mercilessly attacked Miriam Juma Khalifa — an innocent, unarmed, defenseless young woman — grabbed her, dragged her down the stairs leading to the basement of the mosque, beat her, tortured her. All the while, the defendant encouraged and directed the vicious assault and then orchestrated the decapitation execution of the deceased. Thereafter, with his cadre of killers, he celebrated what he had just done in a place he calls holy."

For Karp, the case on trial was not a series of separate, disconnected events. Rather, a trial was one whole, and each individual moment was connected to present a complete picture of the defendant's guilt, like each tile in a mosaic. It all started with the investigation. During that phase, he was already thinking about how the evidence would be presented at trial. The opening statement, the presentation of the People's case, and the closing summation were all integral, connected moments.

Everything Karp did now in the courtroom was designed and planned to accomplish one goal, and only one goal: to persuade the jury that Jabbar was guilty, not beyond a reasonable doubt but beyond any and all doubt. He told the jurors to see his remarks as a "preview" of the evidence. "Think of it like the table of contents to a book presented to help you to follow the evidence with that much more ease, facility, and understanding."

Throughout the opening, Karp kept an eye on Hassan Malik. He was serious and attentive, and to Karp's liking, he was wearing a well-tailored blue pinstriped suit. *So far, score one for the good guys,* he thought.

As Jabbar was charged solely with the murder of Miriam Khalifa and not with any other crimes, the prosecution and its witnesses were prohibited from discussing or even alluding to Jabbar's role in the attack on the New York Stock Exchange. He'd even been prohibited by Judge Mason from using the term *counterterrorism* because of a motion O'Dowd had won, arguing that the use of *terrorism* would "unfairly bias the jury and link my client to crimes he did not commit." Nor was Karp, because of yet another motion, to refer to the young men who had been in the basement during Miriam's murder as *jihadis*, "due to the prejudicial nature of the term."

So Karp limited his comments regarding Tran and Jojola by informing the jury that the young men in the basement were "followers" of Jabbar and that his two eyewitnesses were acting in their capacity as undercover agents for a federal law-enforcement agency investigating a case when they witnessed the murder of Miriam. He noted that the young woman had been cooperating with the investigation. "You will hear for yourselves testimony from the witness stand about what it was like for Jojola and Tran to have to watch this brutal slaughter without being able to act to save her."

Karp had followed his general outline of the prosecution case by briefly reviewing what he'd told the jurors during the selection process about the concept of acting in concert to commit murder. "Whether or not he actually held the knife doesn't matter. What does matter and what we will learn from the evidence is that the defendant participated in the planning and acted with murderous intent to execute Miriam Juma Khalifa."

He'd then concluded, "Keep an open mind until you've heard all of the evidence, because at the conclusion of the case, as the district attorney responsible for presenting the evidence on behalf of the People, I will ask you in the name of the People of the State of New York to find the defendant Jabbar guilty of the crime of murder of young Miriam in the basement of the Al-Aqsa mosque in Harlem, where the defendant desecrated that holy place by ruthlessly and viciously taking her life."

Karp rested his hands on the jury rail and looked at each juror with a solemn expression. The courtroom remained stone silent as he turned, and as he approached his seat at the prosecution table, he informed the court, "The People have concluded our opening statement. Ms. O'Dowd may proceed."

O'Dowd followed Karp's remarks by speaking for nearly three times as long, much of her opening painting a fanciful "alternative scenario" in which "thuggish" government agents "invaded the sanctity of a holy place determined to destroy Imam Jabbar at any cost . . . including murder."

She was able to use the prohibition against referring to the stock-exchange attack to make it appear that Jojola and Tran had "used subterfuge and lies — pretending to be someone they were not — to enter the mosque without a justifiable legal reason but for their own nefarious purposes."

Standing at the lectern in the well of the courtroom, her hands either on her hips or occasionally gesturing angrily toward the prosecution table, she spoke tersely. "They were looking for something, anything, to use to link Imam Jabbar to foreign Islamic nationalists who, while perhaps misguided in their tactics, are trying to throw off the shackles of oppressive capitalist governments like that of the United States. These *agents provocateurs* wanted to silence even

Imam Jabbar's moderate voice in pointing out how the actions of the United States government continue the disparity between haves and have-nots and create enemies for the rest of us peace-loving and fair-minded citizens. But these two spies could not find any legitimate evidence condemning Imam Jabbar, so they concocted a plan to frame my client for a murder he did not commit or participate in planning in any way. In fact, you will hear from another young woman, who, though it will cause her a great deal of embarrassment, will assure you that he was with her on the night Miriam Juma Khalifa was tortured and murdered."

O'Dowd noted that Jojola had been in contact with Miriam Juma Khalifa several times outside the mosque, "where he had ample opportunity to brainwash this simple, semiliterate young woman from a small fishing village in Kenya into helping with his plan to infiltrate the mosque.

"Or perhaps," O'Dowd had said, pausing for effect, "he simply threatened her with deportation, or worse, if she didn't cooperate. After all, she was a trusted employee of Imam Jabbar, who took her under his wing and gave her a good job after her husband died unexpectedly."

Unexpectedly? Karp thought when he

heard the defense attorney's comment. *You think? He probably expected to die when he set off his suicide vest inside the Third Avenue Synagogue.* But O'Dowd didn't have to worry about being called on her statement, as the judge had also acquiesced when she demanded that no references to Jamal Khalifa's murderous attack on the synagogue be allowed. "It would be an unfair 'guilt by association' inference," she'd argued, and the judge had agreed.

"Of course, Mr. Karp will say, 'Look at the evidence,' " O'Dowd said with a sneer. "He will tell you that only he has any so-called real evidence. But I'm here to tell you that the evidence was fabricated — it's all lies — and exactly what you would expect from a racist, oppressive District Attorney's Office."

Although Karp felt the heat rising to his face at O'Dowd's slander, he remained stoic and sat in his seat listening as if to a somewhat interesting dissertation by a first-year law student. However, when the defense attorney implored the jury to "keep an open mind that this case is a frame job," he leaped to his feet.

"I object!" he shouted. "Counsel knows that she has no evidence to support that ridiculous, outrageous statement impugning the honesty and integrity of not only this office but good men and women who put their lives on the line for the citizens of this country! If she has any such evidence, let her describe it now!"

The vehemence of Karp's objection took Mason by surprise. The judge merely looked at O'Dowd and said meekly, "Counsel?"

O'Dowd glared at Karp but shook her head. "I will go no further with this point at this time," she said. "But wait until cross-examination of Karp's 'good men,' as well as what witnesses for the defense will say from the stand, not Mr. Karp's bellowing protestations."

"Then the objection is sustained," Mason ruled, and admonished the jury to disregard Ms. O'Dowd's comments regarding any alleged frame of her client. He went on, "What the lawyers say is not evidence and should not be considered by you to be evidence. Continue, Ms. O'Dowd."

"As I was saying," O'Dowd said, thinly veiling her anger at the ruling, "the so-called evidence the prosecution intends to use to persuade you is fiction. What about this supposed 'meeting' in the basement of the Al-Aqsa mosque with Imam Jabbar and this mysterious cadre of followers, who rather oddly will not be called by the prosecution to testify to this event? You'd think they'd find at least one of them, wouldn't you? But they can't, because it never happened — at least, not to my client's knowledge, because he was visiting a friend that night who will testify to his actual whereabouts when Miriam Juma Khalifa was killed."

O'Dowd paused to make brief eye contact with each juror, then smirked as if she knew they, too, were in on the joke. "And what about this character of the mad assassin who supposedly was the actual killer? This crazy Russian femme fatale, Nadya Malovo? Does she even exist? And if so, where is she? And isn't it just a tad convenient that the killer has gone missing?"

The defense attorney hung her head, which she shook slowly from side to side. When she looked back up this time, her face was grim. "Or is it that Nadya Malovo is another fiction, created by a sinister and secretive government agency to cover up the actions of its own dark servants?"

As she spoke, O'Dowd turned slowly to face the prosecution table. "Perhaps Miriam realized that she was being used to harm a man who'd treated her only with kindness, her employer and spiritual leader. A man she knew had done no wrong, despite the lies the agents were drumming into her head. Maybe she threatened to expose them and had to be stopped. Or perhaps the plan all along had been to murder her and blame it on my client."

Karp started to rise. "I —"

"Don't bother," O'Dowd interrupted with a dismissive wave of her hand. "I withdraw the statement, and we'll deal with such possibilities later during the trial."

O'Dowd turned back to the jurors, whom she told that "without a doubt," the prosecution would call a man to the stand "who, if anyone, deserves to be sitting at the defense table." This man, Jabbar's former attorney Dean Newbury, she said, was under indictment himself. "And he will appear on that stand," she said, waving at the witness stand, "and attempt to save himself, and his powerful friends, by cynically throwing a man of God to the wolves."

Now O'Dowd made a point of looking at the black members of the jury. "Of course, the DA will want you to believe that Dean Newbury — wealthy, white, and one of the most powerful attorneys in the country before his arrest, a man with important friends in high places — is not getting a deal for his lies. That there's no difference between how a rich white lawyer is being treated and my poor, black client. Of course, there's nothing on paper, so we won't know what sort of sweetheart arrangement he'll get until he's actually sentenced. That's how the state does things these days. But some things you just know in your heart; don't be afraid to listen to what your heart tells you is true."

As Karp sat listening, he marveled at O'Dowd's ability to spin something out of nothing. But he knew better than to assume that some member, or even members, of the jury wouldn't buy the big lie. If the first mistake he'd made during that first trial against O'Dowd and the Harlem cop killers was how he approached jury selection, the second had been that he did not believe that a jury would buy into such an outrageous defense based on speculation and the inferences O'Dowd spun off that speculation. He'd thought any rational person would see through such a phony defense. And he had been wrong.

In the retrial, Karp had focused on witness preparation and then hammered away, nail by nail, stroke by stroke, at the defense's illusory fantasy, rebutting it by using hard and corroborating evidence. In doing so, he'd demonstrated that O'Dowd's strategy was an insult to the jurors' intelligence. He'd learned that lesson well, and never again had he taken for granted that jurors would be able to see through the smoke and mirrors. But he knew that if he stayed the course and countered O'Dowd's fiction with fact, the truth would cut through her obfuscation like a sharp knife through cheese.

17

About the same time, in the northern 'burbs of Gotham, Warren Bennett sat hunched over his coffee, alone at the long institutional dining table in the Westchester County Detention Center cafeteria. He'd never been arrested before, so it was all a terrible new experience for him. He flinched and twitched as though he was being assaulted by the cacophony of sound that washed back and forth across the big, open room, bouncing unimpeded off the gray cinder-block walls and security glass of the guard station.

Prisoners jostled, cursed, shouted, and laughed overly loudly, as if by sheer volume they could demonstrate to the other in-mates, as well as the guards, that they were not afraid. So far, the constant noise had been the most surprising and unnerving part of the hell Warren was going through. He never dreamed that even at night there was a constant din of clanging steel gates and irritated guards, as well as the snarls, screams, and cries of incarcerated men.

The noise wasn't the only issue. The whole facility reeked of ammonia, unwashed bodies, and malevolence. He'd steered clear of most of the other inmates. Those who, for one reason or another, tried to engage him in conversation quickly took offense when his Tourette's, which was threatening to flare up under the pressure, caused him to let loose a stream of profanity and twitches.

Already, he'd been threatened with beatings because of words he could not control. However, he didn't think it was his language that was causing other inmates to steer clear of him that morning in the cafeteria. It was the two large, bald Aryan Brotherhood types who sat at a table a row over and stared at him like pitbulls sizing up a toy poodle for sport. One apparently oblivious inmate started to sit down next to Warren but looked up and saw one of the heavily tattooed Aryans shake his head, so he quickly picked his tray back up and moved on.

Great! As if my life hasn't gone down the toilet already, Warren thought. *I'm falsely accused of murdering the only woman besides my sister who was ever nice to me. The only woman I've ever loved. And now I'll be spend-ing the rest of my life in a hellhole like this, only worse.* He glanced up at the Aryans, who continued to glare at him and whisper. *If I live that long.*

Warren was hungry, but he hadn't dared eat the breakfast after one of the cooks handed him a plate of reconstituted pow-dered eggs and ham and then gave his fel-low cooks a sideways glance and a smirk. He recognized the cook as one of the men he'd unintentionally cursed the night before, and he had heard the stories about inmate cooks spitting in the food of men they didn't like. So he'd settled for a cup of coffee and waited to be herded back to his cell with the others. *Maybe I'll just starve to death.*

In some ways, he didn't care what hap-pened. He'd spent much of the time since his arrest on the verge of tears. Some of it was fear, but most of it was for Michelle. Knowing that she'd died sometime after he left Saturday night and before Sunday morning, when her maid found her, he wondered if he might have somehow saved her. *Perhaps the killer had been lurking outside the home when I left. If only I'd turned around and . . . and what? Gone back and professed my love? Get a grip, Warren, you wouldn't have dared. Besides, you're no Da-*

vid Grale. What could you have done against a killer? Cursed him and twitched? . . . I could have tried . . .

Warren jumped when he saw the two Aryans stand. They were both well over six feet tall, with bulging arms and chests. The look in their eyes left no doubt that they were coming for him. He got up quickly and started trying to make his way through the other men milling around the tables toward the closest guard as his pursuers picked up their pace.

The other inmates sensed what was happening and parted like a herd of wildebeest willing to sacrifice one of their number to the lions in exchange for being left alone. Warren started to panic, his head jerking to the side and his shoulders hunching in violent shrugs. He glanced behind him and saw that the assassins were only ten feet away and closing. "Come here, you little freak," one of them snarled.

"Whoop whoop oh boy fuck me queers," Warren replied in terror. The men's eyes registered surprise and then rage as they rushed for him.

Turning to make a last dash, Warren was knocked to the ground by two dark shapes that moved past either side of him toward his attackers. On his hands and knees and still expecting to feel a blade pierce his back, he became aware that for the first time since he'd been in jail, there was silence. Fearfully, he turned and looked back at a sight that made him want to shout with relief and happiness despite the circumstances.

Standing between him and the frothing Aryans was the hulking, bearlike shape of his friend, the Walking Booger, who was so tall and wide that the would-be attacker on the other side of him couldn't be seen. However, Warren could see the face of the second attacker, which was contorted into a mask of fear and hatred as he looked at Booger's companion, a tall, thin man whose gaunt, pale face was framed by long brown hair.

David Grale and Booger came to rescue me!

"Get out of the way, you crazy motherfucker," the visible Aryan growled. He waved a sharp blade of some sort at Grale, but he seemed reluctant to get closer.

" 'Uck coooh!" shouted Booger, whose words were usually garbled even when not encumbered by a large digit stuck up his nose. The giant began to step forward, but Grale put a hand out to stop him.

"Not now, brother," Grale hissed in a low voice. "A time to die will come for these evil ones, but everything according to God's plan." He glared at the Aryans. "But you will leave this man alone," he said, pointing back at Warren, who was picking himself up. His voice was neither loud nor particularly menacing, but it carried a very real threat.

"Or what?" the unseen Aryan spat.

"Or I will cut your stomachs open and leave you squirming on the floor in your own blood and intestines," Grale replied evenly. "Eventually, I will be coming for you and your kind, so if you'd like that time to be now, ignore my request at your own peril."

The Aryan whom Warren could see looked nervously over at his companion and then back at his opponent. "I know who you are. You're Grale . . . you son of a bitch, you killed one of my brothers last year. You cut his fuckin' head off!"

The other Aryan started for Grale but was intercepted by Booger, who grabbed the man's wrist with one massive hand and put him in a headlock with the other arm, then squeezed. The Aryan screamed as his wrist bones were pulverized in the giant's grip and then slumped to the floor, whimpering and holding his damaged arm.

Grale tilted his head to the side and looked at the remaining attacker. It had all happened so quickly the other man had not had a chance to react. "You were saying?"

The Aryan kept the blade out but backed away, leaving his companion to choke and sputter on the ground. He looked past Grale at Warren and said, "We'll be waiting, you freak. Your buddies won't always be around."

Grale started forward, but the man turned and disappeared beyond the circle of inmates who'd gathered to watch the incident. Suddenly, the guards materialized, with their nightsticks out. "Break it up!" a sergeant shouted. "What happened here?" When no one spoke, he pointed his nightstick at the Aryan on the floor and then at Grale and Booger. "I couldn't care less if you assholes want to fuck each other up, but not in my jail. Do you understand me?"

The Aryan grimaced in pain as he gripped his wrist and stood. But he didn't speak as he turned and went in the direction his comrade had fled.

"But of course, brother," Grale said kindly. "And God bless you."

" 'Es, sir," Booger added. "God 'less oo."

The guard sergeant's eyes narrowed, but then he shrugged. "I don't even want to know," he said, and turned to the other inmates. "What the fuck are you numbnuts looking at? Breakfast is over, ladies. Back to your cells. Line up!"

As they stood in line, Grale turned to Warren. "Well, it appears that you're making friends in your new home. Any idea why those two wanted to hurt you?"

"No idea. I don't think I even . . . oh boy nuts balls . . . spoke to them," Warren replied. "I guess they just don't like me. But what are you guys . . . whoop whoop oh boy fuckers assholes . . . doing here?"

"After your arrest, we heard that somebody was willing to pay top dollar to have you killed," Grale responded. "So we participated in a little disorderly conduct in front of the jail. We'll be here for a few days, anyway. Given my . . . vocation, I couldn't risk a felony arrest and more scrutiny."

"I can't thank you enough," Warren said, his eyes welling with tears. "But why would . . . whoo whoo whoop . . . anybody want to have me killed? And who?"

"I don't know the answer to the second question," Grale replied. "As for the first, I'd hazard a guess that whoever killed your friend Michelle wants you dead, too. Any idea why?"

Before Warren could answer, a voice over the intercom announced, "Warren Bennett to the guard station."

"I don't know," Warren said to Grale. "But I guess I need to go. Thanks again."

18

"Sergeant Kreider, you testified that the room appeared to have been used for torture. Why do you say that?"

"There were bloody tools — pliers, a hammer — on the table, as well as what were determined to be . . . ." The police sergeant stopped speaking and passed a hand over his eyes.

A muscular, crew cut, fifteen-year NYPD veteran, Sergeant David Kreider was the SWAT police officer who had discovered Miriam Juma Khalifa's decapitated body in the basement of the mosque. During trial prep, Karp had talked at length with the officer and knew that the man had been badly shaken by what he'd seen in the mosque — a tough thing to do to a SWAT officer with his experience.

Karp walked over to the witness stand and poured water for the sergeant into a paper cup from a pitcher beside the stand. Giving water to witnesses was a touch he'd picked up many years earlier from his mentor, Mel Glass, who believed that such gestures helped "humanize" the authority figure of the prosecutor. After all, Mel would always remind his acolytes, "We are the good guys!"

He felt for the sergeant, who was obviously having a difficult time recalling that horrible scene, and the water was to allow him to regroup more than quench his thirst.

Kreider took the cup from him. "Thank you," he said as he raised it to his lips, his hand trembling.

After opening remarks, Karp had immediately jumped into the prosecution case by first calling a civil engineer who produced a set of diagrams that depicted the layout of the crime scene. The owlish-looking man had been making such diagrams for the DAO for thirty years and had described his work, which Karp hung up on an easel, with all the verve of a funeral director.

Karp had then called to the stand the police photographer who'd responded to the scene. The officer, Carrie Nimmo, was a young woman who testified professionally, but it was obvious that she, too, had been affected by Miriam's death.

When Karp had handed her prints of her

photographs taken at the scene and asked if they "fairly and accurately" depicted what she saw there, she had flipped through them quickly, swallowed hard, and nodded. "Yes, this is what I saw." And even at that, they were not the worst of the photographs she had taken, only the eight he'd felt were necessary.

This jury, he'd told Katz when explaining his reasoning during preparation, would hear plenty of witnesses testify about Miriam Juma Khalifa's suffering and death without traumatizing them with overly graphic photos.

"In a case like this, displaying the more graphic photos panders to jurors' emotions. We're much better off leaving that kind of bottom-fishing and speculation to the defense. And why give O'Dowd a reason to argue that the photographs are so shocking that their value as evidence is far outweighed by their prejudicial effect on the emotions of the jury and unfair to her client?" he'd said. "Leaving them out means fewer grounds for an appellate court to consider." He preferred a photograph of the pretty, smiling victim holding her young son when she was alive as a reminder to the jurors of what had been lost.

With Nimmo, Karp had been able to do a

"double direct," essentially having the photographer testify twice. The first time was to identify the photographs as being fair and accurate representations of the crime scene, and the second was when Karp had her step down from the witness stand and go over to the easel where the civil engineer's diagrams hung.

With each of the crime-scene photographs entered into evidence, Karp would have Nimmo draw a circle on the easel to indicate where she had been standing when she took the photograph. Then he had her place the exhibit number inside the circle and draw an arrow from the circle in the direction her lens was facing. "And where were you standing when you took the photograph of the digital movie camera, People's Exhibit six? And for People's Exhibit seven, the chair with the pool of blood?"

The testimony of the engineer and the photographer had taken up the rest of the morning. Then, after lunch, he'd called Sergeant Kreider to the stand.

As they'd discussed before his appearance on the witness stand, Kreider had let Karp lead him through the tricky business of what an NYPD SWAT officer was doing in the mosque in the first place. With O'Dowd poised and ready to jump to her feet to object to any missteps, they had told the jury that Jabbar had been arrested on another unrelated charge and that the officer and his team were serving a search warrant in connection with that arrest.

Kreider had then described how he'd found the body lying on the floor in a large pool of blood. The head of the deceased, the sergeant had said, his voice growing tight, was on a table in another room "that had apparently been used to torture the young woman."

"Objection!" O'Dowd had shouted. "What this witness knew about the room is pure conjecture! 'Apparently' is just another word for 'I guess.' As your honor knows, we will be presenting witness testimony that my client was not even in the mosque, much less a participant in torture, *if* that is what actually occurred in this room, which has not been established yet."

"He's describing a murder scene that he witnessed personally," Karp had countered.

"There's no reason for this part of the officer's testimony except to inflame the jury's sensibilities with a questionable horror story that has nothing to do with my client," O'Dowd had shot back.

"It has everything to do with your client,

counsel," Karp had replied evenly. "Mr. Jabbar —"

"Imam Jabbar."

"Your client is charged with murder that
included the use of torture and instruments
of torture."

"You have nothing to place Imam Jabbar
in that room!" O'Dowd had bellowed.

Karp had turned to address Judge Mason.
"Most respectfully," he'd said shaking his
head, "there she goes again, your honor. As
counsel well knows since we engaged in
pretrial hearings regarding the torture issue
the People have overwhelming evidence, to
be sure, that puts the defendant at the scene
and as an active participant. So I ask the
court to take the sergeant's testimony
subject to connection to the other evidence
that will be forthcoming shortly. Everything,
as your honor well knows, has an order to
it."

Mason had pursed his lips. While he
would thwart Karp where possible, he
wasn't going to obstruct the DA when the
facts and the law were so clear. It was obvious that O'Dowd had overstepped the limits
of propriety. "You're correct, Mr. Karp, the
record has so reflected. Your objection is
overruled, Ms. O'Dowd," he'd said, looking
sorrowfully at the defense attorney.

Karp had nodded. "Thank you, your honor." He'd waited for O'Dowd to sit back down hard and angry in her seat and then turned back to his witness. "Sergeant Kreider, you said that the room appeared to have been used for torture. Why do you say that?"

As Karp waited for the officer to drink and settle himself, he glanced toward the gallery and happened to catch the eye of the plump middle-aged woman who sat with the defense team in the first bench beyond O'Dowd's table. She gave him a quick, thin smile but looked quickly back down at her notepad as if embarrassed to have been caught looking. He hadn't seen her do much else during the trial except take notes and assist Elijah with the file boxes and folders that had to be toted to the courtroom every morning from O'Dowd's office in Harlem. *Maybe she's learning to be a paralegal,* he thought absently, though surprised that O'Dowd would hire a white woman.

"I'm sorry, where were we?" Kreider said as he put the cup back down on the stand's railing.

"Of course," Karp replied, turning back to his witness. "I had asked you what gave you the impression that the smaller of the two rooms on the diagram was used for torture. And you said there were bloody tools and . . . ?"

"And the fingernails of the deceased," Kreider said, finishing the sentence.

"Tell us precisely what you observed," Karp said.

"The deceased's hands were a mess," the sergeant said. "Her fingers were broken and disjointed. Where her fingernails were supposed to be were just bloody stumps. She'd been beaten so badly she was almost unrecognizable."

Karp paused, waiting for the horror and brutality inflicted on Miriam to filter through each of the jurors. After a few moments, he softly asked the sergeant what, if anything, he had noticed in the room where Miriam's body was discovered.

"There was a large green handwritten banner — about twelve feet long and maybe three wide — taped to one wall," Kreider said.

"Do you know what was written on it?" Karp asked.

"I do not," Kreider replied. "It was a foreign language."

"Was there anything else of note about the room?" Karp asked.

"There was a digital movie camera," Kreider said.

"Where was it in relationship to the rest of the room?"

"It was in front . . ." The officer hesitated to gather himself. "It was in front of the body."

"Was it pointed in any particular direction?"

Kreider tilted his head to the side and looked down at the floor. He looked back up at the jury and nodded. "It was pointed toward the body."

"Were you, or a crime-scene technician, able to retrieve any information from the camera?" Karp asked.

The officer shook his head. "No, the memory card had been removed."

"Do you know where the memory card is?"

"No."

Karp had Kreider get down from the stand and go over to the easel. There he retraced his steps on the diagram of the crime scene, People's Exhibit one in evidence.

After a few more questions, Karp took his seat, and O'Dowd rose and slowly made her way to the lectern for cross-examination. "Sergeant Kreider," she began, "if, say, a white Presbyterian minister had been arrested on some charge, would you have obtained a search warrant and then stormed his church looking for so-called evidence?"

Kreider shrugged. "First, we . . . I mean, our SWAT team, didn't 'storm' anything. And second, it depends if there was a reason to enter the church, any church — say we suspected that whatever the defendant was involved in was tied to the church — then yes, we would have searched the church."

"Or when you say, 'It depends,' do you mean it depends on whether he's a white Presbyterian minister or a black imam of a mosque?" O'Dowd shot back.

Kreider kept his cool. "It didn't matter what color or nationality Mr. Jabbar was when my team and I were assigned to search the mosque," the sergeant replied.

"With a heavily armed, jack-booted SWAT team?" O'Dowd asked.

Rising from his seat, Karp interjected. "Objection! Yet again, Ms. O'Dowd dishonors the proceedings with a political rant having absolutely no evidentiary basis."

"Sustained. Ms. O'Dowd, please let's keep the rhetoric to a dull roar," Mason said with a smile.

O'Dowd returned the smile. "But of course, your honor. I didn't mean to imply that Sergeant Kreider or his men were anything but good soldiers." She turned back to the witness. "Of course, Sergeant Kreider, it didn't matter at all to you, did it, that the imam and his congregation were black?"

Kreider cocked his head to the side and held the defense attorney's stare. "I was unaware that white people are not allowed to be of that faith."

Karp suppressed a smile. It was good to see Kreider fighting back.

The remark seemed to stun O'Dowd for a moment. She cast a quick glance at the jurors, several of whom had smiled at the sergeant's rejoinder. "Thank you for the unnecessary and specious comment, sergeant. But let's stick with actually answering my question: Were you aware that Imam Jabbar and his congregation were African-Americans?"

Kreider nodded. "I knew that he was and that some were. But I did not know that all members of the congregation were black, no."

"And how did you know that Imam Jabbar was black?"

Karp's eyebrows shot up. He saw her mistake before she did, and then it was too late. It was obvious she thought Kreider would have to say he had been informed of that fact by a superior or another agency. She was surprised, therefore, by the answer.

"I saw him on the television after the nine-eleven attacks," Kreider said. "He said that only men of the 'one true faith' would have the courage to attack the World Trade Center."

O'Dowd whirled to face Mason. "Your honor, may we approach the bench?"

"Of course."

Karp rose and walked to the judge's dais, where O'Dowd angrily hissed. "I demand a mistrial. The prosecution witness just painted my client as a terrorist for exercising his First Amendment right and took that statement out of context."

"The First Amendment doesn't protect the defendant from making offensive comments that might come back to haunt him," Karp pointed out. "And the witness did not paint the defendant as anything. He was asked a question about how he knew the defendant was black, and he simply, accurately reported."

"He could have just said that he saw him on television," O'Dowd snarled.

"Your honor, Ms. O'Dowd opened the door, and the witness, in a manner of speaking, slammed it shut," Karp said. "Sergeant Kreider was directly responsive to Ms.

O'Dowd's open-ended question."

O'Dowd glared, and then her face turned red when the judge denied her motion for a mistrial. "Mr. Karp is correct," Mason said. "You opened the door, and, as Mr. Karp said, the witness was directly responsive to your question. My advice is that you should be more careful." Both counsels resumed their places, Karp at the prosecution table and O'Dowd at the lectern.

O'Dowd then addressed the witness. "Sergeant Kreider, is it true that the NYPD sent you to serve the search warrant at the request of a federal law-enforcement agency?"

"Yes."

"Was this agency headed by a man named Stephen Paul Jaxon?"

"I believe that's correct."

O'Dowd walked over to the defense table and picked up a piece of paper. She walked to the witness. "Is it also true that in March 2005, you applied to the FBI Academy at Quantico?"

"Yes."

O'Dowd handed him the piece of paper. "Is this, in fact, a copy of your application?"

The sergeant glanced at it and nodded. "Yes."

O'Dowd held out her hand and took the

piece of paper back from him. "Your honor, I would like this Federal Bureau of Investigation employment application admitted into evidence."

Karp rose to his feet. He had hoped for this attack on the sergeant's credibility. During trial prep, he and the sergeant had covered this issue in depth. "Your honor, I request a *voir dire* on the relevance and provenance of this document. Moreover, your honor, it matters not if the witness applied to the FBI some five years ago."

"It goes to the witness's credibility," O'Dowd retorted. "It is clearly a possible reason why this man might be eager to cooperate with a federal agency in the hopes of getting another job he covets."

"Local, state, and national law-enforcement agencies cooperate all the time," Karp replied. "They're not all auditioning for employment. However, I am entitled to a *voir dire* on this offer of evidence."

"Very well, Mr. Karp, proceed, but I want it to be very limited," Mason said.

Karp turned to the witness and asked, "Sergeant, how are cases assigned to you?"

"Just depends, Mr. Karp, who's on duty at a particular time when a matter arises that requires the SWAT team to respond to a crime scene."

"Have you ever requested a specific assignment when a federal agency was the requesting authority?" Karp asked.

"Never."

"As a matter of fact, is it against the protocols for anyone on the NYPD SWAT team to make such a request?"

"Absolutely."

"So, it's fair to say that you go where you're directed, whether it's at the behest of a federal agency or anyone else — you follow orders. Is that correct?"

"Yes, sir."

Karp walked over to the defense table and held out his hand for the application. "With respect to this application, you filled it out five years ago. Is that fair to say?"

"Yes."

"So, there was a period of time when you felt you might want to work for the FBI. Is that right?"

"Yes."

"But your application for employment with the FBI was rejected. Is that right?"

"Yes."

"And you never made another application again. Is that correct?"

"You are correct, sir."

"Your honor, this whole application issue

is completely irrelevant to any of the issues of importance before this court; it is of absolutely no value and will prove to have a negative impact on the defense. But I'm going to withdraw my objection. Thank you very much," he said. He returned to the prosecution table and, with his back to the jury, gave Katz a wink. When seated, he whispered in Katz's ear, "She took the bait, hook, line, and sinker."

"Very well, then." The judge nodded. "Ms. O'Dowd, you may proceed."

"Thank you, your honor," O'Dowd said. "Sergeant Kreider, what came of your application?"

"I passed the tests . . ."

"And?"

"I was rejected after a background check."

"Oh." O'Dowd feigned surprise. "Why was that?"

"It was a personal issue."

"And what was this personal issue?"

Kreider took in a deep breath and let it out slowly. He and Karp had been over this; they knew it was coming. It didn't make it easier. "I was placed on leave by the NYPD for being drunk on the job."

"And for this, you were not allowed to join the FBI. Correct?"

"Yes."

O'Dowd stroked her chin as though she was trying to put together a difficult picture puzzle. "Does this mean you can never join the FBI?"

"I don't want to," Kreider replied. "I'm happy where I'm at."

"So you say," O'Dowd countered. "But humor me. Could you still reapply?"

Kreider shook his head. "Yes, technically, but . . ."

"But you'd probably be rejected again, unless perhaps they owed you a favor?"

"No. I was going to say that I like what I do. The FBI was a passing fancy."

O'Dowd smiled and turned her back on him as she faced the jury. "So you say." She quickly turned again to the witness. "Sergeant Kreider, was there any particular reason you were the first police officer on the scene when you 'discovered' Miriam Juma Khalifa's body?"

Kreider's eyebrows converged. "It was my assignment to lead the way into the basement. Others were assigned to different parts of the mosque."

"It had nothing to do with you wanting to 'help' the FBI frame my client?"

"Objection!" Karp roared. "Your honor, it is outrageous that counsel continues to make assertions about the integrity of this man without a scintilla of proof, nor will she be able to provide any evidence during the course of this trial. I would like her admonished for this repeated outlandish and disingenuous effort to redirect the jury's attention from the facts and into the realm of pure fiction."

"I am merely asking a question," O'Dowd said innocently.

"Enough!" Judge Mason barked. "I will sustain the objection, though I will choose whom to admonish in this courtroom, Mr. Karp, and will not be bullied by you. Ms. O'Dowd, please continue, but watch the extracurricular stuff."

"Of course, your honor. Sergeant Kreider, did you have information beforehand about what you would find in the basement of the Al-Aqsa mosque?"

"No, I did not."

"You're sure?"

"Objection. Asked and answered, your honor," Karp said.

"Sustained. Move on, Ms. O'Dowd," Mason ordered.

"And you have no idea what became of the digital movie camera's memory card?"

"No, I do not."

"So, if that memory card holds information that might prove my client wasn't in the basement during the murder of the deceased, that information is now missing?"

"Objection, your honor, and likewise, it very well would also show that he was there and engaged in the murder," Karp said.

"Ms. O'Dowd?" Mason asked, looking at the defense attorney with a raised eyebrow.

"Okay, your honor, I'll withdraw the question," she responded.

O'Dowd walked over to the lectern and reviewed her notes. After a moment, she looked up. "Sergeant Kreider, when your heavily armed SWAT team invaded the Al-Aqsa mosque, did you encounter any resistance?"

"We didn't invade anything. We simply entered, and there was no resistance."

"So, the NYPD thought it best to send your Special Weapons and Tactics team, weapons drawn, boots thudding up and down the corridors and rooms, to a place of worship."

"We always approach a search-warrant situation expecting we might meet resistance and better safe than sorry."

"But all you found, as far as people, were peaceful worshipers?"

"That is correct. And the body of the victim."

"Sergeant Kreider, do you have anything

against people of the Muslim faith?"

"No."

"Sergeant Kreider, are you a racist?"

Karp jumped up. "Just a minute, your honor. I demand an offer of proof for the bona fides of the legitimacy of that question. A question that comes out of left field. This is just another defense attempt to smear a witness by asking objectionable questions simply for effect."

"Sustained," Mason shot back.

"No further questions, your honor."

Karp didn't wait for O'Dowd to reach her seat before he was up and walked quickly over to the jury rail. "Sergeant Kreider, how many times have you been shot in the line of duty?" he asked.

"Objection," O'Dowd, as expected, said. "This subject was not part of my cross-examination, and therefore is improper for redirect."

"On the contrary, your honor," Karp argued. "She attacked the witness's credibility. I am within my rights to rehabilitate this man's good name."

Mason thought about it. This was one of those instances where fighting Karp would come back to bite him on the backside. "I'll allow it. The witness may answer the question."

"I've been shot twice in the line of duty," Kreider said quietly.

"Have you received any awards of merit, any decorations for bravery?"

"Yes, sir. I have received five Police Combat Crosses, three Medals of Valor, and one Medal of Honor."

"Was one of the Medals of Valor tied to an incident in which you were shot?"

"Yes, sir."

"What happened?"

"It was a hostage situation. I was trying to get the hostage out of the room when I was shot in the back by one of the kidnappers."

"Did you almost die?"

"Yes, sir. In fact, I did die, but they were able to revive me at the hospital."

"Sergeant Kreider, where did this shooting take place?"

"One Hundred Sixteenth and Manhattan Avenue in Harlem."

"What race was the hostage?"

"She was black."

"Did that matter to you when you very nearly lost your life to help her?"

"No, sir. It did not. She needed help. I did my job."

Karp smiled. O'Dowd had chosen the wrong police officer to attack, though she had little choice based on her defense strategy. But now he would administer the coup de grace.

"Sergeant Kreider, would you please tell the jury how you came to be awarded the Medal of Honor?"

A shadow passed over the man's face, but he nodded. "I really didn't do anything a lot of other guys didn't do. But anyway, I was outside the World Trade Center when it was hit on nine-eleven. I went into the building and brought a few people out."

"A few people?" Karp asked. He walked over to the prosecution table, where Kenny Katz handed him a piece of paper, which he took to the sergeant. "Is this a letter of commendation, signed by the mayor and members of the city council, that accompanied your Medal of Honor?"

"Yes, sir."

Karp took the letter back. "Your honor, I move that this letter be received in evidence."

"Ms. O'Dowd?"

"No objection."

"Very well, the letter is so admitted."

Karp looked down at the letter. "You just told us you went into the burning tower and brought a few people out. Do you consider more than two hundred people to be a few?"

"I suppose not."

"It says here in this commendation letter that you went back into the building three times to bring people to safety, and, I quote, 'at great risk to his own life' and while others stood by and watched. Is that true?"

"It was something like that. I was just in the wrong place at the right time."

"For which more than two hundred people, as well as the citizens of this city, are grateful," Karp said.

Karp stuck his hands into his pockets and rocked back on his heels as he looked up at the ceiling for a moment. "Sergeant Kreider, you just testified that you were turned down by the FBI because of an alcohol problem. When was this problem?"

Kreider hung his head. "End of 2001, most of 2002."

"Had you been a big drinker before then?"

The sergeant shook his head and cleared his throat before he could answer. "No, sir. Hardly at all."

"Do you know why you started drinking heavier at the end of 2001?" Karp asked quietly.

Kreider wiped at his nose and nodded. "My brother . . ." he started, but had to stop and take a sip of water. "My brother, Jon, he was a police officer, too, and he . . ." The sergeant stifled a sob. "He was there, too. We both were. He went in one more time than me, but that last time . . . he didn't come back out."

"Your brother died in the World Trade Center?" Karp said softly but clearly.

"Yes." The sergeant no longer tried to raise his head and look at the jurors. He wiped at his eyes.

"I'm sorry, Sergeant Kreider, I truly am," Karp said. "Was your brother awarded the Medal of Honor posthumously?"

The man's shoulders were shaking as he cried, but he managed to say, "Yes."

"And it was after this that you started to drink?"

Kreider lifted his head, his eyes full of the tears that were not yet rolling down his cheeks. "Yes, sir. I went on quite the bender."

"And you were placed on a leave of absence after you were determined to be under the influence while on the job?"

"Yes, sir. I was drunk pretty much twenty-four/seven."

"What did you do about it?"

"I had a dream . . ."

"I object. Your honor, are we now going to listen to a recollection of a dream as evidence in a murder trial?" O'Dowd asked.

"Overruled," the judge said. "You may

answer the question, sergeant."

"I had a dream in which my brother told me to get my shit, pardon the expression, together," Kreider said, a small smile coming to his face despite the tears. "So I entered rehab, and I've been sober since September 11, 2002."

"But you were still turned down by the FBI?"

"Yes, sir. They get a lot of applications and can afford to be choosy."

"Why not reapply? Surely, now that you've been sober for so long, they might reconsider."

Kreider shrugged. "They might, but like I said, it was just something I did because of some of the memories I have about nine-eleven. I even thought about it again a couple of years ago, but I realized I couldn't leave."

"Why?"

"Because this is my city. These are my people." The sergeant paused, then grinned. "And my brother would kick my ass when I see him again."

19

Marlene paced back and forth in the interview room of the Westchester County Detention Facility as she waited for Warren Bennett to arrive. Her mind was racing ahead. The case she'd taken on the spur of the moment to help a casual friend who needed her help to protect his rights had changed dramatically with her visit to his apartment.

No longer was it just a case of "Did he do it, or did he not?" and making sure he had effective counsel. She was now convinced not only that someone else had killed Michelle Oakley, which is what she believed all along, but that the killer was actively trying to make Warren take the fall. *And that's a whole new ball of wax,* she thought. *Frame jobs take planning.*

She reviewed what she knew, looking for the key to the puzzle. Somebody had tossed Warren's walk-up, which meant they were willing to take a chance that some detective like her cousin would notice and jump to the same conclusion she had. If the murder wasn't somehow connected to Warren, the killer would not have ransacked the apartment.

So, why? . . . Come on, it's obvious, Marlene. The killer thinks Warren knows something . . . No, that's not it, or not all of it . . . They went to his apartment . . . they think he has something they want . . . but what? . . . Something that got Michelle killed and worth going through the trouble, and risk, of framing Warren . . . if he's innocent . . . God damn it, listen to your gut, of course he is!

On the drive over to Westchester County from Manhattan, she'd reminded herself again and again to keep an open mind about Warren's possible involvement in Oakley's murder. It was possible that he had killed her, or maybe he let someone into the house who then killed her. It was also possible that the mess in the apartment was caused by a neighborhood thief who'd heard he'd been arrested and took advantage of the situation. Maybe the burglar got frightened off before he could grab the DVD player and television.

She had to admit to herself that she didn't know much about Warren Bennett, though he'd been part of her family's crazy life for years. But up to this point, he'd mostly existed as one of the many colorful characters who made up New York City's street life — a character in a real play being acted out on the sidewalks, alleys, and thoroughfares of big, indifferent Gotham. She'd talked to him from time to time but always in passing, and neither had delved into the other's personal life beyond "How are you?"

Butch knew him better. It was one of the things she loved about her husband. He was often portrayed by the defense bar, and the bar's friends in the liberal press, as the hardhearted, by-the-book prosecutor, but she knew differently. A person's wealth or station wasn't as important to him as what that person said and did. He would treat the lowliest street person with respect and courtesy, stopping to talk to those who were ignored by the rest of society or to buy a man a hot cup of cocoa from a street vendor on a cold day. And she knew he genuinely enjoyed chatting with Warren and playing their movie-trivia game.

Still, he'd conceded that morning that what he *really* knew about "Dirty Warren" wasn't much other than that he liked movies, was very bright, lived somewhere in the

East Village, was mysteriously connected to David Grale and the city's underground Mole People, and worked hard to make a living.

Butch was also an excellent judge of character. "And it's going to take hard, irrefutable evidence — hell, maybe even a confession — to convince me that he's guilty," he'd said that morning when he called after he got to the office. "But I guess we'll have to let justice take its course."

With maybe just a little push from me, Marlene thought when she arrived at the Westchester detention center in Valhalla.

But she was learning more about Warren, starting when she announced herself to the desk sergeant in the jail lobby. A young woman who'd been standing nearby walked up and introduced herself as Warren's sister, Shannon Bennett. "Are you his lawyer?"

"If he wants me to be," Marlene had replied. "I was trying to protect his rights when he was arrested, so I identified myself as such, but I'll leave the decision up to him when I see him. Has the family retained someone else?"

"No, no," Shannon had replied quickly. "We . . . I appreciate that you are helping him. I wanted you to know that I will pay your fees."

Marlene had smiled. She already liked the pretty young woman with the high patrician forehead, red hair, sea-foam green eyes, and porcelain complexion. "That won't be necessary. If he wants me to stay on, I'm doing it pro bono."

"Pro bono?"

"Latin. Means 'for the good,' which is a fancy way of saying no charge." Marlene had looked around the lobby. "Are your parents here? I'd like to talk to them about Warren."

Shannon had bit her lip and shaken her head. "No. They're . . . well, not here. They love Warren, but I'm afraid they've never handled his Tourette's very well, and his offbeat sense of humor doesn't help. It makes them uncomfortable to be around him, though they ask me about him if they know I've gone to see him in the city. But now this — it's sort of a self-fulfilling prophecy for them; they told him that if he moved to New York City, no good would come of it. Of course, he ignored them." Shannon had stopped and then laughed bitterly. "Sort of ironic, don't you think? He was fine in Manhattan and got into this mess by coming back to Purchase."

Marlene had nodded. "I'm sure this came as a shock to the family. But I'd be interested in anything at all that helps me defend him."

"Well, I probably know him better than anyone," Shannon had replied. "So, why don't you ask me your questions, and I'll see if I can answer them?"

"Let's start with a tough one. Have you ever known him to react violently if he gets angry?"

Shannon had tensed and frowned. "I see you think he could have done this. I —"

Marlene had interrupted. "No, I'm just trying to cover all the bases. If he tells me he's innocent, and that's what he said last night, then that's how we'll go forward, and we'll make the prosecutor prove that he's guilty. But if he tells me that he accidentally, or in a fit of rage, struck Michelle, killing her, then the defense strategy changes. I do have to worry about what the prosecution might try to bring up regarding his past behavior. If there are any issues we need to address . . . ?"

Shannon's shoulders had sagged, and she'd nodded as a tear slipped down her cheek. "I'm sorry. I guess I was being a bit defensive. But no, I've never seen Warren violent. In fact, he's the gentlest person I've ever known. I've often wished he would fight back more, but it's just not his nature."

"What was his relationship with Michelle Oakley?"

Shannon had brightened back up. "He's had a crush on her since junior high school. I think they were pretty good friends for a while. I was quite a bit younger, and, as the snot-nosed kid sister, I wasn't allowed to tag along, but this one summer, they were together all the time. She was one of the most popular girls in the high school, and he was, well, he was Warren. He never felt he could compete with the other boys, and at that age, he probably couldn't have. Michelle was just a teenager, too, and she enjoyed her popularity."

Shannon had paused and looked as if she was going to say one thing but then changed her mind.

"I'm six years or so younger than Michelle, so I didn't really get to know her until this past year when I moved back home after my divorce. I still can't say I know her that well, but I'd see her, and we'd talk at the club or parties in the old neighborhood. She's really nice but struck me as sad. Her parents lost a lot of their money, and her dad was convicted for fraud of some sort; then her mother committed suicide, and her dad died in prison. On top of that, she had several failed marriages. Really just a sad, sad story. I know she was having a hard time making ends meet, though I have to say she seemed to have been doing better lately."

"She get a new job?" Marlene had asked. She'd noticed Shannon's initial change of mind and saw her hesitate again now.

"Not that I'm aware of. We didn't talk about that kind of thing much."

"So, you were telling me about their relationship."

"Yes, of course. There's not much to tell," Shannon had said. "I know she had good memories of Warren and asked about him whenever I saw her. But he's one step away from living on the streets and is pretty much a loner with his Tourette's. Meanwhile, she is . . . was . . . a Westchester County socialite, even if she'd fallen on hard times."

"Did he tell you that he was going to see her on Saturday night?"

Shannon had laughed. "It was all he could talk about after my birthday party. That she had asked him over for dinner. I think he took two showers that day and made me help him with his hair and clothes. I don't think I've seen him that excited ever. Of course, his Tourette's was acting up from the stress; he was cursing a mile a minute and hopping around like the Energizer

Bunny. But I wasn't worried about it. The funny thing is, Michelle always had a calming effect on him when they were younger — more so even than me, and I was pretty much his best friend. I was sure he would be okay once he got over the initial butterflies."

Marlene had reached out and touched the younger woman's arm. "I know you've answered a similar question from me. But could it be possible that Warren hoped that something might happen between himself and Michelle, and if rejected instead, he lashed out?"

Shannon had paused to consider the question but again shook her head. "He's been rejected all of his life — by his friends, by his family, by employers, and, especially, by women — and he's always just swallowed his disappointments and gone on with his life. Why would that change now?" The young woman had held Marlene's gaze. "No, even if he hoped for something more, if Michelle wasn't interested — and I know she would have been nice about it — he would have pretended it didn't matter and then crawled back to New York City with his tail between his legs."

Suddenly, Shannon's eyes had blazed with anger.

"He would not have hurt her and especially wouldn't have done what the newspaper said."

"The alleged sexual assault?" Marlene had asked.

The young woman had nodded but couldn't speak.

"First off, we don't know if that report is even true," Marlene had said.

"Then how can they print something like that?"

Marlene had shrugged. "Because the press — or at least a significant percentage of them — are no longer accountable for what they print and broadcast. They hide behind anonymous sources or no sources at all and simply state their guesswork as fact. They are not their own masters anymore but are the tools of people with hidden agendas. Or they have their own hidden agendas and pretend the opinions, rumors, and stuff they just plain make up are from off-the-record conversations with sources they claim are 'close to the investigation.' But the important thing is how we deal with that information, if it is true that she was sexually assaulted."

Marlene had fished in her purse and found a package of tissues, which she handed to Shannon.

"If it makes you feel any better, my husband doesn't believe Warren did it, and neither do I. We think we know him better than that. I don't know if he's ever said anything about it to you, but he's acted courageously in a couple of incidents that he'll never get credit for, but he actually saved many lives."

Shannon had stopped wiping at her nose and given Marlene an incredulous look. "Really? Warren? Superhero stuff? He never said anything about it."

Marlene had looked at her watch and then at the desk sergeant, who motioned her over. "I guess he's the strong, silent type. Anyway, I've got to go see him now, and I'm sure you know the grand jury is meeting this afternoon. I expect they'll indict him, simply because it's all about what the prosecutor says, and I won't be able to be there to give another perspective." She'd reached back into her purse and produced a business card. "This is my private cell number. Call anytime. And nothing, no detail, is too small to tell me. You never know what piece of a puzzle completes the picture. Then someday, when this is all over, we'll all sit down for a few adult drinks, and I'll tell you about your heroic big brother. Deal?"

Shannon had sniffed and smiled. "Deal."

Marlene stopped pacing when the door to the interview room clicked open and Warren stepped in. He looked surprised, and she could tell that he'd been crying, but when he saw her, he smiled.

"Hi, Marlene! Are you going to . . . oh boy ohhhh boy tits and ass . . . going to be my lawyer?" he asked.

"Hi, Warren. I'd be honored if you'd like me to represent you."

Warren's smile faded a little. "I can't afford much," he said. "I can sell my newsstand, but I don't know what . . . whoop oh boy . . . I'll get for it or how fast I can do it."

Marlene waved dismissively. "That won't be necessary. I'm doing this as a friend."

"I don't . . . whoop ass . . . like taking handouts."

"Well, then, think of it as payback for all that you've done to help my family," Marlene replied. "Especially Butch. Please, we can't repay the debt we owe you, but this would be a token of appreciation."

Warren's smile returned. "I don't know . . . oh boy oh boy fucker . . . about all that, but I'm glad you're here. How's my cat?"

"Brando is fine," Marlene replied. "Which brings me to my first question. This might seem like an odd one, and I don't want you to be embarrassed, but I need you to be as honest as you can. Would you describe how you keep your apartment as neat or messy?"

Puzzled, Warren shrugged. "Well, I'm a little on the obsessive-compulsive side," he replied. "I like everything to be in its . . . my my my balls . . . place. My life is such a mess otherwise because of Tourette's that I probably go a bit overboard with the things I can control."

"Would it surprise you that when the police showed up this morning to search your apartment, your clothes were scattered all over the place, as was your collection of DVDs?"

"I was . . . whoop whoop suck me . . . robbed?" Warren cried out. The muscles around his right eye began twitching violently, making it appear that he was winking rapid-fire at her.

Marlene gestured toward the stool on the opposite side of the table and took a seat herself. "I don't know for sure," she said. "But if you were, they weren't after any of your personal possessions — the DVD player, the television, your movies, nothing appeared to be missing. Did you have any other valuables? Jewelry? Cash? Art?"

Warren snorted, and his head jerked violently to the side so that he was looking at her sideways. "Valuables? I can barely afford kitty litter for Brando." He laughed, then looked worried. "The robber didn't hurt my cat, did he?"

"He's fine. But we did find him outside the apartment. Are you sure you left him inside?"

Warren's shoulders shrugged violently. "Positive. Like I said, I'm pretty compulsive. I always check to make sure . . . oh boy whoop . . . Brando is inside, and I always lock up. I have a pretty heavy-duty dead bolt on that door. Did they kick it in?"

Marlene's eyes narrowed. *Good point, and another piece of the puzzle.* "No, there was no sign of forced entry," she said. "Which means this guy was a pro. He knew what he was doing."

"But why?"

Marlene explained her theory that the killer, or his accomplice — "there might be more than one person involved" — was looking for something he believed Warren had and the break-in was connected to Michelle Oakley's death. "It's obvious you were set up," she said. "But maybe they didn't account for Michelle entrusting you with whatever it is they want? Any ideas?"

Warren looked thoughtful even as his head continued to jerk to the side and occasionally straight back. With an effort, he shook his head no. "I can't think of anything."

"She didn't give you anything — an object or an envelope?"

"Uh-uh . . . whoop whooooop . . . nothing," he replied. "We had a few glasses of wine and dinner, and we talked. That was . . . oh boy piss shit . . . it."

"Did she say anything that might have indicated she felt she was in danger?"

Warren thought about it for a moment. "Well, she said a couple of things about how . . . oh boy . . . if I really knew her, I wouldn't want anything to do with her."

"Did she say why?"

"Not really. She told me she had made some horrible decisions because she was desperate and that . . . whoop oh boy ohhhh . . . she was going to have to pay for them. She said she had to atone. She said she was Shane."

"Who?"

"Shane, the character in the western film by the same name," Warren answered. "We played movie trivia, like I do with Butch."

"Was there anybody else in the house with the two of you?"

Warren shook his head. "No one else was in the house." He paused, then added, "But after dinner, she got a call on her cell phone. She said it was a business client with an emergency. In fact, she called it . . . whoop whoop nice tits . . . a life-and-death emergency. It was why I had to leave when I did."

"Did she say she was meeting someone?"

"No, but that was the impression I got. I could be wrong."

"Did she say she was having trouble with anyone in particular?"

Warren looked troubled. "Well, there were these two guys at the . . . whoop butt ass . . . birthday party my parents threw for my sister. They came up to us when we were talking, and the taller one said that he needed to speak to her. It wasn't a request, either, it was a demand. The other guy just stood there looking at her like he wanted to wring her neck. I asked if she needed help, but she said it was just business. By the way, the other guy's name was Jim Williams."

"You know him?"

"No," Warren replied. "I was introduced to him earlier at the party; he was with some hottie . . . whoooooop . . . named Sherry. But the only reason I know his name now is because it seemed familiar at the time. Then I remembered, Jim Williams is the name of the main character in the movie *Midnight in the Garden of Good and Evil.* He's an art collector and *bon vivant* in Savannah, who shoots his homosexual lover and claims it was self-defense. Kevin Spacey plays him. That's the sort of thing I'm good at remembering."

"And you think this wasn't a friendly business meeting between Michelle and these men?"

"I couldn't tell what was going on, but there was a lot of tension. I'm pretty sensitive to it . . . oh boy ohhhhh boy . . . makes me twitch, in case you haven't noticed." As if to prove his point, Warren's body convulsed, after which he continued as if nothing had happened. "You think they could have had anything to do with her death? But why frame me?"

Getting up out of her seat, Marlene began to pace again. At first, she didn't speak, then she looked at Warren and said, "Maybe you were just convenient. Who knew you were going to Michelle's?"

"Umm, let's see. My folks, Shannon, the cabbie . . . I guess the cook might have heard her say my name." He shrugged and twitched slightly. "I think that's it."

"No one else. You didn't call any of your buddies or say something to someone at your sister's birthday party?"

"No . . . hey, wait a minute," Warren said, his eyes growing wider. "At the party, those two guys heard me ask her out for a coffee. That's when she invited me to her place for dinner." He stopped talking and looked sadly at the floor. "I still can't believe . . . oh boy . . . she's dead."

Marlene noted the hitch in Warren's voice. "How rude of me, Warren. I'm so sorry; I know she was important to you. I met your sister out in the lobby. She's here to visit after we're done. She told me that Michelle was very fond of you, too. Apparently, she asked about you frequently."

Warren's head fell forward as a sob escaped him. Marlene quickly made her way around the table and placed her hands on his quaking shoulders. "Do you want to take a break? I only have a few more questions."

"No, I'm okay," he replied, pulling himself together with a sigh. "Sorry. I keep thinking, there goes your . . . oh ohhh boy piss . . . only chance at love, which is selfish. Michelle lost her life, and I'm worried about me." He stifled another sob with his hand over his mouth. Then, slowly and deliberately, he calmed himself. "Go ahead. Let's finish. Shannon's waiting."

Marlene looked at him for a minute,

impressed by the man's inner strength. "What time did you leave Michelle's house?"

"Not sure," Warren replied. "I don't wear a watch. But I'd say not much after nine."

"Where'd you go from there?"

"I walked home. It's about a mile."

"Why not take a cab?"

Warren bowed his head, and when he looked back up, his pale blue eyes were filled with tears. "It was a nice night, and I was really . . . whoop whoop ass . . . happy about the way our date went. She teased me when I left; she said we'd go out to a movie if I could get the right answer to a movie-trivia question."

"Which was?"

"It's the one I asked Butch about before . . . whoop . . . I was arrested: 'The key goes where the book editor sees his wife and son off to Maine.' That's it."

"Did you figure it out?"

"No. To be honest, I've been a little preoccupied," Warren replied. "And I was trying not to cheat . . . oh boy . . . by looking it up online. I have a feeling I know it, but something's just not clicking. By Monday afternoon, I was stumped, which is why I asked your husband. I would have told her that I cheated and thrown myself . . . whoop nipples oh boy . . . on her mercy."

Warren smiled, but even at that, tears slipped from his eyes and rolled off his cheeks to splash on the table. Marlene patted his shoulders and moved back around to her side of the table to face him, though she remained standing. "I know this is hard, but keep your chin up. We're going to figure out what's going on and beat this rap," she said.

Warren chuckled and wiped at his eyes. "Now you sound like James Cagney. 'You dirty rat.' We're going to beat this rap, ya hear?"

Marlene laughed. "Maybe we've both been watching too many gangster movies." She thought for a moment, then shrugged. "I don't know the answer to the trivia question, either, but it doesn't seem to pertain to Michelle's death. Do you know what time you got home that night?"

"I took my time and sat in a park for a bit. I guess around ten?"

Marlene leaned forward and placed her hands on the table. "Warren, I'm going to ask you an embarrassing question, but it's important, so you have to tell me the truth."

"Go ahead," he replied, lifting his chin slightly.

"Did you have sex with Michelle that night?"

Warren's face turned beet red, and he stammered several times before he could answer. "No. I wish . . . I wanted . . . and she said . . ." He stopped and started again. "Never mind, it doesn't matter. But the answer to your question is we hugged when I arrived, and she kissed me once when I left, but we did not . . . whoop whoop . . . have sex. Now, aren't you going to ask me if I killed her?"

Marlene looked deep into his eyes, so large behind his smudged glasses, and shook her head. "No. I don't need to; I already know you didn't."

After a few more questions, Marlene was ready to go. As she held out her hand, he asked, "What's next?"

Marlene sighed. "Well, the grand jury meets this afternoon, and like I said, I expect you to be indicted for murder. Then there will be an arraignment, probably within a day or so, and you'll be informed of the charges and asked to enter a plea. We will, of course, plead not guilty. Then we'll ask for you to be allowed to get out on bail."

"Won't the district attorney ask for me not to get bail?"

Marlene thought about Harley Chin and

his enormous ego. He was already in the newspapers promising swift justice and about to indict Warren for murder. He wasn't about to appear soft on crime by letting a suspected murderer out on the streets.

"I don't want to get your hopes up about bail," she said. "With a murder charge, they usually . . ."

". . . won't let you . . . whoop whoop oh boy . . . out. I'm a dead man," Warren finished glumly. Then he explained what had happened in the cafeteria. "David and Booger won't be able to protect me for as long as it's going to take to get me out of here."

"I'll demand that they keep you segregated from the rest of the inmates," Marlene said, visibly angered.

"What reason will you give?" Warren said. "Because a couple of street people said there's a hit out on me? I doubt the jailers will see the urgency until I'm already dead. Doesn't matter. This is a jail, and they can't protect me if somebody really wants me dead." Every facial muscle seemed to be twitching now as he looked at Marlene. "I think that's been the plan all along. Frame me and then murder me. They'll just say my Tourette's got me killed — that I said something bad to somebody and paid the price. They might even be right. I might get killed because of my mouth, but you and I will . . . whoop oh boy shit . . . know there's more to it than that."

Warren's grip tightened, and his eyes widened with fear.

"Get me out of here, Marlene! Please!"

20

In the morning before the start of the second day of the Jabbar trial, Karp sat at his desk across from Mahmoud Juma, a small brown man with dark, sad eyes. They'd met before during trial preparations, and he truly liked the man. He was the epitome of the promise of American Exceptionalism, the dream of living in a country in which morality, ethics, and human rights were institutionalized and codified. Not left to the whims of military despots and ayatollahs.

A simple Muslim fisherman from Kenya's east coast, Juma had fled poverty, oppression, and the terrorism of Al Qaeda extremists to find a better life for himself and his teenage daughters. After arriving in America, he'd worked hard at whatever menial jobs he could find while insisting that his girls go to school, learn English, set goals, and become thoroughly American.

And he had even higher goals for his grandson, Abdullah, the child of his murdered daughter, Miriam.

"I would like him to be a doctor, I think. Anything is possible in this country."

As he spoke, the old man glanced over at the subject of their conversation, a toddler whom he'd brought with him to Karp's office. The boy was busy looking at the books in Karp's library and spinning a globe around on its base.

"I've been meaning to ask you," Karp said. "Your English is very good."

"Thank you, Mr. Karp," Juma replied. He explained that when he was a boy, Christian missionaries from America had set up a school in the village a few miles from his own. His father had sent him to the school — walking the six or so miles there and back five days a week — believing that his son would someday need to be educated to navigate a changing world.

"I inherited the truth that education is the key to the future from my father," Juma said. "I passed that to my girls, though some members of the Al-Aqsa mosque — those who think of women as chattel — did not like it." The old man sighed. "My Miriam had dreams of going to college and becoming a teacher someday."

With an effort, the old man steeled himself and quickly regained his composure, submitting, he would say, to the will of Allah. Dabbing quickly at a tear that had rolled down his cheek, he continued. "When we came here, I said we would speak English, even in the house, except around our dinner table, when we spoke the language of my father's fathers. I did not want them to forget where they came from, but I wanted them to be Americans. And so it is now with Abdullah, too."

One of the things Karp had wanted to talk to him about during this interview was the rumor that the Juma family and the relatives of some of the young men who'd been lured into Jabbar's suicide brigade were seeking to avenge the death of Miriam. He wanted to avoid any sort of scene or even an attempt on Jabbar's life in the courtroom.

"I want to discuss the concept of *thar* with you," Karp said.

The old man stiffened slightly, and the smile on his face melted. "*Thar* is an ancient custom, what the Christian Bible calls 'an eye for an eye,' " he said guardedly.

"That's what I've been told," Karp replied. "But I guess what I want to ask you is if you are seeking *thar* in the case of Imam Jabbar. Do you want to cause his death?"

Juma looked hard at Karp for a moment and then shrugged. "Perhaps something will happen to him, and my daughter will be avenged. I will rejoice if that happens."

Karp ran his fingers through his hair and tried again. "Let me rephrase this. Are you going to try to kill Mr. Jabbar or have someone else kill him?"

The man remained silent but finally shook his head. "Because of what he did to my daughter and others, I hope he dies and goes to hell where he belongs. But no, Mr. Karp, I accept that I am a guest in this wonderful country, and I will abide by its laws and customs." Juma reached across the desk with his hand extended. "You have my word as a man of Allah that I will not seek *thar*."

Karp shook the offered hand. "That's all I needed to know."

Moving on, Karp asked Juma about Jabbar. He wanted to know as much as possible about the defendant on a personal level.

"Did you consider Imam Jabbar to be your spiritual advisor?"

Juma frowned. "He was the imam of the Al-Aqsa mosque and led the Namaz, the prayers, five times a day. On Friday mornings, he would give a sermon. But I did not think of him as my spiritual advisor."

"Why not?"

"Because I do not believe that he is truly a man of God."

"Why?"

"He does not understand that Islam is a religion of peace and of obedience to the will of Allah."

"Did you attend his Friday sermons?"

"I attended a few when I first began to worship at the Al-Aqsa mosque, but after that, I stopped."

"Was there a particular reason?"

"I believe it is the duty of the imam at Friday sermon to talk about the Koran or, perhaps, matters that are of spiritual importance to the community. But his sermons were always political and full of hate for white people and this country. They were not the words, or the intent, of the Prophet. The passages of the Koran he did talk about, he twisted and corrupted to fit his hatred. I fled Kenya because of men like that."

"Did you ever confront Imam Jabbar about his politics?"

Juma nodded. "Yes. On several occasions, I told him that I believed he was corrupting the teachings of the Prophet and that Allah did not condone the murder of innocent people or encourage hatred of other people because of their skin color or where they lived."

"And his response?"

"He said I should attend another mosque."

"Why didn't you?"

Juma sighed. "I wish now that I had. But the Al-Aqsa mosque was the only mosque within walking distance of my home. And he is just one man. There were many good Muslims who worshiped there — my friends and neighbors — and there were other scholars who know the Koran better than Jabbar. A mosque is supposed to be the center of the community. I wanted to be part of my community."

Karp asked what Miriam had told Juma about her husband being recruited by Jabbar to join a cadre of young men at the mosque.

"She didn't like it," Juma answered. "He would return from these secret meetings with Jabbar and the other young men, talking about *jihad* and other crazy things. He claimed he was part of something that would make him and the others famous in the Muslim world."

"Did you personally have any discussions with your son-in-law regarding Sharif Jabbar?" Karp asked.

"Yes, Jamal was talking one day about the Al Qaeda attack on the World Trade Center. He was jealous that the killers were famous and said that because of Jabbar, he and other young men from the mosque would be famous, too. I told him that such talk was crazy and against the teachings of the Prophet."

"Why didn't you tell the authorities?" Karp asked.

Juma hung his head. "I thought it was just big talk by young, hotheaded men and that they would eventually listen to older, wiser men. But they were seduced by the words of Jabbar and a desire for fame."

"I understand that your daughter left her husband and came to live with you?"

"Yes. Several months before she was killed."

"Did she say why she left her husband?"

"They were arguing a lot. She did not like his talk of violence and the word of Allah being corrupted to support the teachings of Imam Jabbar. She wanted Jamal to stop attending these secret meetings with Jabbar and the other young men. Then, one night he came home drunk on alcohol; they argued, and he struck her." Recalling the incident, Juma's voice hardened with anger.

"She left him and came to live with me."

"Did she ever say anything to you regarding her feelings about Jabbar?"

Juma nodded. "She did not like him for what he was doing to her husband."

"But didn't she work for Jabbar as a receptionist?"

"Yes. After her husband blew himself up at the synagogue and murdered those poor, innocent men, she needed a job, and Jabbar offered her one. She had a little boy to care for."

"Were you aware that your daughter was working with federal law-enforcement authorities investigating Jabbar and others?"

"Yes, Mr. Karp."

"Did she tell you what it was about?"

Juma shook his head. "No. She said she was giving them information, but she would not say what it was about. She said it was too dangerous for me to know."

"Did there come a point when your daughter told you that she believed she was in danger?"

"Yes, Mr. Karp. She was very frightened."

"Was she afraid of the federal agents? Or did she believe that the federal agents would harm her if she did not help them?"

"No, she told me she trusted them. Especially the man she played chess with. I believe his name was John."

Karp paused. He hadn't heard about the chess and would have to ask Jojola about it. "Did she say they had threatened her, or her family, including you, with deportation if she did not help them?"

"No, Mr. Karp."

"Mr. Juma," Karp asked gently, "when was the last time you saw your daughter Miriam?"

The question seemed to rock Juma, who wiped at his eyes. "The afternoon of the day she died."

"Did she ask you to do something that day?"

"Yes, she asked me to take her son, Abdullah, to Chicago to stay with friends until the danger had passed."

"Did she say where she was going?"

"Yes, to the mosque to worship. It was the first day of Ramadan."

"Did she say any last words to you before she left?"

"Yes. She said, 'No matter what happens here, we will meet again.' " The old man had to stop and take another sip of water. "In Paradise."

"Did her words worry you?"

Juma nodded. "Yes, it sounded to me like she knew she might be harmed or . . . or killed. But she was at peace. Her guardian spirit, Hazrat Fatemah Masumeh, a Muslim saint, had appeared to her and told her that whatever happened, it was the will of Allah."

"And you never saw her again?"

"Only once," Juma said. A sob escaped him before he continued. "I saw her again at the morgue." He covered his face with his hands and began to cry.

Karp waited patiently for Juma to pull himself together, which he did after several minutes. "I am sorry, Mr. Juma, to put you through this."

"I understand," the little man replied. "We are both seeking justice for Miriam. You ask me what you need to ask, and I will do my best to answer."

Karp explained to Juma that in about an hour, he would be called to the witness stand. "But I will only ask you two questions of substance, not including background about you, which are necessary for us to make a legal case. The first is your father-daughter relationship with Miriam, which will be used to establish the basis for the second question, which is that you regrettably had to go to the morgue to identify your daughter. Please understand that in every murder case, there are basically two things that the People must establish beyond a reasonable doubt. The first is that the deceased is in fact dead, and the second is that the deceased died as a result of the criminal conduct of the defendant. You're being asked to establish that your daughter is the deceased, which is presently not an issue, but we must prove it."

"You don't want me to tell the judge about how he recruited young men to murder innocent people?"

Karp shook his head and explained the legal prohibition against hearsay.

Juma looked puzzled. "I am confused. If it's the truth, why must it be hidden?"

Karp smiled. "You make a good point. All I can say is that sometimes, in an effort to be more than fair to a man on trial, the truth must be weighed against an even more important duty. As Americans, we believe that freedom is so important that if we're going to take it away from a man and put him in prison, then we have to give him every benefit of the doubt."

"Guilty beyond a reasonable doubt," Juma said. "I am learning all about the American justice system in my citizenship classes, Mr. Karp."

"And I'm sure you're an excellent student and will make a fine citizen."

An hour later, Juma was called to the stand, where Karp began by asking background information, where he was from, when he had come to America, and how he had chosen the Al-Aqsa mosque.

"Because it was close to my home," Juma replied.

Then he answered the two questions Karp had told him were necessary to prove the case. Yes, the body in the morque was that of his younger daughter, Miriam. And he had told that to the medical examiner that terrible day.

"Thank you, Mr. Juma," Karp said as the old man stepped down from the witness stand.

"*Salaam.* You are very welcome, Mr. Karp."

The remainder of the day was consumed by calling various crime-scene and forensic experts.

A crime-scene technician was called to identify a long, bloody knife found in the basement in the Al-Aqsa mosque. As were, he said, human teeth, fingernails, and a severed head discovered in a small room next to a larger room containing, among other things, the victim's body, a large banner, and a video camera. Karp entered the plastic evidence bags containing the teeth and fingernails, as well as the camera and banner, into evidence.

On cross-examination, O'Dowd ascertained from the technician that there was no physical evidence tying her client to "the so-called torture room or the People's latest exhibits."

An Arab language expert also took the stand to translate the writing on the green banner found in the basement of the Al-Aqsa mosque, now People's Exhibit fourteen. "It says, 'In the name of Allah, the most gracious, the most merciful.' " He also testified that several photographs Karp showed him of Islamic terrorists shortly before the murder of hostages by decapitation in other countries, People's Exhibits eighteen and nineteen, contained banners with the same slogan.

O'Dowd countered on cross-examination by getting the language expert to agree that it was a common saying "and could also simply be an inspirational banner for a mosque youth group that met in the basements on Wednesday afternoons."

The last witness of the day was New York City assistant medical examiner Gail Manning. Karp had worked with Manning before and appreciated the professional yet warm demeanor of the silver-haired, blue-eyed AME in front of a jury. She would testify to a "reasonable degree of medical certainty" the cause and manner of death, highlighting the injuries Miriam had endured.

Manning began her testimony by identifying the teeth, fingernails, and severed head found in the smaller room and the body in the larger room as belonging to the deceased. The tougher part of her testimony, however, was describing the physical injuries of a young woman who had her fingers broken, the nails ripped from their beds with pliers, and the arches of her feet broken with a sledge hammer. Miriam also had puncture wounds inflicted by a small knife on various parts of her head and body.

"And she was beaten about the face with a blunt object and blinded in one eye before she died," Manning said, her voice soft but deliberate. "Four teeth had been extracted . . . also with the use of pliers."

Moving on, Manning testified that the cause of death was "the nearly total loss of blood caused by severing the carotid artery and jugular vein. All of the muscles and all of the structures of the neck, including the spinal cord, were also severed for complete decapitation."

"Other than pain," Karp said, looking now at each member of the panel, "what other uncomfortable sensations would the victim experience?"

"As blood from the wound entered her windpipe, there would have been the sensation of drowning," the doctor replied.

"Drowning in her own blood," Karp said.

"Yes, that's right."

On cross-examination, O'Dowd again had the witness agree with her point that there was no physical evidence linking Jabbar to the torture and murder of Miriam Juma Khalifa. "And is it true that it's actually quite difficult to cut a head off a human being using a knife such as the one marked People's Exhibit fifteen?"

"It's harder than you would think," Manning agreed, "depending, of course, on the size of the muscles and the neck and the sharpness of the blade."

"Is that the sort of thing a middle-aged woman could do easily?" O'Dowd asked.

Manning shrugged. "If she was strong, she could do it. But it does take quite a bit of tough sawing, especially if the victim is living and conscious and therefore bound to move and react."

"Would it more likely take a bigger,

stronger man to accomplish?" O'Dowd asked.

"I don't know if 'more likely' is the way to put it," Manning replied. "The bigger and stronger of either sex would have an easier time severing a human head from the body. I don't think gender has anything to do with it."

If she was strong, she could do it. The thought reverberated in Karp's brain. *Nadya Malovo is certainly strong enough,* he thought. *And ruthless enough. Is there anything she wouldn't kill with pleasure if she was paid enough?* He wondered where the Russian assassin was and, having killed Crawford, how she planned to follow through on any plans to assassinate Newbury, who would be testifying in a matter of days.

And there was the matter of the threat to his family. Fulton's men had it covered — at least, as best as could be expected against a trained killer like the beautiful but deadly Nadya Malovo.

21

Todd Fielding caught himself before he would have otherwise tumbled over backward in the "bloody piece of shit" office chair, which, along with a cheap fiberboard desk, he'd rented when he opened T. X. Fielding Investigations Inc. three years earlier.

"First thing I do is move out of this dump, get a better office, and buy real furniture," he said aloud, although no one else was in the room. He took a deep breath and tried to adhere to his dear old mum's advice about not counting his chickens before they hatched, but it wasn't happening.

Fielding's real middle name was Paul, but he thought the X looked sexier than T. P. Fielding Investigations. In spite of that crackerjack marketing, business had not exactly boomed out of his tiny Chinatown office above a dry-cleaning business on Mott Street, the chemical smells of which permeated every corner of the room. Most months, he had to beg the building owner for "just a wee bit more time" to pay the rent. *However, that is about to change,* he thought gleefully.

A native of Wales, he'd come to the United States fifteen years earlier as a student of the French Culinary Institute with the intention of becoming a world-class sous chef. However, he'd developed a double-barreled habit of cocaine and late-night parties followed by several days of sleeping it off, and he'd wound up getting kicked out of school for poor attendance and falling asleep in class.

He'd since worked a variety of menial jobs, such as short-order cook, bellhop, and theater usher. Then, one day, he'd seen an advertisement, "Learn to Be a Private Investigator," in the back of the *Village Voice,* and he'd liked the thought of the "glamorous and exciting career" the ad for PI Schools Inc. promised. It had also helped that the ad featured a photograph of a good-looking man in a tuxedo standing protectively in front of a beautiful, well-dressed woman with partially exposed cleavage.

The "school" had turned out to be a one-man operation run by a former NYPD detective named Mike Machovoe, who, as

Fielding later discovered using his new-found technical abilities, had been forced out of the department for rolling drug dealers. Machovoe, reeking of stale alcohol and cheap cigars, had taught the two-week course in the basement of a Boys Club in Brooklyn. It had cost Fielding and his five classmates $250 for instruction covering legal and liability issues, the restrictions placed on PIs as private citizens ("No, you cannot go Magnum P.I., waving a gun around and arresting bad guys"), the requirements for licensing in New York (essentially the intelligence to fill out forms), and certain basic "investigative techniques," such as "the lost art of clandestine surveillance," "tailing" (practiced by taking turns following other students about on the streets without being spotted), and how to testify in court.

There had been an evening spent learning basic hand-to-hand combat but — to Fielding's disappointment — no firearms training. "Most of you jokers would just shoot your asses off, so leave the gunplay to the professionals." On the final day of class, a friend of Machovoe, another cop who'd been drummed out of the force and now sold "high-tech electronic surveillance and recording equipment you will need," had been given the floor to demonstrate his products and take orders.

Fielding had spent the next month's rent and then some on gadgets, found a cheap office, hung out his sign, and waited for the fun to begin. Unfortunately, what little there was of the "glamorous and exciting career" mostly consisted of trying to catch insurance scammers and getting the goods on "targets" who were suspected of cheating on their spouses, boyfriends, and girlfriends.

Wealthy clients went to one of the big Midtown firms with dozens of PIs and all the best resources. He was lucky to get clients who could pay him better than he'd made taking tickets for the ferry to the Statue of Liberty. However, there were more perks as a PI. Although admittedly going to seed a bit as he approached his fortieth birthday, he had certainly used his British accent to bang some of his less discerning clients, mostly women who hired him to follow their philandering men and jumped into bed with him to get even.

Sex was a nice side perk, but it didn't go very far toward paying the rent to his landlord, a Vietnamese guy named Tran Vinh Do. However, he wasn't about to turn down a roll in the sack when the young blonde he was now waiting for had first entered his office a couple of weeks earlier. She was definitely a step up from the usual clientele, with a chest that looked as if her shirt had been stuffed with pillows, two bowling balls for an ass, and lips that looked as if they could suck a tennis ball through a hose. He'd also noted that she was wearing a lot of expensive jewelry, and her clothes definitely weren't off the rack at Macy's. She even smelled like sex and money.

He'd tried flirting with Sherry Maxwell at that first meeting. But she wasn't interested in anything except whether her boyfriend, one Jim Williams, address Fifty-sixth and Fifth Avenue, was seeing other women.

"You will be discreet?" Maxwell had asked. "I wouldn't want him to know. But a girl's got to protect herself; there are a lot of female vultures out there who'd like to pounce on my guy."

Fielding had assured her that her secret was safe with him. "I'd take a bullet before I'd give you up," he'd said dramatically. "I've done it before. I don't like to talk about it much, but I was with Special Forces over in the U.K." He'd hoped the lie about his military background, which was nonexistent, would get her steamed up a bit. But again, she'd ignored him and asked how much it would cost.

Fielding had done a quick assessment of the jewelry and clothes and then said, "My retainer is ten . . . fifteen thousand dollars, which covers my expenses — all carefully itemized, of course — and gets us started. For you, because you look like a nice person, I'll take ten up front and the other five after I do my first stakeout; if we have to go from there, my hourly rate is a hundred fifty. Of course, you will want to know the extent of his philandering — though, personally, I think he'd be a fool to cheat on a great-looking woman like yourself — so it might be necessary to gather evidence over a period of time, just to be sure that something that looks bad isn't totally innocent."

Maxwell had frowned. "That's a lot of money."

Worried that he might have scared her off, he'd quickly said, "I know it sounds like a lot, but you might not realize how dangerous this sort of thing is. You probably don't know this — it's the sort of thing we professionals, meaning PIs and the cops, keep to ourselves — but more police officers are shot and killed responding to domestic disturbances than any other call they respond to. And private investigators, such as myself, don't even have the protection of a badge."

"I don't think he's dangerous," Maxwell had replied. "He's just a banker."

"It's always the guys you least expect who go off when cornered," Fielding had said, snapping his fingers for emphasis. "Do you know if he carries a gun?"

The young woman had blinked as if she'd never even considered the possibility, then shaken her head. "I can't imagine Jim with a gun. He can be a little gruff with me sometimes, but he's not violent." She'd leaned toward him and whispered. "To be honest, he's a little wimpy around other men."

Fielding had held up his hands in mock surrender. "Just trying to be careful. You never know what will push even a 'wimpy' man into violent behavior. Love is a powerful emotion, and I've personally seen it turn a mouse into a lion. I hope I won't have to disarm him in order to protect you or myself. But that's why my fees might seem a bit excessive."

Maxwell had thought about it and nodded. "I thought about using one of the big firms in Midtown," she said. "But Jimmy knows everybody who's anybody, so I chose you."

Fielding had let the slight pass and smiled.

"You'd be paying a lot more for those 'department store' agencies without the personal attention I give to my clients, which is why I keep the number of clients at a manageable level."

Barely able to contain his avarice when she wrote him a check for ten thousand dollars, Fielding had accepted it and tossed it into the center drawer of his desk as though he received such largesse on a daily basis. "Now, I'm going to need you to tell me everything about Jim. I can't do my job if you hold back. I'm afraid that means I'm even going to need to know some of the details of your sex life; if he's into anything particularly kinky, it could be important."

Unfortunately for his prurient interest, Williams's sexual interests were pretty vanilla and not particularly geared toward keeping his girlfriend satisfied. Disappointed, he'd asked her what caused her to be suspicious.

"Well, he's always on the telephone, but he doesn't want me to hear him and goes into his office," Maxwell had said. "He leaves the house at all kinds of strange hours, telling me it's business. But what does a banker do at two in the morning?"

Fielding had tilted his head and heaved a sigh as if he didn't want to have to break it to her. "It doesn't sound good. He's showing all the classic signs of a philanderer — secretive behavior, mysterious phone calls, odd hours, and suspicious routines. But let's give him the benefit of the doubt, shall we? There could be another explanation."

Fat chance, he'd thought as Sherry Maxwell smiled weakly and nodded, though her eyes had brimmed with tears. But maybe a few *in flagrante* photographs of her boyfriend would warm up this ice queen, so he'd put on his most understanding face and pushed a box of tissues across the desk to her.

"This is the toughest part of the job," he'd said, "watching innocent hearts get broken. But better to know than to wonder, and better to know now than waste your youth on a man who might not deserve you."

Fielding had stood up and walked over to a locked file cabinet, which he opened with more flair than it deserved, and stood looking inside for a moment as though deep in thought. He'd then looked over his shoulder at the young woman and asked, "How many cars does he drive?"

Maxwell had shrugged. "He has a dozen but only keeps two in the city, a sedan and a Porsche."

Fielding had nodded and pulled out two black boxes the size of cigarette packs.

"These are state-of-the-art GPS tracking devices. With these little puppies, I don't need to worry about keeping him in my line of sight while he's driving and risk being spotted. They are equipped with very powerful magnets, and I would like you to place one of these under each car, doesn't matter where, so long as it's metal. But first, you need to flip this little switch here to activate it."

He'd then told her to give him a call anytime Jim Williams was about to leave on one of his mysterious business trips. "Obviously, I don't want to follow him twenty-four/seven, at least not right away — again, we don't want to be spotted — so we pick and choose our moments."

The first moment had come the past Saturday evening, when Sherry Maxwell had called him to say that Jim had been making mysterious telephone calls all afternoon. "Then I was walking past his office when he thought I was watching television, and I heard him say he would 'be there at ten.' And I just know he was talking to a woman, but he told me he was meeting one of his guy friends for drinks. He's leaving in a half hour."

After that, it had been easy to jump into his own car, an older-model Ford sedan, to follow Jim Williams on the Hutchinson River Parkway into Westchester County to the ritzy burg of Purchase. There he'd almost blown it when the GPS device said his target had stopped, and he'd decided to drive by and check out the lay of the land.

As he'd approached the dark sedan, Fielding saw at the last moment that Jim Williams was still in the car, looking up the street at a gated mansion. He'd picked up his cell phone and pretended to talk to someone as he passed his target. After driving around a corner, he'd parked his car and got out with his small digital camera.

As nonchalantly as possible, he'd walked back and crossed the street to where he could see the target's car. After a few minutes, a man who appeared to be in his mid-thirties, dressed in slacks and a button-down shirt, had emerged from the gate leading to the driveway and walked off on the sidewalk in the opposite direction. He'd noted that Jim Williams had paid particular attention to the other man.

Fielding had been surprised when Williams didn't immediately go up to the house but instead waited nearly an hour before he got out of his car and walked up to the gate. He'd reached forward to press what Fielding assumed was the intercom button.

Aha, Fielding had thought. *Caught you, you dirty bugger. My, but you are the cautious type, waiting for the husband to be long gone before you go make a cuckold of him.*

After Williams had been let in, Fielding crept up to the gate, using everything he knew about the art of clandestine surveillance. Peeking around the corner, he'd seen his quarry at the door and begun taking photographs. He couldn't have been more pleased when a woman answered and let Williams in. *There's an easy five thousand more in the bank,* he thought, *with many billable hours to come gathering more dirt on the wanker.*

He'd decided not to wait for Williams to leave, as he wanted to stretch out the time he spent milking this cash cow. Instead, he'd crept back to his car and called Sherry Maxwell as he made his way back to the city.

"I'm afraid I have some bad news," he'd said, then held the cell phone away from his head when her first scream nearly shattered his eardrum.

"That fucking bastard!" she'd screeched, but then started sobbing loudly.

"Now, now," he'd said, concerned that she might confront her boyfriend before he'd had a chance to make much money off her or get into her pants. "There could be an innocent explanation. I did not see any physical contact. Just suspicious behavior. I took photographs. Why don't you come down to the office Monday, and I'll show them to you — maybe you'll recognize the woman as just a friend — and then we'll chat about what to do next."

Maxwell had sobbed a bit longer but then agreed to come to the office Monday morning.

Now, sitting on his crappy chair in his crappy little office that smelled like dry-cleaning fluids, Fielding sighed. It had been a mistake to ask her to come to the office that day. He'd wanted the remaining five thousand due for his retainer before she changed her mind, but that was before he'd seen the newspaper on Tuesday morning. Or more to the point, the photograph of the front of the house he'd been at Saturday night, only now with police crime-scene tape across the gated drive.

On Monday, he'd shown Sherry the photographs of her boyfriend being invited into the home in Purchase by a beautiful woman. "Her name is Michelle Oakley, a divorcee who apparently likes entertaining more than one man a night," he'd said with a knowing leer.

Sherry had nodded and burst into tears. "I've been faithful," she'd cried, sniffing and reaching for the box of tissues. "I've given him everything he wants, and I try to make a nice home for him. I would have made a good wife."

"There, there," Fielding had said, coming around and sitting on the desk in front of her. "All is not lost, my dear. He just believes that he can have his cake and eat it, too. Maybe you just need to show him that you're on to his tricks and that he stands a good chance of losing you if he doesn't quit his tomfoolery."

The young woman had wagged her head back and forth. "I don't know that he would care," she'd said sadly. "He only says he loves me when I'm naked."

I'm sure of that, Fielding had thought, but said, "My dear ol' mum used to say, 'Men are bound to wander if you don't put up a fence. It's their nature.' But first, I think you need something a little more solid before you confront him. Now that I know where he's shacking up, I should be able to get the proof you need to hold his toes in the fire. And if for some reason, it doesn't work out after that . . ." He'd inched a little closer on the desk. "I'm always here if you need a shoulder to cry on." He'd given her

417

what he thought of as his most winning smile. "Part of that personal service I told you about at T. X. Fielding Investigations Inc."

It had taken Maxwell a moment to realize what he was intimating, but then she'd wrinkled her nose as though offended by some smell. "Not in a million years," she'd said in a voice that could have withered plastic flowers. She'd handed him another check for five thousand dollars, picked up the envelope holding the printouts of the photographs, and got up. "Get me that proof," she'd said, and stomped out as best she could in four-inch heels.

Realizing that he'd been within a lewd suggestion of blowing the last portion of his retainer and whatever hours he could get away with, Fielding had counted himself lucky. Until Tuesday, when he saw the newspaper and realized that he should have waited to tell his client about her boyfriend; that way, he wouldn't have had to bring her in on his little plot to blackmail Jim Williams.

At first, when he read that the police had arrested a suspect on Monday, he'd assumed that it was Jim Williams who'd been taken into custody. But when Sherry Maxwell called that evening to ask if there was an update, he'd realized someone else was being blamed. He'd followed the case and saw that some guy named Warren Bennett had been arrested and indicted for murder.

Poor bastard, he'd thought, guessing that Bennett was the man he'd seen leave Oakley's house at a little after nine. He knew that Williams was the last man to see Michelle Oakley alive. But Warren Bennett wasn't filthy rich, and Williams was.

Sometimes those are the breaks, he thought now as the buzzer on his intercom went off, meaning someone was at the street-level door leading up to his office. "T. X. Fielding Investigations Inc.," he said.

Fielding was still kicking himself, because if he hadn't been so needy about the five thousand and hadn't told Maxwell about Williams's whereabouts, he could have pulled off the blackmail by himself with no one the wiser. But now he was going to have to talk her into going along with the plan.

Then again, maybe she'd see him a little differently. *And why not?* he thought. Her boyfriend had lied to her about where he was going Saturday night, and then, according to what he'd read in the papers he'd had sex with Michelle Oakley before killing her. *Let's see what she thinks about me when I tell her that I'm going to make the two of us*

*very, very rich . . . and she can get even with
the bastard at the same time.*

"It's me," Sherry Maxwell's voice said
over the intercom.

Fielding smiled. This was going to be a
piece of cake.

22

"Mr. Karp, may I have a word with you?"

The dark-skinned man stepped away from the wall outside Part 39 and moved suddenly toward Karp, extending his hand. In a flash, Sergeant Cordova moved past his boss and intercepted the man, grabbing him by his wrist and spinning him back toward the wall, where he was pinned.

"Let me go!" the man squealed. "I'm a journalist! Here's my card." He waved a business card with two fingers of his captured hand.

"Who are you with?" Cordova demanded.

"*Arab World Daily,*" the man replied. "I just wanted to ask a question."

"It's okay, Mike," Karp said, placing a hand on the sergeant's shoulder and plucking the card out of the man's hand. "What can I do for you, Mr. . . . . Mehanna?"

"My readers want to know if you are trying to convict Imam Jabbar because he is

Muslim or because he is black."

"How about because he murdered a young woman who also happened to be black and a Muslim?" Karp replied. "Now, if you'll excuse me, I have a killer to prosecute."

Entering the courtroom, Karp glanced around the gallery. The benches were packed as usual. Many of the faces were the same, but there was a sprinkling of new, eager visages anxious to be able to report later to friends and family that they'd been at the "Macabre Mosque Murder" trial, as it had been labeled by the *Post.*

Casually, he shifted his gaze to the defense table, where Jabbar and O'Dowd sat with their heads together engaged in animated conversation. At that moment, Jabbar looked back and, seeing him, glared. But the defendant quickly dropped his eyes when his stare was met and returned without wavering.

In the first row behind the defense table, O'Dowd's three large bodyguards glanced back, looking bored and sleepy from whatever they'd had for lunch. Elijah and the young man with the dreadlocks were also engaged in conversation, but from their smiles and faces, they appeared to be two young men discussing the previous night's social engagements. The middle-aged woman was missing, but she had come and gone several times during the trial, often returning with papers or even coffee during breaks for O'Dowd and Jabbar.

Turning to the right, Karp caught the eye of Sergeant Mike Cordova, now sitting next to John Jojola in the first row behind the prosecution table. The police officer gave him a slight nod. So far, the threat-assessment reports had been quiet. Other than the same half-dozen protesters outside the Criminal Courts Building, there'd been no real shows of support for Jabbar, certainly no attempts by followers to disrupt the proceedings in the courtroom. And according to his last briefing from Fulton that morning, there had been no threats more credible than the usual closet vigilantes who called radio talk shows and wrote e-mails to the newspapers about the trial being "a waste of taxpayer money" and that "(racial epithet) Jabbar should be strung up."

However, Nadya Malovo had disappeared off the radar screen, which worried Karp. She wasn't the type to give up. *Tomorrow will be the most dangerous,* he thought. That's when he'd be calling Dean Newbury to the stand and the old bastard would be most vulnerable.

Fulton had said he was chiefly concerned

with getting Newbury to and from the courthouse. They knew from hard experience that the Sons of Man had tentacles in the NYPD and, therefore, it could be assumed within the jail, too. So Newbury had been moved to an isolated safe house in Brooklyn instead of the Tombs, because Fulton couldn't control everything that went on in the jail. NYPD would clear the sidewalks and streets ahead of the motorcade that would deliver the old man to the Franklin Street side of the Criminal Courts Building, where he'd be whisked onto a private elevator normally reserved for the DA and judges making their way to the courts.

By prior arrangement with Jaxon, after Newbury testified, he was to be handed over to the U.S. Marshal's Office for transport to the maximum-segregation unit at the Varick Federal Detention Center. "I understand that Jen Capers will be heading up the detail," Fulton had said at lunch. "She's still recovering from being shot and probably should be on leave. But Espey told me that she'd insisted, and he backed her."

As he pushed open the gate to enter the well of the courtroom, Karp smiled to himself and put on his game face. He was a

424

competitor who loved the strategy that went into the game as much as winning it. *I hope I set this one up right,* he thought as court clerk Al Lopez announced the arrival of the judge.

After the jury was seated, John Jojola was recalled to the witness stand for O'Dowd's cross-examination. He settled into the chair, his long black hair pulled back from his wide bronze face and tied behind his head, and surveyed the jury with his deep-set brown eyes.

Direct examination of the witness had taken the entire morning, which Karp had begun by asking Jojola to give a "brief" rundown of his background. That had entailed little more than noting that he was a full-blooded American Indian from the Taos Pueblo, where he'd been raised as a boy and later as an adult had become its police chief.

Purposefully, Karp had only briefly touched on the fact that Jojola had served in the U.S. Army and then moved on. Only slightly more time was used to describe how, as the chief of police, he'd been investigating the abduction and murder of several boys from the reservation, which had led to his current occupation as an agent with a small federal law-enforcement agency.

With Jojola on the witness stand, Karp had delicately worked around the edges of what had brought Jojola to the mosque: his agency had been investigating criminal activities connected to Jabbar at the Al-Aqsa mosque, and during that investigation, his team had been contacted by Miriam Juma Khalifa, who had divulged certain information about these activities.

Karp had to leave out that Miriam had brought Jaxon's team a videotape made by her husband shortly before he blew himself up in the Third Avenue Synagogue. It was his "last will and testament" but contained enough clues about his association with Jabbar and his cadre of other young *jihadis* that the attack on the New York Stock Exchange had been thwarted.

It was with considerable more force that Karp had Jojola testify about the night Miriam was murdered. In vivid detail, with only the flintlike hardness in his eyes revealing his emotions, the witness had recalled how the young woman had been dragged into the main basement meeting room wearing a hood and how she'd looked when the hood had been removed.

Throughout it all, Jojola had kept his voice

even and unemotional, until he'd reached the moment before the knife was drawn across her throat by Nadya Malovo and Miriam had looked him in the eyes. Then his voice had caught, and he'd had to take a drink of the water Karp had poured for him before he could go on to describe the sight and sound of the brutal execution.

"Why didn't you attempt to stop it?" Karp had asked as gently as he could.

Jojola had hung his head. The truth was that he'd heard a voice telling him that Miriam didn't want him to interfere, that her death was necessary to save other lives, and he'd seen that truth in her eyes even as her blood had spurted from her throat. But that would not be part of his testimony. "It would have meant revealing my identity and the failure of my primary mission," he'd said instead.

"And do you believe the failure of your mission would have placed more lives in danger?" Karp had asked.

"Many more."

Karp had turned to the defense table and looked at Jabbar, who had shaken his head as if he couldn't believe the lies that were being told about him. "And where was the defendant, Sharif Jabbar, during these events?"

"In the room," Jojola had replied. "He was organizing the others and making sure the digital movie camera was set up properly."

"Did he make any attempt to dissuade or stop Malovo?"

"No. In fact, he was leading the other men in demanding her execution."

"And after Nadya Malovo cut Miriam's throat, how did the defendant react?"

Jojola had glared at Jabbar, who'd stopped shaking his head and looked down at a legal pad, suddenly remembering that he wanted to make note of something. "He led the celebration, including chanting *'Allahu Akbar,'* which means . . ." Jojola had paused and taken in a deep breath before releasing it and finishing. "God is great."

Karp had cut his direct examination short, which seemed to catch O'Dowd by surprise. She'd asked the judge for an early lunch break, "so that I can have a few moments to consider the government's rather brief examination of this witness."

O'Dowd walked up to the lectern, eyeing Jojola as if he was some sort of dangerous animal who might jump out of the witness box. She placed her notes on the stand and then shook her head sadly. "That's a pretty incredible story, Agent Jojola," she began.

"Let's see if I got this straight. You said you and your partner, this mysterious Mr. Tran, are working for a federal law-enforcement agency investigating alleged criminal activities at the Al-Aqsa mosque when you just happen to be contacted by Miriam Juma Khalifa. Is that correct?"

"It is," Jojola replied.

"She just found you out of the blue?"

"She'd met another agent, also a young woman, at the mosque and contacted her on her own."

"Oh, right." O'Dowd scoffed. "They met during a friendly social gathering at the mosque, which this other agent and her boss attended, also under pretense of being someone they were not."

"That's correct. It was all part of the same investigation."

"And after this one brief meeting, we're to believe that Miriam Juma Khalifa developed such trust that she was suddenly willing to divulge deep, dark secrets about her spiritual advisor, friend, and employer Imam Jabbar?"

"That's what happened."

"Uh-huh," O'Dowd said. "I believe it was your testimony that you met Ms. Khalifa several times in secret. Am I correct?"

"Yes."

"And were any other people present during these meetings?"

"Sometimes. At other times, we were alone."

"I see. And if I recall from your testimony, you and Ms. Khalifa were 'pretending' . . ." O'Dowd used her fingers to sarcastically put the quote marks around the word. "To be lovers in order to throw off any watchers."

"Yes, that was the idea."

"Did you, in fact, have sex with Ms. Khalifa?"

Karp saw Jojola stiffen. They'd gone over the likelihood that O'Dowd would try to imply that Jojola had sex with Miriam to gain control over her.

"No, I did not."

"Then what did you do all this time?"

Karp smiled to himself, recalling how Mahmoud Juma had answered this in his office.

"We talked, and we played chess."

O'Dowd looked incredulous. "You played chess?"

"Yes."

"So, I take it this young woman from a fishing village in Kenya was a chess grand master," O'Dowd said with a smile to show her disbelief.

430

"No, she was a beginner," Jojola replied, smiling himself but at the memory of Miriam. "But she was getting the hang of it. She was very smart."

"Perhaps, Mr. Jojola, but she was also very young and also in this country illegally," O'Dowd said. "So, I'm asking you, did you lure or badger her into cooperating with you?"

"No, she came to us and then insisted on continuing to help with our investigation."

"You didn't threaten to have her and her family deported back to Kenya?"

"No, I did not. She believed that she was doing the right thing."

"Uh-huh, so you say, but of course, we have to take your word for that, don't we?" O'Dowd said.

"That's true," Jojola answered as Karp rose to object.

"Your honor," Karp said, "the witness is quite correct, unless, of course, Ms. O'Dowd has independent evidence to rebut it, instead of her flawed, snide innuendos."

O'Dowd immediately turned away from the witness and stared at Karp. "I resent that disrespectful comment."

"Just a minute, counsel," Mason interrupted. "The witness has answered. This colloquy is over. Proceed, Ms. O'Dowd."

"Mr. Jojola, you snuck into the Al-Aqsa mosque by pretending to be one of these other criminals, correct?"

"Correct. My partner and I assumed the identities of two men my agency had just arrested."

"Yes, you and this mysterious partner, whom we have yet to hear from to see if his story jibes with yours — though I'm sure it will if you rehearsed it often enough."

"Objection," Karp said, rising to his feet again. "Counsel is making argument that is best left for summation."

"Sustained," Judge Mason said. "However, I will admonish the jury to remember that what the lawyers say is not evidence. The only evidence you are to consider is from the sworn witnesses and those exhibits admitted into evidence. Proceed."

"Mr. Jojola, you testified that Miriam Khalifa was afraid of my client?"

"That is true."

"Then can you explain why she never said anything to anyone else — at least, no one who has testified in this courtroom, including her own father — about being afraid of the man who befriended her after her husband's untimely death and gave her a job so she could support herself and her child?"

"Objection," Karp said. "Question assumes facts not in evidence, your honor, and asks for this witness to speculate on the deceased's state of mind."

"Overruled. I'll let the witness answer if he knows."

"I don't know what she told anyone else," Jojola replied. "I know what she told me and other members of my agency."

"If she was so afraid of Mr. Jabbar, why did she return to her job and act in a friendly manner toward him?" O'Dowd asked.

"She volunteered to help us by reporting on activities by Mr. Jabbar and others at the mosque."

"So you talked her into helping you."

"She wanted to help."

"And you didn't threaten her and tell her she would be deported if she didn't."

"Absolutely not."

O'Dowd went back over to the lectern to check her notes. Looking back up at Jojola, she then asked, "Did you see Ms. Khalifa in the mosque prior to her murder?"

"Yes, once."

"How did she react?"

"She obviously recognized us but was a little surprised. However, she carried on as if she didn't know us."

"Were you worried that she might identify you?"

"No, we trusted her."

"You trusted her? Is that because you had her brainwashed or so cowed that she didn't dare open her mouth?"

"Yes, we trusted her, and no, she wasn't brainwashed or coerced."

"So you say," O'Dowd replied. "But of course, we have only your word for that."

"Yes, it's my word against yours."

For a moment, O'Dowd seemed stunned by the retort. Karp himself winced slightly without showing it. He didn't want Jojola to get into arguments with O'Dowd where she could try to twist what he said. But when he thought about it, the timing with the judge's admonition about what the lawyers said was just about perfect.

"So, if my client was to take the stand and say that the deceased had come to him troubled and wanted to talk —"

"Objection!" Karp roared. "If her client is going to take the stand and testify, then let him do so. But counsel can't testify for him."

Mason shook his head. "Sustained. Ms. O'Dowd, please, you know better than that."

"I'm sorry, your honor," O'Dowd replied facetiously. "I just get a little irate when the government pulls this sort of —"

"Objection!" Karp roared again. "You just admonished her, and she's ignoring your ruling."

"Sustained," the judge said, now scowling at his former compatriot. "Ms. O'Dowd, you will refrain from making another remark on this matter, or on any other matter after I've ruled limiting you, as I have here."

"Yes, your honor," O'Dowd replied flatly before turning back to Jojola. "Do you know of any living witnesses — other than yourself and this mysterious partner — who could verify that what you're saying is not one big lie?"

"The defendant, Jabbar," Jojola said.

"Of course." O'Dowd scowled, her hands on her hips like a schoolteacher scolding a child. "You had to have someone to blame."

"And Nadya Malovo. At least, I assume she is still alive."

O'Dowd smiled and raised a bushy eyebrow. "Ah, yes, another mystery nonwitness. The infamous Nadya Malovo, or I believe you testified that she also goes by the name Ajmaani, is that correct?"

"You're correct."

"Where is this dangerous, vicious woman killer?" O'Dowd asked.

"I don't know," Jojola replied.

"You don't know," O'Dowd repeated. "In

fact, isn't it true that everyone who was supposedly in this room — another dozen men, I believe you testified — is allegedly dead, except as otherwise noted a moment ago?"

"To the best of my knowledge, yes."

O'Dowd strolled for a moment in front of the witness stand with a puzzled look on her face. "I'm curious. This Nadya Malovo, is she a great big strongwoman?"

"She's not particularly large. But she is well trained as an assassin and physically fit."

"And do I understand that you've allegedly met her several times, including at the mosque?"

"Yes."

"But despite all these contacts, you just can't seem to apprehend her, isn't that right?"

Karp might have been the only one in the courtroom who saw the muscles of Jojola's jaw clench. He knew that Jojola had sworn after Miriam's death that he would hunt Malovo down. But so far, he'd missed in the few chances he'd had or had found the tables turned and was hunted himself.

"Not yet," Jojola answered.

"Not yet?" O'Dowd scoffed. "Is it because she doesn't exist?"

"She exists."

"Really? But all we have is your word for that."

"Objection, your honor," Karp said. "Does Ms. O'Dowd really want to open the door on this one and give us the opportunity to establish certain facts about Nadya Malovo?"

"Sustained. Ms. O'Dowd, I've warned you before about having a door slammed shut," the judge said, "that prudence suggests you never should have opened. Since this is a collateral matter and will only serve to distract the jury from its primary focus, I am ordering you to continue on a different subject."

"Very well," O'Dowd growled. "You claim that this horrific crime was recorded on a digital movie camera. Is that correct, Mr. Jojola?"

"I never saw the recording, but yes, they at least went through the motions of filming, and I believe that is what was done."

"You believe," O'Dowd repeated. "And you expect these twelve jurors to believe that there was such a recording and that it depicts what you claim happened. So, where is the memory card that contains this recording, Mr. Jojola?"

"I don't know."

"Was this memory card found on my client when he was arrested?"

"No."

"Was it located in any subsequent search of his apartment or the mosque?"

"No."

"Who would have taken it, Mr. Jojola?"

"I don't know who removed the memory card," Jojola replied. "I wasn't present."

O'Dowd chuckled as if he'd told a joke. "Uh-huh. But it makes it easy to claim that if the jurors could just see this alleged recording, they would be convinced that a dozen young men, as well as my client, 'celebrated' the brutal murder of a beautiful young black Muslim woman at the hands of a mysterious Russian spy whom you just can't seem to get your hands on?"

"There isn't anything easy about any of this," Jojola replied, again surprising O'Dowd but not Karp.

"Yes, keeping lies straight is hard work," O'Dowd retorted. "And once again, we have only your word that any of this is true. Mr. Jojola, are you lying now?"

"No, I am not."

"Mr. Jojola, did Miriam Juma Khalifa threaten to reveal your true identities to her spiritual leader, employer, and friend, Imam Jabbar?"

"No."

"Wasn't she going to expose your plan and so you silenced her?"

"No."

"And did you then settle on my client to take the fall, knowing he was an unpopular figure with the government and the media for speaking the truth about the oppression of blacks and Muslims in America?"

As she said this, O'Dowd looked quickly over at Hassan Malik and the other blacks on the jury.

"That's not true."

"And did you, in fact, kill Miriam Juma Khalifa?"

"No."

"Did you and your partner force her down into the basement of the Al-Aqsa mosque, torture her to find out what she might have told her friend, Imam Jabbar . . ."

"No."

"And then cut her throat to make it look as if she'd been executed, all the while setting up this devious plan to pin it on my client?"

"That is absolutely not true," Jojola said.

O'Dowd glanced over at Karp as if surprised that he hadn't objected to her questions. He didn't react. *Stay with the game plan,* he reminded himself, though he seethed at the defense lawyer's low tactics.

"Then why didn't you try to help her, Mr. Jojola? You told us you have some military experience, and as a police officer, you've been trained for violent confrontations."

"There were too many of them, and I was unarmed," Jojola responded. "I would have died without completing my mission." He paused, looking down for a moment before returning his gaze to the jurors, the sadness in his voice unmistakable as he said, "And I couldn't have saved Miriam."

"But you could have tried, couldn't you, Mr. Jojola?"

John Jojola nodded. "I could have tried."

"Yet you expect the jury to believe that a law-enforcement officer, sworn to protect people, just stood there gawking while one woman nearly cut another woman's head off!"

"That's what happened."

"Are you a coward, Mr. Jojola?" O'Dowd asked. "Or are you a liar?"

Jojola sat still in the witness chair, a dark emotion crossing his face. But with an effort, he held his head up and replied, "Neither."

O'Dowd smirked. "Of course not." She turned to the judge. "I have no more questions for this man."

■ ■ ■ ■

If O'Dowd had expected Karp to look troubled or worried as he rose from his seat for redirect, she was sorely disappointed. He roiled with anger, but his demeanor displayed righteous indignation writ large.

"Mr. Jojola, you testified that before you became the chief of police of the Taos Pueblo, you served in the military," Karp began.

"Yes, sir," Jojola replied. "I served in the United States Army from 1967 to 1971."

"Were you stationed overseas?"

"I served in Vietnam from June 1967 through August 1971."

"Did you see combat?"

"Pretty much from the time I got there until the time I left. I belonged to a special unit known as a LURP, a long-range reconnaissance patrol."

"Objection," O'Dowd said, scowling as she stood. "Counsel already ascertained that Mr. Jojola was in the army. Of what relevance is all of this additional detail regarding this man's participation in an immoral war?"

"Well, your honor, perhaps for Ms. O'Dowd there are no moral wars," Karp retorted. "Only acquiescence to bullies, dictators, mass murderers, and terrorists. But that's hardly on point with what this trial is about. I am merely responding to counsel's attack on this good man's reputation, which is entirely proper rehabilitation permitted during redirect examination."

As he spoke, Karp looked at the jury to see how they were absorbing all of this. He noted in particular that Malik was sitting on the edge of his chair, his eyes narrowed as he glanced at O'Dowd. Katz had been right about one combat veteran's reaction to an attack on the courage of another combat veteran.

"Overruled, Ms. O'Dowd," Mason said. "But Mr. Karp, you will keep this brief."

"Yes, your honor," Karp replied, turning to face Jojola. "Would you 'briefly' explain what duties you performed as a LURP?"

"We worked as two-man teams, operating for long periods of time away from the base camp to intercept and disrupt enemy activity."

"When you were alone, deep in enemy territory, was death a constant possibility?"

"Yes, in fact, my partner — a childhood friend — was killed while we were on patrol."

"Were you ever wounded in combat?"

"I suffered combat-related wounds on three separate occasions."

"Did you receive any sort of commendations in relation to these wounds?"

"I received the Purple Heart for the first incident and two oak-leaf clusters for the subsequent wounds."

"Did you receive any other commendations while in the service of your country?"

"Yes, sir. I was awarded the Silver Star . . ."

"The Silver Star is for gallantry?"

"Yes, sir."

"Any other medals or commendations?"

"I also was awarded the Bronze Star."

"For bravery. Any others?"

Jojola smiled. "Well, when I got back stateside, they handed me a Good Conduct Medal, which I call the 'no discovered criminal activities medal.' "

The spectators in the gallery and the jurors laughed. Even Malik, Karp noted with satisfaction.

Through questioning, he now established that Jojola had achieved the rank of sergeant before being honorably discharged from the army and returning to the Taos Pueblo.

"As the chief of police at the Taos Pueblo, were you ever in physical danger?"

"Quite often," Jojola responded.

"Did you ever testify at trials on behalf of

the prosecution?"

"Frequently."

"Were you ever accused of lying?"

Jojola chuckled. "Whenever the defense attorney had nothing else to use."

For a moment, the courtroom remained in stunned silence. Then O'Dowd rumbled to her feet and shouted, "Objection! Who is this *agent provocateur* to besmirch me?"

Karp thundered right back. "Defense counsel, without evidence to the contrary, labeled this man a coward and a liar! I expect that if she has proof of this — whether in this trial or in previous trials Mr. Jojola has testified at — she had better present it during the defense case, or the jury will know who the liar is in this court-room!"

O'Dowd made a sound as if she was about to explode, but Mason rapped his gavel until she and Karp were both silent. "Enough! Ms. O'Dowd, you did attack the witness's credibility and should expect that he might shoot back. Your objection is over-ruled. But Mr. Karp, we are near the end on this line of questioning."

"Yes, your honor," Karp replied amiably as if he'd just been complimented. "Mr. Jojola, why didn't you help Miriam Juma Khalifa?"

444

Jojola's head fell forward for a moment, and he sighed. "I had to weigh the outcome. I couldn't have saved her, and many others would have died if I had tried."

"Mr. Jojola, you were asked this once by defense counsel, but I'm going to ask you again. Did you kill Miriam Juma Khalifa?"

"I did not."

"Who did?"

Jojola turned in his seat so that he was facing the defense table. "Nadya Malovo cut her throat, while that man" — he pointed at Jabbar, whose eyes grew large before he ducked his head — "planned, encouraged, and celebrated her death."

23

Marlene paused next to the elevators in the lobby of the new Westchester County Courthouse in White Plains to check the directory. She was looking for the office of District Attorney Harley Chin, hoping without much hope to prevent her client from being railroaded.

"Dirty Warren" Bennett was due to be arraigned in one hour on the charge of murder. At that point, her client would be slated to go on trial for his life in a setting where Tourette's syndrome would automatically put him at a disadvantage with a jury. Even if he never took the stand, which would be suicide, his tics and outbursts just while sitting in his seat at the defense table would prejudice the jury against him.

If he even makes it to trial, Marlene reminded herself for the hundredth time since visiting Warren in jail two days earlier and hearing about the Aryans. After she had left him that day, she'd gone to the jail administrator and demanded that Warren be placed in protective custody. But the man had just given her a baleful look and explained that every one of his segregation cells was filled by "some schmuck who's already been knifed, hit, raped, and otherwise attacked. Your guy's still in one piece."

"And if he's not when this is all over, I'll hold you personally responsible," Marlene had replied angrily.

"Yeah, you and the lawyer for every 'innocent' character who has the misfortune of being given into my care," the man had said. He'd then sighed in such a way that she almost felt sorry for him, and he'd added, "Squeeze some more money from the taxpayers, and we'll build more cells. Until then, sorry, but if you could see yourself out, I have a jail that's bursting at the seams, and I've got to go put my finger in the dike."

Marlene had talked her concern over with her husband when she'd seen him in his office during lunch break. "He's walking around with a target on his back. If he dies, the Michelle Oakley case goes away."

Butch had commiserated, but there wasn't much he could do in the middle of his trial. So she'd come to Westchester County an hour early, hoping to talk Chin out of arraigning Warren or at least into not opposing bail. She didn't think it would work. Chin had announced the indictment to the media within minutes of the grand jury returning it, citing "incontrovertible evidence."

Dropping the charges, or even putting off the arraignment, would be the same as admitting he'd been wrong. Not very likely with Harley Chin, whose bid for the soon-to-be-vacant state attorney general seat seemed to have gained steam since the indictment was announced.

But I have to try, Marlene thought as she pressed the button to summon the elevator. As she waited, she compared the district attorney she was going to see to her husband, whom she'd spent the morning watching as he questioned John Jojola at the Jabbar trial.

With Butch, everything at the New York DAO was very methodical, and there was never a rush to judgment until all the facts were in. Certainly, nothing like the unnecessarily swift indictment of Warren Bennett. Like her cousin the detective had noted, the police investigation wasn't even completed before Chin had wanted to go to the grand jury. She chalked it up to a rather desperate and pathetic grab for publicity to help his cause for the AG position. He obviously wanted to appear tough on crime and swift to mete out justice, knowing that the general public had no concept of how the system worked, only the perception that it was hopelessly bogged down and generally unable to protect innocent citizens. But there could not have been time to receive the police reports on the Oakley murder and properly evaluate the evidence.

At the New York DAO, the case would have been put through a rigorous process to ensure that the right man had been charged and that there was legally admissible evidence to prove the case beyond a reasonable doubt. That included having to pass through the weekly bureau meeting, where the top trial lawyers at the DAO, who were the top trial lawyers in the state, would gleefully rip apart cases presented to them by assistant district attorneys.

Harley had cut his teeth in that system and had the benefit of Butch's personal attention. *But Harley Chin is no Roger Karp,* she thought as she got off the elevator. She walked down the hall and opened the door leading into the reception area of the Westchester County District Attorney.

"May I help you?" asked a pretty young woman wearing a headset, who sat in front of a large photograph of Chin that hung on the wall behind her.

"Yes, thank you. My name is Marlene Ciampi," she said to the receptionist. "I called ahead. I'm here to see Harley Chin."

The receptionist pressed a couple of buttons and spoke into the microphone of her headset. "Marlene Ciampi here to see you," she said in a sweet voice, then giggled at the response. She looked up at Marlene. "He'll be right out."

Five minutes later, Chin emerged from the back of the office area with a grin on his face and his long, effeminate hand held out like a fishmonger on Fulton Street holding out the morning's catch. "Marlene Ciampi! It has been *such* a long time. How is that husband of yours? All wrapped up in a doozy of a trial, I hear. What's the prognosis? Hey, hope there are no hard feelings about the past. I know I was young and brash, and Butch, well, Butch is Butch — heh heh — hard-nosed bastard but one hell of a trial lawyer."

"No hard feelings, I'm sure," Marlene said, shaking his hand, which was soft and slightly damp. She did her best to keep a modicum of a smile on her face, though she was repulsed by his transparent glad-handing.

450

"Good. Good. So I guess I owe the pleasure of your visit to the Bennett case? I was a bit surprised when I heard that you were the defense attorney," Chin said. "But I hear his parents are rich, and we all have to make a living, don't we?"

Marlene wanted to punch him in the face, but instead, she forced a slightly larger smile and pointed in the direction from which he'd come. "I suppose. And yes, I'd like a moment of your time regarding the Bennett case. Would you mind if we went into your office?"

"But of course; come on back." Chin made a sweeping gesture with his hand. He winked at the receptionist, who giggled knowingly. "I'd *love* to hear what you have to say."

Chin led the way back to his office with Marlene staring daggers into his back. Once they were settled in chairs across the desk from each other, he placed his elbows on the desk and clasped his hands. "I'm all ears, though we only have forty minutes before we're to appear in front of Judge Jack Kingston, and I'd like thirty minutes or so to prepare." He looked at his watch.

"Doing the math, I have ten minutes . . . or so," Marlene said.

"Exactly," Chin said with another grin.

"Then I won't waste any more time. I'd like you to drop the charges against my client."

Chin threw his head back and laughed. He looked back down at her, barely suppressing a lingering desire to chuckle. "Oh, that's rich. Drop the charges? Marlene, I got an indictment hardly lifting a finger."

"That I believe," Marlene replied, dropping any pretense at friendliness. "At the very least, consider delaying this arraignment and letting my client out on bail before he gets killed."

Chin let his jaw drop dramatically, then shook his head. "Are you kidding? Let a cold-blooded killer out on the streets? The press would crucify me."

"Who cares what the press thinks?" she said, though the little voice in her head immediately chimed in: *He does.* "This is the life of an innocent man."

Chin's face grew serious. "Do you have something that clearly controverts the overwhelming evidence gathered by the police thus far? Something that proves his innocence?"

The little voice continued telling Marlene that she was wasting her time, but she went ahead anyway. "Proves his innocence? I didn't realize the standard had changed," she said. "But no, I don't have proof . . . yet. But I know this guy. He's just a sweet, little man who runs the newsstand in front of the Criminal Courts Building on Centre Street . . ."

Chin waved a dismissive hand. "Yes, yes, I met him once or twice when I was still employed by your husband," he said. "I found him to be annoying and shifty. Typical street person."

Marlene frowned. "He'd never hurt a fly."

"Till now," Chin said. He reached down and opened a thick manila folder on his desk. Picking up what looked like a police report, he began to read. " 'When informed that he was under arrest, suspect voluntarily made the following statement, "Michelle! . . . Whoop oh boy fucking bitch," and "dirty whore whoop whoop." ' "

"Oh, come on, you know he has Tourette's syndrome," Marlene retorted.

"So I've been told," Chin said, placing the report back in the folder and clasping his hands again. "To be honest, I thought back then that a lot of it was a put-on for sympathy and to get away with saying whatever he wanted. A little nuts, maybe, but still competent to stand trial for murder. I suppose you could put him on the stand during the trial and let the jury decide if he's faking."

Marlene bit her lip. She imagined jumping over the desk and strangling Chin just to get the smirk off his face, but her client's life hung in the balance. "Look, Harley." She tried to placate. "I don't want to get in a pissing match here with you. I do appreciate you hearing me out. But I want to tell you that something's just not right here."

"And why do you say that?" Chin asked, as if still willing to listen to reason.

"For one thing, his apartment was tossed by an intruder sometime after his arrest," she pointed out.

Chin's eyes narrowed. "How do you know that?"

"I was there at the tail end of the search," Marlene said. "The place looked as if a tornado had gone through it — drawers and closets flung open, clothes and personal belongings scattered everywhere. But my client is obsessive-compulsive about keeping his things orderly. Somebody went through there looking for something."

Chin shrugged. "Maybe you don't know him as well as you thought. Have you ever been to his apartment before this?"

"No," she admitted. "But the deceased had told him that she'd made a mistake and was going to have to pay for it."

"Even if I believe she said that, and I

don't, she could have been talking about one of her many divorces. What else have you got?" Chin looked at his watch to make his point.

"But why would he kill her? They were going to go out on a date," Marlene said. "He loved her."

"Which was probably his motive," Chin said. "Not that I have to prove why he snapped, but love is responsible for more murders than drugs. And what's he going to say, 'I asked her out. She turned me down. So I stabbed her to death and raped her'? No, he's going to claim that this beautiful, wealthy woman wanted to go out with a foul-mouthed, twitching newspaper boy and willingly had sex with him. Go ahead, Marlene, I dare you, put him on the witness stand, and see if the jury will believe him." Chin tapped the thick manila file on his desk. "Maybe you ought to know what's in here," he said. "You will soon enough, after I charge him with murder, so here's what I got: a cab driver who dropped him off at seven P.M. The driver says he was agitated, angry, cursing up a storm."

"That's the Tourette's. He was excited," Marlene countered.

Chin ignored her and held up a second finger. "There's no record of a cab being called to pick him up."

"He wanted to walk home."

"Yeah, right. And he says he left a little after nine. But his parents say he didn't come home until after ten. That's a long walk. Time enough to clean up, maybe." Holding up a third finger, Chin said, "He is the last one to see Michelle Oakley alive."

"Except for the real killer."

Chin snorted. "Nice try. His fingerprints are all over the place, including one very nice lift from the murder weapon — a steak knife. And by the way, he raped her, too. Such are the ways of 'true love.' "

"You're an ass, Harley," Marlene swore. "You always were, and nothing has changed. You have DNA proof from the body that proves Warren had sex with her? A used rubber?" She was pleased and relieved to see the shadow that passed across her opponent's face. *No, he doesn't,* she thought.

"Oh, we have the right man, Marlene. And believe me, I'm going to enjoy taking Butch Karp's bitch wife apart in court," Chin said with a sneer. "Your motion to dismiss is denied. I'm going to charge and convict your client and send this disgusting bum's ass to Attica, where one day he'll say the wrong thing to the wrong animal and justice will be served. Now get the fuck out of here."

Marlene stood but leaned over the desk. "I'll see you in court, Chin," she snarled. "You didn't learn a damn thing from my husband, which is good for my client, because I'm going to tear you a new one in front of the jury, your peers, and the media. And when I get done with you, you won't be able to run for dog catcher and win."

It wasn't much, but she enjoyed the momentary look of doubt in Chin's eyes. She was confident that she could take him in court if the playing field was level.

Unfortunately, that was put into question in the courtroom when the judge — a tan, handsome man with long silver hair combed back — who would be presiding over the case entered. After they were told they could sit back down, Warren slumped into his seat and put a hand over his eyes. "I'm so . . . whoop whoop bite me . . . fucked," he mumbled.

"What?" Marlene asked. "What's wrong? We'll enter a not-guilty plea and ask for bail."

"It won't matter," Warren replied. "The judge . . ."

"What about him?"

"He's the one Michelle was arguing with at my sister's party."

24

Standing at the rail waiting for Dean Newbury to enter the courtroom, Karp was
momentarily distracted by a familiar aroma.
It was the delightful bouquet of cherry-
cheese coffee cake, and not just any version
but cherry-cheese coffee cake from Il Buon
Pane. He'd have recognized that particular
smell if he'd been walking down a dark alley during a Gotham garbage strike.

His eyes followed the scent back to its
origin, a piece of which was just about to be
deposited into the mouth of the middle-
aged paralegal sitting behind the defense
table. Her eyes locked on his at that moment; she hesitated, then smiled and made
a gesture as if to offer him the bite. He
returned the smile but waved away the offer. His eyes returned to the back of the
courtroom as the entrance doors flew open
and Kenny Katz marched in.

Karp knew that the news wasn't going to

be good from the way Katz hurried down the aisle. *What now?* He glanced at his watch. It was ten o'clock, and the jury had yet to be called into the courtroom.

Up to this point, the morning had been taken up with a new O'Dowd motion demanding an "offer of proof" hearing to address once again the attorney-client privilege as it applied to Dean Newbury's testimony. Her motion to prevent Newbury from appearing had been denied at the pretrial hearing where Katz had wondered why she wasn't making more of a fuss about his testimony.

But an "offer of proof" hearing was different. In it, Newbury would be called to the stand and sworn in; however, the jury would not be present. Instead, Newbury would be questioned first by Karp and then by O'Dowd. She ostensibly would be trying to elicit testimony from Newbury that if prejudicial to the defendant she would argue was the result of privileged confidential communications and therefore inadmissible.

Generally, these types of testimonial, evidentiary hearings benefited the defendant. The prosecution necessarily has to preview its case through the witness under oath, giving the defense a better shot, a roadmap to prepare its cross-examination attack.

Karp figured that as much as anything, O'Dowd had made the motion to preserve the record for an appeal, as well as to make it appear that she was fighting tooth and nail for her client. This was, of course, good advertising, especially if she lost the trial and needed to show potential clients that the odds had been stacked too high against her.

However, Karp hadn't opposed the hearing for two reasons. One, he wanted Newbury on the record in case the old man later refused to testify before the jury or tried to recant. And two, the evidentiary hearing would preserve the record on appeal. Unless the court engaged in an abuse of discretion when ruling on the motion after an evidentiary hearing, the court's fact-finding would withstand appellate review.

Without opposition, Judge Mason happily granted the motion. It was no skin off his teeth. He would look as if he was being fair to both sides, and O'Dowd couldn't use it against him to have the case overturned. And he'd still rule against her opposition to Newbury's testimony before the jury, keeping Karp off his back.

That settled, everyone had taken their places, and Karp had asked that Newbury be called to the stand. When he didn't immediately appear, Karp had sent Katz to find out why not. Now he was about to learn.

Karp motioned Katz over to the front of the empty witness stand. "What's up?" he asked in a low voice.

"He wants to withdraw his plea," Katz said in a low voice.

Karp smiled, but it was all show, as he gritted his teeth and said in a low voice, "Okay, I'll go have a talk with him." He turned to the judge. "Your honor, I just need a moment to produce the witness."

Mason frowned but nodded. "Five minutes, Mr. Karp, and then he's on the witness stand, or you move on to your next witness."

"Thank you, your honor," Karp said as he moved toward the side door of the courtroom that led to the witness room. By the time he opened the door, he was steaming, and it showed.

Before the trial, Karp had, of course, had several long discussions with Newbury regarding his testimony and his "deal." But he knew the old man might pull something, thinking the federal government would save his bacon from Karp. And they'd tried in the person of Espey Jaxon, who'd appeared in Karp's office one day that spring asking for a favor.

Jaxon had said he wanted Newbury, the one man who could bring down the Sons of Man. The old bastard would dearly give up his former colleagues, insisting that in exchange for his cooperation, he be enrolled in WITSEC, the federal witness-protection program. But once in the program, he'd demanded that he be given special privileges and not just a new identity. His other requirements were that he be sent to live in a place of his choosing with plenty of money to live on for the remainder of his days. All the while being protected by the U.S. Marshal's Office.

The only problem with that plan was that Newbury was in the custody of the New York DAO, whose chief planned to prosecute him for murder. So Jaxon had come to Karp. Now Dean Newbury was not going to cooperate unless he was granted immunity in the New York County cases — meaning that he couldn't be prosecuted for his role in Miriam Juma Khalifa's death or the multiple deaths caused by the attacks on the New York Stock Exchange and the Brooklyn Bridge. It also meant that he would be free and clear for murdering his own brother, Vincent Newbury, the father of Karp's great friend and colleague V. T. Newbury.

Karp had scowled and shaken his head after Jaxon broached the subject. "Is he really worth one life, much less dozens of others that he's at least partly responsible for? And those are just the ones we are aware of. Who knows the extent of the evil this man has done?"

"I don't like it any better than you do," Jaxon had replied. "But we have to weigh what has already been done against what could still happen. The Sons of Man came within seconds of crashing this country's economy, which would have caused rioting, lawlessness, and anarchy, the likes of which we have never seen before. And they also came within a few hundred yards of incinerating the Brooklyn Bridge and a mile of real estate and humanity on both sides of the East River. All that death, disorder, and destruction so that they can create a scenario in which they step in to 'restore order,' through martial law, which means the end of democracy in this country."

Jaxon had sighed. "We know who some of them are but not all. They have insinuated themselves into every facet of American life — the government and its agencies, including law enforcement and national security, the justice system, the military, and even the entertainment industry. They are organized, secretive, and resilient, which is why they've lasted a couple of hundred years with no one the wiser until now. And if we don't get all of them at the same time, those who are left will go to ground, reorganize, and go on with their plans."

"But aren't they going to ground now? They know we have Newbury," Karp had pointed out.

Jaxon had nodded. "I imagine they're scared to death. They know he hasn't talked so far and won't until he's disappeared into the WITSEC program. But they only have two choices if they want to survive — rescue him or kill him — because otherwise he will take them down. We've only seen a sample so far, but Newbury collected information and documents on his group like nobody's business. He apparently didn't trust anybody and kept files on every single member of the Sons of Man, their families, and their associates. He can identify them, tell us where they are, and where they rank in the organization and their responsibilities. This group was never working on just one plan, and he knows them all and how they fit together — past and present. Most important, he has the financial records for the

Sons of Man going back a hundred years. The crimes and conspiracies we might be able to link to them by following the money are staggering. And we will be able to freeze their assets, killing the beast by depriving it of sustenance."

Jaxon's voice had trailed off. Karp knew that even with everything he'd just said, the former prosecutor turned FBI agent was uncomfortable with the thought of a murderer like Dean Newbury getting away with it. He'd held up his hand.

"Let me save you the trouble," Karp had said. "I'm sorry, old friend, but my answer is no way in hell. You've made your 'greater purpose' argument deftly, but it falls on deaf ears. I'm not going to get into a 'situational ethics' debate. If it makes it more difficult to dismantle the Sons of Man, then we'll all just have to work that much harder. But he's not walking away from murders he committed in New York County. He can plead guilty to murdering his brother, Vincent Newbury, and count himself lucky that I don't make him plead to a dozen other murders. *And* he will testify honestly and completely at Jabbar's trial. In exchange, I will make no recommendations for or against him at his sentencing; I will only tell the judge whether or not he testified truthfully. As far as I'm concerned, he's going to get twenty-five to life. Now, if you feds work out something with the judge after sentencing when he goes into WITSEC, that's on your heads."

Jaxon had stood and stuck out his hand. "I told the boss that would be your answer, but I was sent to ask. I asked."

"Well, Mr. Karp, good morning," Dean Newbury said as he entered the witness waiting room, as if they were a couple of lawyers meeting to work out a settlement. The old man started to stand with his hand extended.

Karp ignored the gesture. "Don't get up, Newbury," he spat. "I'm not here for any pleasantries."

The old man shrugged and sat back down. He had not become one of the top white-shoe attorneys in the country, head of a powerful Fifth Avenue law firm, and the leader of a powerful clandestine cabal without having a spine. "Fine. I've decided I want to withdraw my plea in regard to the death of my brother. I won't be testifying unless I get complete immunity from New York State charges. I'm not taking a chance that the feds will be able to work out a deal with the judge."

Karp glared and then leaned across the table so that his face was only a foot from Newbury's. "Happy to hear that," he said. "Because I intend to prosecute you for capital murder. You'll be convicted, no question, and sentenced to death. In fact, I'll be the one who pulls the lever that pumps three different kinds of poisons and sends you straight to hell."

Karp let the lethal-injection image sink in. "Now, I'm two seconds from walking out that door and telling Judge Mason that you will not be appearing," he said. "And when this trial is over, I am going to immediately ask for a trial date for you."

For a moment, Karp considered whether to just let Newbury swing. He was confident that Jojola's testimony was all the jurors needed. All he wanted from Newbury was to provide the nexus among Sharif Jabbar, Nadya Malovo, and the "criminal activities" fomented by the Sons of Man. He would place himself, Jabbar, and Malovo in the same room as they planned the events leading up to Miriam's murder.

Newbury's testimony probably wasn't even necessary. Karp planned to hammer O'Dowd's case during summation as nothing but an exercise in speculation and inferences spun from that rank speculation. He didn't see how the jury could do anything except convict after he was done.

However, he'd made that mistake before. Having prosecuted scores and scores of murderers to verdict, he was tempered by the understanding that he could not quantify evidence and know precisely when the jury would return a guilty verdict. No jury bell rings and informs the prosecutor that he has proven the case beyond a reasonable doubt. That, of course, only happens after all the evidence has been submitted and after jury deliberation, so he made sure he used every bit of piercing evidentiary proof available to get the desired verdict. To do otherwise and wind up with a not-guilty verdict would put the prosecutor in the inevitable position of second-guessing psychological torment.

In that first trial against O'Dowd and her self-proclaimed Black Liberation Army cop killers, he'd refused to believe that the jury would buy a case based on sheer speculation replete with "big-lie" inferences. Yet at least one juror had, and the jury hung. A fast learner, he'd come back in the second trial. Like Joe Louis in his second fight with Max Schmeling, Karp was relentless throughout. He'd hammered away at O'Dowd's big-lie defense mercilessly, keeping her on the ropes, so that the jury was convinced beyond any and all doubt of the defendants' guilt. He wasn't going to take a chance now, either, not when he could pound one more nail into Jabbar's coffin.

Wanting nothing so much as to toss Newbury to the wolves in the state penal system, Karp instead looked him in the eyes and without equivocation stated, "Just so we understand each other. You are going to take the witness stand today. You will testify truthfully and completely. If you lie, I will impeach you and thereafter prosecute you." He pointed toward the door. "Now, get the fuck out there and get up on that witness stand. Am I clear?"

As Karp spoke, Newbury's facial expression turned grim. Brittle hatred sparkled in his eyes, but so did fear. "Very."

Two hours later, Karp finished his redirect examination of Newbury, satisfied that the old man had told the truth and provided all the linkage the jury would need between Jabbar and Malovo. He'd also removed any doubt regarding Malovo's existence. And O'Dowd had done little to limit what he'd say and its devastating impact on the defense.

When Karp took his seat, Judge Mason

looked at his watch and announced that he was calling a lunch break. "When we return, the witness will return to the stand, and we'll call in the jury."

Back in his office, Karp and Katz went over what could be expected from Newbury's testimony in front of the jury. "It should take up the rest of the day, and then that's it for our case," Karp said. "I'm guessing the judge won't want to jump right into the defense case, so we'll probably start tomorrow morning with her 'expert' witnesses on government conspiracies and then on to his supposed alibi witness, this young woman, Alysha Kimbata. Then they're going to have to decide whether to put Jabbar on the stand."

"That would be a mistake," Katz noted. "You'll take him apart."

"Maybe, but it might be their only hope," Karp replied. "A last-ditch effort to appeal to that one juror who can identify with the oppressed black Muslim preacher and believes that the government is out to get all black men."

Karp excused himself, saying he wanted to spend a few minutes in the courtroom going over his notes from his questioning of Newbury and the expected tactics of O'Dowd. "I'll see you up there in ten minutes," he said, looking at his watch.

On the way to Part 39, Karp took a call from Marlene, who asked him about the movie-trivia question Warren had asked before his arrest. She seemed excited about something but hung up before he got a chance to ask much, saying she'd explain more at home.

As he approached the courtroom, Karp greeted the guard on duty who opened the door for him. He was surprised when he looked up to see the middle-aged defense paralegal just walking away from the witness stand. "I didn't know anybody else was in here," he said.

The woman, who was dressed in one of her usual dowdy brown pantsuits, grabbed a black three-ring binder. "I was checking on the water for the witness," she replied. "Ms. O'Dowd sent me to get this."

As she left the well of the court and drew close, Karp noticed for the first time that the woman actually had an attractive face if she would put a little effort into her makeup and hairstyle. He heard the slight accent and wondered where she was from, but then he spotted the paper bag she clutched along with the binder. He pointed and smiled. "Il Buon Pane?" he asked, knowing the answer.

The woman hesitated and gave him a curious look. "Yes," she said with a smile. "Is very good. And they were such a nice old couple." With that, she moved past him and left the courtroom.

Karp watched her go and shrugged. *An odd duck,* he thought, and placed his notepad and trial folder on the prosecution table. He walked back to the witness waiting room to remind Newbury that he had two options: the truth or prison bars for what remained of his life.

Ten minutes later, the courtroom had filled again with spectators and officials alike. The defense attorney and her client were seated at their table and seemed eager to get started.

Judge Mason entered and told Dean Newbury that he could resume his seat in the witness stand.

"Are you ready to proceed?" Mason asked the witness.

Newbury nodded and reached for the water pitcher. Karp immediately popped up from his seat and walked over to the stand, where he filled Newbury's cup. He glanced over at the defense table, where, oddly, O'Dowd and Jabbar both looked as if they were waiting for a movie to start.

The judge nodded to the court clerk. "You may bring in the —"

Suddenly, the quiet courtroom was jolted awake by the appearance of John Jojola, who burst in through the doors and rushed forward.

Jojola walked swiftly up to the prosecution table where Karp was standing. "I was just out front with Jen Capers," he said. "She's sure that she just saw Nadya Malovo leave the courthouse and get into a cab headed north, uptown. Jen jumped into another cab and is pursuing."

"Do you have a description of Malovo?" Sergeant Cordova, who joined them, asked. He pressed the button on the radio microphone clipped to his lapel, ready to relay the information and summon his team to start searching for bombs.

"I do, but it has to be a disguise," Jojola replied. "I personally didn't get a good look at her face. But she was wearing a brown pantsuit — padded, or Malovo has gained a lot of weight since I last saw her. What is it, Butch?"

Both of the other men were looking at Karp, whose eyes registered understanding and alarm. He looked over again to the defense table, where Jabbar sat licking his lips nervously and O'Dowd scowled. The pieces were falling into place in his mind like the tumblers in a bank safe. The frumpy paralegal sitting behind the defense, except when Jojola was testifying. His mind flashed to the last time he saw the woman, leaving the well of the court, and the misplaced water pitcher.

Karp glanced over at Katz, who was just about to take a drink of water. The pitcher had been moved. "Put the cup down!" Karp shouted. He spun toward the witness stand, but he knew in that moment that it was already too late.

Dean Newbury was grasping his throat with both of his hands, but no words came out, just white foam and a strangled, gargling sound. "Call an ambulance!" Karp shouted to Cordova as he rushed for the witness stand.

Court clerk Al Lopez beat him to Newbury, who had collapsed to the floor, and was about to start CPR when Karp stopped him with a hand on his shoulder. "I can't let you do that," he said as Newbury gasped one more time and then went limp.

"He's dying!" Lopez cried out, and tried to continue to help.

Again, Karp restrained him. "He's been poisoned, and it might be strong enough to affect you touching his lips to yours."

In horror, Lopez stood up and backed away. At the same moment, another tumbler clicked into place in Karp's mind. The cherry-cheese coffee cake from Il Buon Pane. "They were such a nice old couple," with an emphasis on the word *were*.

Karp swore. "Sergeant Cordova, I think she's headed to Il Buon Pane on Twenty-ninth and Third. Get somebody there as fast as possible. Suspect is a woman, heavyset, last seen wearing a brown pantsuit. And be careful, she's a trained killer!"

At the same time, Karp pulled his cell phone out of his pocket and hit the speed dial for Moishe at the bakery. He was relieved when his friend picked up.

"Hello, Butch."

"Moishe, close your shop, get Goldie, and —"

"Butch, she is already here. She wants to speak to you."

Karp's hand trembled with rage and fear for his friends as he listened to Nadya Malovo's voice in his ear. "You might as well call off the police, Karp. Your friends will be dead before they arrive, and I will be gone. But I wanted you to know that soon it will be your sons and daughter and then your bitch wife you will be mourning. And only then will I come for you." And the phone went dead.

25

Marlene got out of the cab on Forty-ninth Street and stood for a moment looking up at the looming gray façade of the Saks Fifth Avenue department store. It seemed an odd meeting place. *But better than the usual dark alley,* she thought.

Warren Bennett's arraignment on the indictment the day before had taken about an hour. Generally, an arraignment lasted only a few minutes, with the defendant entering a plea either to a prearranged plea bargain, meaning to a lesser charge with a less severe sentence than the original, or a plea of not guilty. If the latter, the case was sent to a trial courtroom, where pretrial motions addressed to the indictment were heard. Then the case was set for trial at some future date.

However, Bennett's case for many reasons was unusual. DA Chin craved ink, so he'd asked the lead investigating detective, James

Meadow, who had similar inclinations, to give a synopsis of the People's case against Warren, ostensibly to justify Chin's request for remand of Warren and no bail for the duration pending trial.

All the while, Marlene had sat pondering the coincidence that the same man Warren had witnessed confronting Michelle Oakley at his sister's party would be presiding at his trial. Her first inclination when her client had made his comment about Judge Jack Kingston was to jump up and demand that the judge recuse himself because of his personal connection to the victim and the defendant. But something had cautioned her to wait. If the judge was somehow part of this conspiracy to commit murder and set Warren up for the fall, she needed to figure out why first.

Better I don't tip my hand, she'd thought. *If it does turn out to be just a coincidence, I can always make the motion at a later time. But for now, let's play dumb.*

All that was required to have Warren bound over for trial was the grand-jury indictment that satisfied a "probable cause" finding that a crime had been committed, that the defendant had committed it, and that if the evidence went uncontradicted or unexplained, the defendant would be found

478

guilty beyond a reasonable doubt.

The judge had asked Marlene if her client was going to enter a plea. Rising, she'd given Harley Chin a venomous look before answering. "Not guilty, your honor," she'd said.

Knowing it was a waste of time, she'd still asked for bail, citing Warren's Tourette's, "which places him at great risk in the jail population. He has already been the victim of one attempted assault. He is the owner of a small business in New York City with strong ties to that community, as well as having family in Purchase. He has no criminal record and is not a flight risk."

However, Chin had requested that Warren be remanded without bail to await trial. "Given the severity and brutality of the crime, the safety of this community demands that he be removed from the streets until such time as this case can be adjudicated."

After encouraging Warren to keep his head up, Marlene had left the courthouse with her mind whirling. She'd reminded herself that the confrontation at the party between the judge and Michelle could be a false lead. And if she put all of her eggs in that basket, she might miss something important. She didn't believe that Warren had killed his friend, but it didn't mean that some intruder intent on burglary or rape hadn't surprised Michelle and killed her.

Warren could have just been in the wrong place at the wrong time, and this is all just a tragic misunderstanding, she'd told herself. . . . *And you don't believe that for an instant.*

Leaving White Plains, Marlene had driven to Purchase and the home of Warren's parents, Clare and Wesley. She'd called ahead so they were expecting her, and she was invited into the library. The Bennetts had clearly been uncomfortable at first, but they'd answered her questions without hesitation.

Warren had not appeared to be angry when he left the house for his date with Michelle. "Quite the contrary," his mother had said. "He was actually dressed nicely and seemed very happy. He even spoke civilly to me without that dreadful sense of humor. Of course, he was so excited about seeing Michelle that his other 'issue' was acting up. But that happens."

Marlene had asked how they knew that Warren arrived home a little after ten P.M., as Chin had told her. "I always watch the evening news," Wesley had said. "And I remember hearing him come in shortly after it began."

"Did you see him or talk to him?" Marlene had asked.

Both parents had shaken their heads. "No," the mother had replied. "I did hear him puttering about in the kitchen, getting a late-night snack, I suppose. He used to do that a lot as a boy . . ."

As the woman's voice had trailed off, tears sprang to her eyes, which she wiped at angrily, as if they were annoying insects. "Pardon me, there must be something in the air."

"It's okay," Marlene had said gently, and she was touched when Warren's father reached over and patted his wife's knee. "Mothers never stop loving their children."

The other woman had looked up, grateful. "Do you . . . do you think . . ." she'd stammered.

"That he did it? Absolutely not," Marlene had said.

Some of Clare Bennett's icy demeanor had returned. "I know he didn't do it," she'd said thinly. "Despite our . . . 'differences,' I know my son, and he is not a killer. What I meant was, do you think he'll be convicted?"

Marlene's lips had twisted. "I, of course, can't say how this will go for sure. I haven't seen, examined, or had a chance to challenge the prosecution evidence, but I think we can beat this."

"Do you need a retainer?" Wesley Bennett had asked.

Marlene had shaken her head. "No, I'm doing this pro bono for Warren. As I told your daughter, your son is more than he seems and has helped a lot of people, including my family."

Both parents had exchanged surprised looks. "I'd like to hear about that sometime," Wesley had said.

"And in the meantime, what can we do?" Clare had asked.

Marlene had looked her in the eyes and said, "You can go see your son and tell him what you told me about knowing he is not a murderer. Right now, what he needs most is the support of his family."

Clare Bennett's head had tilted back slightly as though she'd taken offense. But then she'd smiled. "We'll see what we can do."

As she'd stood up to leave, Marlene suddenly froze as a new thought sprang into her mind. "You know, it just struck me," she'd said. "I've seen the evidence log from the items the police seized in connection with this case, and it lists the clothes he was wearing when he was arrested — jeans, a sweatshirt, a T-shirt, and socks. But other than that, there's no mention of any other clothing items; apparently, there was nothing in his apartment they considered worth taking to be tested or kept as evidence. But if I just heard you right, and from what I recollect from talking to your daughter, Shannon, Warren was wearing nice clothes for his date."

"Yes," Clare had replied, puzzled. "We bought him a jacket, tie, shirt, and slacks for Shannon's party; otherwise, he dresses like a street person, and that just wouldn't do for the occasion. I do know he was wearing the new shirt and slacks when he left for his date; I was watching from an upstairs window. And I believe he hung them back up in his closet upstairs before he left for Manhattan."

"The police didn't want them?"

"They didn't ask."

"May I see them, please?"

Clare had led the way to Warren's room. Marlene had smiled as she entered. It was definitely a boy's room, the walls covered with posters for films such as *Star Wars, The Godfather, Indiana Jones,* and *The Searchers.* There were also poster-sized photographs of Marilyn Monroe and John Wayne.

"Warren loves his movies," his mother had said.

"I know." Marlene had chuckled. "He and my husband play a movie-trivia game with each other." The aside had reminded her of the trivia question Warren was supposed to solve for his date with Michelle. *The key goes where the book editor sees his wife and son off to Maine.* She'd wondered if Butch had ever figured it out or if it had slipped his mind as it had hers.

Clare Bennett had walked over to the closet and opened the door, pointing out the shirt and pants her son had worn on his date. Marlene had carefully picked them off the rack by their hangers and laid them on the bed so she could see the front of both clearly. She'd bent over to look at the sleeves of the tan shirt. "No blood," she'd said, mostly to herself.

"What?" the Bennetts had asked at the same time, just as Shannon had entered the room.

"Umm . . . it could be nothing," Marlene had replied. *Except,* she'd thought, *the autopsy report said that Michelle Oakley had been stabbed several times in the back, piercing her lungs and heart; in fact, cause of death was loss of blood. And yet there are no discernible flecks of blood on the shirtsleeves or chest or on the front of the pants. But that media-hound Detective Meadow didn't think to ask Warren's parents for the clothing their son wore the night he saw Michelle, just in case? Cousin Bobby said he was lazy, but that's just plain shoddy detective work!*

"Would you have any plastic bags around, like what you'd get from the dry cleaner, that I can use to protect these? I'd like to take them with me to be tested," Marlene had said.

A few minutes later, Marlene had left the house with the clothes in plastic bags, escorted by Shannon. When they'd reached Marlene's pickup truck, Shannon cleared her throat. "I . . . uh . . . wanted to talk to you about something I've been thinking about."

"Sure. What's on your mind?"

"I don't want to speak ill of the dead," Shannon had begun, "and knowing the way Warren felt about Michelle, I hope I'm wrong. But I don't think I am."

"Go on," Marlene had said. "Maybe it's nothing, but we can't afford to overlook anything."

Shannon had nodded. "Okay, well, I guess this would fall into the category of rumor or partially overheard conversations and guesswork. But anyway, I was at the club a month or so ago, having a drink with a friend, when I saw Michelle come in and sit down at a table with two of the wealthy — and married, I might add — members. She didn't see me, and she didn't stay long, just shook their hands, talked for a few minutes, and left. I'm probably making too much of this . . ."

"Finish your thought," Marlene had encouraged.

"Well, after she left, I went outside to smoke a cigarette and was standing on the lawn below the raised patio when those same two men came out. They were right up above me, but they didn't see me. I couldn't hear everything they were saying, but I did catch one of them telling the other, 'It's expensive, but they're beautiful, discreet, will do whatever you want, and best of all, you don't have to live with them.' They laughed, and then the guy who was talking said, 'Want me to tell Michelle you're in?' And that was all I heard."

Marlene had let it sink in for a moment. "You're saying you think Michelle Oakley was running an escort service."

Shannon had bitten her lip and nodded. "It took me some time to believe it, but then it all made sense. I told you that I knew she was struggling financially — her house was up for sale, and the neighborhood gossips were telling Mom, who is one herself, that she was letting her staff go and selling some of her possessions. Then suddenly, the for-sale sign came down, she bought a new car, and I'd been seeing her out again, shopping and attending parties, obviously wearing new clothes."

"Is this what you started to tell me the first time we met at the jail?"

"Yes. It just seemed so outlandish. Then again, after what the governor of our state did, I guess anybody could be involved in that sort of thing."

Anybody indeed, Marlene thought now, as she made her way to the expensive-perfume counter inside Saks. *Maybe even a judge?* She'd asked her husband what he knew about Jack Kingston, and he'd said that the dapper, extremely well-heeled and politically-connected-up-the-wazoo judge was apparently headed for a seat on the federal bench, maybe even the Second Circuit U.S. Court of Appeals. "With an eye on the U.S. Supreme Court."

So why kill Michelle? Was she blackmailing him? She didn't seem the type, and Warren said she was looking to "atone" for her mistakes, not make new ones.

Marlene knew that the key to solving the murder and saving Warren was Jim Williams. But that wasn't going to be easy. Warren's parents knew Judge Kingston, but they only vaguely recalled Jim Williams and his date who had accompanied him to Shannon's party.

"We could call Jack and ask if he has the man's number," Wesley Bennett had offered. But Marlene had declined that offer. If the judge was involved in any way, she didn't want to tip him off or have him warn Williams.

Marlene had tried looking up Jim Williams in the Westchester County phone book, but there were nearly a hundred entries for Jim, James, and Jimmy Williams and another two hundred in Manhattan. *The proverbial needle in a haystack,* she thought. *I need a break.*

It had come with the telephone call she'd received that morning.

"Is this Marlene Ciampi?" the woman on the other end of the line had asked.

"Yes, and who are you?"

"I don't want to give you my name, not yet. I got your telephone number by calling the Westchester courthouse and asked for Mr. Warren Bennett's lawyer. He didn't kill that woman, but I think I know who did."

Marlene had made a mental note to call the courthouse and tell them not to give out her cell-phone number willy-nilly. There were always amateur sleuths who had it all figured out and were generally nutcases. But what the woman had said next changed her opinion in this case. "I think the killer was my boyfriend, Jim Williams."

The woman had said she wanted to meet and show Marlene something. "But I'm afraid. Meet me at Saks, at the perfume counter."

As she approached the counter now, Marlene picked out a pretty, buxom blond woman who was wearing sunglasses, a floppy hat, and a raincoat as her contact. She walked over to her and, in a low voice so as not to startle the woman, said, "My name is Marlene. Did you call me?"

The young woman nodded. "Meet me at King's Cafeteria on Fifty-first and Seventh in about ten minutes," she said in a stage whisper. Then she turned and strolled away.

Marlene wasn't exactly sure what the woman thought she was accomplishing by the subterfuge, but she waited a few minutes and then walked to the cafeteria. Twenty minutes later, she knew she had her man.

Sometimes in tears and sometimes angry, the woman, who identified herself as Sherry

Maxwell, talked about how she'd become suspicious that her boyfriend, Jim Williams, was seeing other women. So she'd hired a low-budget Chinatown private investigator named Todd Fielding to follow him. "Todd's a slimy bastard and has been hitting on me from the moment I walked into his office," she said. "But he did what he said he would do."

Sherry handed Marlene a large envelope. She opened it and removed several photographs. The first showed a man walking up a long driveway toward a large house that Marlene recognized as Michelle Oakley's. The lighting wasn't good, as he was illuminated only by ground lights along the drive. However, the next photograph was better. It showed the man standing in the porch light and being met at the door by Michelle.

Sniffing and dabbing at her eyes with a tissue, Sherry pointed to the man in the picture. "That's Jim."

Marlene looked down at the time and date indicator on the bottom righthand corner of the photograph. *Nine fifty-eight P.M.,* she thought. *Warren was just about to walk in the door of his parents' home a mile away. Not impossible if a cab had been waiting for him but impossible if he walked home.* Even

Harley Chin would have to sit up and take notice. *Or will his ego make him ignore even this?*

The third shot was a close-up of the faces. Neither looked happy to see the other, and Marlene could almost feel the tension of the moment.

"I can't believe he was cheating on me," Sherry said, shaking her head sadly. "What did she have that I don't?" Several tears leaked out from beneath the dark glasses.

"I think that's a better question than you know," Marlene replied. "This probably won't make you feel any better, but I don't think this was a social call."

Sherry looked puzzled. "What do you mean?"

"I don't think he was there to see her for anything sexual," Marlene said.

"But the paper said . . ."

"A red herring," Marlene replied. "Meant to make it look like something other than what it was, which was a murder for hire."

"I don't understand," Sherry said. "Jim is an investment banker."

"Another ruse," Marlene said. "I think your guy's a pro and knew exactly what he was doing. You just asked me what she had that you don't. Well, I think she had something — information, a photograph, documents — that someone doesn't want anyone else to see. So they hired your boyfriend to retrieve it and make sure Michelle never spoke about it again."

She tapped on the photograph. "He had it set up perfectly, with the perfect scapegoat. Except he didn't count on a jealous girlfriend having him followed."

"Todd said he saw your client leave a little after nine," Sherry noted.

Marlene smiled. "Oh, really?" she said. "Between this photograph and putting Fielding on the stand to say just that, it could be the break we needed."

Sherry smiled and wiped at her tears. "You might want to talk to Todd right away," she said, and then explained his plan to blackmail Williams. "At first, I was so angry that he had cheated on me, I almost went along with it. I even said I'd think it over and let him know this afternoon. But then I thought about the poor man in jail . . . what's his name? Warren? And, well, I couldn't do that no matter how much money I could get."

Suddenly, Sherry put her face in her hands and began to weep. "What am I going to do? I came to New York to be an actress, and I end up just being a kept woman for a murderer."

Marlene reached across the table and gave the young woman's arm a squeeze. "You should be proud of yourself," she said. "You could have taken the money. Or you could have just decided to keep living with Williams and pretending you didn't know. But because you have a conscience, an innocent man won't have to spend the rest of his life in prison, and we might be able to get a killer off the streets. You're a real hero in this."

Sherry looked at Marlene's face, searching for the truth. "Yeah, I guess I am a little, huh? Thanks. You can have the photographs. Are you going to arrest Jimmy now?"

Marlene considered the question. Maybe it was time to call her cousin, Detective Sergeant Bobby Scalia. But if Williams was arrested, whoever he was working for might get away with his role in the murder and whatever else it was that they didn't want out.

"Soon, I think," Marlene said. "I want to do a little more digging before the bad guys get wind of it. When are you supposed to give Fielding your answer?"

Sherry looked at her watch. "It's noon. I told him that I'd come by at two if I was going to help blackmail Jimmy. I think he's hoping to get laid, too . . . like that's going

493

to happen. Not in this lifetime."

Marlene thought about it for a moment. "If you don't mind," she said, "I think I'll pay a visit to T. X. Fielding Investigations in your place. Will you be okay going home?"

The tears sprang to Sherry's eyes again. "Yeah, I've known about this for days, and he doesn't suspect. Like I said, I wanted to be an actress — and to be honest, I've had to do a lot of acting with Jim Williams, if you know what I mean." She sighed, took out a small notepad from her purse, and wrote something on it. "Here's my number. I'll just pretend you're a girlfriend if he's around when you call. Are you going to see Todd now?"

"I have one stop I want to make first," Marlene said. "I'm going to Warren's apartment in the Lower East Side."

"Why?"

Marlene smiled. "To feed a cat . . . and look for whatever it was that Michelle Oakley had that you don't."

26

"You might as well call off the police, Karp. Your friends will be dead before they arrive, and I will be gone. But I wanted you to know that soon it will be your sons and daughter and then your bitch wife you will be mourning. And only then will I come for you."

Nadya Malovo flipped Moishe Sobelman's cell phone shut and laughed. Her main objective was accomplished — the death of Dean Newbury. All it had taken was a couple of tablespoons of powdered aconite root placed in the water pitcher she'd watched Karp use throughout the trial.

It had been risky staying in the courtroom while Newbury testified that morning. She'd met the old man on several previous occasions, and there was the chance he'd recognize her. The same reason she'd stayed away on the day the Indian, Jojola, took the stand. But he was younger, sharper, and a lot more dangerous than Newbury.

The disguise as Natalie Stiefelmaier, the dowdy, middle-aged paralegal, was a good one, although the extra padding in the support hose and around her hips, buttocks, and breasts was uncomfortably warm. It did its job, however. Early on, starting with some of the pretrial hearings, it got her through the shorter, less intensive court-personnel security line with O'Dowd and Elijah. By the time the trial got under way, the guards were used to seeing her come and go, though Karp's men still kept them on their toes for weapons and strange packages.

Malovo was also counting on the way most men looked at women. Even old men like Newbury would hone in on an attractive blond woman like heat-seeking missiles, but a plain, overweight spinster was just background noise. Her prey never noticed her sitting behind the defense table, which he avoided looking at most of the time anyway.

Unable to locate Newbury in the months before the trial, she'd hoped to take him out as he was being transported. But Detective Fulton had kept the security detail small so that there'd be no leaks about when he was being moved and by what routes. So she'd moved on to the idea of getting some suicidal idiot to drive a panel truck in front of the court building and ignite a fertilizer-fuel bomb, as Timothy McVeigh had done to the Murrah Building in Oklahoma City. But one look at the solid, looming edifice that occupied 100 Centre Street, and she knew that it would withstand a fairly major blast, and there was no guarantee that Newbury would be killed. And the Sons of Man had made it very clear that they expected her to succeed this time, or they would find someone else.

No, she was going to have to get as close to Newbury as she did with Congressman Denton Crawford, and that meant getting him into the courtroom. The first step had been a call from the Varick Detention Center to Karp's office, pretending to be an anonymous federal agent with a tip about Jabbar being moved. After that, it was not difficult to talk Megan O'Dowd into going along with the plan for "paralegal" Stiefelmaier to accompany her, as well as to ensure that Newbury testified — opposing his appearance but only enough to avoid raising suspicions.

The defense attorney considered it a win-win situation. She was tired of taking on political cases with little to show for it except a diminishing reputation as an activist lawyer, and the Sons of Man were going to make her wealthy. She would also get her revenge on Karp, a man she hated as much as Malovo did.

Still, even with O'Dowd's cooperation, it was no easy task to accomplish the assassination. The assumed identity got her into the courtroom, but she wasn't going to be able to smuggle a bomb or a gun. Nor was she willing to commit suicide to kill Newbury; she needed an exit strategy that would provide for her own escape.

The idea of how to make it all work had come from watching Karp pour water for witnesses, his co-counsel, and himself. Once he'd even poured a cup for Megan O'Dowd, who'd glared at him with her back to the jury but accepted the drink rather than make a scene in front of them.

It was easy enough to get the small packet of powdered aconite root past the metal detectors and bomb-detection dogs. The question had been whether Newbury would drink on the witness stand, and that's why she'd chanced attending to watch Karp's questioning. She'd been pleased to note that Newbury frequently sipped water on the stand. She knew he would do the same thing when O'Dowd questioned him after lunch.

The plan was nearly foiled when Karp returned from the break early and almost caught her pouring the packet into the water pitcher. She'd heard him greet the guard at the door just in time to grab one of the defense folders, so that she would have an excuse for being on that side of the bar.

Then there'd been another close call when she saw Jojola and a woman approaching the front of the Criminal Courts Building. Recognizing the woman as the U.S. marshal she'd shot in Colorado, she'd quickly ducked into the nearest cab and hoped she hadn't been spotted. As soon as the cab pulled away, though, she'd relaxed and laughed as she stripped out of her "fat suit."

"You okay, lady?" the cab driver had asked, glancing in his rearview mirror and obviously wondering what kinky event was going on as his new fare took off her clothes in the back of his vehicle.

"Yes, all part of a Broadway production," she'd said with a coy smile, which satisfied the cabbie, who kept watching her finish dressing in a blouse and jeans, amazed at the transformation from plain to gorgeous.

As the taxi had made its way uptown toward Twenty-ninth Street and Il Buon Pane, Malovo had laughed out loud at the delicious irony of Karp becoming her "accomplice" by pouring the fatal cup of water for Dean Newbury. She'd been dropping hints purposely throughout the trial. She'd even brought the cherry-cheese coffee cake from Il Buon Pane into the courtroom hoping he would notice. It was an unnecessary risk, but she wanted Karp to know that she'd been sitting there right under his nose the whole time, plotting her revenge. And he would know without a doubt that there was nothing he could do to prevent her from making good on her promise to kill him and his family.

She imagined Newbury wrinkling his nose at the slightly bitter aftertaste of the poisoned water. But he'd quickly forget about that as he began to experience a severe shortness of breath and constriction of his airway, followed by pain and tightness in his chest. He might wonder if he was having a heart attack — and indeed, the "Queen of Poisons" over the centuries had often gone undetected as anything but death from natural causes. No amount of resuscitation effort would save him.

Of course, Sharif Jabbar was going to be disappointed in the actual outcome. O'Dowd had been led to believe, and passed on to her client, that "Natalie" would assassinate both Newbury and Karp. With the district attorney dead, the judge would be forced to declare a mistrial, and powerful people within the federal government could then insist that Jabbar be turned over to them. And, according to what O'Dowd was told, the original deal to ship him off to the Saudis would be back on.

However, while there was the chance that Karp would drink the water — something she had not seen him do during the trial so far — the Sons of Man were paying her to kill Crawford and Newbury. Unless Karp happened to die, too, Jabbar would be on his own to beat the charges. If he won, he'd be off to Saudi Arabia; if he lost, the plan was to make sure he didn't survive his first month in the penitentiary.

Malovo had actually hoped Karp wouldn't drink the poison, because she wanted to kill everything he loved before she came for him. And she would start with the old couple who owned the bakery. She'd learned of their existence, and their place in Karp's life, by following him. She'd seen him on his weekly visits and saw how they greeted him like a long-lost son and he returned the affection as if they were his parents.

A rare twinge of guilt had nagged at

Malovo as she visited the bakery to learn the couple's routines. The old man, Moishe, she could not have cared less about; she didn't like Jews, and killing him wasn't going to trouble her. However, the old woman, Goldie, had been extraordinarily kind, even if she spoke with her hands and her actions rather than words. Malovo had even considered just killing the husband, but she knew it would be the death of the woman that would eat at Karp, who would know that he'd led his enemy to them. And in her own admittedly twisted way, she also thought it would be cruel to murder one and not the other.

So she'd resolved to kill them both and let Karp absorb the guilt. On the way to the bakery, she'd called her accomplice, a muscle-bound idiot the Sons of Man had provided for her, and told him to move ahead with the plan. As a result, when she'd reached Il Buon Pane, he was standing guard near the door with his gun trained on Moishe, who stood with his hands in the air behind the counter, trying to shield his wife.

Malovo had just walked up to the old man when the cell phone in his top apron pocket began to ring. She'd reached over the counter and plucked it out, smiling when she read the caller ID. "It's your friend, the district attorney," she'd said, handing the phone back. "Answer it. Then let me talk."

Moishe had done as he was told. "Hello, Butch," he'd said, and then added, "Butch, she is already here. She wants to speak to you."

After hanging up with Karp, she flipped the cell phone shut and laughed. She was going to be a wealthy woman. Now it was time to begin her revenge. She stepped back from the counter and nodded to her accomplice, who leveled his gun at Moishe.

Two things happened next, neither of which Malovo had counted on. The first was Goldie Sobelman screaming, "Nooooo!" The only word she'd ever heard the old woman say. The second was the ear-shattering roar of the .45-caliber pistol that had appeared in Goldie's hand, the bullet from which caught the would-be executioner in the chest, knocking him backward into a table as customers screamed and panicked.

Malovo didn't panic. Instead, she dove for the gun her partner had dropped and rolled back to her feet with the sights now trained on Goldie, who was trying to hold her own gun steady.

The two women stood looking at each

other over the barrels of their guns. Then Goldie placed hers on the counter and raised her hands. "Please, child," she said, her voice hardly more than a whisper from self-imposed silence. "If you must shoot, then I beg you, me first. I cannot stand to see him hurt."

"Goldie, no!" Moishe cried. He picked up a baker's knife and raised it above his head as if to threaten the assassin. "Shoot me, but spare her!"

Nadya Malovo moved the gun from Moishe and back to Goldie. Her finger had begun to exert pressure when, for the first time in years beyond which she could remember, a voice from deep within stopped her. She lowered the gun and stood still, her eyes locked on Goldie's.

The front door of the bakery was flung open. "Drop the gun," U.S. Marshal Jen Capers shouted as she entered, her gun aimed at Malovo's head.

For a moment, Malovo considered whirling and shooting the marshal. She knew she stood a good chance of winning the duel. But Goldie shook her head slightly and smiled. The gun clattered to the ground as she returned the smile and raised her hands in the air. She turned to face Capers. "Shoot — get it over with," she said.

Capers shook her head. "Not today, dang it. Today you live."

27

At the sound of the buzzer, Todd Fielding smiled and popped a breath mint into his mouth. He pressed the button for the intercom and, using his best British savoir faire, answered. "Do come up, love."

You still have it, old chap. He chortled to himself as he stood and quickly checked his hair in the beer-commercial mirror hanging on the wall. He wondered if he should have downed a Viagra tablet. *No time now, she's here. Just going to have to score this goal on your own.*

He hoped she wouldn't mind that he'd already gone ahead and called her boyfriend, Jim Williams, that morning and suggested that he meet him in the evening "regarding certain photographs I took outside the residence of one Michelle Oakley last Saturday evening a little before ten." He'd felt immensely clever using the electronic voice changer that he'd purchased at his last PI Schools class. And of course, he'd also placed a "restricted number" on his cell phone so that he wouldn't be identified; then he'd walked several blocks away from his office to Sara Roosevelt Park off Chrystie Street to make the call so that his location couldn't be pinpointed by GPS.

"I'll want five hundred thousand dollars in small unmarked bills, for which you'll get my camera's memory card and all the printouts. Oh, and my word as an English gentleman that you'll never see or hear from me again."

That good old drunk ex-cop Mike Machovoe taught me well, Fielding had thought as he walked back to his office. He'd made sure that the meeting that night would be in a very public place — outside Madison Square Garden, where any hanky-panky on the part of Williams would be witnessed by a few thousand spectators attending the Knicks game, as well as a couple dozen cops. They'd make the exchange, and he'd disappear into the crowd, head down the escalator to Penn Station, and be off on the first train out of Dodge.

Never to be seen in this part of the country again, he mused. *And if that fine little tart Sherry wants to go along for the ride with her half, which I'll tell her was two hundred thousand, so much the better.* He wasn't worried about the money running out; he'd downloaded and kept a flash-drive copy of the Oakley photographs in case he ever needed to dip into that well again.

Fielding glanced around the office in anticipation of the arrival of his beautiful client. He tossed an old pizza box off the couch, unlatched the door, leaving it open just a crack, and then half sat, half leaned against the front of the desk with what he thought was his finest Humphrey-Bogart-as-Sam-Spade pose. He was concentrating on the type of smile he should employ — *friendly, suggestive, but not gloating, I think* — so at first, he didn't grasp the enormity of the situation.

Jim Williams was standing in the doorway with a finger to his lips and a gun with a silencer attached pointed at his head. "Shhh," the gunman said quietly. "If you so much as squeak, I'm going to blow your fucking head off."

Standing and raising his hands, Fielding was suddenly aware of a warm, wet sensation running down his right leg as his bladder voided. He was shaking too much to consider doing anything else when two young, muscle-bound men rushed past Williams. One of them plastered a piece of duct tape over Fielding's mouth, while the other spun him around and violently shoved him down onto an old wooden office chair normally reserved for clients. It took only a few more seconds and more duct tape for the pair to bind his wrists to the arms of the chair and his ankles to the front legs. All he could do was try to suck in enough air through his nose and roll his eyes wildly as Williams walked around the desk and sat in the chair, with the gun still pointed at his face.

"Now, you and I are going to have a conversation," Williams said quietly yet firmly. "If all goes well, you may live to see another sunrise. If it doesn't, you won't. Am I clear?"

"Mmmphff," Fielding replied, nodding his head rapidly.

"Good. I need to fix some things, and you're going to help me do it."

Watching the Brit pansy wet his pants and shake like a wet dog, the Fixer wondered how such a complete idiot had come so close to messing up his plan.

Some of it, of course, had to do with his decision to deal with the Michelle Oakley problem by himself. If he'd had the usual team together, someone would have been on lookout and surely spotted a bumbling spy creeping around the residence. Then again, he would have had to share the wealth for the additional work, and he did, after all, have other expenses. *That new Lotus Elise SC I want will run me at least ninety thou, but with 219 supercharged horses under the hood, it will be worth it.* At least, that was what he'd been thinking when he went alone to the Purchase mansion.

The Fixer also knew he'd committed the sin of being overconfident, which in the spy game could result in capture or death. *But it was such a perfect setup,* he consoled himself.

Originally, when Judge Kingston called and said they had a problem with Oakley's "discretion," the Fixer had hoped that she could simply be bought off or "discouraged" with implied threats. Either was always preferable to murder, which carried with it a whole new set of issues with the police and crusading family members. But Oakley had proved difficult.

She was the sole proprietor of a high-end call-girl service that she'd run out of her family home in Purchase. From what he'd been able to gather from Kingston, as well as what she'd told him before he killed her, the whole thing had started when one of the upstanding members of the country club, knowing she was desperate for funds, had offered her a generous sum for sex.

Despondent from the breakup of yet another marriage and nearly broke, she'd decided *why not* when her benefactor introduced her to a couple of other members of the club, including his Honor. At some point after that, Oakley had been approached by several bored, wealthy twenty-somethings, the children of her clients, one of whom had found compromising e-mails on her father's computer. Rather than being upset, the girls, including Rene Hanson, had wanted to go into business with Oakley; they'd done their research and had been impressed with the financial opportunity. "Better than screwing college jocks for free," Rene had apparently once told Kingston.

Oakley had demurred at first. But when the younger women had said they were going to go forward anyway, she'd acceded. The girls, like Rene, had seemed attracted to the fantasy of seducing powerful men and making their own way out from under their parents' financial thumb, as well as rebelling against their pampered, comfortable lives. At least there'd be one wiser head to run the service like a business, including setting up the "arrangements" to protect the girls' identities and safety while providing discretion for the clients.

Things had apparently been going along swimmingly until Judge Jack Kingston choked the life out of Rene in a frenzy of sexual ecstasy. Unfortunately, the girl was the child of wealthy parents with a lot of political and social clout, who'd applied a great deal of pressure on law enforcement from the federal government on down. The media had obliged by going into full "missing blond white girl" syndrome and made Rene's disappearance a national story. Seeking to redirect attention, he'd supplied the false lead by feeding the press the story about Mexican drug trafficking, and it had seemed to work. Guadalajara had received more adverse media attention than even that city was used to getting.

Oakley had not been so easy to fool. She knew Rene and how enamored the girl had become with Kingston and his promises to divorce his wife and marry her.

"There was no way she was going off to Mexico with a stranger, especially without telling me," Oakley had told the Fixer the night he murdered her. "I went back and looked at her accounts and noted that she was seeing Kingston pretty much exclusively and spent every night with him that week before Christmas when his wife was out of town. Except there's no entry for the night she disappeared. At first, I was fooled when Kingston kept calling, demanding to see her. It didn't make sense that she'd just left town, but I wasn't sure what else to think. Until I overheard him talking about his trip with the wife and kids at the same time he was supposedly so desperate to see Rene. That's what confirmed my suspicions."

With confirmation of what she'd had a hand in creating, her conscience — whose voice she had heard but ignored — returned. Then she'd become a blackmailer, but not the usual sort who wanted money, a job, or some special favor. Instead, she'd demanded that Kingston come clean on his own — claim it was an accident if he wanted and that he was giving himself up because his conscience was haunting him. But he would have to admit his guilt and throw himself on the mercy of the courts. And there was one more thing. He would have to reveal where Rene Hanson's body was located so that her parents could have the closure of a burial.

If Kingston didn't do it on his own, she was going to the police with documentation, including deposited checks from traceable bank accounts, a calendar of dates when he'd met with Rene, plus the blood test Kingston had taken, which could be traced back to him through DNA, and even his last two voice messages asking to meet with Rene. And if the judge didn't think that was enough to worry about, or at least open up an investigation with him as the prime suspect, there was one more piece of evidence, she'd said, that she wasn't going to reveal yet. "But it will finish him."

Sitting in her library, facing the Fixer across her desk, Oakley had sighed, and for a moment, he'd almost felt sorry for what he was going to have to do. She'd looked haunted and incredibly sad. Obviously, when her conscience had resurrected itself, it had done so with a vengeance.

"I should have stopped it when I realized she was falling in love, because he was only going to use her until he moved on. I didn't even consider that he would kill her," she'd said. "Of course, I should have stopped the whole thing, the Gentleman's VIP Club, before it got started. What was I thinking? Victimless crime? A win-win opportunity?"

Oakley had looked him deep in the eyes then, and he'd realized that she already knew what was going to happen to her. Then she'd said something curious. "And now I have to atone." With that, she'd picked up her cell phone. "I'm calling the police."

Surprised by the sudden turn of events, Williams had thrown himself over the desk with the steak knife he'd picked up from the dining room table when he'd first come in. It *had* been the perfect setup. The weird little man was easy to frame. The taxi driver an added bonus. The availability of the murder weapon, which he'd surmised would have his scapegoat's fingerprints ready and waiting. But he hadn't wanted to finish her yet. He'd still needed to know where she kept all the incriminating evidence.

However, she'd fought like a tigress, and he'd had to kill her too soon. Her ferocity had taken him by surprise, and he didn't like surprises, as they could lead to mistakes. He'd sat down, looking at her body for a moment, to recollect his thoughts. When he'd been satisfied that his mind was back on track, he'd stood and gone to work.

After setting up the murder scene, including a sexual assault with a candlestick, the Fixer had hacked into Oakley's computer, where he'd found the files to the Gentleman's VIP Club. She did indeed have the documentation she'd claimed, including the testing clinic in New Jersey where the blood sample had been sent. But there had been no indication of what secret she had not revealed that would "fix" his client.

His concerns about the unknown piece of evidence had soon been overridden by another. Her computer's log had indicated that a little after nine P.M., the files pertaining to Client 032355-JK — which he immediately recognized as the birthdate and initials of Jack Kingston — had been downloaded, presumably onto a disk or flash drive. Cursing, he'd inserted a disk of his own that introduced a computer virus into Oakley's machine and would crash the memory system the next time it was turned on. He'd then searched for the downloaded material, to no avail, leading him to one conclusion: She'd given it to her date, Warren Bennett, the man he'd set up to frame.

The Fixer had had to wait until Sunday afternoon to get a friend at the Agency to get him Bennett's address in New York City. He'd then watched the apartment the rest of that Sunday, hoping the occupant would leave long enough to have Josh and Lex search the place while he watched. But Bennett, who seemed to have a steady stream of homeless bums for visitors, had stayed inside all day and hadn't left until very early Monday morning.

Only then could Josh and Lex toss the place, working quietly and quickly to search while purposefully making it appear to be a burglary. But they hadn't found anything of value. *No matter,* he'd thought. *This case will soon be closed.*

He'd waited until after Rob, who'd been parked down the block from the Oakley mansion, reported that the maid had discovered the body and run out of the house screaming. Then he'd called the Westchester County police and asked to be put in touch with the lead detective on the Oakley case.

Good fortune had smiled again when Detective James Meadow had come online. The Fixer had identified himself as a "concerned citizen" who wanted to report that Michelle Oakley had entertained one Warren Bennett on Saturday night, the latter arriving by taxi. "Which you can check out," he'd said. "I don't want to be a snitch, but I heard this sleazeball talking about raping and killing this broad." He'd then hung up and was satisfied to learn that Bennett had been arrested that afternoon as he was closing his newsstand.

The next step was to contact the powerful people who were paying him to protect Kingston and to put the pressure on District Attorney Harley Chin and make sure they wanted this case resolved quickly. If he wanted to come within sniffing distance of the soon-to-be-vacated state attorney general's seat, Warren Bennett needed to be indicted forthwith.

As expected, Chin had jumped through the hoops like a circus poodle. Then all that had remained was for Jack Kingston to get himself appointed to the case. When the judge had pointed out that the defense attorney was likely to demand that Kingston recuse himself because of his personal knowledge of the deceased and the defendant's family, the Fixer had told him it wouldn't matter. He'd left it unsaid that this case would never make it past arraignment, and the only way Warren Bennett was getting out of the Westchester County jail was in a body bag.

Then, when the defendant was murdered in jail, Chin would declare the case closed. And whatever secret incriminating evidence Michelle Oakley had against his client would go to the grave with her.

There'd been a flicker of concern when Marlene Ciampi unexpectedly took on Bennett's defense. Not only was she the wife of the incorruptible district attorney of New York County, but his contacts had told him that she was a formidable adversary in her own right. She had quickly deduced that the apartment search was no ordinary burglary. But after considering his options, the Fixer had decided that however competent Ciampi might be as an attorney and investigator, it was going to be too little, too late.

It was the perfect setup, he told himself again. Except for this moron Todd Fielding and his camera.

When he'd first received the call from the blackmailer, he'd worried that it was a professional working freelance for one of the agencies. Maybe someone hired to get a little dirt on one of the rich and powerful assholes from the country club whose influence might come in handy at some point in the future. But instead, whoever it was had snapped photographs of the Fixer and, realizing what he had, had decided to supplement his income.

However, it was soon apparent that the blackmailer was a rank amateur. Of course, this Fielding had no idea who he was dealing with or that he had all the latest countersurveillance and tracking gadgetry. As soon as the "caller unknown" had come up on his private cell-phone number, the Fixer's equipment had immediately started tracing the call. The GPS tracking system found in most late-model cell phones had placed the caller on Chrystie Street. But another search had come up with the caller's real phone number and linked into the Agency's database, which said it was owned by Todd Fielding with an address on Mott Street.

If I'd wanted to, I could have probably beat him back to his office, the Fixer thought now as he sat looking at the frightened man. He nodded to Lex, who pulled a pair of pruning shears from his pants pocket and placed the business end around the first knuckle of the pinky finger on Fielding's left hand. The private eye squealed and began to hyperventilate.

"We'll get to your photographs in just a moment, but first I want to know why you were spying on that house," the Fixer said calmly. "So I'm going to ask Josh to remove the duct tape covering your mouth, at which point you will quietly, yet clearly, tell me the truth." He let his eyes flick tellingly to the endangered pinky and added, "I think you know the consequences of lying."

It took every bit of willpower and the dual threats of shears and gun for Fielding not to scream when the Fixer's man ripped the tape off his face.

Although he'd once been evaluated by the headmaster at the boys' school he'd attended in Wales as "not the brightest bulb in the room," he was smart enough to know that as soon as these men got what they wanted, he was a dead man. He tried to recall if old Mike Machovoe had covered this sort of circumstance in class. The man he knew as Jim Williams, who he'd assumed had killed Michelle Oakley in some sort of fit of passion, had turned out to be some sort of mob guy, complete with henchmen, guns, and shears.

You need to stall, old man, until you can figure a way out of this pickle, he told himself. It was risky, but he considered himself a consummate liar and thought he ought to be able to talk himself out of this. *Maybe we can still work out some sort of deal,* like gentlemen, *where I get paid for my troubles.*

"I was working for some old broad who thought her hubby was banging the decedent," he said, trying to sound sincere and professional. He even added what he thought was a relaxed smile for good measure. *That ought to throw them off.*

As he spoke, Williams leaned forward and studied his face. The man then sat back with a rather disconcerting look of disappointment.

"Did you know that when people lie, their pupils dilate, and their eyes involuntarily shift from side to side?" Williams asked. "And that when your smile is sincere — meaning that you've told the truth — you use all the muscles in your face, including those around your eyes. But if you're insincere, you only use the muscles around your mouth. And Mr. Fielding, your eyes aren't smiling."

Fielding felt the scream building up inside, but it didn't get a chance to erupt before Josh slapped the duct tape back across his mouth and Lex squeezed the shears. There was a sickening snap, a lightning bolt of pain, and then he passed out.

The Fixer looked at the lolling head of his captive and rolled his eyes. "Jesus H. Christ, what a pansy. Wake him up!"

Josh stepped around and slapped Fielding's face until the captive came to. However, it took him only a couple of seconds to feel the searing pain in his left hand and attempt to scream despite the tape. He looked as if he might pass out again.

"No, no, now stay with me here, Todd," the Fixer said. "Just tell me the truth, and this will all be over. But don't lie to me, because I'll know it. You won't lie to me again, will you, Todd?"

Fielding gagged and shook his head violently. He started to cry when Lex handed the shears to Josh, who placed the sharp edges around the same knuckle of the pinky on his right hand.

"Good. Now, Lex will remove the tape from your mouth, and I want you to tell me truthfully who you were working for," the Fixer said, leaning forward again.

"Your girlfriend, Sherry," Fielding blurted out. "She thought you were cheating on her."

The Fixer looked as if somebody had hit him on the head with a two-by-four. *I knew I should have dumped that bitch the moment she mentioned marriage.* He blinked twice and looked up in time to see Lex and Josh exchange a look and knew what it meant. The boss had made a bad mistake. He was getting soft, which made him dangerous to work with. But he would have to deal with that later.

Pointing to the digital camera on the desk, the Fixer asked, "Is this the camera you used?" Without waiting for an answer, he opened the port on the side and removed the memory card. "Now, in just a moment,

I'm going to look at your computer, and it will tell me if you've stored or made copies and prints of these photographs. But you could save me the trouble of having to search your office, and perhaps remove more pieces of your fingers, if you'd just tell me where everything — and I mean everything — is located."

Fielding sniffed and whimpered. "All the prints are in the folder in the filing cabinet marked Jim Williams," he said, and paused.

The Fixer smiled encouragingly. "Come on, spit it out."

"I made a copy of everything and placed it in a safety-deposit box at a bank!" Fielding cried, certain that he was about to lose the tip of another pinky.

The Fixer studied his victim's face. *Damn, he's telling the truth.* But before he could say what would happen next, a buzzer sounded. Somebody was at the door downstairs.

"I guess this would be the female company you were expecting," the Fixer said. He pointed to the intercom. "You're going to tell her that you're busy and to come back later." He pressed the button on the intercom and nodded.

"Sorry, love, I'm a . . . I'm preoccupied!" Fielding shouted, trying to sound normal. "Come back later, please."

The Fixer looked at Lex. "Go have a look through the peephole," he said.

Lex returned a minute later and reported. "It was some MILF," he said. "Actually pretty good-looking for a wuss like this guy. How do you do it?"

"It's the accent," Fielding mumbled.

The Fixer actually laughed. "I'll have to remember that one. Now, back to the bank. You were being naughty, weren't you? If 'Jim Williams' had paid, he was going to have to pay again and again. So it's only fair that since you were caught cheating, you tell me which bank and give me the key."

The Fixer was surprised when Fielding shook his head. "Sorry, old chap," the Brit replied, "but if I give you the key, you'll simply kill me now. And I'd rather like to see that sunrise you talked about. I will, however, take you to the bank. You get what you need, and I get to walk away. Very far away, I assure you."

Fielding cringed and shut his eyes as Josh tightened his grip on the shears and waited for the order to start cutting. The Fixer considered his options. The Agency tended to look the other way regarding his activities, but they frowned on the murder of civilians. If it came out that he was responsible for Oakley's death, he would have to call in all sorts of favors to get off — favors he might need some other day.

"Okay, Todd, we'll play it your way," the Fixer said, nodding to Josh, who pocketed the shears while Lex tore the tape off his mouth.

"Ow! Fuck!" Fielding swore. "Bloody wankers!" He was obviously feeling good about his little stand.

The Fixer shot him a hard look. "Don't get carried away, you moron. We're going to the bank to retrieve the flash drive," he said. "Josh will accompany you. If anything goes wrong, we'll be watching, and I promise you that Lex and I will find you in the not-so-distant future and take you apart joint by joint. A very long, gruesome, and painful way to die. Am I clear?"

Fielding swallowed hard. "Quite."

28

"I thought you said there would be a mistrial!" Imam Sharif Jabbar groused as he paced around the holding cell adjoining the courtroom, waiting for the "crime scene" to be cleared and court reconvened.

"She was supposed to wait and kill Newbury after Karp put him on the stand in front of the jury," O'Dowd replied. "Then, if I wasn't able to cross-examine him, the judge would almost have to have declared a mistrial. And if he didn't, we'd certainly win an appeal."

"Appeal? It could take years to win an appeal, and I can't spend no more time locked up," Jabbar complained. "Somebody is going to put a screwdriver in my kidney before I get out on an appeal." He stopped pacing and shook his head as if he couldn't believe this was all happening to him. "The deal was, I would stick it out for this trial so that those rich white motherfuckers could get their bitch close enough to kill Newbury. Then there'd be a mistrial, and the fucking U.S. government would take over and get my ass out of this damn country."

Jabbar stopped and glared at his attorney. "Maybe if you hadn't filed that motion for an 'opportunity of proof' hearing, things wouldn't have got fucked up."

O'Dowd knew that her client had a point, but only in hindsight. She had been surprised when Karp did not oppose her motion for an "offer of proof." If he had, the judge would have probably rejected it, as he had her previous attempt to keep Newbury off the stage. Then the jury would have been brought in and the old man put on the stand to testify in front of them. He would have been murdered after the lunch break and before she could cross-examine him, and *voilà,* a mistrial.

But everybody was covering their asses, she thought, *including me.* She realized that Karp had acceded to her demand to take away one more appellate argument from her, probably so that he'd have his reluctant witness on the record.

On the other hand, O'Dowd had felt she needed to make the motion, and indeed had to defend Jabbar, as she would have regardless, if the Sons of Man planned to assassinate a prosecution witness and cause a mistrial. *Just in case what happened happened,* she thought.

At an early-morning meeting at O'Dowd's office in Harlem, Stiefelmaier, or whatever her name was, had explained that she planned to strike immediately following the lunch break by putting poison in the witness stand's water pitcher. But first, she'd wanted to observe Newbury on the stand to make sure her plan would work.

Of course, the plan also called for Stiefelmaier to dump the poison in the water without being seen. Then Newbury's death would have been attributed to a heart attack — at least, until toxicology reports came in. Even then, aconite was supposedly difficult to detect unless the medical examiner chemist was looking for it specifically.

But O'Dowd knew that if it was discovered that paralegal Natalie Stiefelmaier had murdered a prosecution witness, all eyes would turn to the defense attorney who had brought her into the courtroom. So O'Dowd had wanted to be able to point out that she had been zealously representing her client, unaware that an assassin had been planted on her team. And that if she'd been involved in the conspiracy to kill Newbury, then why was she doing more than going through the motions? Motions that included demanding an "offer of proof" hearing to keep Newbury off the stand, as well as preserve the record for appeal.

However, two things had gone wrong with the plan. First, Karp had not opposed the hearing, so that they actually got through the questioning of Newbury without the jury present before the lunch break. She had asked Stiefelmaier to wait until the afternoon break, but the assassin had shaken her head. She'd pointed out that the courtroom was cleared of people during lunch — she would need an excuse from O'Dowd to get past the guard herself — but there were often many people who remained during breaks. "It has to be lunch," the assassin had said. "And besides, what does it really matter to you?"

O'Dowd had known what the killer was getting at. She was being paid far above any legal fees she could have charged to set the stage for Newbury's murder. The money people didn't really care what happened to Jabbar. If Newbury's death caused a mistrial, then that was his reward for helping out, though the defense attorney had a gut feeling that her client would never live to reach Saudi Arabia. It was just a fantasy to keep him in line.

The second problem had occurred when Karp saw Stiefelmaier at the witness stand, "checking" the water. And then she'd been identified leaving the Criminal Courts Building.

Glaring at the defense table, Karp had asked one of his detectives to seize all the water in the courtroom to be tested. "And I'll put you on notice right now, O'Dowd," he'd snarled. "There will be an investigation into what role you played in getting your 'paralegal' into this courtroom to commit murder. I will get to the bottom of this, and if you're involved, you'd better have your toothbrush with you the next time I see you, because you're going away forever."

O'Dowd had protested that the murder of Newbury was a government conspiracy to make her a scapegoat for the death of a man "whose testimony under oath when cross-examined might have embarrassed, or even condemned, people in high places." She'd also suggested that Stiefelmaier was a plant sent to her office by the New York DAO who had noticed her advertisement for legal help to assist with Jabbar's trial.

When word had come back that Stiefelmaier had been apprehended, Karp had looked at O'Dowd and smiled. Then she'd known such a pang of fear that she'd felt suddenly light-headed and had sat down without a word.

The judge had asked Karp if he wanted to wait until the next day to regroup and call someone else to the stand. "No, your honor, Mr. Newbury was our last witness," he'd replied. "That's the People's case. Now we'll see what other tricks the defense team has up its sleeves."

O'Dowd had mustered what indignation she could and replied, "I resent Mr. Karp's implication that I am in any way responsible for the unfortunate circumstances of Mr. Newbury's death. And I would remind him that his story about seeing this woman near the witness stand after lunch, which, by the way, was witnessed by no one else and might not even be true, is hardly incriminating. If Natalie Stiefelmaier isn't a plant, then I wonder if this is an elaborate plan to frame an innocent woman and then claim that she's this mysterious Nadya Malovo."

"Resent all you want, counselor, the truth will out," Karp had retorted. "But in this case, it might definitely not set you free."

Judge Mason had quieted the two attorneys and then brought the jury into the courtroom long enough for Karp to say that the People's case was concluded. The judge had then announced that there would be another short break, "after which the defense will begin its case."

In the holding cell now, Jabbar stopped pacing and pointed his finger in O'Dowd's wide frowning face. "And I thought she was supposed to kill Karp, too!"

"That's what I was led to believe," O'Dowd answered. "But it didn't happen."

Actually, she was well aware that Karp wasn't a target yet. There was no poison in the water Kenny Katz nearly drank. The best scenario was to have everyone believe that Newbury died of a heart attack, and it would have been too much of a coincidence for two men to succumb simultaneously.

"I told you there was always the possibility that we'd have to go through the entire trial," O'Dowd retorted. "The death of Newbury, and even Karp, was no guarantee that the case wouldn't go forward. That's why we've been fighting this thing as if it was going forward, and we'll still win it."

Jabbar licked his lips. He was sweating profusely and gave her a doubtful look. "What makes you so sure?"

"Well, for one thing, Newbury won't be testifying against you," O'Dowd pointed out. "And he's the only person outside of

Jojola, an *agent provocateur,* who can put you together with Nadya Malovo. It will be your word against his."

"What about my alibi witness?" Jabbar said. "Is she going to hold up?"

O'Dowd nodded. When Jabbar first suggested that a certain young woman from his congregation had been "persuaded" by her father to testify that she was with him that night, O'Dowd had been hesitant. Even if she put off telling Karp that she had an alibi witness — as she eventually had — it was risky to put someone on the stand, as Jabbar had put it, "to tell a greater truth for the good of Allah."

But she had met with the girl, Alysha Kimbata, and was convinced that the twenty-year-old was frightened enough of her father, an immigrant from Yemen who shared the same radical views as Jabbar, to stick with her story. She would testify that Jabbar had come to her house late that afternoon; they'd had dinner, and then he'd had sex with her.

"I think she'll be fine," O'Dowd said. "Karp won't want to be seen as roughing up a young woman on the stand. He'll try to discredit what she says, but he won't be too hard on her."

While initially frightened by Karp's

threats, O'Dowd was actually relishing the fight now. In fact, the only thing she had not liked about being paid a ridiculous amount of money to help kill Newbury was that if it had caused a mistrial, she would not have the opportunity to beat her despised rival. She'd hated him ever since he'd come back in that second trial against her black nationalist cop killers to win four guilty verdicts, and he'd beaten her again every time they'd met after that. She was convinced that she could at least get a hung jury now.

She truly believed that government in the United States from the federal level down, including the local district attorney, was racist and oppressive. If she or her client or their witnesses lied, or even if a young black woman like Miriam Juma Khalifa was murdered, it was for a good cause. "The sins of the state were worse than any one life is worth," she mumbled.

"What? The sins of the state?" Jabbar said with a frown.

O'Dowd smiled. "Nothing. Just thinking aloud." She stood and looked him in the eye. "I think you're going to have to take the stand."

Jabbar rolled his eyes. "But won't Karp get into my past . . . you know, like the armed robbery and manslaughter?"

"You merely say that you are a changed man," O'Dowd replied. "You never had a chance growing up . . . poor, fatherless, a victim of the state. But you found Allah in prison and turned your life around."

"I don't know," Jabbar said. "People don't like some of the things I've said, like about the World Trade Center."

"Exactly," O'Dowd said. "I want him to attack you. Our whole defense is that you've been accused of this crime because of your political and religious beliefs. That you are being singled out."

"All of those jurors aren't going to believe that," Jabbar said. "I can tell already that some of them hate me."

"The white ones, maybe," O'Dowd countered. "But your brothers of color, the blacks and Hispanics? We don't need all of the jurors; we just need one who believes that a black Muslim man cannot get a fair trial in this country. A hung jury will work as well as a mistrial."

O'Dowd could see that her speech was having an effect on Jabbar. The man had an ego all out of proportion to who and what he was, and it was showing in his face now. She wanted this battle against Karp, but she needed Jabbar to testify to have any chance of throwing it back in his face. "And aren't you the man who persuaded more than a dozen 'freedom fighters,' the Al-Aqsa Martyrs Brigade, to give their lives up for Allah and their race? I would think convincing just one juror that you're not the criminal here, you're a victim, would be easy."

Jabbar tilted his head back and smirked. "Let's do this thing!"

An hour later, O'Dowd had to hide her sneer behind a hand as she watched Karp rise from his seat to cross-examine her "leading expert on the government conspiracy behind the September 11, 2001, destruction of the World Trade Center and Pentagon." Braxton Howe, a thin, bearded professor of political science at Columbia University, had written two books on his September 11, 2001, theories, and the district attorney made no attempt to disguise the contempt he felt for the man.

At a previous "offer of proof" hearing without the jury present, Karp had argued that Howe shouldn't be allowed to take the stand, because whatever he had to say about September 11 was irrelevant and untrustworthy — the two benchmarks for admissibility — in Jabbar's trial. He'd listened to O'Dowd's questioning of Howe and told the judge that "whatever the government may or may not have done in the past has nothing to do with the matter before this court. It's just highly speculative nonsense based on flawed, mindless rhetoric and ideology."

Mason had disagreed. "The defense is contending that the government engaged in a conspiracy to frame an otherwise innocent defendant. I am going to permit the defense to go forward with this witness and leave it to the jury to decide what weight to give his testimony."

Now, with the jury present, Karp went on the attack. "Mr. Howe, you just told the jury that you believe that the United States government planned, conspired, and carried out the September 11, 2001, attacks on the World Trade Center and the Pentagon. Am I correct?"

"Well, yes, that or allowed it to happen," Howe replied with one bushy eyebrow arched.

"Well, which was it?"

Howe gave a puzzled look. "What do you mean?"

"Did the government plan and carry out the attacks? Or did the government know about the plans and do nothing to prevent the attacks?"

"I think there is evidence to support either theory," the professor replied.

"Evidence? Other than speculation and a loose assembly of rumors, innuendos, and disconnected facts, what hard evidence do you have?"

"Well, as I discussed a few minutes ago, there is the manner in which the buildings collapsed and the ease with which the alleged hijackers accomplished their mission —"

"All of which is based on conjecture and guesswork. Am I right?" Karp interrupted.

"It is based on the examination of thousands of documents, witness interviews, and, yes, educated postulations," Howe retorted as though correcting a student in one of his classrooms.

"And not one scintilla of incontrovertible evidence that would be accepted into a court of law," Karp shot back.

"The government controls the courts."

"I see, so Judge Mason and all the other judges and attorneys who are part of the justice system are also part of this enormous and yet incredibly secretive conspiracy."

"I don't know if they're all doing it consciously or subconsciously, but yes, many are going along —"

"Thank you. 'I don't know' is the first

factual thing you've said today. Isn't that right?"

O'Dowd rose quickly from her seat. "Objection! Counsel cut off the witness's answer and is improperly arguing with him."

"I'm just trying to determine exactly how far his conspiracy theory goes, and it would appear to include every man, woman, and child in the country."

"Sustained. I get your point, Mr. Karp. I think we all do," Mason said with the hint of a smile. "But let's not engage in debate with the witness. Just ask your questions."

"Yes, your honor," Karp replied before turning back to Howe. "So whatever theory you're operating under today, it still amounts to the U.S. government — the police officers, military personnel, airline employees, building janitors, and security personnel, as well as hundreds of passersby who would have had to look the other way for this massive conspiracy to work — being responsible for the murder of 2,993 people, most of them U.S. citizens?"

"That's correct," Howe said, lifting his chin defiantly.

"I have one final question, Mr. Howe," Karp said, letting his anger show as his voice rose. "What bearing does all of this unsubstantiated speculation and pure fantasy have on whether that man" — he turned and pointed at Jabbar — "murdered Miriam Juma Khalifa in the basement of the Al-Aqsa mosque?"

Howe shrugged and frowned at O'Dowd, who he apparently felt was not leaping to her feet often enough to object. "I believe I am here today to testify regarding a government that is capable of committing crimes against those it considers its enemies."

"Then you show us right here and now the hard, factual proof — beyond whatever divining rod you normally use to separate fact from fiction — that the government participated in any way in the death of Ms. Khalifa," Karp demanded.

"Well, I understand that there was a federal agent or possibly two who were in the mosque at the same time," Howe said. "It's possible they may have had a hand in it."

"Possible doesn't cut it here, Mr. Howe," Karp said. "You're just theorizing again. Am I right?"

"I guess you could call it a theory."

"You guess? You seem to do an awful lot of that," Karp said with disdain. He turned his back purposefully on Howe and looked at the jurors. "I have no further questions for this man."

It was near the end of the afternoon, and O'Dowd was ready to call it a day. Her expert government conspiracy witness had ended up looking like a nutcase. She just hoped that as Karp stood at the jury rail and began his cross-examination of Alysha Kimbata, the alibi witness would hold up better.

Kimbata was a young, pretty black woman with an oval face, green eyes, and a voice that hardly rose above a whisper. In fact, she had to be told several times when O'Dowd was questioning her to speak up so that the court reporter could hear her.

O'Dowd thought she'd done a good job during direct examination of recalling her rather simple story. The girl did have a habit of looking back at the defense row in the spectator section where her glowering father was allowed to sit, so O'Dowd had addressed it.

"Ms. Kimbata, during the course of your testimony, you have looked frequently toward the gallery where people watching this trial are sitting. Is there a reason?"

Kimbata had nodded and needed to be reminded to speak up. "Yes, my father is there."

"Are you frightened of him?"

"Yes."

"Why?"

The young woman had bowed her head and appeared to cry, but then she'd answered. "He is angry because I slept with a man."

"Because you slept with Imam Jabbar?"

Kimbata had nodded, lifting her head so that her tear-stained cheeks were visible, and then remembered she had to answer aloud. "Yes."

Then it was Karp's turn, and O'Dowd had hoped he would go after the young woman the way he had gone after Howe. But his tone was gentle when he asked his first question.

"Ms. Kimbata, what time approximately did Imam Jabbar arrive at your apartment?"

The young woman glanced quickly toward her father and shrugged. "I don't know exactly."

"Was the sun still up, or was it down? And Ms. Kimbata, please, either look at me or at the jurors and not the spectators. The truth is not over there," Karp said.

"I . . . I don't remember," she said.

Karp smiled while standing at the jury rail and held up a transcript. "Ms. Kimbata, do you remember being interviewed by Assistant District Attorney Kenny Katz last week?" he said, pointing to the prosecution table. "The gentleman seated next to me in the court?"

"Yes."

"Good. Now, do you also recall when Assistant DA Katz spoke with you, he asked questions and you gave answers that were recorded by a stenographer who was present?"

"Yes."

"Now, I am going to read to you, starting from page three of that transcript, some questions that were asked of you and answers that you gave. Okay? Question: 'What time did Sharif Jabbar arrive at your apartment?' Answer: 'I don't know exactly. It was late afternoon.' Question: 'How do you know that?' Answer: 'Because it was still light outside.' Question: 'The sun was up?' Answer: 'Yes. I remember children playing in the sunlight in the courtyard.' "

Karp put the transcript on the jury rail. "Do you remember being asked those questions and giving those answers?"

"Yes, I remember that now. The sun was up, and the children were playing."

"And after the imam arrived at your apartment, what did the two of you do first?"

"What do you mean?"

"Did you offer him something to drink? Or eat? Did you kiss? Or did you have sex first?"

"Objection!" O'Dowd roared. "Counsel is just trying to embarrass this girl and confuse her with multiple questions."

"Sustained," Mason said. "Mr. Karp, one question at a time."

"Yes, thank you, your honor," Karp replied. "Ms. Kimbata, when Imam Jabbar arrived at your apartment, did you kiss him?"

The girl looked puzzled and started to look at her father before remembering Karp's admonition and averting her eyes. "Yes, I kissed him."

"And did you give him something to drink?"

The girl nodded. "Yes, I gave him tea."

"And did you offer him something to eat?"

"Yes, we ate something . . . I don't remember what."

"And did you then have sex?"

Kimbata blushed and dropped her head again. "Yes. We went to bed until he got up to pray."

"You went to bed when the sun was still up?" Karp asked.

The young woman nodded. "Yes, I could still hear the children playing outside."

"And it was light in your apartment from the sun?"

O'Dowd was suddenly conscious of Jabbar leaning toward her. "Stop this!" he whispered urgently.

"Why?" she whispered back. "She's doing a fine job."

"Because —" But it was already too late.

"Ms. Kimbata, you are obviously mistaken about all this, aren't you?"

She tried to look past Karp to her father, then thought a moment and shook her head. "I don't think so."

"No?" Karp said. "You mean that you did not know that it was the afternoon of the first day of Ramadan?"

Kimbata couldn't help herself. She threw frightened glances at Jabbar and her father, both of whom were watching with a dawning realization that Karp had set a trap and now it was being sprung.

"I'm not sure."

"You mean the chief imam of your mosque, the man responsible for the spiritual guidance of the mosque and for keeping the holy days, did not realize it was the first day of the holiest month of the Muslim calendar?"

The woman's lips trembled, and tears poured down from frightened eyes. "He must have forgotten."

"Indeed, he must have, because there are certain things a good Muslim does not do from sunup to sundown on Ramadan. Isn't that true?"

The young woman looked as if she'd just been told that she was to be shot at dawn. Finally, she nodded and said, "Yes."

"Are you supposed to drink anything, including tea, before sunset?"

"No."

"Are you supposed to eat?"

"No."

Karp strolled over to the witness stand and, looking up, smiled kindly. "Ms. Kimbata, I know you find this embarrassing, and so I apologize, but are you supposed to have sex before sunset during Ramadan?"

Alysha Kimbata burst into tears. "No. No, you are not."

Karp reached up onto the rail around the witness stand and moved a box of tissues closer to the weeping girl. "Let me know when you're ready," he said gently.

After several minutes, the young woman wiped her nose and finally looked up again. "I'm ready," she said softly.

"Thank you," Karp said. "You just testified that Imam Jabbar drank, ate, and had sex before sundown on Ramadan. Is that true?"

The young woman hesitated, then passed a hand over her eyes. "Yes. Yes, it is all true."

"Are you sure, Ms. Kimbata? A few minutes ago, defense counsel asked why you were looking at your father in the spectator section, and you said you were frightened. And that you were frightened because he was angry that you had slept with Mr. Jabbar."

"Yes."

"Are you sure, Ms. Kimbata, that you're not frightened because you've been told to lie on the stand to protect Imam Jabbar?"

Kimbata bowed her head and sighed. She glanced over at the gallery and then at the jury. "No, I'm telling the truth."

29

The "good-looking MILF" was sitting in the small bakery across Mott Street from the Chinese laundry, watching the door leading up to the office of T. X. Investigations Inc., when four men emerged. Three moved with military precision around a fourth — the one in the lead signaling to a dark sedan down the block, while the other two scanned the street and kept control of the man in the middle.

Marlene assumed from the description she'd received from Sherry Maxwell that the fourth man was Todd Fielding. *Thinning blond hair. Paunch.* He looked around, frightened, as he shambled down the sidewalk toward the approaching sedan, holding a towel around his left hand.

Frightened with good reason, Marlene thought. The man in the lead was a professional killer; she'd recognized him from the photos Sherry Maxwell had given her. *Hello,*

Mr. Williams. Are we doing a little investment banking today? she mused as he got in the front passenger side of the car while Fielding was shoved into the back between the "muscle."

"Excuse me? Did you need more coffee?" asked a waiter near the door.

Marlene smiled. "I do, but I've got to run."

After the sedan pulled away, Marlene hurried across Mott, digging into her purse and removing a small black case that contained various picks and other burglary tools. *If Butch knew I still had this,* she thought with a twinge of guilt, *he'd flip. One of those things best left out of pillow talk for a peaceful marriage.*

Reaching the door, she picked the lock in less than fifteen seconds and headed up the stairs. She replaced the burglary kit and pulled out a small .380 Beretta instead. *Another one of those things best left in the dark.*

The door at the top of the stairs was ajar. With the gun held out in a two-handed stance, she moved swiftly into the room. Seeing that there was no one else present, she relaxed until she looked at the wooden office chair. There were remnants of duct tape still attached to the arms and legs, where it had apparently been used to secure Todd Fielding. But it was the pool of blood beneath the left arm that caught her attention, particularly when closer inspection revealed that the red lump in the middle was the tip of a human finger.

Marlene guessed that Fielding, who did not seem the strong, silent type, had told them everything they wanted to know. She wondered why Williams hadn't simply killed him. After all, it wouldn't be the first time the police had come across a sleazy private eye who'd been executed by an angry husband. Then it came to her that Fielding might have told them everything, but it was possible that he still had something they wanted.

She swore. Fielding was the witness who could clear Warren and convict Jim Williams. She still had the photographs from Sherry, but without the corroboration of the photographer, it could be dicey. The photographs weren't the best quality, and maybe Chin, or eventually a defense attorney, could claim they were doctored. But she wouldn't have stood a chance against the four men on the street, and she had no idea where they'd taken him. She'd have to hope that they kept him alive for a reason that would last a while longer.

Think, Marlene, you've got to do this right.
Suddenly, a plan began to coalesce in her head, and implementing it began with a series of telephone calls.

The first was to Sherry Maxwell. If Fielding had talked, he would have told them who hired him.

"This is Marlene," she said when the other woman answered. She described what she'd seen and what it meant. "Get out of the apartment now. He could be on his way. . . . No, Sherry, he is not an investment banker. He is a killer, and he's not going to be happy that you had him followed to a murder scene. . . . Sherry, I need you to stop crying and move. . . . Take a taxi back to Saks, then walk through the store and catch another taxi. Take it to the corner of Grand and Crosby. I'll meet you there. No, there's no time to pack. . . . Okay, grab the jewelry, but then you've got to go!"

Marlene hung up and shook her head. It was all falling into place. After meeting Sherry, she'd gone back to Warren's apartment and, identifying herself as Warren's attorney, persuaded the building manager to let her in to feed the cat and birds. While Brando was busy eating, she'd carefully looked around the apartment again. She'd jumped at the sound of a voice behind her.

"How's Warren?" asked the building manager, who'd appeared in the doorway.

Marlene had calmed herself and replied. "He's in a tough spot right now, but I think he's going to be okay."

"Did he do it?"

"No. He didn't do it, but we've got some things to do to prove it."

The manager had nodded. "I'd hate to lose him," he'd said. "Always paid his rent on time. Nice and quiet. Didn't complain much . . . and you sort of get used to the mouth." He'd turned to go but then remembered something and held out a small bundle of mail. "This is everything that's arrived since his arrest. Would you give it to him, please?"

Marlene had accepted the mail. *I'll have a quick look to make sure no bills have arrived,* she thought to herself. *But I'll leave most of it here for Warren to look at when he gets out.*

The manager had left, and Marlene had laid the bundle on the kitchen counter and quickly gone through it. She hadn't seen anything that seemed to need immediate attention until, near the bottom, she'd come to a small padded envelope. It appeared to be the size and shape of a DVD, so at first she'd assumed it could be a new film he'd ordered. But then she'd looked at the addresses on the front.

It had been addressed to Rick Blaine, and the return address said it had been sent by Ilsa Lund. *Why are those names familiar?* She'd looked up at a poster from the movie *Casablanca,* starring Humphrey Bogart and Ingrid Bergman. *As Rick Blaine and Ilsa Lund.* She'd smiled. *That was a nice touch, Michelle. Now let's see what you sent Warren.*

Marlene had slit open the package with a kitchen knife, and a small key attached to a note had fallen out. She'd recognized it as a locker key; it had a number on it but nothing else, and there wasn't anything in the note that told her where the locker might be located. All the note said was: "Answer my question."

"Answer my question." What question? Marlene had asked herself as she left the apartment and hailed a taxi. When it dawned on her what Michelle was saying, she'd called her husband. He'd said he was just walking to the elevator to return to the courtroom for the Jabbar trial.

"We spent the morning on an 'offer of proof' hearing for Dean Newbury," he'd said. "Now we'll finally get him in front of a jury."

"Go get him, tiger," Marlene had replied. "But first, do you happen to remember that movie-trivia question Warren asked right before he was arrested?"

"Yeah, funny you should ask," he'd said. "I woke up the other night thinking about it. 'The key goes where the book editor sees his wife and son off to Maine.' That was a tough one."

"You solved it?" Marlene had practically shouted.

"Well, sort of," Butch had responded. "I think the part about 'where the book editor sees his wife and son off to Maine' is a reference to *The Seven Year Itch,* starring Marilyn Monroe with Tom Ewell as Richard Sherman the book editor."

"And?"

"And it's a reference to the place where Sherman put his wife and son on a train for their summer vacation in Maine."

"And?"

"The train left Penn Station. But the part I don't get is the reference to a key going to Penn Station."

Marlene had laughed. "I do. Thanks, baby. I'll explain when I get home. I've got to go see a man about some photographs."

The next stop had been Mott Street and T. X. Fielding Investigations. However, Todd Fielding had seemed to be otherwise engaged, shouting, "Sorry, love, I'm a . . . I'm preoccupied!"

Her first thought had been that Fielding was "entertaining" some other poor woman who had fallen for his shtick. She'd trotted across Mott, intending to walk the few blocks over to Grand and Crosby, where her loft and, she hoped, Sherry Maxwell waited. She'd make sure the young woman was safely inside and return for Fielding.

At the sidewalk on the other side, however, Marlene had pulled up short. Something didn't make sense. *This guy Fielding thinks he has a knockout like Sherry coming to jump his bones and go in with him on a half-million dollars in blackmail money. And instead he's boinking some Village housewife? I don't think so.*

Marlene had slipped into the bakery to see who came out of the door across the street. She'd intended to call Sherry and tell her she'd been delayed and to wait. But first, she'd needed to make another call.

Now, glancing one more time at the fingertip lying in the pool of blood, Marlene punched in the number. "Hey, cousin," she said when Sergeant Bobby Scalia answered. "Can you meet me at Penn Station ASAP? It's important. . . . Love you, too. *Ciao.*"

30

The atmosphere in Part 39 courtroom the next morning reminded Karp of what it must have been like at Yankee Stadium in 1938 before the second Louis-Schmeling heavyweight battle. It was the so-called fight of the century. The immortal Joe Louis had been beaten in the first fight in '36 by the German, Max Schmeling. Shocked and humiliated, Louis felt that he had let down his country. He had always been the gracious champion; the Nazis, however, played it up that Schmeling's victory was vindication of the superiority of the Nazi system.

Louis's preparation for the second fight was a paradigm for laser focus and concentration. Without bravado or bluster, Louis was determined to pummel Schmeling into oblivion with unremitting ferocity. Indeed, from the start in round one, Louis tore into his opponent, putting him on the ropes, and wouldn't let him fall to the canvas until the

German was thoroughly beaten and unable to stand.

Psychologically, Karp prepared his case and, particularly, his summation with the notion that the defendant, Jabbar, would feel the same helplessness and frustration that Schmeling had known once the evidence was presented in a compelling and persuasive fashion.

Although no one was shouting, cheering, or jeering, the air buzzed with intensity as the spectators, media, and even courtroom personnel debated who would deliver the knockout blow. Everybody was aware of the disasters that had struck both sides the day before, once the media "legal experts" weighed in on television and in the newspapers regarding who they thought had suffered the most damage.

As the media had breathlessly reported, a prosecution witness — one of the city's most prominent attorneys, Dean Newbury — had apparently succumbed to a heart attack or, some claimed, something more sinister.

According to one of the tabloids, which quoted an unnamed source "present at the death," Newbury, who had already scandalized Gotham by pleading guilty to the murder of his own brother, "took a sip of water and just keeled over. He was dead before he hit the floor." The paper's source theorized that the water had been poisoned; however, the District Attorney's Office, as well as the NYPD, would say only that no comment would be forthcoming pending the outcome of the trial and leaving the medical findings to the Medical Examiner's Office.

Alleged legal experts were sure that Karp's case was now in trouble. He no longer had Newbury to support the testimony of federal agent Jojola. A well-known liberal defense lawyer opined sanctimoniously on a national cable news network that "it will be tough for the district attorney to get a unanimous jury for what amounts to the word of a shadowy federal agent against that of a Harlem firebrand whose attorney, civil rights lion Megan O'Dowd, has not been afraid to play the race card, and justifiably so."

However, other pundits were just as adamant that Karp's dismantling of defense witnesses Braxton Howe and Alysha Kimbata had staggered the defense with a one-two combination. "One was made to look like a member of the Tinfoil Helmet Society and the other a liar." Most of the so-called experts of this ilk predicted that for Jabbar to walk, he was going to have to take the stand and appeal to that one juror who "believes that pigs can fly."

Scanning the stories in the morning newspapers, Karp had been pleased that no one in the media had made the connection between Newbury's death and a small story buried in the inside pages about the "attempted robbery" of a Twenty-ninth Street bakery that had been thwarted when one of the proprietors shot and killed a male perpetrator. According to the story, the second robber, a female, had been taken into custody.

Now, as he waited for Judge Mason to enter the courtroom, Karp allowed himself a moment away from focusing on Jabbar to reflect on the events of Nadya Malovo's capture. He marveled at the irony that with intelligence agencies, the FBI, and Interpol hunting Malovo, also known as Ajmaani, it was a little old Jewish lady, herself a holocaust survivor, and a wounded female U.S. marshal who had brought down the assassin.

After court the day before, Karp had Fulton drive him to Bellevue Hospital, where Goldie Sobelman had been taken after she collapsed following the shooting. He'd found Moishe sitting next to his sleeping wife, his head on her shoulder and his eyes closed as he held her hand. The old man had opened his eyes and picked up his head as Karp entered the room.

"How is she?" Karp had asked.

Moishe shrugged. "She was pretty shook up. I think killing that man was the worst part for her; it is such a violation of her values to harm another human being. But it was him or me. Before the drugs put her to sleep, she signed that she had chosen love over conscience. And then she cried herself to sleep."

Pausing, Moishe had caressed his wife's arm and pressed her hand to his lips. "She saved me, you know. The bad woman, the one I told you about who made me nervous, was going to kill me, but Goldie spoke to her and melted even that evil heart. She said, 'Please, child, if you must shoot, then I beg you, me first. I cannot stand to see him hurt.' " Starting to sob, Moishe, barely whispering, had said, "Those were the first words she's spoken since the concentration camp."

Karp had felt the emotion rise within him. "What do the doctors say?"

"They say that there is nothing physically wrong with her, but she probably has post-traumatic stress syndrome, and right now she needs to rest. So that's what she's going to do until she can come home." He'd turned to look at his wife's resting face, his eyes brimming with tears.

"You know that the two of you were almost killed today because you know me and I frequent your shop," Karp had said.

"Not another word," Moishe had replied before Karp could go on. "We do not turn our backs on our friends because of danger." He'd chuckled. "God forgive me for saying this, but we would not be Jews if we allowed evil people to say who we will or won't have as friends. Do not stop coming to our shop, or we will be very hurt."

Karp had smiled, the guilt he'd been feeling since hearing about Malovo's vicious plan subsiding. "What? And miss out on the best cherry-cheese coffee cake in the five boroughs? Never!"

As he'd headed home from the hospital an hour later, Karp had looked forward to a quiet evening with his wife and boys to decompress for a bit. He was feeling the effects of a physically taxing and emotionally charged day. But it was the weariness of a boxer drawing near the end of the fight, tired but satisfied that his pace and stamina would carry him through to the final bell. In the first case against O'Dowd, he hadn't been psychologically prepared for the physical and mental rigors of the trial. He'd allowed it to wear him down and let O'Dowd carry the fight to him. But ever since that second trial, he'd steeled himself to go the distance, no matter how many rounds the opposition wanted to go with its rope-a-dope delaying tactics or list of inane witnesses.

An evening at home represented a breather between rounds. Yet when he'd arrived home, he'd learned that the day wasn't over for Marlene. He'd walked through the door of the loft just as she was preparing to leave with an attractive young woman she'd introduced as Sherry Maxwell. She'd given him a brief rundown on what was happening in Warren Bennett's case.

Karp wasn't terribly pleased that his wife was tangling with yet another professional assassin. However, he'd been somewhat mollified when he heard that instead of her usual "go it alone" tendencies, she'd actually involved the police in the person of Detective Sergeant Bobby Scalia. He'd met her cousin before, a tough guy and a sharp cop, who would, he hoped, keep the love of his life safe from harm.

"The twins have had dinner, yours is in the oven," she'd said, and kissed him. "Play your cards right, and I might even let you and Clay Fulton in on the glory tomorrow night. Now I need to run to save a sleazeball named Todd Fielding." She'd hurried out of the loft with the young woman before he could ask any more questions.

Marlene hadn't returned home until long after he'd gone to bed. Nor had there been much time to talk to her in the morning before he left for the Criminal Courts Building just after dawn. And what he'd found waiting for him outside the building had made him forget all about Warren Bennett for the moment.

Standing in the early-morning light was the hard right cross to the chin that would put his opponent on the canvas. He'd just needed to figure out how to land it.

As expected, O'Dowd's direct examination of Sharif Jabbar concentrated on painting the illusion that he was the victim of a racist, paranoid government that was trying to silence him. But first, she'd dealt with his past criminal history to lessen the blow they expected on the subject from Karp's cross-examination.

"Imam Jabbar, have you ever been convicted of a crime?" O'Dowd asked, as if she wasn't sure of the answer.

"Yes, when I was younger. Before I became a Muslim, I ran with a rough crowd," he replied. "I committed many crimes, including two I was convicted for — armed robbery and manslaughter."

"Have you been convicted of any crimes since your conversion many years ago to Islam?"

Jabbar shook his head. "Nothing worse than a parking ticket."

After further exploring his poverty-stricken, fatherless childhood, misguided teenage years, and felonious young adulthood, O'Dowd launched into the meat of her questioning. "Imam Jabbar, have you been an outspoken critic of the government of the United States?"

"Yes," Jabbar admitted. "You cannot be a black person raised in Harlem and not know that racism is a fact of life in this country and that the main perpetrator of this offense is an oppressive government controlled by wealthy Christian white men and Jews. Once I became a Muslim, I learned it was doubly hard to be a person of color *and* a follower of Islam."

"But you're a spiritual leader as an imam?"

"Yes, but I am also a leader of my community," Jabbar responded. "And I take it upon my own shoulders to speak out against injustice and oppression for those who have no voice or are afraid of the government."

"Are you afraid of the government, Imam Jabbar?"

Jabbar laughed sardonically. "I am now," he said with an embittered smile. "I had not realized to what extent the government would go to silence me."

"Well, don't you say things that make you unpopular with the government and people in general?" O'Dowd asked. "For instance, weren't you interviewed after the September 11, 2001, attacks on the World Trade Center in which you described the hijackers as heroes and the people who died there as, and I quote, 'pawns of the U.S. government, and therefore legitimate targets'? Did you say that?"

Jabbar bowed his head. "I'm not proud of those comments," he replied as he lifted his head and looked at the jurors. "I wasn't thinking about the pain other people were in. I was just voicing a hope that now people of good conscience of all races and religions would sit up and take notice of the suffering caused in the world by this government. Suffering that would lead young men to sacrifice their lives to wake up the people of the United States to the fact that many more human beings die throughout the world every year as a result of U.S. bombs — many of them delivered by murderous Israelis — than died in the World Trade Center. Still, I was not thinking of the families and friends who lost their loved ones, and it was wrong. I've prostrated myself before Allah ever since, seeking forgiveness for what I said."

"Does that mean you no longer believe that what you said — however harshly — is not true?"

"No. The words I used were wrong. But as Allah is my witness, the United States government, not its people, but the government and its agents are unjust and murderous."

After several more minutes of exploring Jabbar's political beliefs, O'Dowd switched gears. "Imam Jabbar, do you know anyone named Nadya Malovo, who also, according to the government *agent provocateur* Jojola, goes by the name of Ajmaani?"

"No. I never heard either name until after my arrest," he replied. "And I've never met anyone who matches the description of such a woman."

Through O'Dowd's questioning, Jabbar explained his theory of how Jojola had infiltrated the Al-Aqsa mosque through deception and lies, hoping to discover evidence of serious wrongdoing on the part of Jabbar. But failing that and having heard that Jabbar was leaving on a trip to hand-deliver donations raised by the mosque's congregation for Muslim charities in Africa, the agent had come up with a plan to frame him for murder.

"Imam Jabbar, did you in any way help plan the murder of Miriam Juma Khalifa?"

"No," Jabbar replied angrily. "She was one of my flock. And a friend."

"Did you assault or torture Miriam Juma Khalifa?"

"No, I did not."

"Did you participate in any actions encouraging the murder of Miriam Juma Khalifa?"

"No."

"Were you present in the basement of the Al-Aqsa mosque when Miriam Juma Khalifa was murdered?"

"Absolutely not."

"Where were you?"

Jabbar paused and hung his head as if overcome with shame. "I was seeing my girlfriend, Alysha Kimbata."

"Are you proud that you have a young woman for a girlfriend whom is not your wife?"

"No. I have sinned in the eyes of Allah

and hurt my wife, whom I respect and love."

"You were here when the jury heard the district attorney make a big deal that it might or might not have been sundown on the first day of Ramadan. What do you say to that?"

Again, Jabbar's head fell forward. "He might be right. I believe that it was already sundown, but I am willing to concede that as an imam and a Muslim, I am sometimes lax with the prohibitions regarding food, drink, and sex during Ramadan. Again, I am an imperfect, sinful man."

"You are an imperfect, sinful man who believes that it is his place as a religious leader to speak out against injustice," O'Dowd repeated, "but did you participate in any way in the murder of Miriam Juma Khalifa?"

"I did not," Jabbar said, looking from one black member of the jury to the next.

O'Dowd's direct examination had taken up the entire morning and the first hour after the lunch break. But the crowd in the courtroom was as eager to see how Karp would respond to the jabs from the defense team as they had been that morning when he rose for cross-examination.

"Mr. Jabbar, if the United States government, or any other government, wanted to shut you up, why not just assassinate you?"

The question created a stir in the courtroom. But Jabbar had his answer ready. "I believe you all wanted to make an example out of me with a big trial. Then it will be easy to kill me in prison and make it look like just another inmate-to-inmate fatality. That way, the government can claim it had nothing to do with my blood on its hands."

"Really? A government capable of — as your own expert witness testified — secretly carrying out the attacks on the World Trade Center, assassinating several presidents and other leaders, could not simply murder the imam of a local mosque and get away with it?"

"Like I said, you all want to make an example out of me," Jabbar retorted. "A warning to any black man who dares speak out against racism and oppression."

"Like the Reverends Al Sharpton or Jesse Jackson? Why haven't they been framed or murdered?" Karp replied.

"They're black, and so they, too, feel the sting of racism's whip," Jabbar said. "But they're Christian and have large followings, so it's not as easy as going after the imam of a small mosque in Harlem."

"Mr. Jabbar, the jury heard testimony

about the digital movie camera that was found at the crime scene in front of the chair where Miriam Juma Khalifa was murdered," Karp began.

"Yes, we often make recordings of my Friday sermons to share with the faithful who could not attend," Jabbar responded.

"I see. And as we heard from the People's witnesses, the memory card from the camera is missing, and the inference from your direct examination is that Mr. Jojola or some other nefarious agent of the government, such as a police officer, removed it. Is that correct?"

Jabbar shrugged. "They must have — that's how they operate."

"Why?" Karp asked. "Why would someone working for the government, such as Mr. Jojola, record the murder of Ms. Khalifa, if that's what was done, but then remove the memory card?"

"I don't know," Jabbar replied. "Maybe to show it to his Jew masters."

"Or maybe you and your followers recorded the murder to send to radical Islamists in other parts of the world?" Karp suggested.

"That's what you want these people to think!"

"Or maybe it was removed because you,

or Nadya Malovo, wanted to make sure the evidence of your part in this heinous crime wouldn't be found, at least not until you were out of the country with your cash." Karp continued, "Mr. Jabbar, are you absolutely sure that you were not present in the basement of the Al-Aqsa mosque when Miriam Juma Khalifa was tortured and then cruelly decapitated?"

"I was not there."

"Are you as sure of that as you are of the rest of your testimony?"

"Absolutely. May Allah be my witness."

"Did you lead a group of men in calling for her murder and then celebrate when this atrocity was accomplished?"

"I did not."

"You were eating and having sex with Ms. Kimbata. Is that what you said?"

"Yes."

Karp paused and looked as though he was at a loss for where to go from there. He looked up and shook his head. "You've certainly come a long way from your humble beginnings."

Jabbar smiled. "*Allahu Akbar.* Yes, God is great."

"Ah, yes, God is great," Karp repeated. "But God does not like to be mocked." He turned to Judge Mason. "Your honor, at this time, I have no more questions for the defendant."

O'Dowd rose and informed the court that she had concluded the defendant's case. She renewed her perfunctory motions to dismiss the case, which she had already tendered when Karp concluded the People's case.

Judge Mason turned to Karp and asked, "Do the People wish to proceed by way of rebuttal?"

"Yes, your honor. The People call Alysha Kimbata to the stand," Karp said. He turned to the back of the courtroom as the doors opened and the young woman entered.

"Your honor I object to this travesty of justice!" O'Dowd shouted. "I have no doubt that the government was able to put the screws to Miss Kimbata in order to force her reappearance here to lie for them."

"Your honor, the court and jury will learn from this witness as part of the People's impeachment-rebuttal case that the only people who 'put the screws' to Miss Kimbata were the defendant and defense counsel," Karp shot back angrily. "As well as her father, who was acting on behalf of the defendant."

Karp looked up at the frightened young woman as she took the witness stand. He admired her courage. When he'd arrived at the Criminal Courts Building that morning, Kimbata and several other older women wearing traditional Muslim clothing had been waiting along with Mahmoud Juma.

The older man had stepped forward. "Mr. Karp, Miss Kimbata has something she would like to say to you, as well as something she wants to give you," Juma had said.

Karp had surmised as he invited the group up to his office that Miss Kimbata had had a change of heart and wanted to recant. That was part of it.

"All day, I could not get out of my head that Allah hates a liar more than any sinner, because all sin starts with a lie of some kind," Kimbata had told him. "My father tried to convince me that lying if it was for the good of Allah was okay. But I knew in my heart that it was not. Miriam was my friend, and it was horrible what they did to her. Then when I went to bed, I had a dream that the great Muslim saint, Hazrat Fatemah Masumeh, came to me and told me what I needed to do to make amends."

Dreams, divine intervention, or guilty conscience, Karp didn't care. What she'd handed to him was a knockout punch, but he had to set up his opponent to land it.

Now, Karp asked, "Miss Kimbata, when

you appeared on behalf of the defendant yesterday, did you tell the truth about him being with you on the night in question?"

"No," she replied.

"Why not?"

"I was afraid."

"Of who?"

"My father and Imam Jabbar."

"Why?"

"My father said that I had to lie to help Imam Jabbar, because that is what Allah wanted me to do. He said if I did not lie, he would disown me and send me back to Yemen, where I would be stoned to death as an adulteress."

"Are you an adulteress?"

"No. I am a virgin." As she spoke and the courtroom started buzzing, the young woman kept her eyes downcast.

"Miss Kimbata, after you came to my office with some of the women from the Al-Aqsa mosque this morning, did you agree to a medical examination arranged by my office and conducted by a physician?"

Kimbata nodded her head. "Yes," she said softly.

"And did that examination determine that you are, indeed, a virgin?"

"Yes."

"So, you have never had sex with a man,

including the defendant?"

"No."

"Thank you, Miss Kimbata. I understand that this was terribly embarrassing for you," Karp said gently. "Now, I need to ask you another question. This morning, you gave me something that was wrapped in a plastic bag. Is that correct?"

"Yes."

"Where did you get this item?"

"My father kept it in his desk."

"How did you know it was there?"

"On the night of Miriam's death, Imam Jabbar came to my family's home, and I saw him hand it to my father."

"Was anything said?"

Kimbata nodded. "I heard Imam Jabbar say something about martyrs and Miriam. And then he told my father to keep it safe and that someday when the world was converted to Islam, it would prove who had fought for Allah in this country."

"You took this item from your father's desk?"

"Yes."

"Do you know what it is?"

"I read in a newspaper that a memory card was missing from a camera in the mosque, and —"

"Objection!" O'Dowd thundered, seeing

too late the haymaker Karp had thrown. "We're witnessing firsthand the furtherance of the government conspiracy against this imam."

"Your honor, the People will call more witnesses in a moment who will testify to the authenticity of the memory card, as well as the fact that a single thumbprint was located on it belonging to the defendant," Karp replied calmly.

"Overruled," Mason ordered, and waved O'Dowd to sit down. "Please proceed, Mr. Karp."

Glancing over at the defense table, where O'Dowd slumped back into her seat with hatred for him writ large on her face while Jabbar merely looked sick to his stomach, Karp turned back to Kimbata. "You were saying?"

"Yes, I read that the memory card was missing from the camera. I believe that what I gave you is that memory card."

"Thank you, Miss Kimbata," Karp said, walking over to the prosecution table, where Kenny Katz handed him a plastic bag containing a small black square. "Your honor, the People request that this memory card be marked for identification People's Exhibit thirty-two. Miss Kimbata, is this the memory card that you observed the defendant give to your father, as you previously testified?"

"Yes."

"And this is the same card you gave me this morning?"

"Yes."

"Just a moment here," O'Dowd objected. "I demand a *voir dire* on the authenticity of this evidence."

"No objection, your honor," Karp said.

"Proceed, and be brief," Judge Mason instructed O'Dowd.

"Miss Kimbata, you have no idea if this card is the one you gave the district attorney. Isn't that a fact?" O'Dowd said.

"No, that is not true," Kimbata answered.

"Look, Miss Kimbata, I'm not suggesting that you didn't give a card to the district attorney. Do you understand that?"

"Yes, I understand what you're saying."

"But really, child, you don't know whether or not the district attorney is showing you this card, I believe People's thirty-two, for identification. He switched it. Isn't that possible?"

Before the witness could answer, O'Dowd glanced over at Karp and wondered why he hadn't objected. She looked back at the witness, who said, "No, Ms. O'Dowd, I know this is the same card I gave Mr. Karp."

Scoffing, O'Dowd said, "Well, my dear, what makes this memory card any different from any other?"

"May I see the memory card again, please?" Kimbata asked.

O'Dowd handed it to her.

Kimbata held up the bag and nodded. "This morning, Mr. Karp asked me to scratch my initials on the middle of the disk. It's hard to see, but they're there."

The courtroom was completely silent. Judge Mason shook his head at O'Dowd. "I assume, Ms. Dowd, you have no further questions."

O'Dowd shook her head and plopped down in her seat.

Karp then requested that the memory card be received in evidence and said, "I have no further questions, either. Your honor, the People now recall John Jojola."

Kimbata quietly climbed down from the witness stand and walked quickly to where the other women waited in the aisle to escort her from the courtroom. As she left, Jojola returned, but instead of taking the stand, he walked over to where a screen had been set up at the far end of the jury box.

"In just a moment," Karp explained to the jury, "with the court's permission, I will play part of the material captured on the memory card in the basement of the Al-Aqsa mosque, taken from the desk of Bakr Kimbata by his daughter Alysha Kimbata. At times, you will notice that either the sound or the picture will be turned off so that comments that do not pertain to this trial cannot be heard and so that you will not be unnecessarily accosted by gruesome images. This has nothing to do with the quality of the recording."

Karp made a signal, and the courtroom was darkened. The screen next to Jojola came alive with the images of men, their faces covered with scarves and ski masks, some of them holding assault rifles, chanting slogans. Jojola, who was standing next to the screen, used a pointer to tap one of the men on the screen. "This is Sharif Jabbar."

The chanting stopped when the camera's point of view swung to a statuesque woman, also with her face partly covered, standing with a small Asian-looking man. "That is Nadya Malovo," Jojola said, pointing to the assassin. "And this is my partner."

On the screen, Tran began reading from a statement the woman handed him. "All thanks are due to Allah. We ask for his help and guidance, and we ask his forgiveness for any sins we commit."

As everyone in the courtroom's attention was fixed on the screen, Karp stole a look at the jurors. They were as rapt as those in the courtroom gallery. Tran ended his speech with *"Allahu Akbar!"* As the other *jihadis* joined in shouting *"Allahu Akbar!"* the camera panned out, showing the man Jojola had identified as Jabbar leading the chant. *"Allahu Akbar!"*

The picture cut out, and when it came on again, a young woman, bound and hooded, her hands and face bloody, was on her knees in front of a man. "This is . . . this is Miriam Juma Khalifa," Jojola said, choking up as he used the pointer. "And of course, the man is me."

On the screen, Jojola was tense, his face clouding with anger and horror as Malovo, a knife clenched in her hand, moved into the picture and began reading a statement of her own. Jojola appeared ready to attack Malovo but then looked back at Miriam. A moment later, his body relaxed, and he nodded almost imperceptibly and said something in an unknown language.

"What did you say there?" Karp asked quickly.

"It was Vietnamese. I said to my partner, 'Do nothing. This is as it should be.' "

Next to the screen, Jojola stood with his

head bowed as, on the recording, Malovo demanded to know what they were talking about. "Is there a problem?" she said, and made a signal to the cameraman. The screen went black again.

This time, when the images returned, Malovo was pulling back Miriam's head by the hair, exposing the young woman's throat.

Then, disconcertingly, the victim smiled up at her assassin. "*La ilaha illal lah!* There is no God but God," Miriam said.

The response seemed to enrage Malovo, whose face contorted. She placed her knife at Miriam's throat and started to cut. The screen went black again.

"We purposefully have spared you seeing the actual murder," Karp explained, then looked at O'Dowd, who leaned on her elbows with her face in her hands. "Unless the defense wants to object and force us to show it to you."

"No objection," O'Dowd mumbled without bothering to lift her head.

The screen once again filled with the images of the men in the room. But instead of celebrating, they appeared subdued. Only one continued to chant.

The camera pulled in close. Although a scarf covered his face from his nose down, the excited, bulbous eyes of Sharif Jabbar were clearly visible as he alone shouted triumphantly, *"Allahu Akbar! Allahu Akbar!"*

Looking at the jurors, Karp knew that they were recalling hearing that same man a half hour earlier, shouting the same thing from the witness stand.

Allahu Akbar, Karp thought, turning his attention to Jabbar, who sat slumped in his chair, staring disconsolately at nothing at all, like a pummeled, beaten fighter who could no longer answer the bell. *God truly is great.*

31

The Fixer spotted his team waiting for him outside Madison Square Garden and took a deep breath to calm himself as he crossed Thirty-first Street to reach them. One of the two men, Jason, had his hand resting on the handle of a black rollaway suitcase, as though he planned to catch a train from Penn Station beneath the Garden.

Calm yourself, he thought. *You can fix this if you stay calm.* It wasn't going to be easy; he was used to being in control and having his plans follow a logical order like moves on a chess board. *But the whole Kingston job has been one big clusterfuck from the jump. Every time I fix something, it comes undone.*

Some of it he blamed on the client. *If that idiot hadn't been bragging about his travels in the presence of Michelle Oakley, she would still be in the dark.* Some of it he blamed on bad luck. But he knew that ultimately, most of the blame fell on his own shoulders.

Either because he hadn't anticipated problems, not as he was paid to do, or he'd ignored the warning signs that he was losing focus.

Maybe he was a little too preoccupied with his toys and living the good life. And he'd broken the rule about jealous girlfriends: get rid of them. It was particularly galling that he'd told himself at Christmas that it was time to send Sherry packing. But he'd also become lazy. Sherry met his needs, and it was always tough to find a young woman with her attributes, as well as convenient limitations, and then break her in.

Only now, it's all coming back to haunt me. He had to fix this. The people who'd hired him and already paid him an outrageous sum of money didn't tolerate failure, and they had a very long reach. In fact, he'd heard through channels the previous night that one of their other independent assassins had eliminated a government witness in a Manhattan courtroom during a trial!

After accompanying Todd Fielding to his bank, where he and Josh had retrieved the flash drive of the photographs taken of him at the Oakley mansion, he'd left them at a Bronx apartment he maintained as a safe house. He planned to keep the private investigator, who was drugged up on pain pills for his amputated finger, alive only until he could interrogate Sherry and make sure their stories jibed. Then they'd both be on their way to that New Jersey hog farm.

But when he'd reached his Fifth Avenue apartment, there was no sign of Sherry. She hadn't answered her cell phone, either, and apparently had turned it off, because his buddy at the Agency couldn't trace it.

The mystery had been cleared up somewhat a few minutes after he arrived, however, when his office phone had rung and the caller ID said his girlfriend was on the line. "Hi, babe, where are you? You have me worried," he'd said as though nothing was amiss.

"You ought to be, fucker," replied a deep male voice. "You took my partner *after* you cut one of his goddamned fingers off. Well, two can play at that game. We got your girlfriend, and if you want to see her again, you're going to do it our way now."

"What makes you think I want to see her again? She betrayed me," the Fixer had replied dryly. He'd glanced at his computer to see how the tracking of Sherry's cell phone was progressing.

"Well, if you don't care about her," the man had said, "maybe you'd be interested in certain photographs."

"I have all the photographs I need," the Fixer had replied. "Our mutual friend was kind enough to hand them over to me, including the extra flash drive."

"We ain't talking about the same photographs." The man had chuckled. "These are of you and your three gorillas leaving a certain Chinatown office. Todd thought you might try coming at him. I'm sure you or your goons must have seen our associate, an attractive brunette, come to the door. You're pretty good but apparently not good enough to spot me and my camera in the bakery across the street. Todd figured he might need a little insurance so that he don't end up in some New Jersey swamp. And by the way, if that happens, these photos go to the cops along with the address of your swanky little Fifth Avenue pad."

The Fixer's smile had disappeared. "Okay, so what's the game?"

"Hold on, Cochise, that's not all I'm offering," the man had said. "You're going to give me Todd and a significant sum of money — by the way, for fucking with us, the price has gone up to one million — and in exchange, you get your girlfriend and a certain flash drive containing certain state secrets we got from the house of that broad you killed. Does Client 032355-JK mean anything to you?"

The Fixer had never wanted to strangle someone personally as much as he did Judge Kingston at that moment. "I believe we might be able to make a deal," he'd said. "But I won't be able to get that kind of money together until tomorrow."

"You got till tomorrow night," the man had said. "Just so we're clear. My pal Todd stays healthy, including keeping his remaining fingers and toes, or the deal's off. *Capice?* I realize that you're going to slap him around a bit for this. He's a tough cookie, but tell him he can go ahead and give me up. I'll be long gone before you come looking."

At that moment, the location of Sherry's cell phone had come through on his computer. "God damn it!" the Fixer had sworn. The signal was coming from the underground parking garage in his building.

The caller had laughed. "I guess you figured out where I am," he'd said. "Just so you know I mean business, I'm leaving you a calling card on the windshield of your Porsche. Nice car, by the way, but it could use a paint job."

The Fixer had slammed the phone down and yanked open his desk drawer, seizing the 9mm gun inside it. A few moments later, he was sprinting out of the apartment for the elevator. *If that asshole so much as leaned up against that car, I'll* . . . he'd thought as he waited impatiently for the elevator to reach the parking garage.

When the door had opened, he'd emerged with the gun out ready to shoot, not caring if any of the other residents were in the garage or not. Seeing no one else, he'd moved quickly to where he'd parked the Porsche. Beneath one of the windshield wipers was the "calling card," a severed finger still wearing a ruby-encrusted ring (but not *the* ring) he'd bought Sherry for her birthday. If that wasn't bad enough, what really infuriated him was that the bastard had keyed a long scratch along the side of the car from hood to trunk.

It had taken him several minutes to control his anger. After which he'd walked to the building's security office, where he'd demanded to see the garage security tape for the past hour. But the young officer, a new guy, had apologized and said that "a glitch of some sort" had knocked out the building's security cameras for an hour, and he was waiting for the repairman.

"Glitch! You dumb son of a bitch!" the Fixer had screamed at the young man. "Didn't you think to go check to see if maybe someone was breaking into cars?"

The caller had phoned in again that morning, this time, according to the GPS locator, from the sidewalk outside the Oakley mansion. *Rubbing my face in it,* he'd thought after the conversation was over.

He'd hoped that the twenty-four-hour delay would buy him enough time to track down the caller — either someone on the streets would hear something, or the caller would make a mistake, leading to a swift bullet to the head. But he had to admit that Fielding and his associates were better at this game than he'd thought.

The most surprising was Fielding himself. He'd come off as a pansy, but he was a tough nut to crack. As the caller had surmised, the Fixer had his men slap the Brit around and finally resorted to cutting the tip of the pinky off his right hand. The crazy bastard had screamed, cried, and passed out, but he'd stuck to his story: he didn't have a partner or an attractive brunette as an associate. *He's a hell of a lot tougher than the act he puts on,* he'd grudgingly conceded, looking down at the unconscious figure of PI Todd Fielding.

The caller had left specific instructions. One of the Fixer's men would enter Madison Square Garden with the rollaway suitcase containing the money and wait to be contacted. The Fixer was to head down into the bowels of Penn Station beneath the Garden, where he, too, would be met. Once the caller's associate had verified that the money had been delivered, "you'll hand over Todd Fielding, and we'll give you your nine-fingered girlfriend back and the key to a locker that contains what you killed the late Miss Oakley to get."

"How do I know it's the only copy?" the Fixer had asked.

"I'm sure you'll bring a laptop to verify what's on the disk. And if you're as good as I think you are, you'll have software that can determine if it's been downloaded again. If I'm messing with you, your guy walks off with the money."

Twenty-four hours later, the Fixer patted his suitcoat to feel for the plastic-wrapped finger in the inside pocket. He intended to feed it to the son of a bitch who had dared to damage that most exquisite example of German engineering.

The Fixer looked at his watch. "It's time," he said to Jason and Lex. He looked down at the rollaway suitcase, which, in addition to a million dollars in counterfeit money a friend with the U.S. Secret Service had loaned him, had a false bottom beneath which was an acetone peroxide bomb. "Be careful with that thing. It doesn't take much to set it off. The contact is going to want to take it into a restroom stall to count it. Let him go. Then, when I have what I need, I'll give you the word, and you blow his ass into the next century."

The Fixer and Lex walked into the Garden and made their way to the entrance to Penn Station. The plan was to wait until he had the evidence of Kingston's involvement and the blackmailers were all together counting their money and congratulating themselves. If anything happened before that, Jason would set the bomb off, and they'd all make their getaway in the confusion.

The nice thing about the acetone peroxide bomb was that it was a favorite of terrorists. In fact, within an hour of the detonation, several shadowy overseas "radical Islamic" groups would claim responsibility. *Allahu Akbar,* he thought as he entered Penn Station. *Let Al Qaeda take the rap; they'll appreciate the publicity.*

The caller had said to head for the Long Island Railroad ticket office, where they would be contacted. As they reached the area, Lex tapped the Fixer on the arm and nodded at an attractive brunette walking toward them with a big Italian-looking brute. "That's the MILF I saw in China-town," he said.

Marlene and her cousin, Detective Sergeant Bobby Scalia, gave each other a high five when they received the report from Clay Fulton, who was waiting with Sherry in a limousine that had been parked on Thirty-First Street, that Jim Williams had arrived and was conferring with two associates.

"One of them has the suitcase," Fulton said over the radio. "Williams and his pal are going inside. The guy with the suitcase has split off, but he's going in, too. I love it when a plan falls together."

"This one's not there yet, Clay. Be care-ful," Marlene said. "I don't like you taking this risk."

"Is that a nice way of saying I'm getting too old for this? Besides, darlin', I'm *always* careful," Fulton replied with a chuckle. "And I think we all owe Warren a little for services rendered. Taking this bad dude down is going to be a pleasure."

"Has anybody seen Todd Fielding?" Mar-lene asked.

"Sherry says no sign of him up here," Ful-ton replied. "I'm off to do my part."

Scalia nudged Marlene. "This is our guy, right?" he said, looking at the pair of men who were approaching the LIRR ticket office.

"Yeah," Marlene replied. "But where's Fielding? We need him to ice this guy for sure."

Scalia shrugged. "Let's go ask him."

Like gunfighters in a western movie, the two pairs of antagonists eyed each other carefully as they walked up to within several yards. "Where's my partner Todd?" Scalia demanded.

"He'll be along shortly," Williams replied. "Where's Sherry?"

"She'll be along shortly," Scalia shot back. "I take it you found my little calling card and my artwork." He made a gesture and a screeching sound, as though scraping paint off a Porsche 993 with a key, and laughed.

For a moment, Marlene thought Williams was going to attack her cousin, even though he wasn't nearly as big a man. Bobby was doing everything he could to provoke him, acting out the part of the tough Italian wiseguy and laying the Queens accent on heavy.

Responding to her call, Scalia had met her the day before at Penn Station after Marlene had left Sherry at the loft for safekeeping. She'd quickly brought him up to date on everything she knew. "You want to go check out what's in locker 3412?" she'd said, holding up the key that had been sent to Warren by Michelle.

"You bet." He'd smiled. Locating the locker across from the Long Island Railroad ticket counter, they'd opened it, and her cousin had carefully placed what they found in evidence bags.

Worried that Detective Meadow might see them if they returned to Westchester County, they'd gone down instead to the Criminal Courts Building in lower Manhattan, where Marlene had explained what was going on to the chief of the DAO detectives, Clay Fulton. "Can we borrow an office and a computer, please?"

"Only if I get to play, too," Fulton had replied.

Inside the locker at Penn Station, Marlene and her cousin had found a flash drive containing the files for numerous documents, including an appointment calendar with the name "Brandy Fox" at the top and "Client 032355-JK" listed on nearly all of the dates since the previous October. The client had apparently been so taken with the young woman that he saw her several times a week, including every day during the week and a half leading up to two days before Christmas, when Brandy Fox's calendar suddenly went blank. The files also contained images of canceled checks from the account of "John Klein" deposited into the account of Gentleman's VIP Club Inc., as well as results from a company Marlene recognized as a DNA-testing laboratory.

And finally, there was a letter from Michelle Oakley explaining what it all meant. It had been addressed to Marlene's client.

Dearest Warren,

If you're reading this, it means that I'm gone. And if so, I'm okay with that, and I want you to be, too. I will have paid for my sins and hopefully redeemed myself a little. I am meeting tonight after our date with a man named Jim Williams, who works for Judge Jack Kingston; you might remember meeting both men at your sister's party. For reasons that will become clear, I believe Williams intends to try to silence me, and I'm counting on you to make sure my voice gets heard.

What I'm about to tell you will come as a shock. As I said, I'm not the girl you remembered from that wonderful summer so long ago. I have been, for more than a year, the proprietor of a call-girl service that offers sex and companionship to men with lots of money.

I won't try to make excuses for what I've done. I can only try to atone now.

In my business, called the Gentleman's VIP

Club, I had a number of young women who worked for me. One of them was Rene Hanson, the young woman you'll remember who disappeared shortly before Christmas. For many reasons, some of which you'll find documented elsewhere here on this flash drive, I doubted the "official" version that she had climbed aboard a plane bound for Mexico, never to be seen or heard from again. That simply was not Rene.

Rene was in love with one of her clients, 032355-JK, a rather simple code for the birth-date and initials of Judge Jack Kingston. I believe that when you turn this evidence over — and I would suggest that you do so to your friend District Attorney Karp, who seems to be one of those increasingly rare creatures known as an honest man — the police will find plenty of evidence to implicate Kingston in her death. And there is one more item that should do it, if it can be located . . .

Michelle explained that her plan was to force Kingston into admitting his guilt in Rene's death so that her parents would "learn the truth about her fate" and perhaps retrieve her body for burial.

And if he won't do that willingly and intends instead to keep his secret by killing me, then I hope my death will bring about justice for Rene.

In closing, I don't expect you to forgive what I've done. But I wanted to thank you for that summer we had long ago and reminding me at your sister's party, and I'm sure our date tonight, of the girl I used to be.

You were a wonderful friend then, Warren Bennett, and I can tell you've become a wonderful man. Maybe in the next lifetime, I'll make smarter choices.

Love always, Michelle

Apparently, Michelle had put the flash drive in the locker at Penn Station the day she was murdered. At first, while driving with her cousin to 100 Centre Street, Marlene had wondered why the other woman hadn't just given it to Warren for safekeeping. But the more she thought about it, the more she was convinced that Michelle hadn't wanted to endanger Warren, not knowing that he'd already been set up to take the fall for her murder.

Michelle had sent the key to Warren and given him that riddle to solve just in case something went wrong during her meeting with Jim Williams, Marlene thought. If nothing had happened, she would have retrieved the key from Warren while on their date, with no one the wiser.

After a quick scan of Michelle's materials,

Marlene, Scalia, and Fulton had quickly come up with a plan. They wanted to nail Williams for Michelle Oakley's murder and clear Warren. But now they also wanted to bring down Judge Kingston, who had precipitated the whole thing by killing a young call girl in his home.

Using Sherry's security card, they'd entered the underground parking structure off Fifth Avenue and called Williams. The severed finger had been Scalia's idea. He had a friend in the New York City Medical Examiner's Office who'd loaned it to him from the morgue. He'd placed it on the car and then scratched the paint.

"A guy like that loves his cars more than his mother, if he had one," Scalia had said. "I want to get him so pissed off that he can't see straight."

Leaving one of Fulton's men in the security office to play the part of the guard waiting for the camera repairman, they'd returned to Penn Station and replaced the flash drive in the locker.

Now, despite the circumstances, it was everything Marlene could do not to laugh as Bobby chomped loudly on a stick of gum and smirked at Williams about damaging his car.

"That's funny," Williams said with an effort. "I'm going to have to remember that one."

Scalia quit chewing. "Let's do this," he said, pulling out a cell phone, punching in a number, and then speaking into it when it was answered. "Clay, we're with our friend. Do you have the suitcase?"

"I'm going into the restroom to do a little counting," Fulton replied.

Scalia turned to Williams and handed him the key. The detective pointed to the lockers. "Over there."

The four of them walked over to the locker, which Williams opened. He leaned in, removed the flash drive, and handed it to his partner, who quickly placed it in a small computer he was carrying. The younger man scanned the files, pressed a few buttons, and nodded. "It's here, and it hasn't been downloaded anywhere else," he informed his boss.

"Now, hand over my partner," Scalia said, "and we can all be on our merry way."

Williams pointed down a concourse to where two men were approaching, one of them with his hands bandaged. "Where's Sherry?" he asked.

It was Marlene who answered by pointing back in the direction Williams and his man had come from. He looked in that direction and saw a tall white man accompanied by a large black one approaching. "She's upstairs with detectives from the New York Police Department, you son of a bitch," she replied. "In the meantime, I'd like to introduce you to District Attorney Roger Karp and Detective Clay Fulton of the NYPD."

Williams snarled and turned back toward Marlene, his hand reaching under his coat for the gun in the holster. "Blow it!" he yelled into the microphone pinned to his shirt pocket.

However, there was no corresponding sound of a bomb going off. Instead, he found himself looking down the barrel of a gun held by Scalia. "You and your boy put your hands where I can see them," Scalia snarled. "Or I'm going to save the taxpayers a lot of money. You're both under arrest for the murder of Michelle Oakley."

As her husband and Fulton hurried up to help secure the pair, Marlene looked down the concourse to where Todd Fielding and his captor were surrounded by plainclothes detectives with guns drawn.

"You'll never make it stick," Williams said when she turned back to face him. "You have no idea who you're dealing with. I'll be out by morning."

"Maybe so," Karp said as he stepped

between Williams and his wife. "Bobby, you want to read him his rights?"

"With pleasure, Butch," Scalia said. "Then I think I'll go get his Porsche and drive it to the impound lot." He looked at the prisoner. "Hope you got good insurance."

EPILOGUE

The victory party was well under way in Karp's office when his secretary, Darla Milquetost, announced, "Mr. Hassan Malik is here, and he'd like a moment of your time." The room had immediately gone quiet. Even Ray Guma, who had liberally spiked a dash of water with generous portions of Jack Daniel's, and V. T. Newberry, who'd been downing martinis, raised their eyebrows and took another sip.

No one knew what this unexpected appearance could mean. Was the juror there to report an irregularity on the jury that might void the guilty verdict for Sharif Jabbar?

O'Dowd had tried an ineffectual surrebuttal counter to the prosecution's rebuttal case, an unusual tactic, rarely granted, but Judge Mason had figured he owed the hapless O'Dowd last rites. He was well aware that she'd blundered and had seriously crossed the line.

Regarding the filming of Miriam's murder and Jabbar's jubilant participation in it, Karp had made a note for his summation to inform the jurors with as much righteous indignation as he could muster. "The defense argues, 'Don't believe your lying eyes.' The ultimate defense big-lie tactic and insult to jurors' intelligence."

First, O'Dowd had called Alysha Kimbata's father to the stand to deny that he'd pressured his daughter to lie or that he'd received any memory card from Jabbar. However, his contempt for the prosecutors and all things Western had been so obvious that Karp had hardly bothered on cross-examination to do much more than let the man hang himself with his radical ideology.

O'Dowd had also recalled Jabbar to the stand to argue that it wasn't him in the movie. It was, he'd insisted, another man — one who had actually died in the New York Stock Exchange attack so that he couldn't be called to the stand — who was shouting *"Allahu Akbar!"*

O'Dowd's summation had never got off the ropes. She'd insisted that a government "capable of planning and carrying out the attack on the World Trade Center" was also capable of manufacturing a digital recording, "a recording in which perfectly legitimate free-speech sermons given by Imam Jabbar were spliced in with the heinous crime committed by the *agent provocateur* and his associate, Nadya Malovo."

Watching the jurors during O'Dowd's summation, Karp had known he had nothing to worry about. Judging from their dead eyes and blank expressions, her desperate arguments were falling on deaf ears.

The defense attorney's last-ditch plea had been that Jabbar was the victim of "an oppressive, racist government that has made all of Islam its enemy."

When O'Dowd had slumped back into her seat, it was Karp's turn. A younger, less experienced prosecutor might have shortened his summation and let the weight of the evidence resonate in the jurors' minds. That was old school, by the book — keep it short, precise, and colorless, and don't elaborate too much for fear of boring the jury. Karp had thrown out that book long ago.

Having learned his lesson all those years ago, Karp was taking no chances — and no prisoners. He was relentless as he pounded his opponent with jabs, hooks, body blows, and right crosses, citing the evidence against which he'd challenged the jurors to find "a single real piece, a scintilla, of evidence offered by the defense that wasn't based on speculation and fantasy, wrapped inside the big lie.

"Finally, ladies and gentlemen, in this case, the evidence screams out that it is about one thing and only one thing." He'd walked over and stood directly in front of the defense table, where neither occupant could look him in the eye. "It is about the vicious, brutal execution murder of helpless, innocent Miriam Juma Khalifa, which this man, the defendant Jabbar, and his henchmen helped plan and carry out even as he celebrated by asking God to condone such a terrible sin. That is not part of any religion we know — not Christian, not Jewish, and not Muslim."

The jury had hardly taken any more time to reach its verdict than it would have taken to fill out the verdict form, which was then given to the court clerk, Lopez, who in turn had handed it to Judge Mason. The only surprise when the judge had read the guilty verdict was when Jabbar turned suddenly and lunged at O'Dowd, trying to strangle her, only to be set upon by her bodyguards, who'd managed to pummel him pretty good before court security officers rescued him.

Now everyone in Karp's office wondered

if Hassan Malik was going to make him go through it all over again. But Malik entered the office, looked around, and smiled. "Looks like one of my old 'mission accomplished' celebrations, and you earned it," he said as he crossed the room and extended his hand to Karp. "I won't take up your time, but I wanted to stop by and say thank you."

"For what?" Karp said, puzzled.

"For showing enough respect to leave a black Muslim on this jury," Malik said. "I understand I might have been the lesser of some other potential evil, but I appreciate it nonetheless. Reminds me of what I was fighting for."

"There's no reason to thank me; in fact, quite the opposite," Karp said. "I should be thanking you for your service on the jury, as well as to our country."

"I guess then we're both welcome," Malik said, then excused himself.

The juror was just leaving when Marlene walked in. "I'm on my way to the Westchester County jail," she announced. "Warren's being released on personal recognizance until the charges can be formally dropped. I'm going to put him in a cab back to the city. Then I'm going to pay Harley Chin a visit."

"I'd like to be a fly on the wall for that one." Guma laughed.

"Not unless you're fireproof, too," Marlene said with a wicked smile. "I'm going to light that little bastard up."

"Then, I take it, it's on to Judge Kingston?" Karp asked.

"Yes, saving the best for last." Marlene smiled again. "I'll tell you all about it when I get home."

"Oh, that reminds me. Espey Jaxon was trying to reach you," Karp said.

A strange look passed across his wife's face, but she nodded. "Yes. I got the message."

As Marlene drove to Westchester County, she relived the Penn Station encounter. *It could have turned out worse, much worse,* she thought.

Fulton had taken the suitcase bomb into the bathroom, which, unknown to Williams's man outside, had been cleared of civilians and was occupied solely by several members of the NYPD SWAT and bomb squads. "Nice thing about peroxide bombs," the detective had told her later, "is that they might be simple to make, but they're also easy to defuse. In this case, it was getting into the false bottom and removing the

608

detonator. Still, we probably only had a few minutes before Williams's guy came rushing in to find out why the dang thing hadn't blown me past Saint Peter's gates."

Fulton had laughed. "You should have seen the look on his face when he found himself staring at the business end of a half-dozen guns held by nervous and angry cops. Priceless!"

There'd been another humorous moment when Todd Fielding, who obviously saw himself as the hero in much of this tale, had come up to Marlene and Sherry and, slurring because of the pain pills, asked, "So, would either of you lovely ladies — or perhaps both — care to join me for a celebratory cocktail?"

The two women had looked at each other and burst out laughing. "Fielding, I think we need to look into getting you to a hospital. And by the way, you'll be escorted there by a police officer," Marlene had said. "I think Detective Scalia here is about to tell you that you're under arrest for your part in all of this, though I think if you play nice and agree to testify about your photographs, you might find they'll go easy on you."

As she'd told the group back at the Criminal Courts Building, her first stop was the jail, where Warren was already waiting. He burst into tears when he saw her. "Thank you, thank you . . . whoop bitch oh boy . . . for everything."

"You're very welcome," she replied, hugging him. "By the way, I saw Booger on the way out of the courthouse and passed a message on. You might want to get in touch with David Grale when you get back to the city. Oh, and I almost forgot, I brought this for you." Marlene handed him a piece of paper. "The original letter is on a computer file, and it's now considered evidence, but I made a copy for you."

Warren looked at the letter and saw who it was from. A tear fell from his eye. He tried to smile. "What's the saying? Better to have loved and lost, eh?"

Marlene hugged him again and felt him stifle a sob. "It is never too soon or too late to love someone. It is what it is. So, anyway, I have some business to conclude here, but I was going to get you a cab back into the city."

"Won't be necessary," Warren said with a smile, and pointed to a limousine parked at the curb in front of the jail. Shannon Bennett and his parents were standing on the sidewalk next to it. They waved. "Mom and Dad showed up to offer me a ride in style and dinner. I said it had to be an early night, because I have something I need to do, too."

Marlene left Warren and headed over to Harley Chin's office, where the young receptionist couldn't have been more eager to please. And Chin showed up less than twenty seconds after her arrival was announced.

"Boy, quite a turn of events," Chin said after he took a seat behind his desk while Marlene remained standing. "I, of course, will want to review the evidence that has come to light, but it appears that this office might have made a mistake regarding your client. If it all checks out, I believe I will move to have the charges against Mr. Bennett dropped. As you know, though, we've had to release Jim Williams — if that is his name; you never know with these spooks. Some suit with the U.S. Attorney's Office produced a *habeas corpus ad prosequendum* warrant requiring his immediate release into federal custody, national security and all that. But it doesn't negate some really fine work on your part —"

"Cut the crap, Harley," Marlene snarled. She had been incensed by Williams's release "into federal custody," which apparently was no custody at all, according to Espey

Jaxon, who'd passed the news to her. "I'm not here to listen to your bullshit. I'm just letting you know that I'll be demanding an official investigation and a special prosecutor to look into your actions. And that you can look forward to a civil lawsuit that I'll be filing shortly on behalf of Warren Bennett for false imprisonment and malicious prosecution."

Chin swallowed hard. "Come on, Marlene," he said. "I can make it tough on your boy. After all, I have an indictment, and —"

"Cram your indictment. We both know now that it has the impact of a feather," Marlene interrupted. "In fact, if you dare go forward with this case, it will only add to the punitive damages by demonstrating your additional bad faith in the reckless manner in which you rushed to judgment for nefarious, narcissistic reasons."

Leaving Chin pale and quivering, Marlene proceded to the office of Judge Kingston, where she was met by two detectives. When they reached the outer office, they barged right past the judge's startled clerk and entered without knocking.

"What is the meaning of this outrage?" Kingston demanded.

"This will only take a moment," Marlene said as she held up an eight-by-ten photograph of Rene Hanson. "Ever seen this girl?"

Kingston blanched. "It's the Hanson girl. Of course, I've seen the photograph in the newspapers and at fundraisers."

"Never met her personally?"

"I'm afraid not," the judge said. "Now, I'm going to demand that you leave, and I will report this to the bar association."

"She's never been in your house?" Marlene continued.

"Not to my knowledge," Kingston said, nervously eyeing the two detectives who waited behind Marlene. "Perhaps one of my daughters had her over . . ."

"Yes, we'll ask them," Marlene replied sarcastically. "And maybe they'll want to know what their father — also known as Client 032355-JK, also known as John Klein — was doing paying for sex with Rene Hanson."

"That's a lie," Kingston said. "I've had no personal contact with that woman."

"That woman? You're starting to sound like Bill Clinton," Marlene said with disgust. "Look, it's over, Kingston. We have you signing checks as John Klein to the Gentleman's VIP Club, which a handwriting expert has already verified. And I don't think the bank officials will have any problem identifying you as the man who set up that account. Then there's the blood test you took to test for sexually transmitted diseases . . . too bad they can't test for murderers."

"It will never hold up," Kingston said.

"Oh? I forgot to tell you that Jim Williams, or whatever his name really is, made a videotaped confession," Marlene said. "We have it all. The kinky sex in the master bedroom. The call your associate, Peter, made. The police are looking for him now."

Just then, the judge's telephone rang. "I suspect that will be your wife," Marlene said, "letting you know that the Westchester County police are going through your house with a search warrant."

Marlene's cell phone also rang. "Hello, Bobby, anything interesting?" She listened for a few moments and then smiled as she hung up. "Really, Jack, you kept the pendant with 'JK' and 'RH' on the back? That some sort of trophy?"

"What pendant? I have no idea what you're talking about," Kingston said, getting up from his chair.

Marlene shook her head as she recalled Michelle's letter. *And there is one more item that should do it, if it can be located . . .*

"That was Detective Sergeant Bobby Scalia on the phone," Marlene said. "They found the pendant in your desk drawer, and he says there's a great latent thumbprint on the back that appears to be a woman's. Want to take bets it belongs to a woman you said you've never met, never had in your house, never paid for sex?"

Kingston's face changed to a mask of anger and desperation as he came out from around his desk and pushed past Marlene. "I don't have to put up with this," he said. "I'm leaving."

That was as far as he got, as the two detectives grabbed him. "You're under arrest," one said, "for the murder of Rene Hanson, as well as Michelle Oakley. Please turn around, sir, so that we can place you in handcuffs. If you resist, we'll do this on the floor."

Kingston looked at Marlene and cried, "I need to go home!"

"The only place you're going, your honor," Marlene said with a smile, "is to jail and then, someday in the not-too-distant future, straight to hell."

The shadows beneath the trees in Central Park were dark and impenetrable when the Fixer emerged from his apartment building across the street dressed in a jogging outfit. He carefully looked around as he stretched in preparation for his evening run, nodding to Josh and Lex, who were waiting across the street on the sidewalk next to the park.

As he'd told that bitch Marlene Ciampi the night before, he'd been freed from the Westchester County jail in the morning. The spineless creature known as Harley Chin had put up a minimal protest, but he'd known better than to stand in the way when an assistant U.S. attorney produced the warrant for his release. *There's the benefit of knowing too many secrets that too many people don't want me talking about,* he thought, smiling as he trotted across Fifth Avenue to join his men. *Ha, I'm too big to incarcerate.*

There'd been a price to pay. He'd had to give a videotaped "confession" to the locals regarding the murders of Michelle Oakley and Rene Hanson. And, of course, the U.S. Attorney's Office, while invoking the "national-security" coverall, had assured those same locals that he would be dealt with at the federal level. That was a laugh. He'd never see the inside of a federal prison. Instead, "Jim Williams," a.k.a. the Fixer, would disappear and lie low for a while — preferably on some warm, tropical beach — before reincarnating himself at a later time and place.

It was unfortunate that Jack Kingston would never sit in a courtroom again, except from the wrong side of the defense table. A "little bird" had called to tell him that the judge had been arrested that afternoon. There would be no seat on the federal bench and no more help in enabling his benefactors' schemes. They wouldn't be happy with Jim Williams, either. It could be dicey for a bit, but he'd throw them a few freebies, and they'd eventually be mollified.

In the meantime, he had to be careful. Not only were Kingston's backers not going to be happy, but according to his sources, District Attorney Karp and his bitch wife had gone ballistic when they learned about his release. The thought did bring a smile to his face as he jogged into the park.

The Fixer had been running about ten minutes and was nearing the boathouse when he noticed that the park seemed unusually deserted, even for nighttime. He glanced back and was satisfied to see the two figures of his bodyguards trailing. He didn't like lugging a weapon while running and left that to his men.

Twenty yards farther along the path, he saw a small, dark figure approaching from the other direction. He wasn't too worried; he was more than capable of handling one potential mugger even without his backup. He moved a little to the right so that he could pass the stranger, who was walking down the middle of the path. But the other man moved as if to block his way; he veered to the left, and the stranger moved to block him again.

The Fixer slowed and then stopped about fifteen feet from the other man, whose facial features were hidden by a hooded sweat-shirt. "Do you have a problem?" he asked.

"Yes, I have a . . . whoop whoop oh boy asshole . . . problem with murderers," the stranger answered.

The Fixer peered hard. "You," he said with a smirk. "Looking for revenge? Josh, Lex, you want to take care of my friend here?"

"I am not . . . scumbag shit whoop . . . your friend," Warren Bennett replied. "In fact, at this moment, I don't think you have any . . . oh boy . . . friends."

The Fixer whirled, expecting to see his men. Instead, a dozen dark shapes emerged from the shadows behind him. One of them was enormous and in the dark looked like a bear — smelled like one, too. But the figure who made him quail was wearing a hooded monk's robe, only the pale, gaunt features of his face visible in the dim light of the lampposts.

"Josh! Lex!" the Fixer yelled, his knees threatening to buckle in fear. There was no answer. "Who are you?" he demanded of the robed man.

"Your judges and executioners," the gaunt man said. "You are an evil man, and Satan waits for you."

"What the fuck are you talking about? You're crazy!" the Fixer cried out. He turned back around to Warren. "Look, it was nothing personal. I can make it worth your while to forget the whole thing. You'll be a rich man!"

"You already took from me all that matters," Warren replied. "You are nothing now."

As Warren spoke, he was joined by David Grale, chief among those who lived in the tunnels beneath Gotham, who produced a long, wicked knife from the folds of his robe. At the same time, the Fixer's arms were pinned from behind by the Walking Booger.

"Let me go, damn you!" the Fixer whimpered. "My people will hunt you down. You don't know who you're dealing with!"

"Oh, but I do," Grale responded. "You are a dead man." He turned to Warren and held out the knife. "His blood is forfeit to you."

Warren looked at the weapon, the light glinting off the cold steel; he started to reach for it. In his other hand, he clutched a copy of the letter Marlene had printed out for him. *You were a wonderful friend then, Warren Bennett, and I can tell you've become a wonderful man. Maybe in the next lifetime, I'll make smarter choices. Love always, Michelle.*

Marlene had dropped by his apartment that day to let him know that the Fixer had been released from jail. "I don't want to know what you'll do with this information," she'd said. "But I'm told that he goes for a run every night about ten P.M. in Central Park."

As he'd waited in the park with Grale, Booger, and the Mole People, Warren had imagined the blood of Williams spilling on the ground. But now he sighed and shook his head. "No, but thank you, David," he said. "He's all . . . whoop whoop . . . yours."

With that, he turned away. He was no killer, and his cat, Brando, was waiting for him. *Maybe I'll watch* Casablanca *again,* he thought as a shooting star crossed the sky. "We'll always have Paris," he said aloud, and walked into the night.

ABOUT THE AUTHOR

Robert K. Tanenbaum is one of the country's most respected and successful trial lawyers and legal experts. He has never lost a felony case. He has taught Advanced Criminal Procedure at his alma mater, the Boalt Hall School of Law, University of California at Berkeley. He has held such prestigious positions as Bureau Chief of the Criminal Courts and Chief of the Homicide Bureau for the New York District Attorney's office and Deputy Chief Counsel for the Congressional committee investigations into the assassinations of President John F. Kennedy and Dr. Martin Luther King, Jr. He has also conducted continuing legal education (CLE) seminars for practicing lawyers in California, New York, and Pennsylvania. He is the *USA Today, Los Angeles Times,* and *New York Times* bestselling author of twenty-two novels, including *Capture, Escape, Malice, Counterplay, Fury, Hoax, Abso-*

lute Rage, and *Enemy Within.* He is also the author of the true-crime books *Badge of the Assassin* and *The Piano Teacher: The True Story of a Psychotic Killer.*